Lonely Hearts

John Harvey is the author of the richly praised sequence of ten Charlie Resnick novels, the first of which, *Lonely Hearts*, was named by *The Times* as one of the '100 Best Crime Novels of the Century'. *Flesh and Blood*, his first novel featuring retired Detective Inspector Frank Elder, was published to great acclaim in 2004 and won the CWA Silver Dagger Award. *Flesh and Blood* is now available in Arrow Books.

John Harvey is also a poet, dramatist and occasional broadcaster.

Praise for *Lonely Hearts*

'John Harvey's beautifully down-beat crime novel . . . Mr Harvey captures the anxiety and tedium of modern police work with skill, his characterisation is excellent – particularly when they are underdogs or victims' *The Times*

'In *Lonely Hearts*, John Harvey . . . brings depth of character study and beautiful imagery to the police procedural' *Washington Post*

'Charlie Resnick is one of the most fully realised characters in modern crime fiction; complex and capable, a man who not only loves justice, jazz and cats, but one who can turn the construction of a sandwich into a work of art' Sue Grafton

D1322568

Find out more about John Harvey by visiting his website at:
www.mellotone.co.uk

Lonely Hearts

John Harvey

arrow books

The lines on page 111 are from 'I Got It Bad and That Ain't Good',
by Keith Jafrate, published in *Jump!* (Slow Dancer Press, 1988).
The lines on page 228 are from 'I Don't Stand a Ghost of a Chance
with You', © 1932 American Academy of Music Inc., reprinted by permission
of Columbia Pictures Publications/International Music Publications.
The lines on page 266 are from 'These Foolish Things Remind Me of You'
by John Strachey, reprinted by permission of Boosey & Hawkes.

Reissued by Arrow Books in 2002

5 7 9 10 8 6

First published in the United Kingdom in 1989 by the Penguin Group

This edition first published in 1995 by Mandarin Paperbacks

Arrow Books
The Random House Group Limited
20 Vauxhall Bridge Road, London SW1V 2SA

Random House Australia (Pty) Limited
20 Alfred Street, Milsons Point, Sydney
New South Wales 2061, Australia

Random House New Zealand Limited
18 Poland Road, Glenfield
Auckland 10, New Zealand

Random House (Pty) Limited
Endulini, 5a Jubilee Road, Parktown 2193, South Africa

The Random House Group Limited Reg. No. 954009

www.randomhouse.co.uk

A CIP catalogue record for this book
is available from the British Library

Papers used by Random House are natural, recyclable
products made from wood grown in sustainable forests.
The manufacturing processes conform to the environmental
regulations of the country of origin

ISBN 0 09 942152 6

Printed and bound in Great Britain by
Cox & Wyman Ltd, Reading, Berkshire

For Dulan Barber – whose help and friendship in the
early stages of this book were invaluable

One

She hadn't thought of him in a long time. The way he would hunch against the doorway, watching her as she dressed. Waiting to see which sweater she would choose, the soft green or maybe the red. *You know it, don't you?* His voice, as she stood before the mirror, as clear inside her now as it had been those years before. *Watching you like this, the way you do those things; I can't keep my hands off you.*

After they had started living together it had seemed that he could never leave her alone. She would wake in the night and he would be propped up in bed on one elbow, staring down at her. Once, he had parked his car across the street from the office building where she had been working and had sat there the whole day on the chance that she might walk past one of the windows. Whenever she had passed within reach of him inside the flat they had shared, his hands had moved for her, wanting to touch, to hold her. Just when she had become convinced it was going to be that way for ever, he had changed.

Tony.

Small ways at first, barely perceptible: he no longer held her hand when they were watching television; failed to dip his head into the corner of her neck as she stood at the stove, making Sunday morning scrambled eggs. She realized that she had dressed five morn-

1

ings in a row without his coming through from the bathroom, shaving lather on his face, to watch.

After that there had been other things, clearer, impossible not to recognize.

'Tony?'

'Uh?'

'Are you okay?'

'Does it look like I'm okay?'

'No. That's why I . . .'

'Then why ask?'

She looked at herself now in the mirror. A plain grey sweater over a calf-length black skirt; the boots she had had repaired for the second winter running. Her hair was dark, almost black, and she wore it down to her shoulders at the sides, the front cut thicker and short, clear of her forehead. This evening she had been more than usually careful with her make-up, not wanting to send out the wrong signals, certainly not too soon.

Something was not quite right. She pulled open the top drawer of the dressing-table and took out a thin wool scarf, deep red; tying it loose at the side of her neck, rearranging it several times until it was right.

A smile came to her face.

'Shirley Peters, you are not a bad-looking woman.'

Her voice was loud in the small room, a rough undertow as if she might be going down with a cold.

'Still.'

The letter lay on the coffee-table in front of the couch, a single sheet of notepaper, pale blue. Maybe the only reason she had read this one twice was that it had been written with a fountain-pen. Black ink. Isn't it strange how things that should be insignificant affect what we do?

2

Please be there between eight-fifteen and eight-thirty.

She carried it over to the narrow kitchen. A bottle of Italian red had been opened and recorked and she rinsed a glass under the cold tap before pouring herself a drink. The writing was distinctive, lower-case letters that were small and rounded, the capitals more pronounced and florid. The *P* of *Please* large enough to contain the whole word within its loop.

Shirley checked her watch again, plenty of time. Back in the living-room, she pushed a cassette into the tape deck and swung her legs up on to the cushions of the settee. One of her friends had told her it wasn't fashionable to like Sinatra so much, but she didn't care. There were not so many things she did like that she could afford to pass them up for the sake of fashion.

She smiled and, as Sinatra's voice rose against a bank of strings, leaned back her head and, for no longer than a moment or two, closed her eyes.

The first ring of the phone merged with high-flown phrases, bits of a dream. As she went to pick it up, Shirley thought against logic it might be her date, cancelling the evening. But then, removing one ear-ring, that wasn't the way it happened, no way for him to know her number, not yet; what happened was, he simply didn't turn up.

'I thought I'd missed you.'

'Tony . . .?'

'Thought you'd left early.'

'I don't understand . . .'

'Monday night, isn't it? When did you ever stay in on a Monday night?'

She had a sense of her bones, fragile, pressing against

the lightness of skin. Across the room a glimpsed reflection, the red scarf bright against the grey.

'Where are you? What do you want?'

'Long time since we talked.'

'We didn't talk, we shouted.'

'That temper of mine . . .'

'I told you I didn't want to see you again.'

'You did more than that.'

'I had to protect myself.'

'Oh, yeh . . .' His voice softening into a smile she could still see. 'Tell me something, Shirl.'

'Go on.'

'Tell us what you're wearing.'

Her eyes were closed as she set the receiver back in place. Damn him! In the kitchen she uncorked the bottle a second time. Court orders couldn't free her from that look that had come back to his face after they had separated, couldn't disguise the tone of his voice. She clunked the glass down in the sink and went to the wardrobe for her coat. He was right and it was Monday night and when had she stayed in on a Monday night these last twenty years? It was what got her through the rest of the week.

Careful, she released the catch, turned the key.

Two

It was several moments before Resnick realized that one of the cats was sitting on his head. The radio was tuned to Four and a woman's voice was trying to tell him something about the price of Maris Piper potatoes.

'Dizzy, come on.'

He turned slowly, coaxing the animal down on to the pillow. The clock read six-seventeen. A second cat, Miles, purred on contentedly from the patch in the covers where Resnick's legs had made a deep V.

'Dizzy, cut it out!'

The cat, unbroken black and with its tail crooked in greeting, continued the rhythmic movement of its claws in and out of Resnick's arm.

'Now!'

Finally, he lifted the cat away, lowering it to the floor as he swung his own legs round, hesitated for no more than seconds, finally bracing himself on to his feet. Rain clipped against the window and when he pulled the curtains aside it did little to raise the level of light.

Standing under the shower, Resnick massaged shampoo into his hair as vigorously as he dared; eyes closed tight, face tilted upwards, he lowered the temperature of the water until it reached minimum. When he looked into the mirror, his breath came back at him a mixture of German beer and sweet pickled gherkins. He was the usual eight pounds over on the scales. Cats swayed around his bare legs, almost slid under his feet as he pulled on his dark grey trousers, light grey socks.

By the far wall of the kitchen, Pepper peered out at him from between the leaves of the rhoicissus on top of the fridge.

Dizzy, Miles and Pepper – where was Bud?

The runt of the unrelated litter appeared, splay-legged and startled, as Resnick opened a tin of chicken and liver cat food and forked it into four bowls: green, blue, yellow and red. Whenever he changed the position of the bowls, the cats would go to their usual one without fail – who was it claimed that cats were colour-blind? Or maybe the answer lay in the way each one had its name, printed in inch-high red ink, taped to the side of each bowl.

Too early for anything more strident, Resnick set a guitar album on the stereo and kept the volume turned low. He got the coffee-pot going, cut three slices of rye bread for toast and sat down to read yesterday's paper. Both of the city's soccer teams had played and lost; one was treading water in the Third Division, the other keeping close to the top of the First until the inevitable winter retreat. It went without saying that Resnick supported the former. Off-duty Saturday afternoons he would stand on the terraces with half-a-dozen refugees from the Polish delicatessen and search with growing desperation for something to applaud – a cross-field pass, a tasty back-heel, a shot on goal was almost too much to ask for.

Using one sock-covered foot to dissuade Dizzy from finishing the contents of Bud's bowl, Resnick thinly sliced some mozzarella and placed it on the toast. Coffee he drank black and without sugar: there were days when he wondered exactly why it was that he didn't lose weight.

'You ought to get married again, Charlie.'

Superintendent Jack Skelton was on his way out of the station, executive briefcase under his arm and something of a gleam in his eye. Greying hair, still thick, had been brushed meticulously into place. Bugger's probably back from a three-mile run already, Resnick thought.

'I'm still waiting for the first time, sir,' he said.

'A wife would do things for you.'

'That's what I've heard.'

'Like make sure you didn't leave the house in the morning with breakfast on your tie.'

Resnick glanced down. 'It's not mine, sir.'

'You've got someone else's breakfast on your tie?'

'Someone else's tie.'

Skelton continued down the steps and round into the car park with a step that managed to be unhurried and urgent at the same time. Resnick wondered if the superintendent would be back in the station for the nine o'clock briefing, or whether the chief inspector would be sitting in for him. He'd rather Skelton's briskness than twenty minutes of Len Lawrence doing his man-of-the-people act.

The CID office was L-shaped. Desks were pushed together along the centre of the room, four and then six and four more around the corner; spaces left between them for access. A row of desks lined the window that ran the length of the left-hand wall. Four detective sergeants and sixteen constables used the office in shifts; somehow, between them, trying to make an impression on the five thousand plus crimes that had been reported so far that year – it was early November – and that was only one section of the city.

Resnick's office was the missing section of the rectangle, partitioned off from the rest by chipboard and glass.

Patel had drawn the early shift, seven till three, and was bending over his desk, making final adjustments to the files that would bring Resnick up to date with what had happened through the night. One detailed the movement of prisoners, in and out of the cells on the ground floor; the other logged messages and Patel would have sorted these into local and national. And he would have put on the kettle for tea.

'Anything I ought to see urgent?' Resnick called through the open door.

'Sir, there were six robberies, sir.' Patel stood at the entrance to Resnick's office, one file under each arm, sheets of computer paper folding back at top and bottom.

'Six? You're going to have your work cut out.'

As officer on the early shift, Patel was responsible for all burglaries. He looked at Resnick, unable to relax, uncertain if he was supposed to smile.

'Let's have a look, then. Before the army gets here.'

The DC placed the files on Resnick's desk, opening each in turn. 'Sergeant Millington, sir. He is here already.'

Resnick nodded. What was the matter with everybody today? Had they done something to the clocks without telling him? He was certain he'd changed all his when Summer Time had ended.

'That tea won't mash by itself, lad.'

Patel scuttled out and Resnick did no more than glance at his sergeant, knowing he had to finish reading the files before the meeting. Graham Millington took a cigarette from its packet, transferred it from one hand to another, put it back unlit. He could never understand

8

it. There he was, ten years in uniform, seven as a DC; four years now since passing his promotion board to sergeant. Not only that, he had a couple of commendations and a medal for bravery, a three-piece suit that didn't strain to fit, a wedding ring on his finger, an internal clock like Greenwich Mean Time and a clean tie. What more did it take to make detective inspector?

'Anything the matter, Graham?' Resnick closed the files.

Millington sniffed and shook his head. 'No, sir.'

'Somebody's been busy along the back of the boulevard.'

'I just had a word with uniform. Night inspector said some kid rang in about five. Just got back from a party. Got out of a taxi and into the drive and realized the front door's open to the wind. Takes him another five minutes to realize there's a space where the TV used to be.'

'Anyone else in the house?'

'Family. All upstairs in bed. Fast off.'

Lucky for some, Resnick thought. 'Much else missing?' he asked.

'VCR, couple of good cameras – the kid's getting himself into a state on account his entire James Brown collection's been lifted.' Millington sighed. 'Five others so far, and there'll be more when folk wake up to it. All the same.'

'All mourning their James Brown, eh?'

Millington felt one side of his mouth shaping into a grin and willed it to stop. He wanted to call Resnick's bluff but didn't quite dare. For all he knew, his superior went home and kicked back the carpet, tossed down a few glasses of schnapps and boogied the night away to 'Papa's Got a Brand New Bag'.

Bodies moved past the doorway, snatches of early

conversation, a loud laugh and then a groan as Mark Divine's voice rose above the rest, boasting about the night before to the other officers.

Resnick glanced over his shoulder at the round-faced clock between pinboard and his pair of filing cabinets: four minutes past eight.

'Okay, Graham,' said Resnick, standing. 'Let's get to it.'

Superintendent Skelton had not returned from Central Police Station, so, after briefing his men, Resnick had reported to Chief Inspector Lawrence, together with the uniformed inspector in charge. Both men had kept it as short as possible and by a quarter-past nine, Resnick was back in his own office, phoning through to the detective chief inspector at headquarters.

'Lively night down your way,' the DCI observed, pleasantly caustic.

'Yes, sir.'

'Getting any help from uniform on this?'

'Two men for house-to-house, sir.'

'Right you are, then, Charlie. Talk to you tomorrow. You'll likely have a result by then.'

Resnick set the receiver down and the door to his office opened.

'Didn't know if I should remind you,' said Graham Millington. 'You're in court this morning, aren't you?'

Resnick closed his eyes, pinched the bridge of his nose between forefinger and thumb. The door to his office closed quietly. Beyond it phones rang and were answered. Somebody swore, softly, repeatedly, and no one appeared to notice.

He had been trying to wipe from his mind the fact that he was due, that morning, to give evidence. There were cases that seemed to make no impact at all, others

10

that brought their share of sleepless hours, and then there were those that bit deep.

This had started with a call to the station. A child's mother had rung in, pretending to be a neighbour. She had alleged that her husband was consistently forcing their daughter to take part in sexual acts. That was what it had come down to, when all the pretence, the play-acting were over. Remembering, Resnick's mouth went tight. It all seemed a long time ago, the first stumbled words, the investigation, the child who had sat quietly before a video camera and played with dolls. *Yes, he did, he took this and he put it there.* Seven years old. Was that what people got married for, Resnick asked? Had children?

On his way into the city-centre he tried not to answer the questions, tried to clear his mind of the case altogether. Once in the witness box it would come back soon enough.

There was time to walk up to the indoor market and take his usual seat at the Italian coffee stall. The girl slid an espresso in front of him without waiting to be asked and Resnick drank it down in two and ordered another.

'How's it going?' she asked.

Resnick slid the coins across the counter and shrugged. How was it going? Phones rang and were answered. It was part of the job, it was what he did.

The courthouse had been newly built from pink stone and smoked glass, and from the foyer entrance you could watch the buses pulling out of the station and into the traffic, one every couple of minutes. Hiss of brakes, hiss of rain. Resnick turned and saw the couple, child and mother, sitting on a bench seat, clear space between them. Had he thought about it, he would have

11

known they would be there, known he would see them, but he had stopped himself thinking about it. These things took a long time. He wondered if the little girl would recognize him and how she would react if she did.

A woman stood beside them, bending down to talk to the mother, her hand brushing the fall of the child's hair as she straightened away. Resnick dismissed her as being a relative, put her down as a social worker, not the same one who had been at the station when they had been asking their questions.

'*Yes, it hurt me.*'

This woman was tall, tall enough; she had a way of standing that said I know who I am and what I'm doing here and if you don't, well, I don't give a damn. The deep collar of her camel coat was pulled high, the belt looped loosely over. Resnick caught sight of tan boots with a heel, a glimpse of blue skirt where the hem of the coat separated out.

When he realized she was looking back at him, Resnick slid one hand inside his jacket and left it there, resting on the fastened button, covering the stain on his tie.

He felt the need to walk over and talk to the mother, say something calming and trite. What stopped him was not knowing how to speak to the little girl, sitting there plucking at a button on her sleeve and tapping her toes against that newly polished floor. What stopped him was knowing that his reason for doing it was to appear sympathetic in front of the woman in the camel coat.

Rachel Chaplin rested her right hand on the back of the bench and watched Resnick walk away towards the door of the court. She didn't know his name, but knew his rank; she knew him for a police officer. She knew that he had been looking at her and not at the clients who were sitting on the bench. When he had been about to approach them she had guessed that he had been involved in the arrest and in a moment she would ask Mrs Taylor if that had been so. Meanwhile, she was wondering what had made him change his mind.

He was an overweight man in his early forties, whose narrow eyes were bagged and tired, and who couldn't find the time to drop his tie off at the cleaners.

Now Rachel Chaplin was wondering just why she was smiling.

Giving evidence, Resnick stumbled over a date and had to flick back through the pages of his notebook for verification. Yes, that did mean that the child was examined by a doctor precisely seven days after he had received the initial call. Yes, the delay was in part due to the manner in which the mother had elected to inform the authorities. Did he think that the mother had been to any degree complicit in the father's behaviour towards their daughter?

Only once did Resnick allow himself to look directly at the man standing between two officers in the dock. He had been asked to describe the accused's emotions when faced with the offence. Had he shown unusual emotion? Had he broken down? Wept? Asked for forgiveness? He stood there now much as a man might stand, bored, in the Friday-night queue at the supermarket.

'Detective inspector?'

Resnick's eyes never left the father's face as he answered. 'The accused said, "She's just a bloody kid!" And then he said, "The lying little bitch!" '

Rachel could have been waiting for him, but she wasn't.

She was by the exit, talking to a ginger-haired man Resnick recognized as the probation officer to the court. She was talking earnestly, her oval face serious amidst curls.

'Inspector . . .' The soft leather bag that hung from her right shoulder hit against the glass door as she moved.

Resnick turned towards her, nodding to the probation officer as he did so.

'I won't keep you a moment,' Rachel said. There was an unevenness at the bottom of her front teeth, as though a piece had been chipped away.

'I'm Rachel Chaplin, I'm . . .'

'You're the Taylors' social worker,' Resnick interrupted.

'Yes.'

The probation officer raised a hand that neither acknowledged and walked between them, down and into the street.

'How are they coping?' asked Resnick.

'In the circumstances it's difficult to say.'

'The girl . . .'

A barrister hurried behind Resnick, stuffing his gown down into a sports bag as he went. The step which the inspector automatically took forward placed him close enough to Rachel Chaplin to see his reflection clearly in the red-framed glasses that she wore.

'Ask me again in six months, a year. I might have an answer for you. Ask me after the father comes out of prison, after therapy. I don't know.' She looked away from him and then back and asked, 'How are you?'

Taken by surprise, Resnick didn't know what to say.

'You seem tense,' Rachel said. 'You've got frown lines cluttering up your eyes and you haven't been sleeping properly.'

14

'I haven't?'

'Uh-huh. You've probably got a bed that isn't firm enough to take your weight and if you told me you drank Scotch before trying to sleep, I'd believe you.'

'Suppose it's coffee?'

'The effect's the same.'

He couldn't decide if her eyes were more green than blue.

He said: 'Is this why you called me over?'

She said: 'It's what I've ended up saying.'

'But when you stopped me . . .?'

'I wanted to tell you that Mrs Taylor . . . this morning, before court, I asked her about you.'

'Yes?'

'She said how understanding you'd been.'

'Then she's wrong,' Resnick said. 'I don't understand at all.'

Instead of leaving the building with her, the two of them walking down the steps side-by-side, Resnick was on his own. The corner outside the court was jammed with people waiting for the lights to change. He hadn't thought about turning away from her, he had just done it.

He was heading for the underpass that would take him through the shopping precinct and back into the city centre when the bleeper clipped inside his jacket sounded and sent him in search of the nearest telephone.

Three

Resnick had lived here, this part of the city, when he had been a uniformed sergeant, straining to get back into CID, eager to improve his status, move on up. Now the terraced streets had two-tone 2CVs parked at the kerb and, through painted blinds, glimpses of parlour palms and Laura Ashley wallpaper: maybe he should have stuck around a little longer.

There was an ambulance outside number 37 and Resnick pulled in between it and a maroon saloon which he recognized as belonging to Parkinson, the police surgeon.

The rain had stopped but the air was still damp enough to make ageing bones ache. A few people stood around on the opposite side of the street, hands in their pockets, shuffling their feet and speculating. Faces stared out from windows, several with lights already switched on in the rooms behind.

DC Kellogg stood talking to a youth with a shaft of black gelled hair in the doorway of number 39, listening and making notes. By the entrance to number 37, a young constable stood with hands clasped behind his back, embarrassed to be the temporary focus of so much attention.

Millington met Resnick in the narrow hallway.

'How did it go at court?'

Resnick ignored the question, looked past his

sergeant at the partly open doorway ahead. 'Scene-of-crime here yet?'

'On their way.'

Resnick nodded. 'I want a look.'

A grey top-coat had been dropped across the back of an easy chair; from behind it the toe of a red shoe poked out. On the glass-topped coffee-table were a couple of wine glasses, one with an inch of red wine at the bottom, and a single red and white ear-ring. A thick glass ashtray held the stubs of three cigarettes. Above the fireplace, a few tan-and-orange lilies had started to throw off their petals, curled like tongues.

There were several posters on the walls, clip-framed; from one Monroe looked out, slump-backed on a stool, black clothes, white face. Resnick glanced into her empty eyes and turned away. Words from a song of Billie Holliday nudged away at his mind, images of winter through the slight distortion of glass.

Parkinson stood up and half-turned to acknowledge Resnick's presence; he took off his bifocals and slid them down into a case he kept in the breast pocket of his suit jacket.

'You're finished?' Resnick asked.

'For now.'

'Any idea of time?'

The police surgeon blinked and sounded bored; Resnick guessed the weather had kept him off the golf course for too long. 'Somewhere in excess of twelve hours.'

'Last night then?'

'The wee small hours.'

Resnick nodded and moved a little closer. The rear of Shirley Peters's skirt had become rucked up behind her and one leg was folded beneath the other, as if she

17

had been sitting on it and then lain slowly back. Her grey sweater had been loosened from the waist band of the skirt and was pushed up at one side towards her breast. Maybe, Resnick thought, it had first been pulled all the way up and later drawn, imperfectly, down. The dead woman's head lolled back sideways on a cushion, angled over towards the fireplace. Her eyes – mouth – were open. The line of red, taut and twisted, ran from beneath the rich dark of her hair: a red scarf knotted at the throat and pulled tight.

'Who found her?'

Millington cleared his throat. 'Patel.'

'He's still around?'

'Supposed to be helping Kellogg with . . .'

'I want to see him.'

The scene-of-crime squad was filling out the corridor. During the next hour or so, a practised search would be carried out, samples lifted with tweezers, scraped from beneath the painted fingernails of Shirley Peters's hands; wine glasses, surfaces would be fingerprinted; photographs taken, a video film shot and prepared for Resnick's briefing.

Clear out of the way and let them get on with it.

'We were knocking on doors, that run of break-ins, the nearest was down the street at number 62.'

'Two constables and yourself.'

'Yes, sir.'

Resnick watched the slim fingers of Patel's hands slide back and forth along his thighs, intertwine, free themselves and move again. He wondered if it was the first time Patel had come upon a dead body – and decided that probably there would have been a grand-parent or an aunt, some relative back home in – where was it? – Bradford.

18

'I rang the bell, knocked. Nobody came to the door, so I made a note to call back and that was when the neighbour came out from number 39.'

'Neighbour?'

Patel opened the small black notebook, the right page marked by a rubber band. 'MRS BENNETT.' The name had been written in capitals, neat and black and underlined. 'She said somebody should be in, Shirley, that was the name she used. She said she often slept late.'

'You tried again?'

Patel nodded. Resnick thought how different it would have been coming from any of the other officers. The young Asian's diffidence came from years of stepping through conversation as through minefields, aware of how little it took to make everything go up in your face. Without it, he would have been unlikely to have survived in the Force.

'I went round to the back . . .'

'To ask a few routine questions about a burglary?'

Patel looked into Resnick's face: the first time he had done so directly. 'I thought it would do no harm to check. Only a minute. There is an entry at the end of the street.'

You followed a hunch, you bugger, Resnick thought. Good for you!

'The back door, it wasn't quite closed. Pulled to. I tried the handle.'

'You went in?'

'There were grounds for believing . . . at least, I thought . . .'

'From what the neighbour had said, someone should have been at home.'

'Yes, sir. I opened the door wide enough to call out.

19

Several times. Loud enough, I think, to have woken most people.'

Not this one, Resnick thought, seeing again the savage turn of the woman's head, back against the cushion.

'With the other burglaries in the area...' Patel ceased talking, the words drained from him. Resnick knew that inside his head the officer was walking again through the kitchen, past the sink, electric cooker, the painted chipboard units, on towards the living-room door.

'Your suspicion now,' Resnick finished for him, 'was that the neighbour's assumptions were wrong, the house was empty, there had been a break-in, illegal entry through the rear, just like the rest.'

Patel nodded.

'But that wasn't the case?'

'No.' Patel shook his head. 'No, sir. It was not.'

Resnick touched him briefly on the arm. 'Outside and get some fresh air. Right?'

Resnick watched him walking slowly back across the road, head bowed a little and his helmet held by his fingers between arm and hip. If he hadn't already vomited, he would before long.

'Graham?'

Millington walked over from where he had been watching a scene-of-crime officer loading a fresh cassette into his video camera. 'Shouldn't be too long now.'

'Where's Lynn?'

Millington pointed beyond the ambulance. Lynn Kellogg was sitting on a low wall, talking to a couple of kids of barely school age.

'Send her over. And, listen, if there's nothing more

you can do here, run Patel back to the station. He ought to get home but he'll as like say no.'

'If it was anybody else, I could take him to the pub and buy him a large brandy.'

'Anybody else, that body might have been mouldering away in there for days.'

Millington looked at him sharply, looking for offence. 'I hope you're not including me in that?'

'You, Graham?' said Resnick, straight-faced. 'You're a sergeant.'

Lynn Kellogg was a stocky, red-faced woman of twenty-eight with soft brown hair and the still distinguishable burr of a Norfolk accent. Her mother and stepfather owned a chicken farm between Thetford and Norwich and each Christmas for the past three years Resnick had found a capon in a plastic carrier-bag inside the metal waste-paper bin beneath his desk.

Like many women officers, she tended to get shunted into certain areas: so many cases of child abuse and rape that there were whole weeks on end when she thought she'd joined Social Services. But she was good with other women, kids too, and that didn't mean Resnick forgot seeing her wade into the crowd at the Trent End and haul out a youth in a red and white scarf who'd just hurled a half-brick at the visiting goalkeeper.

'Important witnesses?' asked Resnick, nodding in the direction of the five-year-olds.

'Public relations.'

'There's a woman in number 39, Mrs Bennett. Sounds as if she might be the eyes and ears of the street. According to Patel, she was pretty knowledge-able about the dead woman's movements – or thought she was. Have a chat, will you? If you turn up anything that seems important get in touch with Sergeant

21

Millington or myself at the station. If there's any chance of closing this one down quickly, so much the better.'

He spoke with the officer in charge of the scene-of-crime team for no more than ten minutes. When he got their report through, there might be something to go on. The small crowd of onlookers had got cold and bored and had mostly drifted away. The street lights stood out clearly now. On the horizon the reflections of the other lights threw up an oddly violet glow over the heaped shadow of the city. Resnick shivered as he headed back towards the house; he hated those evenings where dusk hardly seemed to exist; you blinked and there it was, night.

Whatever in the room had been touched, had been replaced with care. Shirley Peters's face looked like the painting of a face. When the Home Office pathologist performed the post-mortem, what he did would be careful, too, and terrible.

'Sir . . .'

The constable was at the entrance to the room, more awkward now than embarrassed, fidgeting from one foot to another as if his trousers were suddenly too tight.

'There's somebody outside, sir . . . to see . . .' He nodded towards the corpse. 'It's . . . I think it's her mother.'

Resnick started to move. 'For God's sake, keep her out.'

'Yes, sir.'

As the constable turned, the woman slipped beneath his arm and Resnick had to set his body in front of hers to keep her from the room. She had hair that was a shade of platinum blonde you didn't see much any more, and, if it hadn't been for the way it had been piled up on top and the size of her heels, she would have been less than five feet tall.

'What's happened? Shirley. Oh, my God, Shirley!'

'I think we should go back outside, Mrs Peters. And you,' he called over her head, 'stop dithering and find DC Kellogg. Next door. Now.'

The woman tried to wriggle past him and Resnick grasped her shoulders.

'Let me go!'

'I don't think that's a good idea.'

'You've got no right ...'

He was slowly forcing her back along the hallway, trying not to force his fingers too hard against her upper arms, hurt her, bruise her.

'My Shirley!' She screamed up into Resnick's face and he loosened his grip until his hands were not quite touching her arms. They were inside the front doorway and Lynn Kellogg was waiting by the metal gate at the pavement.

'I think we should go and sit next door,' Resnick said, talking to the DC as much as Mrs Peters. 'Maybe a cup of tea?'

All colour had left the woman's face; her eyes were blinking involuntarily and, at her sides, her hands were beginning to shake.

'Come on,' said Resnick, touching her gently.

'No, no ...'

'I think you might be going to faint.'

'No, I'm not. I'm all right. I ... I think I'm going to faint.'

Resnick stooped and swept an arm behind her legs and caught her before she struck the ground.

Four

The sandwich was tuna fish and egg mayonnaise with some small slices of pickled gherkin and a crumbling of blue cheese; the mayonnaise kept dripping over the edges of the bread and down on to his fingers so that Dizzy twisted and stretched from his lap in order to lick it off. Billie Holliday and Lester Young were doing it through the headphones, making love to music without ever holding hands. Resnick couldn't stop thinking about the fact that he had lied to Skelton, wondering why.

His marriage had neither been so bad that he had stricken it from the record of his memory, nor so lacking in incident that he would have truly forgotten. Something over five years and she had walked in while he was painting the woodwork in the spare room and announced that she wanted a divorce. Each year of their marriage he had redecorated that small room at the back of their own bedroom in the hope that one day she might walk into it with a glow in her eyes and announce that she was pregnant. Why else did he use alphabet wallpaper in primary colours? Why else the paintwork in bright reds and greens?

All she had been able to say was that she needed space to grow, room to find herself and she didn't mean the one he was so obsessively turning into a succession of nurseries. Her horizons, she felt, were being limited, foreshortened.

Fine, Resnick had said, let's sell up, move. There's nothing special to keep us here. I'll forget about making babies for a few years and you concentrate on your career. Better still, throw in your job. Retrain. Get a place at university. Go abroad. Only last month someone from CID got a transfer to Billings, Montana; doubled his salary for the price of a ticket across the Atlantic, one way. Now he's got a house on the edge of town that looks over miles of prairie and all he had to do was learn how to ride a horse.

None of that was what she had in mind.

Whatever growing Resnick might be going in for, and she made it more than clear in those last weeks that he had a lot of potential in that area, he was going to do it in his own time and company. She was going to stretch her new-found wings alone.

Within six months she was remarried, her new husband an estate agent who changed his car every year and spent weekends at a holiday cottage in Wales. Resnick used to scan the papers, eager for reports that it had been burnt down. For a while he even subscribed to the fighting fund of Plaid Cymru. Now it was as if he had never really known her, as if nothing but their bodies had ever really touched. He had realized that in all the five years they had lived under the same roof, he had never known what she had been thinking or feeling and the truly frightening thing was realizing that he had never really cared. She would have said that was why, finally, she had to leave him. He had never been able to find her, so she had better try to find herself.

But what do you find, Resnick had used to wonder, down behind the rear seat of a new Volvo or at the bottom of an exclusive estate's swimming-pool after the water has been drained away?

He used to think it very sad; then, as more years

passed, he scarcely thought about it – about her – at all.

Maybe his denial to Jack Skelton had not been as much of a lie as he had thought.

He cleaned those parts of his fingers the cat had ignored, leaned forward and set the plate on the floor and then removed the headphones. As he did so, he realized that the telephone was ringing. He made a lunge towards it and lifted the receiver and, of course, the line went dead the moment it got close to his ear.

The receiver still in his hand, he dialled the station: no, no one had been trying to contact him. Lynn Kellogg was alone in the office, catching up on some paperwork. Her voice sounded more Norfolk the more tired she became and now Resnick had difficulty making out what she said.

'How's Patel?' Resnick asked.

'White as a mucky sheet. The sergeant told him to go home.'

'Home to Bradford, or home to his digs?'

'Digs, I suppose.'

'You do the same.'

'I've moved on from digs long since.'

She had moved to a housing association flat in the old Lace Market area of the city, where she lived with a professional cyclist who spent most of his spare time pedalling over the Alps in bottom gear and much of the remainder shaving his legs to eliminate wind resistance.

At least it allowed her space.

'Go home yourself,' Resnick said. 'Get some sleep. And remember your box of plasters as well as your sensible shoes tomorrow. You'll be doing house-to-house.'

Resnick went into the kitchen area and shifted Pepper far enough from the stove to set the kettle on the gas. He was spooning a mixture of dark continental and mocha into the filter when he realized he had been thinking about Rachel Chaplin for some minutes. Partly it was because of the little lecture she had delivered on caffeine before bedtime, but mainly it was the way he remembered her eyes. The way they held his gaze and refused to fade away. In some way or another she meant trouble for him, this Rachel Chaplin, and Resnick was unable to resist the feeling that a little trouble was his due.

He poured the boiling water over the ground coffee, reached for a clean glass and a bottle of Scotch and poured some of that, too. If he wasn't going to be able to sleep, at least he could enjoy staying awake.

'Don't say it!' warned Resnick. 'Don't say a thing.'

He leaned his back against the corner of the stair-well, breathing heavily, unsteadily. DC Kellogg turned her head and gazed out over the park with its pitch-and-putt course, the domed church on the hill opposite, beyond that houses and the first glimpses of open country.

'Bloody lifts never work! It's all right for youngsters like you. Take the stairs three at a time and keep smiling.'

Lynn Kellogg smiled. 'First time I've ever heard you plead getting old, sir.'

Resnick levered himself away from the wall. 'I'm not.'

Still smiling, she followed him along the landing, negotiating their way past two prams, one holding a sleeping child, the other a half-hundredweight of coal and the inside of a television.

Olive Peters showed them into a small living-room, dralon and plastic, a damp stain spreading out in dark,

27

wavering rings from one corner of the ceiling. Her cheeks had sunk deep into her face and her mouth had all but disappeared, as if the dentures she normally wore had been mislaid, forgotten. Lacking yesterday's make-up, grey creases strayed across her skin. The platinum blonde hair had been pinned-up haphazardly; her body shrunk inside a buttoned cardigan and skirt.

'I could make some tea . . .'

'Don't trouble yourself.'

'It seems wrong,' she fidgeted. 'When you've come out, like . . .'

'Mrs Peters,' said Lynn Kellogg, getting up. 'Why don't I pop into the kitchen and make us a pot? Would you mind?'

She leaned back into her chair, relieved. 'That's it, duck, you mash.' And then, 'There's a packet of biscuits somewhere, you'll see.'

'Lovely girl,' she said, turning to Resnick, and the tears began to flow again, easing themselves down her face.

Resnick leaned across and gave her his handkerchief, looked at the photograph of mother and daughter on the mantelpiece, crooked in a perspex frame, waited for the tea and biscuits.

Shirley Peters's mother didn't wait that long. 'What makes me sick, when you catch the bastard he won't swing for it!'

Something about the way she spoke jogged Resnick awake, made him realize that when she said 'he', she didn't mean some anonymous, still-to-be-identified killer. She meant somebody specific.

'Tony,' she said, looking Resnick in the face, reading his thoughts in return. 'He always said he'd do this to her. Tony. The bastard!'

In the kitchen the kettle whistled and then was still;

Resnick quietly took out his notebook and fingered the cap from his pen.

DS Millington swung into the car park, driving too fast, as Resnick and Kellogg were closing the doors of the black saloon. Before there was time to climb the steps into the station, Millington was hurrying between them.

'Six witnesses. Six. All willing to testify to Peters's common-law husband threatening her with violence.'

Resnick pushed through the glass door, nodded to the uniformed officer on duty and moved on towards the stairs.

'One couple, black, but never mind, can't have everything, they remember it clearly, date, time, everything, wedding anniversary, that's why. Got back from some do and there was all this going on in the middle of the street. *You as much as sniff another man and I'll bloody strangle you!*, that's what he came out with. They'll swear to it.'

They were standing inside Resnick's office now, Resnick's face expressionless as he nodded, listening to the sergeant's excited voice. Off to the side, Lynn Kellogg watching, a smile ready at the corners of her rounded mouth.

Millington clapped his hands emphatically. 'Open and sodding shut!'

'Tony Macliesh.' Resnick's tone was level, matter-of-fact.

Millington's eyes grew wide, then narrowed to a slit. Resnick continued to look at a point some six inches above his sergeant's head.

'If you knew...'

'I've sent Naylor and Divine to bring him in.'

Lynn Kellogg excused herself, hand to her mouth,

bottling up the laughter as best she could until she reached the privacy of the ladies.

'Open and shut, Charlie. Is that what you think?'

Resnick was sitting in Skelton's office, trying not to get annoyed at the way both in-tray and out-tray were arranged a precise quarter-inch from the edges of the desk, the blotter with its fountain-pens, each containing different coloured inks, pointing towards it at an angle of forty-five degrees. Equidistant from the silver-framed calendar, photographs of Skelton's wife and daughter, also silver-framed and smiling.

'Looks that way.'

Skelton nodded. 'Run me through it.'

Resnick uncrossed his legs, crossed them again the other way. 'Shirley Peters, thirty-nine. Last four years she'd worked for a computer software company near the old market square. Typist, switchboard, nothing specialized. Up till about eighteen months ago she'd been living with this Tony Macliesh. Her mother says they were together the best part of three years – though to hear her tell it, the best part was when she finally chucked him. He went off to Aberdeen to work on the rigs, she got on with her life and inside six months he was back and making a nuisance of himself. Arguments, threats; he'd be banging on the door in the middle of the night. She changed the locks, spent some nights with her mum, only of course that made it worse because he thought she'd been with a bloke.'

'Any complaints through us?' Skelton interrupted.

'Kellogg's checking the files. There must have been something; a little over a year back she got a restraining order against him.'

'Effective?'

'Didn't need to be. Macliesh got lifted for aggravated

30

burglary and earned himself nine months in Lincoln. He's not long out. One of the neighbours told Millington she saw him pacing up and down the street no more than two days back.'

Skelton leaned backwards, flexing his fingers and then cupping his hands behind his head. 'File it away under domestic violence.'

'I think so.'

'No need to panic.'

'No.'

'You'll get your other evidence?'

'Scene-of-crime turned up some hairs on the woman's sweater that weren't hers, scraping of skin under the forefinger of the right hand, male pubic hair around the pelvic . . .'

'I understood her to be fully clothed?'

Resnick looked at him. 'Some people prefer it that way.'

The look he got in return was of no great interest, only mild surprise. Resnick had worked with Skelton for almost two years and if his superior's self-control had slipped during that time, Resnick had not been aware of it.

'How does this fit in with your theory about Macliesh?' Skelton asked.

'If what was driving him was sexual jealousy, anything's possible. And all traces of semen were outside the body, her abdomen, her . . .' Resnick left it there; if Skelton wanted to use his imagination, he could give it a try.

'All right, then, Charlie. You're bringing him in?'

'I sent two men down to his digs. He'd got himself a room in Radford. They phoned in an hour ago to say he wasn't there, but most of his stuff's still in the room.

They're nosing around, other lodgers, the local. They'll turn something up.'

Skelton stood up, glancing at his watch. Resnick wondered if, the second the door to the office was closed, Skelton would be logging the exact time the interview had finished in his Filofax.

Kevin Naylor spread the colour charts across his desk and couldn't remember whether Debbie had said peach or apricot. What was the difference anyway and how much did it matter? Something to do with the way it had to match the terracotta she'd already chosen for the tiles. Jesus! He'd always thought that getting married was a matter of finding a girl with the best qualities of your mother, but who wasn't going to turn into her own at half-time. Then it came down to choosing your moment, plucking up courage, will you . . .? A bucketful of tears and a gold ring later and you put the deposit down on one of those new houses across from the canal.

All of which showed how naive a young DC could be once clear of his own territory.

Drawing the down payment out of the Nationwide had been simply the beginning. Now every weekend, every off-duty moment, was filled with papers and paints, carpet samples, swatches of curtain material – he could have described the layout of every large furniture store and warehouse, every DIY emporium within a fifteen-mile radius of the city.

He refolded the charts as Mark Divine came into the office with two mugs of tea. Why couldn't he be like Divine? The world divided into three equal parts: you drank it, fly-tackled it or got your leg over it.

'Boss back?'
'Not yet.'

'Think we'll get to go up to Scottyland?'

'Who knows?'

'Good beer. Heavy, they call it. Pint of heavy. First time I heard that I thought . . .'

Both men stood up as Resnick came in, biting into a cream-cheese and gammon sandwich and balancing one styrofoam cup of black coffee on top of another. He nodded in the direction of his office and a chunk of gammon squeezed out and bounced from Resnick's cuff to his trouser leg and then to the floor.

'Where is he?' Resnick asked, using a brown envelope to swab up the spilt coffee.

'Aberdeen, sir,' Naylor and Divine answered, more or less in unison.

Resnick closed his eyes for a moment. 'Am I supposed to say good work?'

'Bloke across the hall,' Divine stepped in swiftly, 'bumped into him the other night after the pubs turned out. Macliesh said something about going back up to work on the oil rigs.'

'There was a train from Midland Station this morning,' said Divine. 'Quarter-past eight. Booking clerk recognized him from the photograph.'

Resnick remembered the picture the dead woman's mother had lifted out from beneath worn cardigans folded into a drawer. Shirley Peters wearing a white suit and holding a bouquet of pink flowers in front of her. Had she caught them, Resnick wondered, when the bride had tossed them through the air? 'Three times she were bridesmaid,' Mrs Peters had said. And then: 'At least she never married the lousy sod!' Tony Macliesh stood beside her in a borrowed suit, his eyes unable to focus. If the clerk had known him from that, he was doing well.

'The train's in when?' Resnick asked.

'Three forty-seven, sir,' said Naylor.

'Forty-nine,' corrected Divine. 'Sir.'

'Of course, you've been in touch with Aberdeen?'

'There's a Detective Inspector Cameron, sir. Says he'll make sure the train is met. He'd like you to give him a bell.'

Resnick nodded, wrote the name on a pad. 'Get yourselves up there. Catch some sleep. Bring him back down, first thing.'

'You want us to charge him, sir?' Divine sounded eager.

'Just bring him back down.'

'Not arrest him?'

Resnick looked at him evenly, holding his gaze until the constable looked away. 'No point in hurling ourselves into this. Let's get him in and ask some questions.'

'Sir, I thought . . .' Divine blurted.

'No, Divine, that's what you didn't do. What you did was see the obvious and not look beyond it.'

'Yes, sir.' Divine wasn't looking beyond anything now; he was studying his feet on his inspector's carpet.

'If you want to be any good as a detective, Divine, that's what you've got to learn to do.'

'Yes, sir.'

Standing alongside, it required strenuous effort from Naylor not to smirk.

'We're lucky he's getting picked up in Scotland,' said Resnick. 'England or Wales and the twenty-four hours we can hold him starts the moment he's arrested. Coming from Scotland, it doesn't start till we get him back in the station. But I expect you both knew that.'

Naylor and Divine exchanged glances.

'Yes, sir,' they said without conviction.

'*Police and Criminal Evidence Act, 1984*. Take a copy with you. It'll keep you awake on the journey.'

He waited until he was on his own before prising the lid from the first of the cups. Whatever the knack was of managing this without the coffee running down the insides of your fingers, he hadn't yet acquired it.

Five

It was five minutes short of five o'clock when Resnick called Rachel Chaplin. She was in the middle of discussing a long-term fostering breakdown. The kid was a fourteen-year-old West Indian lad, who, after months of stealing systematically from his foster mother's purse, had neglected to send her a card on her birthday. The petty theft she'd been able to understand, even expected; the ignoring of her birthday, purposeful or merely forgetful, she found more difficult to take.

'What are the chances of finding him a hostel place?' asked one of the other workers.

Rachel picked up her phone on the second ring. 'Social Services,' she said.

'Hello, this is Charlie Resnick.'

'I'm sorry. Who did you say?'

'Resnick. We met in court. You were there with Mrs Taylor.'

Charlie, Rachel was thinking. His name is Charlie!

'What can I do for you, Inspector?'

'I was just wondering . . .'

'Look, I'm in a meeting at the moment. Can I ring you back?'

'A drink,' Resnick said. 'How about a drink after work?'

'We might be able to get one of the project foster parents to take him on short-term,' someone near her suggested.

'I don't know what time this will get sorted,' Rachel said into the phone.

'You don't think there's any chance at all of keeping things as they are?' Rachel said into the room. 'Are we all saying that that's just not on?'

'How about six-thirty?' asked Resnick.

'Make it seven.'

'Where?'

'Could we try Buxton?' Rachel said.

'Isn't fifty miles rather a long way to go for a drink?' said Resnick.

'I wasn't talking to you. Unless you'd like to foster a wayward but charming teenager.'

'Not tonight.'

'All right then. You know the Peach Tree?'

'Yes.'

'Seven o'clock.'

She put down the phone and got on with her meeting.

All over the city, these past few years, local pubs had been stripped and gutted, painted and refitted, finally re-emerging as wine bars, cocktail bars, theme bars, simply bars. Resnick reckoned the manufacturers of strip lighting and nostalgia posters must have their Christmas holidays in the Bahamas on permanent reservation. This place was less than two hundred yards from his station, yet he hadn't been inside it since the day the refurbishers had moved in.

Now he pushed between a pair of frosted glass doors and found himself among a crowd of fashionable young people shouting at each other over pre-recorded music. Ah! thought Resnick knowledgeably, the Happy Hour crowd. One thing about browsing the colour supplements – it kept you up-to-date with life the way some folk lived it.

It was three-deep to the curve of the downstairs bar, so Resnick found the stairs at the back and climbed up into a 'living' video. Set amongst hi-tech furniture, green plants and cream-coloured blinds was a vision of money wearing money.

He had turned and was starting on his way back down when he saw Rachel at the foot of the stairs.

'Don't believe in waiting long, do you?' She was wearing a white shirt, large and loose, belted over deep blue cords, a black blouson jacket with wide epaulettes. Only the boots appeared to be the same as before.

'I thought I might have missed you downstairs.'

She glanced back over her shoulder. 'D'you want to come down?'

'Not really.'

A smile came to the edges of her mouth. 'You want to stay up there?'

'Not really.'

Rachel marched up the steps smartly, turned him round and moved him towards the bar. 'Come on, since we're here, I'll buy you a drink.'

They found a small table at the front, looking down at the traffic driving up the hill from the city through the rain that had started to fall again.

'Last time I came here,' Resnick said, 'it was an Irish pub with cheese and onion cobs and good Guinness. The backroom downstairs was carved straight out of the rock and they had a juke box in there with the best selection of rock 'n' roll in the city. Played it so loud on a Saturday night, pieces used to flake off the walls and fall into your pint.'

Rachel listened, sipping her white wine and soda. 'When you phoned, I couldn't think who you were.'

'I know. I make that impression on people.'

'At work sometimes, it's impossible to think about

38

anything else. I mean, outside.' She lifted her glass but set it down again. 'It must be the same for you.'

'With me it's the opposite.'

She thought about that a little and smiled. 'I don't believe you.'

'Ah,' said Resnick, leaning back in his chair.

Why were they talking like this?

'Anyway,' said Rachel, 'I'm sorry you don't approve of the pub. At least it's pretty quiet up here. You can usually get a seat if it's early enough.' She stopped talking abruptly, struck by the thought that she was saying too much, filling the silence. She looked at him, waiting until he looked back at her. 'I come here with Chris sometimes.'

'Who's she?'

'He.'

Resnick was still looking at her; he took a couple of swallows from his glass.

'Who's he?'

'The man I live with.'

He drained his glass as he stood up. 'I'll get you another.'

'No, I'm okay,' Rachel said.

He brought her one anyway. Typical bloody male, Rachel thought, making sure he saw her pushing the glass away and continuing to sip at the first.

'It's not against the law,' she said. 'Living with somebody.'

'No.'

'You don't approve.'

'Don't I?'

'Your face didn't.'

'I wasn't being moral.'

'I'm relieved.'

He shrugged his shoulders. He might not be too

bad-looking, Rachel was thinking, if only he'd lose a little weight.

'Maybe I was surprised. I didn't think of you as living with someone, that's all. It wasn't the picture I had of you.'

'Not the way I present myself?'

'No.'

'It doesn't mean you have to wear purdah, you know. Being in a relationship.'

'No,' said Resnick. 'I don't suppose it does.' More the hair shirt, he thought, sackcloth and ashes. He didn't say so; he didn't imagine she'd go for the poor chest-beating male routine.

'What picture did you have of me?' Rachel asked.

There were people standing between the tables now, uncertain whether it was more important to be overheard or overseen.

Resnick was holding his glass against his chest; for a few moments she was afraid he was going to try and balance it there. 'I don't know.'

'But it didn't include myself and a man... and Chris?'

'No.'

'I give off that sort of aura, do I? I must watch out. Some woman on her own, just about getting along. Home at nights to hot chocolate, a moth-eaten teddy bear and reruns of *Rhoda*.' She had started on the second glass of wine without really noticing. 'That's it, isn't it? That's what interests you. You thought I was some woman like the one I read about in today's paper. The case you're investigating. Single woman in her thirties found murdered in her own living-room. What was her name?'

'Shirley Peters,' Resnick said, leaning forward.

'Right. Well, that's it, isn't it? That explains the

sudden invitation to a drink. Instant analysis, part five. I thought when I put the phone down in the office, hello, Rachel, you've made an impression this time. But, no. What you see in me is a bit of living insight. Sex and the single girl. Well, sorry, Inspector, but I'm not volunteering. I live with a social worker so I take the job home too often as it is. I've had stereotypes and syndromes and role-play re-enactments with my Shreddies for so long I just cover them with sugar and they all go down the same way.'

She was close to shouting; a few people were looking round but no one seemed to notice overmuch. Resnick didn't respond; he sat there looking across at her as she sank back the rest of her wine, swung her bag up from the back of her chair and on to her arm and pushed her way through the crowd.

One hell of a way to end the day! thought Resnick. One hell of a way to start the evening! And he hadn't even wanted to talk to her about Shirley Peters: he had hoped she might be able to get him some information about Tony Macliesh. Through the blur of the window he watched her cross the road to her car and wondered what was putting her under so much pressure.

Patel saw the red Porsche at two hundred-plus yards, despite the rain driving in on his face. Seen anywhere else, he might not have given it a second look, but there, in that street, parked in front of that house.

Leave this one alone, Resnick had told him that morning, get back to the break-ins. You know the routine: question and answer. The same numbing procedure that had gone on too long. Houses where all the occupants were at work, no use in calling until way after six. Now there was a pain stretching across between his shoulder blades – all those kitchen tables he had leaned over, filling in the forms. Question and answer. Officially, he'd come off duty at three that afternoon.

'Is it Mrs Peters you're looking for?' Patel asked.

The woman who turned from the door, sheltering beneath a transparent umbrella, surveyed him with her head held to one side.

'Shirl, yeh. Why, sunshine?'

Patel took out his warrant card, shielding it from the rain as best he could. The woman looked at him with surprise, her glossed mouth forming a soundless, 'Oh!'

'You are a friend, perhaps?'

'No perhaps about it.' She nodded towards the Porsche. 'Just drove up to see her.'

'I wonder if . . .'

She beckoned him with a glitter-red fingernail. 'Come closer then. No point in getting wet for nothing.'

She was wearing, thought Patel, too much perfume, too much make-up; below her short white fur coat, her legs shone in shiny black plastic trousers. For a young man of simple tastes, she was altogether too much.

'What's happened then?' And seeing the pain flinching at the back of Patel's soft brown eyes, she touched his arm lightly with her free hand. 'You can tell me, you know. I ain't about to throw a wobbler or anything.'

Patel sucked in air. 'There was a . . . your friend is dead. She was . . .'

'Don't be bloody stupid!'

'I'm afraid she was murdered.'

The umbrella slipped from the woman's hand and, automatically, Patel caught it and held it close above her head. He looked into her face for tears and all he saw was anger.

'The stupid, stupid bitch! The stupid sodding cow!

How many times? How many times did I tell her this would bloody happen?'

She stared at Patel hard, their faces close together, rain springing back from the plastic of the umbrella, the concrete below their feet. He watched her mouth open and for one delirious moment thought she was about to sink her teeth into the soft flesh of his lip.

'All right,' she said. 'I'd better follow you up the station.'

She pulled her umbrella away from Patel and he turned full-face into the rain.

Six

Chris Phillips was stretched out on the settee in front
of the fire, one leg hooked over its low back. A beige
labrador was spread across the rug between settee and
fire, growling lightly into the towel that Phillips had
used to dry the dog down after their evening walk. A
card-index box balanced on Phillips's stomach and a
brace of pink files was clamped between his knees;
pieces of stationery, all bearing the name of the local
authority, were scattered within arm's reach. If he
hadn't been writing on one of the cards when Rachel
came into the room he might have looked up and seen
the expression on her face, in which case he might not
have spoken at all. He certainly would not have called
out, 'Surprise, surprise!' in his usual tone of affectionate
irony.

'What's that supposed to mean?' said Rachel.

Phillips looked up at the sharpness in her voice.

The labrador took its piece of towel and dropped it
across Rachel's feet.

'I wasn't expecting you back so soon, that's all,' he
said.

'I'm sorry.'

'I didn't mean that. I . . .'

'I can sit in the kitchen if you're working.'

Phillips released a breath, close to a sigh. 'I thought
you were meeting someone.' He lifted the box and

folders away and turned round. 'I thought you were going for a drink.'

'I was,' Rachel's voice came back from the kitchen.

'And?'

'And I had a drink and now I'm back here.'

He leaned forward and retrieved the card he'd been writing on, quickly finished making his annotation, slotted the card back into place. He knew how he should react to Rachel when she was like this, knew that what he had to do was leave her alone, let her sort her own way out of it.

'I was just about to have a Scotch,' he said, leaning against the kitchen doorway.

She swung her head towards him as if to say, good for you.

'Want to join me?'

'No.'

'Might make you feel better.'

'No.'

Somehow he'd managed to close out the sound of the rain so completely that when he went out into the garden the fierceness of it took him by surprise. The dog had run out after him and now hunched back near some roses that were waiting to be cut back, looking at him hopefully through the gloom. You want to play ball, don't you? You want to go for another walk?

Through the blurred square of the window he could make out the dark twist of Rachel's hair as she moved back and forth between the cooker and the sink.

The labrador's coat was soaked already, his nose slick and his eyes bright.

All right, he knew she was having a tough time at work, this placement breaking down on top of everything else, a kid she'd really struggled for. But why did she have to hold so much into herself, why try so hard to keep him out, as if admitting any kind of weakness was showing a crack through which he could slide his hand and hang on? And besides, his day hadn't exactly been a cakewalk. A couple of kids with so much solvent up their noses that breathing was more or less impossible; a woman who'd barricaded herself into her flat on the thirteenth floor and threatened to chop off her fingers if she weren't left alone; an old man all but dead from hypothermia, who'd fallen over and lain for two days with the carpet wrapped around him until Meals on Wheels raised the alarm. She wasn't the only one with things to feel bad about.

When he walked back into the house, water running down his face, Rachel had left the kitchen and the kettle was coming up to the boil, beginning its shrill whistle.

In the bathroom Rachel stood quite still, staring at her reflection in the mirror. Where her cheekbones touched her skin, she was still flushed from the rain and the cold. After some moments she began to pull the comb down through her hair and then stopped. Why was she behaving like this? Because she'd allowed herself to get annoyed by a man she scarcely knew? A stupid policeman. It was ridiculous.

'I'm sorry,' she started to say.

'It's okay. Nothing.' Phillips closed the living-room door with one foot, a mug in each hand.

Rachel tried for a smile. 'What is it? Coffee?'

'Tea.'

The smile became real. 'Just because your wife told you it was what women needed when they were premenstrual.'

'Oh, so that's what it is.'

46

'Part of it.'

'I should have known.'

'I told you those little red dots should be in your diary.'

He waited until she had sat on the settee, handed her the tea and sat beside her, careful not to crowd her too close. 'How did it go, the meeting?'

'It went.'

'No way of holding it together?'

Rachel sat with the mug cradled between both hands. 'No,' she said. 'No way.'

Resnick had driven home from the Peach Tree and fed the cats. The post comprised a letter from his bank urging him to apply for the one credit card he already had, several pieces of disposable junk mail and a reminder that his dues to the local Polish Association had not been paid. He was tearing everything but the last in half when he noticed a leaflet offering three free trial sessions at a new health club.

You never could tell.

Resnick folded the leaflet neatly and slid it between the tabasco and the Worcester sauce. Bud was sulking because Dizzy had stolen her food again, so Resnick picked the cat up and set her down near the draining board, tipping a handful of chicken Brekkies quietly out of the palm of his hand in front of her.

A few minutes later he was back in his car and heading for the station.

Graham Millington had a small hand mirror propped up on his desk and was using a pair of nail scissors to trim his moustache.

'Graham. The house-to-house?'

Millington nearly cut a generous slice out of his lip

when he jumped. 'Reports are on your desk,' he said, scrambling to his feet, his voice a shade muffled.

Resnick leafed through the forms, summaries of the calls Kellogg and Patel had made that day. 'Give me the gist of it,' he said, not looking up.

'Lot more stuff about threats from Macliesh, hammering on the door at all hours, calling her all the names under the sun, at least two claim he'd wait down the end of the street for her of an evening...'

'Recent?'

'Most of them before he went down, but not all.'

'This one here,' Resnick said, lifting one sheet away from the rest. 'Man at 42 – that's across the street, isn't it? – says he saw Shirley Peters leaving the house the evening she was killed. Eight o'clock.'

'Says he knew the time because of the television.'

'Saw a taxi pulled up and she went off in that.'

'Thinks there was only the driver in the cab but he couldn't swear to it.'

Resnick glanced down at the report. 'Didn't know which taxi firm either.'

'No particular reason for him to notice, sounds as if she was always off out, this one.'

Resnick looked up sharply at the censorious tone in his sergeant's voice. 'Not about to voice the opinion that she was asking for it, Graham?' he said softly.

'No, sir.'

'And we're following up the taxi?'

'DC Kellogg, she's been phoning round. Nothing definite yet, but they're usually pretty good, things like this.'

Resnick pushed the reports back together, glanced at his watch. 'Off duty, aren't you?'

Millington shrugged. 'Wife's night for her Russian

class. She's dropped the boys off at her mother's. I'll probably just have a quick pint and then get back.'

Resnick nodded and the sergeant turned to leave.

'Graham?'

'Yes?'

'Peach Tree, that's your pub, isn't it?'

Millington nodded.

'Shouldn't go in there looking like that. You've got blood down the front of your shirt.'

Resnick checked through the reports again, making notes here and there. A call had been logged from Aberdeen informing him that Tony Macliesh had been taken into custody off the train. The DS on the second shift had been called out to clear up a couple of assaults at a private family party. The owner of a second-hand shop on the Alfreton Road had called in to say that a couple of youths had been round offering him three VCRs; they were coming back tomorrow and an officer would be there to greet them. If the owner hadn't already been sentenced twice for receiving stolen goods, it would have been altruistic.

When Resnick realized he had been thinking about Rachel Chaplin for some minutes, he called down to the desk and asked the sergeant to send one of the uniforms past Reno's to pick him up a pizza – pepperoni, anchovies, extra olives.

He'd hardly put the phone down when Patel came in with the woman.

Grace Kelley sniffed the room for the smell of Brut and was disappointed. She'd been inside police stations before but never into CID and somehow it wasn't living up to her expectations. She'd anticipated a mixture of shower gel and Benson king-size, men with jock straps snug beneath the polyester weave of their off-the-peg blue suits, but all she got were some uncovered typewriters, a couple of dying pot plants and, on the desk nearest to her, a photograph of a wife and two kids with a mirror resting against it. She might as well, she thought, have been back in the typing pool.

Leaning sideways on to the desk, Grace took off one of her high-heels and massaged the arch of her foot. She could see the young Asian talking to another man in a side office. The man was standing, listening, now sitting, pushing his chair back and getting comfortable without taking his eyes from the Asian's face. Only once did he glance away, eyes drifting across hers, then quickly back.

Grace pushed her other shoe free and shimmied her black trousers on to the edge of the desk. Two hours it had taken her up the motorway, sodding roadworks, panting to show Shirley the new motor, watch her face as she stood there creaming herself. What Shirley wouldn't have done for a Porsche, red and all – likely a sight more than she'd done herself. Given the chance, poor cow!

The door to the office opened and she pushed herself off the desk and started to wiggle back into her shoes. She caught the unmistakable smell of sweat and realized that it was coming off her own body.

'The Inspector would like to talk to you.'

Grace wobbled and reached out a hand to grasp Patel's shoulder, smiling as he flinched. 'Thanks, pet,' she said, jamming her heel down into her right shoe.

Resnick was standing, gesturing for her to sit down. 'Miss Kelley?'

'That's right.' She sat down, pulling the sides of her white fur out to the metal arms of the chair.

Resnick looked at her appraisingly. 'Grace.'

She opened the small black bag that hung from her shoulder and took out a pack of cigarettes. 'My mother had ideas above my station.'

Resnick smiled. He looks good when he smiles, she thought, younger. She stopped, waiting for him to light her cigarette, then did it herself, using a slim gold lighter which she dropped back into her bag, drawing in the smoke as she leaned her head back before exhaling.

'New Cross,' she said.

'Sorry?'

'My station. You're supposed to say, when I say my station, you're supposed to say . . .'

'What station?'

'And I say New Cross.' She wiped her left hand through a slow curve of blue-grey smoke. 'Even that isn't quite the truth. Deptford, really.' She remembered to keep her head level, hide the looseness that was starting to show beneath her chin. 'D'you know London, south of the river?'

'Not really.'

'Haven't missed a lot. I got out as soon as I could.'

'Gracefully,' Resnick smiled.

'You can't get over that, can you?'

'Mmm?'

'The name.' She looked at the ash forming at the tip of her cigarette and Resnick fished an ashtray from a drawer and slid it towards her.

'My mum used to spend every spare minute she had at the pictures. Deptford, Lewisham. Anything with Grace Kelly in it, she'd be there, three, four times in a week. Spent half of my time as a kid, I did, sitting in Greenwich Park listening to her telling me what happened, over and over again. *Fourteen Hours, High*

Noon, Mogambo. It was only when I saw some of them later, on the telly, I realized she'd got the plots all in a twist. That one, *Dial M for Murder*, where Grace Kelly's husband's out to . . .'

She leaned forward awkwardly and stubbed out the cigarette. A shiver ran through her and when Resnick saw her face again she was crying.

' . . . out to murder her. Jesus!' She stood up, tried to, the pocket of her coat catching on the end of the chair so that it tore when she tugged at it. 'Shirley – that bastard! – I must have talked myself hoarse trying to get her to come down to London, move in with me for a bit, anything to get clear of that pig when they let him out.' She smeared tears across her make-up. 'She couldn't see it, reckoned it'd be all right, sitting around in that poxy place waiting for some bloody Prince Charming to appear at the end of the rainbow. As if he'd ever let her have a life with someone else, not while he knew where to find them. She couldn't live with him, and he was going to make good and sure she didn't live with anyone else.'

'Macliesh,' Resnick said.

'Who bloody else?' Grace said. And then she grabbed hold of the back of the chair with both hands and said: 'I don't suppose you've got a drink?'

Resnick got up and went into the main office. He took the half-bottle of Bell's from Divine's desk drawer and poured some into a styrofoam cup.

'I could send for some coffee,' he said.

'It's just starting to sink in,' she said. 'Delayed shock, isn't that what they call it?'

Resnick sat back down. 'I think my young DC had almost as much of a shock as you did.'

'Poor love! Don't know what he thought I was going to do to him.'

'I meant when he found the body.'

There was a knock on the door and a West Indian constable came in carrying Resnick's pizza.

'Equal opportunities round here, isn't it?' she said when the constable had gone.

'Want a slice?' Resnick asked, sliding it out from the box and on to his desk.

'I don't think ... My God! Anchovies and sausage, that's disgusting!'

Only slightly shamefaced, Resnick lifted a piece to his mouth, wondering if for once he would be able to eat it without getting strands of cheese stuck to his chin.

'How well did you know Shirley Peters?' Resnick asked, between bites.

'We were good mates. Good as you can be when you don't live in the same place, not any more. I met her about six years ago. I'd been living in Birmingham and then I come over here, some sales promotion job or other, you know, poncing around between new cars in the shopping centre, sticking out your tits and getting your ass felt up by the sales reps at the same time. Shirley was there too, moonlighting from the office job she had, Tony would have ... would have killed her there and then if he'd known. We just hit it off, you know, kept in touch. When she finally got rid of Tony, I came up and stayed with her for a couple of weeks.' She helped herself to some more of Divine's whisky. 'Not the place for me, though. Too quiet. Everyone's tucked up in bed by half-twelve.'

Resnick had had too much experience outside the city's discos at three in the morning to believe that, but he didn't contradict her. 'She was living with Macliesh then, was she?'

'Yeh, and he never liked me one little bit. I was always getting her to stand up to him, that's why. One of those blokes who reckons he can wipe his hands all over you like you're a box of Kleenex and goes spare if you as much as cough in front of another man. He hit her once in Tesco's, not like a push, a real slap, hard across the face because she smiled at some feller pushing his trolley out of the way to let her past.'

'Why . . .?' Resnick began, but he knew the question was never any good. Why did women stick with men who knocked them around? Why did so many men get off on it, need it, the owning, the forcing, the feel of skin breaking beneath their own? In twelve hours, a little more, he would be back in court, facing a man who had abused his seven-year-old daughter as if he had the right.

'Did you ever hear him threaten her, threaten Shirley?'

'Now you're kidding.'

'Incidents you can remember, clearly I mean. Things he said.'

'And did.'

An olive rolled off the side of Resnick's slice of pizza. 'If you wouldn't mind coming back in the morning and making a statement?'

'Anything to put that bastard back where he belongs.' She looked at Resnick keenly. 'You have got him, haven't you? He hasn't done a runner?'

'Only as far as Aberdeen. He's in police custody.'

'Pity he was ever allowed out of it.' She stood up. 'Pity he won't swing.'

On the stairs, Resnick asked, 'Are you all right for tonight? I mean, have you got somewhere to stay?'

The smile was almost real, but the red gloss had been wiped across one cheek and on to her teeth. 'That an offer?'

'If it's a matter of finding a hotel . . .'

She touched his arm, but for no more than a moment. 'I'm used to finding hotels.'

There were two half-drunken lads at the desk, nothing over their short-sleeved check shirts in spite of the weather; their eyes followed her to the door and they were about to come out with some remark until one look from her made them feel almost as young as they were and they stayed quiet.

'What time d'you want me in the morning?'

Resnick shrugged, aware that the desk sergeant was watching him with amusement. 'Half-nine, ten.'

'Goodnight, Inspector. Thanks for the drink.'

The sergeant was still looking at him. 'You owe me two-fifty for the pizza,' he said.

Resnick nodded and went back up the stairs.

Rachel Chaplin was in bed when the phone rang. Phillips called her from the bottom of the stairs. 'It's for you.'

She came down wearing a sweat shirt and leg warmers, at least she hadn't been asleep.

'What time is it?' she asked, taking the receiver.

'Nearly twelve,' Phillips said, walking away.

'Hello,' Rachel said into the phone. 'Who is this?'

Resnick said, 'I figured the chances were we'd bump into one another tomorrow and I just, well, I didn't want it to be awkward, that's all.'

He didn't say anything else.

Rachel hung up the phone.

Phillips looked over from where he was writing a

final draft of his report, head angled to one side as if to say, who was that?

'Nobody important,' Rachel said, and went back upstairs to bed.

Seven

Mark Divine sat in the reception area across from an enquiry desk that had been enclosed with contiboard, leaving space for a sliding glass window that would have admitted a man's head but not his shoulders. Not without the head being pulled very hard. Jutting out from beneath the window was a formica-topped counter edged with cigarette burns. Posters asking for information about missing children had been pinned to the walls beside and behind the wooden bench on which Divine sat, thumbing through the pages of the *Sun*. Fifteen, no, twenty minutes they'd been kept hanging about and not so much as a cup of tea.

Kevin Naylor came through the door past the desk and Divine folded his newspaper and stood up. 'About time,' he said.

'Macliesh, is he . . .?'

'I thought that's what you'd been to find out.'

Naylor shook his head. 'I was on the phone.'

'Reporting in?'

'No. Debbie. Thought I'd give her a quick call, that's all.'

Divine grunted as he sat back down and shook open the paper. 'Afraid she'll disappear or something?'

'What's that supposed to mean?'

'If she doesn't hear your voice, she'll go up in a puff of smoke.'

'Don't be soft.'

'Me? Soft? You're the one who has to phone his missus every other five minutes.'

'I don't *have* to phone her at all.'

Divine turned a page, then another. 'No, you don't have to call, of course you don't. What d'you find to say to one another all the time, that's what I'd like to know?' He grinned up at Naylor. 'That lovey-dovey, newly-wedded, darling-I'm-missing-you-I-can't-live-without-you mush, is it? Sweetheart, I'm lost without . . .'

'Stuff it, Divine!' Naylor lashed out with his arm and knocked the paper from Divine's hands.

'Oooh, now, now!' Divine smirked.

'I said, stuff it!'

Divine was on his feet with dangerous speed and looking at Naylor hard.

'Up here we usually leave that kind of thing to the customers,' said a uniformed sergeant from the window.

Naylor lowered his eyes first and the two men stood apart.

'You're here for Macliesh, aren't you?'

They nodded.

'Come through with me and I'll take you down to the cells.'

The custody sergeant was sitting behind a small curved counter, a leather-bound book open in front of him, lines ruled and crammed with letters in black ink. Behind his right shoulder was a dark green board on which arrivals and departures were chalked in and out. The smell, freshly splashed disinfectant overlaying the sweetness of sewage, came up the steps on the cold air.

'These two are for Macliesh.'

'Aye.'

Aside from the allegations they'd heard and that single photograph, neither Naylor nor Divine had any clear idea of what to expect of Macliesh. So when he walked slowly up the stone steps they were surprised to find that he was slight. Seemed it, until they saw the tightness of the muscle on arms almost without body hair, the flatness of his stomach. Not a pound of spare flesh on him.

'That all he was wearing?' Divine asked.

A grey pullover without sleeves, a black T-shirt beneath it; jeans from which the belt had been removed, worn-down scuffed shoes without laces.

A hold-all was pulled up from behind the counter, an envelope opened and its contents tipped out: some coins, stub of pencil, a five-pound note, a watch on a clear plastic strap.

The officer held out a pen.

Naylor signed for the belongings and they were returned to the envelope, the envelope pushed down under the zip of the hold-all. Naylor signed again and the sergeant handed him the custody record. 'Go careful with him.'

The sergeant clicked one cuff over Macliesh's right wrist, the other to Divine's left.

'Shit!' hissed Divine as it pinched skin.

'Sorry,' said the sergeant with a grin and loosened the ratchets before locking it fast again.

'Right, then?' asked Naylor.

The sergeant nodded as Naylor and Divine took their prisoner out to the waiting car; they weren't going to get much out of him on the drive back home. Smiling, he used a bright yellow duster to wipe Macliesh's name from the board.

'At which point did you establish that the woman who first reported the alleged offence was not, in fact, a neighbour but the girl's mother?'

Resnick had briefed Millington on the procedure to be followed when Macliesh arrived: made sure he would be at the station to interview Grace Kelley and take her statement. He would far rather have been there himself, anywhere rather than back in court under cross-examination.

'Inspector?'

Resnick finished checking his notebook. 'Three days after the initial report.'

'Three days?'

'Detective Sergeant Pierce went back to the home with DC Kellogg and on that occasion Mrs Taylor agreed that she had made the allegations herself. Then, after some discussion, she further agreed to bring her daughter in for a medical examination.'

'And this examination, Inspector, where did this take place?'

'At the City Hospital.'

'Who was present at this examination?'

'A consultant paediatrician, the police surgeon, Mrs Taylor of course, and the social worker assigned to her case.'

'But not Mr Taylor?'

Resnick shook his head. 'No.'

'Not the child's father?'

'No, for obvious . . .'

'Your mind was already made up. As to his guilt? Yourself and Social Services between you had determined . . .'

'Nothing,' Resnick interrupted.

The defence counsel smiled. 'You would say that you enjoy a good relationship with the Social Services department, Inspector?'

Resnick wanted to shift his gaze to where he knew Rachel Chaplin was sitting. He knew she was wearing a dark blue suit with a fine stripe running through it, the jacket tucked in slightly at the waist, padded at the shoulders. A pale blue blouse was buttoned high at her neck. Today her hair had been pulled back off her face to be held by matt silver combs.

'Given that our aims are not always identical, I'd say, yes, it's a good working relationship.'

He was looking directly at the defence counsel, face giving nothing away. The barrister hesitated, drawn to pursue the issue of aims, wanting to, but not allowing himself, ploughing on instead.

Rachel Chaplin shifted back on the bench seat, recrossed her legs, right over left. In the quiet of the court, she could hear the sound of nylon sliding across nylon. 'Not giving evidence today, are you?' Phillips had said as she was leaving. 'I shouldn't think so, why?' 'Just you're looking extra smart.'

She had held her breath when she heard the question, waiting for Resnick to look across the courtroom and seek her out. How would you describe your relationship with Social Services? She was certain that he wanted to look in her direction, just a glance, and it impressed her that he did not. Only later did it occur to her that was his intention, the effect he'd been working on.

Yes, she thought, all right, I'd like to sit down with you some time and talk about aims, intentions, sit down and talk some things through.

'Now, Inspector,' counsel was saying, 'I should like to draw your attention to those photographs, entered as Exhibit A, which were taken by the police photographer subsequent to the girl's initial medical examination.'

Resnick pinched the bridge of his nose and, for little more than the space of a second, closed his eyes.

'Underpowered,' Divine said sideways.

He was doing eighty-five in the outside lane, flashing full-beam at the Volvo fifteen yards in front.

'Stop at the next services,' said Naylor.

'Again?'

'Again.'

On the previous occasion, the two men had changed places, leaving Naylor in the rear with the prisoner. Almost a hundred miles of sitting less than comfortably, feeling your left leg growing numb above the knee; fidgeting your buttocks without wanting to move around too much because the man who was handcuffed to you was not moving at all, only breathing, his eyes staring through the offside window at the patches of green that rose and fell dully away between the swish of traffic.

'You're not going to make another phone call.'

There was one thing you'd have to say about Divine, Naylor thought, once he got an idea into his head, no matter how pathetic, he didn't let it go easily.

'I want a leak,' Naylor said.

'A couple of those doughnuts,' Divine said over his shoulder. 'Lemon curd.'

'Only two?' said Naylor.

'For starters.' Grudgingly the Volvo shifted into the centre lane and they accelerated past. 'How about happy-bollocks?' said Divine. 'He'll be wanting to go by now.'

Naylor looked at Macliesh.

Macliesh continued to gaze out of the window like a man who'd found himself in another land surrounded by another language.

They parked alongside a VW Polo and waited while a baby was strapped into a car seat and then three other children aged between three and seven were packed aboard, arguing and pushing their way between suitcases, assorted games, a blue plastic potty and a Yorkshire terrier. By the time the parents had got into the front, they looked too tired to drive out of the car park.

'That'll be you in a few years' time,' grinned Divine, opening the door so that Macliesh could get out.

'It doesn't have to be like that,' said Naylor, following close behind.

'Oh, yeh?'

'There are other ways of doing it.'

Divine smirked and raised one eyebrow.

'It all depends on the way you treat them, the kids I mean. Set about it right and the more kids you have the more help they are. Within reason.'

'Debbie tell you that?'

'Common sense tells me that.'

They were standing close to a line of video games and slot machines, a couple of bikers leaning up against the wall making gestures of solidarity towards Macliesh, who didn't acknowledge they were there. An elderly woman went slowly past using a Zimmer frame, staring at the handcuffs all the way.

'Realize how much it'd cost bringing a family like that in here? All those fish fingers, burgers, cobs and chips. Set off on holiday and you'd be spent up before you were off the motorway.'

Then what you do is pack up your own sandwiches before you leave, Naylor said to himself, big bottle of Coke and a Thermos. He knew better than to say it out loud.

'Cheaper sticking to condoms,' laughed Divine. 'Not that I use them myself, take away most of the enjoyment.'

'Get us something and bring it out to the car,' said

Naylor, nodding towards the cafeteria. 'I don't want to go in there like this. We'll go to the Gents and see you back in the car park.'

'Sure you'll be all right?'

Naylor nodded at Macliesh and started to walk him towards the toilet.

'Better hope he's left-handed,' Divine called after them.

Just once, Naylor was thinking, just once it would be nice to get sent out with Patel, he wasn't such a bad bloke, Lynn Kellogg even. There were even times when he found himself quite fancying Lynn. And that was something else that had taken him by surprise. Get hitched, he'd thought, and all that lusting after other women'll go by the board. For the first few years anyway. God, he wondered what Debbie would say if he ever plucked up the courage to tell her, which, of course, he wouldn't. She wasn't even good-looking, Lynn, not in the way women were supposed to be, but that didn't stop him catching a sideways glance at her sometimes in the squadroom and wondering what she looked like underneath those loose-fitting clothes she usually wore. Not long after she'd been promoted into CID, Divine had taken her out. Mouth flapping away as usual beforehand. On and on about how he was going to see she was made good and welcome, getting her properly initiated, crap like that. He didn't know what had happened, but Divine had clammed up like a stone afterwards. Like a stone. He . . .

Naylor felt something suddenly warm and turned his head. Macliesh had shifted sideways in his stall and was standing, quite solemnly, holding himself in his left hand and directing a steady stream of urine down the left leg of Naylor's trousers.

'And at no point, Inspector, did it occur to you to doubt the truth of Mrs Taylor's allegations?'

'It's for the court to establish truth. What I needed to be certain of was that there was a real possibility that an offence had been committed.'

'Which you were?'

'Yes.'

'Beyond any doubt?'

'If there was any possibility of a child being at risk, it was my duty to see that the allegations were properly investigated.'

'Speedily.'

'Yes.'

'Hastily.'

'That's your word,' said Resnick flatly.

Good for you, Rachel said to herself and smiled.

'I don't consider it necessary for you to debate semantics with the legal profession,' said the judge, leaning slightly forward. 'Simply answer the questions.'

'I'm sorry, your honour,' replied Resnick, 'I thought I already had.'

'I suggest that what you have done,' said the counsel for the defence, 'is to marry together two convenient pieces of evidence. That which proves, all too sadly and conclusively, that this unfortunate child was the victim of sexual misuse on more than one occasion, and the accusations of a highly wrought and distressed mother who may have had any number of other reasons for electing to blame her husband for those same offences.'

There were angry shouts, two of them, bitter and prolonged, from different sections of the public seating. Rachel realized that she had risen halfway to her feet and made herself slowly sit down.

'You took the first solution because it was the easiest,

because it has become almost axiomatic in these increasingly well-publicized cases to see the father or stepfather as the perpetrator, and because, as you so revealingly said earlier, the good relationship you enjoy with the Social Services would have encouraged you to come to the same convenient and fashionable conclusion.'

'I did not say . . .'

'Inspector, your evidence is now a matter of record.'

'I did *not* say that the views of any members of the Social Services . . .'

'Inspector, please. The court is fully aware of what it was you said.'

'Nothing was said by any outside agency that convinced us to put Mr Taylor under arrest.'

'Then what did?'

Resnick held back his response, held his breath. He could feel the dampness of his shirt where it clung to the small of his back, the itch of perspiration beneath his arms and between his legs. 'The girl,' he said clearly.

'The seven-year-old girl.'

'Yes.'

'Upset, intimidated . . .'

'No.'

'Asked so many leading questions . . .'

'No.'

' . . . that, like all little girls do, she gave the answer she had come to realize was wanted.'

A sound broke from Resnick's mouth, somewhere between a roar and a laugh. 'I watched,' Resnick said, 'watched through a two-way mirror, watched seven-year-old Sharon Taylor sitting with a social worker and with nobody else in the room . . .'

'Inspector,' said the barrister, 'there is no need.'

'Yes, there is!' Resnick's hands were gripping the

66

front of the witness stand and even from near the rear of the room Rachel could see that his knuckles were white. 'There is a need.'

The judge bent towards him. 'Inspector Resnick, I do realize that this is a disquieting case.'

Resnick faced the judge and when he spoke again his voice was low and even. 'The only other things that mattered in the room were a microphone and two dolls.' He pointed towards the table where the dolls lay. 'Those which have already been examined by the court. And what I heard and saw was Sharon Taylor using those dolls to explain what it was the accused had done to her. What he had made her do to him.' Resnick's eyes fixed on the barrister's face. 'Her father.'

Eight

At first he thought she wasn't there and felt a flush of disappointment that ran close to anger. It was something he almost believed he had earned, that his testimony had deserved. He had allowed himself to picture how she would be standing there, the smile coming up on her face to greet him. When would he learn to stop fooling himself?

Resnick nodded at someone he knew, skirted round a couple of solicitors, diaries out, arranging their weekly bridge game, and there she was. Off to the side, her head mostly turned away, of course, Rachel was talking to Mrs Taylor and Resnick could imagine her tone, even and reassuring.

He slowed his pace, not wanting to reach the exit before she noticed him.

'Inspector.' Rachel left Mrs Taylor with a smile and crossed the foyer.

Resnick took his time about turning, so that Rachel was almost up to him when he looked at her.

'How are you feeling?' Rachel asked.

Resnick nodded past her shoulder. 'How's your client?'

'She's spent the best part of the day in court, listening while a highly paid smoothie with a wig on his head does everything he can to prove she's a vindictive and hysterical liar. How do you think she's feeling?'

Rachel lowered her head for a moment and the corners of her mouth broke into a smile. 'I'm sorry,' she said. 'You don't deserve that. Mrs Taylor's coping pretty well. The positive thing about that kind of display is that it makes her feel angry too. Angry at what they're trying to do to her. Whereas you . . .' The smile was in her eyes now.' . . . she thinks you're the bee's knees.'

'Did she say that? The bee's knees?'

'No, I did.' She moved a half-pace towards him. 'Look,' she said, touching her finger to her mouth. 'Watch my lips move.'

'I'm sorry about the other evening,' Resnick said, trying not to keep watching her mouth now and finding it difficult.

'You said.'

'I hope I didn't dig you out of bed when I phoned?'

'You did.'

'But not – what's his name?'

'You know very well. It's Chris. And we're not going to start that again, are we?'

'I thought we might go and have a drink.'

'I've promised Mrs Taylor I'd go along with her and collect Sharon. I ought to stay with them for a while.'

'Later then?'

Resnick watched her weighing it up, uncertain what was being held in the balance.

'Seven?' Rachel said finally.

'Okay. Where d'you want to go?'

'You'd better choose this time,' she said, amused.

'D'you know the Partridge?'

'Mansfield Road?'

'That's the one.'

Nodding, she turned away and walked back to where Mrs Taylor was waiting. Resnick figured he would have ample time to check back at the station and find out what progress Millington had made with Macliesh. In all likelihood, he'd been bearing down on him so hard that by the time Resnick arrived there'd be a confession, signed, sealed and witnessed. It might be enough to earn the sergeant his promotion and get him off Resnick's back.

On his way to the street, Resnick checked his watch. If he was lucky there'd just be time to nip home and feed the cats as well.

'Bloody hopeless!'

Graham Millington was sitting on the centre block of desks, one foot pushed out against a convenient chairback; he had a plastic cup in one hand, a cigarette in the other and looked as though he'd thrown his clothes in the tumble drier without bothering to get out of them first.

'Thought you'd given up,' Resnick said.

Millington stared down at his hands. 'Which one?'

'Can I have a word, boss?' The late-shift sergeant was hovering close to Resnick's shoulder, three plastic bags and a half-dozen ten-by-eight photographs in his hands.

'Come on in.'

Ten minutes later, when Resnick and the sergeant emerged, Millington was still in the same position.

'Are we drinking Divine's Scotch again?' Resnick asked.

Millington nodded.

Resnick took the bottle from the drawer, thinking as he did so that come January First he would have to say something to Divine about his taste in calendars. Surely he wasn't the only one in the office who found month after month of jutting breasts objectionable? Maybe he should have a word about it with Lynn Kellogg.

He tipped a little of the whisky into the sergeant's cup.

'How about you, sir?'

Resnick shook his head. 'Later.' And then: 'I take it he didn't break down and reveal all.'

'I was the one fit for sodding breaking down.'

'How come?'

Millington looked at him. 'What d'you think it's like spending the entire afternoon with a man who won't answer a single question?'

'Quiet?' Resnick said quietly.

Clever bastard! Millington thought.

'Why isn't he talking?' Resnick asked.

'If he won't open his bloody mouth, how'm I supposed to know?'

'Take it easy, Graham.'

'Sorry, sir.' Millington levered himself off the desk, started feeling in his pockets for his cigarettes. 'It's so bloody infuriating. Sitting there listening to the clock ticking round. You want to reach across the desk and shake it out of him.'

Resnick took the cigarette out of Millington's fingers and slid it back into the packet for him; the packet he dropped down into the side pocket of the sergeant's rumpled jacket.

'You didn't?' Resnick said, only just a question.

Millington shook his head. 'I think he'd have been more than happy if I had. Had a go at him, I mean.'

'Pretty cool for a man who's supposed to have a violent temper.'

'Perhaps he's only tough with women.'

Resnick felt an echo of something inside himself, too distant to be clear what it was. 'Maybe,' he said.

'The one thing he did say,' Millington began.

'Yes?'

71

'When Divine and Naylor were taking him through to the cells.'

'Yes.'

'He said, "I know that cow set me up for this and I'll fucking kill her!" '

'Who did he mean?'

'He didn't say.'

'Who d'you think he meant?'

'The girl's mother?'

'Probably,' Resnick said, but he was thinking about Grace Kelley.

Across the room a phone rang and Millington picked up the receiver, 'CID.' Then, 'Right, sir. Yes, sir. The superintendent,' he said to Resnick. 'Will you pop up and see him before he goes?'

Resnick was already on his way.

The newspaper was spread across the superintendent's desk, open at the report of the trial. Most of page two and a run-on to page three: child abuse was still big news. Resnick looked down at an out-of-date press photograph of himself, blurred and upside-down.

'Not a very good likeness.'

'No, sir.'

'And the report – any more accurate, would you say?'

Resnick lifted the paper from the desk and skimmed it through. Skelton studied the station roster on the side wall. You could have fitted Resnick's office into the superintendent's several times and still had room to do fifty push-ups during the lunch break. Rumour had it that an over-zealous inspector had come bursting in one day and found Skelton standing on his head beside the filing cabinets. But that was only rumour.

'Yes, sir,' Resnick said, replacing the newspaper. 'I suppose it's fair.'

Skelton made a sound pitched somewhere between a cough and a grunt. 'It doesn't usually serve our purposes to become combative in court.'

· 'He was trying to steamroller me. Make an impression in front of the jury.'

'Which you didn't want him to do. Unopposed.'

'He'd been practising this one in front of the mirror. Look sharp, score points and bugger the truth.'

'You've got the monopoly, have you, Charlie?'

Resnick didn't answer.

'Emotionally involved, Charlie?'

'Yes, sir,' Resnick said. 'Of course I am.'

Skelton's eyes grazed the picture of his wife and daughter, safe in their silver frame. 'How about the jury? Any idea which way they'll go?'

Resnick thought about their faces, solemn, apprehensive: the bald man in the sports jacket who made notes with a ball-point pen on the back of an envelope; the woman who gripped her handbag tighter during portions of the evidence and whose lips moved rapidly, silently, as if in prayer.

'I don't know, sir.'

Skelton slid back in his chair and stood up, a single fluid action. He had been in the building for close to nine hours and his clothes looked as if they'd come from the dry cleaners within the past twenty minutes. Sensible shoes, sensible diet: Resnick didn't suppose Skelton ever left the house without first buffing up his brogues and enjoying a smooth bowel movement.

'You've seen Macliesh?'

'Not yet, sir. I was just talking to Millington.'

'Frustrating afternoon.'

Resnick nodded.

'I can't delay on intimation much longer. There was the threat against a witness, the custody sergeant heard that as well, loud and clear. But I can hardly claim that we're securing evidence by questioning – not expeditiously, at any rate. Come morning, we're going to let him make his call and he's got to have a solicitor. If he refuses to request one, we'll take whoever's duty solicitor on call.' He nodded briskly and Resnick stood up.

'All right, Charlie. You'll be looking after things here in the morning?'

'Yes, sir.'

'Try talking to Macliesh yourself.'

'Yes, sir.'

'Oh, and Charlie?'

'Sir?'

'Do you ever do anything – in the way of exercise?'

Resnick looked at the superintendent a shade blankly. Weekend before last he'd lugged that Hoover all over the house, up and down stairs, rooms whose only function was to gather dust and the dried remains of dead birds. Was that the sort of thing Skelton meant?

'No, sir,' he said. 'Not really.'

'Maybe you should.' He looked appraisingly at Resnick's figure. 'You're starting to look a little plump.'

The pub was round a couple of corners from Central Police Station and Resnick had sometimes used it when he was stationed there. The road that led away from it, up the hill towards the cemetery, was a mixture of pork butchers and Chinese restaurants, second-hand shops with rusting refrigerators and Baby Bellings in the window and a dozen paperbacks outside in an apple box, ten pence each. Its clientele was a mixture of locals who lived in the narrow terraced streets that spawned off to either side and students stretching out their Polytechnic grants or in for a quick half before or after their adult education classes opposite.

Rachel Chaplin was already there, sitting at the rear of the right-hand room, squeezed up into a corner of the upholstered bench that ran along the wall. She had a book open on her lap, a glass of white wine close by her hand. The buttons at the front of her blue suit jacket were undone. All she has to do is sit there, Resnick thought, all she has to do to make me feel like this.

Rachel was aware that he'd arrived before she glanced up, felt his eyes upon her, just as she had before. The way she'd known in court that turning towards her was what he had wanted to do. She finished the sentence she was reading, lifted the wine and soda towards her mouth.

A group of kids from the Poly pushed past Resnick as he walked towards where she was sitting. One of the girls – short skirt, grey, up around her hips over ribbed tights – collided with him and moved, giggling, away. He was nothing to her: an older man filling space. Sexless.

Was that how she saw him? Rachel thought. Even in his best courtroom suit, his trousers were bagged at the knee, the knot of his tie had become twisted round so that the short, thinner end hung down in front.

'Sorry I'm late.' Resnick found space beside her. 'Work.'

His leg touched hers lightly and pulling it away he banged against the table, not hard. 'It'll thin out in a bit. A lot of these'll be off to the WEA.'

'I know,' Rachel said. 'I used to go to yoga.'

Seeing his expression, she continued, 'It's okay. I didn't live up to the stereotype very well. Packed it in after the first three weeks.'

'How come?'

'Whenever she told us to lay down on the floor and relax, I went right off.'

'Asleep?'

'Sound.'

'I thought I was the one whose nights were in need of repair?'

'When I gave up the class, I got myself a new mattress.'

And a new man to share it with, Resnick guessed. 'Yoga's not so bad,' he said. 'I was afraid you were going to own up to transactional analysis.'

Resnick's wife had gone to TA. Positive strokes, negative strokes, he had felt like a cat on an electric fence. He stretched an arm behind Rachel's shoulders and pressed the button set into the woodwork.

'I didn't know anywhere had those any more,' Rachel said as he withdrew his arm. 'Bells and waiters.'

'Used to be all there was,' Resnick told her. 'Every lounge bar in the city.'

She looked away and immediately Resnick wished he hadn't said it, didn't like the way it made him sound, hankering after a past where a shilling was a shilling and all the telephone boxes were red and none of them were working. Nostalgia was arthritis of the brain.

He ordered a Guinness, draught, in a straight glass. The woman waiting-on was wafer-thin and her back curved like old paper left in the sun. She knew Resnick by sight and nothing more: each time she served him as though it were the first.

'Any sandwiches left?' he asked.

'Cobs, duck. Cheese, cheese and onion, onion.'

'Cheese and onion.' He angled his head towards Rachel and she raised her hand, no.

They talked about Mrs Taylor and how she was

faring, how quiet the little girl had become, furled in upon herself. She asked him how the murder inquiry was progressing and he said they'd brought in a man for questioning.

'Husband?' Rachel asked.

'Good as.'

She drank some more of her wine. 'One of the things I'm involved in, a women's refuge here in the city.' She looked at Resnick carefully: 'Are you married?'

The waitress leant over them, setting down Resnick's drink and roll.

'Can I have another white wine and soda?' Rachel asked.

'And Worcester sauce,' added Resnick.

'I'm not putting that in no wine,' the woman said.

'For the cob,' Resnick explained.

'There's them relishes. Mustard.'

He shook his head. 'Worcester sauce.'

When she brought the bottle to the table, the waitress did so with her eyes squinting off to one side as if not wanting to see what use he was going to put it to.

'So?' Rachel pressed.

'Gives it a bit of bite,' Resnick said.

'Why are you avoiding the question?'

Resnick blinked. 'I was married for five years. It was a long time ago.'

'Any children?'

'No. You?'

'Children or married?'

'Either. Both.'

'Yes, I was married. That seems like a long while ago as well, although I suppose it wasn't. We didn't have any kids, I haven't had any since.'

He wanted to ask her about that, about having – not

having – children. Instead he said, 'Why did you get unmarried?'

Rachel turned the wine glass round between her fingers. 'It was like trying to breathe under water.'

He watched her come back from the Ladies. She still wore her hair pinned up, silver pendant ear-rings like slim cylinders accentuating the line of her neck. It made her jawline seem stronger, her mouth fuller.

Watch my lips move, she had said.

'I shall have to go soon,' she said, sitting back down.

Resnick nodded, asked her the same question that Skelton had asked him, about the jury. She didn't know either, not for certain.

'A year ago,' she said, 'I think I would have been. Six months even.'

'You think attitudes have changed that much?'

'Don't you?'

She knew the figures: an increase in cases of reported sexual child abuse that ran close to a hundred and forty per cent. Local Authorities with over three thousand children on their abuse registers. In the wake of the Jasmine Beckford case, extra staff had been appointed with special responsibilities in that area, special knowledge. The same after Cleveland.

The trouble is,' she said, 'it became fashionable.'

'Didn't that encourage a lot of kids to speak out?'

'Of course it did. But the trouble with fashions is that they change. Pop stars, styles. The big thing used to be that we were never acting quickly enough. Read a newspaper and you'd think the whole country wanted us to go charging in at the least sign of danger and whisk kids away from home.'

'And now it's gone the other way,' Resnick said. They

thought about the police in much the same way, the public.

'D'you know,' Rachel said, leaning a little towards him, 'that, when one of those children up in Cleveland was taken off a Place of Safety Order, there was a headline in one of the papers, inches deep – THE FIRST CHILD IS SET FREE.'

'So you think the jury's going to find for the father if they can?'

Rachel just looked at him.

Resnick shifted back on the seat, drank some more of his Guinness, assumed she wanted the subject dropped. Busman's holiday.

'It's the guilt they won't accept,' Rachel said suddenly, her voice rising up a tone. 'Their guilt.'

'Theirs?'

'It used to be, anybody who abused a child, sexually abused them, they were psychopaths. Push them off to one side, lock them up. Criminally insane. People used to think Myra Hindley, Ian Brady.' She touched her fingers to her cheek, where it was beginning to burn. 'Now it's all over the place, everywhere. Ordinary people. That's what they don't want to believe. It's them, their friends, their kids. Them.'

Rachel lifted her glass and emptied it in one long swallow. Those who had been turning round and listening went back to their own conversations, their own silences. Resnick watched as the colour slowly began to fade down again on her cheeks, the light began to leave her eyes.

'I'm sorry,' Rachel said, 'I didn't mean to treat you to an outburst.'

'That's okay,' Resnick said.

Rachel stood up. 'I must go.'

'Thanks for the drink,' she said, out on the pavement.

Traffic was moving down the hill at a steady rate, twin lines of headlights sliding into the centre. Groups of men and women, strictly segregated, were gathered on the far side of the street, outside Huckleberry's, Zhivago's, The Empire.

'Thanks for coming,' Resnick said.

She smiled, something of a smile. 'It was supposed to help me unwind.'

'It's probably not too late for a yoga class.'

She pushed both hands down into her pockets and hurried away. The same group of students who had entered the pub with Resnick emerged and stood near the doorway, laughing. The lads were all wearing long raincoats, shapeless as the one the insurance man had always worn when he'd called to collect on the penny-a-week policy his mother had taken out for him when he was born.

Nine

If Dizzy had been human, Resnick thought, he would have spent days meandering drunkenly around shopping centres, splashed through municipal fountains with a red and white scarf dangling from his belt. He would have travelled back and forth across the Channel barricading himself behind a wall of lager cans in the ferry bar. Resnick blinked at the insistent wailing, eased his body from beneath the covers without disturbing the somnolent Miles, and barefooted to the window.

The leafless black of the tree yielded up the softer blackness of the cat. A soft thump against the ledge and yellowed eyes stared through the pane. Something hung down from the mouth, inert. Resnick pushed up the window and Dizzy moved with a quick pad across the room, tip of his tail crooked. Outside, the rain had not long ceased: sheen of water under the street light; soughing of wind.

Glancing at it, Resnick had taken Dizzy's prey for a bat, but no, a field mouse, grey in the smudged hollow of the pillow. Its back broken, a brief trail of pink and palish yellow slipped from the puncture of its underside.

From the floor beside the bedside table Dizzy looked up at him, daring rebuke.

Resnick used a tissue to lift the mouse away. Stripped the cover from the pillow and took it to the bathroom. Pepper was curled around the lid of the laundry basket and when Resnick switched on the light, lay one paw across his eyes.

It was not yet a quarter-past four.

Resnick made tea.

He remembered his grandfather: collarless shirts and cardigans that hung past the cave of his chest; grey trousers always with a flap sewn to the front and held in place by two large safety pins. Two things he would do in the house: he would make a fire each morning in the blackened range; he would make tea. Thin fingers would rub the strands of tea between them then sprinkle them across the bottom of the enamel pan like droppings. When the water boiled, he would pour it over the leaves and let it stand. Always the pan at the side of the range, tea growing thicker and blacker. All day.

He could scarcely recall his grandfather's voice. Little else about him. A slow-stepping figure that would move between the kitchen and the outside lavatory, where strips of newspaper, torn in two and two again, hung from a metal skewer bent into a hook. Once, on a Sunday, the rest of his family had brought a stranger home from church and Resnick had seen his grandfather struggle into a collar and tie – Resnick had used his young fingers to press the collar stud home, had twisted straight the knot of tie – and shiny coat and gone into the parlour with them, closing fast the door. From the hallway, between the banisters on the stairs, he had listened to the clamour of voices and then his grandfather, angry, bitter and pitched oddly high, forcing out all argument.

And since he knew, then, little Polish, having stopped his ears to it, old-fashioned nonsense, Resnick had never known what those heated words were about.

Thinking back now, he did not think, in all the years

they had inhabited the same house, that his grandfather had even spoken to him directly as much as a single word.

'Jesus! What's happening to him?'
   'All right, just take it easy.'
   'I want to know . . .'
   'A minute while this gets sorted.'
   'Not . . .'
   'Sir, I think you should take a look.'
Resnick looked at the warning expression on the custody sergeant's face, the solicitor standing inside his small room, alongside the desk. A uniformed constable was bringing a prisoner out of the toilet opposite the row of three cells. Inside the nearest of those a fist was being worked against the door, a metronomic rise and angry fall. A policewoman with a shining bob of fair hair was talking softly to a young black man who was handcuffed to the radiator. Divine and Naylor were standing at the furthest end of the corridor, by the open door to the third cell. Telephones were ringing: all over the building telephones were ringing.
   'Sir . . .'
   'Okay, sergeant.' He squeezed his way along the corridor.

He heard the solicitor's voice calling after him and shut it out. Outside the cell, Naylor looked as pale as Divine was flushed. Ignoring them, Resnick pushed the door fully open. Tony Macliesh looked up at him from where he was sitting on the narrow bed and smiled.

Blood leaked from his left cheekbone where the skin was broken; a swelling the shape and size of a blackbird's egg already broke the hairline over his left temple. His lip was cut. Still smiling, he stood up and a channel of blood ran from nose and chin on to his black T-shirt, his jeans, the soiled suede of his shoes.

No wonder, Resnick thought, the bastard's smiling.

'My office.' He spoke to Naylor and Divine without looking at them, turning away. 'Now.'

The solicitor was still in the custody sergeant's office, still making the same demands. Out of sight, somebody was whistling 'Moonlight Serenade'.

'Inspector . . .' she said.

'A doctor?' Resnick said to the sergeant.

'On his way, sir.'

'Inspector Resnick . . .'

'Ring through to the desk, see if someone can't fetch Ms Olds a cup of tea.' He glanced at the solicitor quickly. 'Make that coffee.'

Resnick had only run across Suzanne Olds once before. She had been representing a thirteen-year-old on a charge of malicious wounding and had had the lad's confession thrown out of court, and, likely, quite right too. He remembered a few things about her and one of them was that she liked to be addressed as Ms.

'I should have thought my client was the one in need . . .' she was saying.

'How long has Macliesh been your client?' Resnick asked.

Suzanne Olds drew back the sleeve of her beige linen jacket in order to look at her watch.

'All right. Don't bother.' He picked up the phone on the desk and dialled an internal number. 'Patel, get yourself down to the cells. I want you with Macliesh, door open, nobody in or out till the doctor gets here. Understood?'

Without waiting for a response, he put the receiver down and moved away.

'During all of which my client's injuries will remain unattended, I suppose?'

Resnick held her gaze for one, two, three seconds before walking to the inquiry desk and returning with a first-aid box in his hand. He sorted through it in front of her, finding a cellophane envelope of plasters, a tin of Germolene, the remains of a roll of cotton wool. Patel appeared at the doorway and Resnick pushed the things into his hand. 'If the doctor's not here in the next ten minutes, see if you can do anything with these.'

Naylor was wondering if they were likely to get more than a good bollocking but he wasn't worrying about it. After all, what had happened was down to Divine and if push came to shove that's exactly what Divine could do with any ideas about loyalty in the ranks.

What was worrying him was Debbie's announcement that morning – causing him to bite so fiercely into his toast that it disintegrated into brittle fragments – that she was four days late. Late! What was she talking about, late! Why was she talking about it at all, when normally such things weren't even referred to? When they went shopping together in Sainsbury's she would push her box of Tampax down to the bottom of the trolley and contrive to cover it with a packet of tagliatelle parmigiane. And that tinge of accusation in her voice when she'd said it, as if somehow he might have slipped something past her defences.

Besides, late was hardly the word: according to Debbie's five-year plan, anything in that line was three-and-a-half years early. They hadn't even got as far as choosing the best-value microwave.

Mark Divine was reminded of the time he'd been carpeted by the rugby association for breaking another player's nose in the scrum. Mouthing off at him all through the game he'd been. Needle, needle, needle. It had been easy enough for Divine to duck in close, quick yank of the hair, there, right on to his fist. Something satisfying about the sound that cartilage makes when the tissue ruptures across. Divine straightened his shoulders back as he heard Resnick approaching. Shame the bloke had been in his own team.

'What happened?' Resnick began his question as soon as the door opened and was standing behind his desk before either officer made a reply.

'Sir, Macliesh, he sort of . . .'

'Yes, Naylor?'

'He went berserk, sir.'

'Somebody did.'

The two men glanced at one another.

'Those injuries, sir,' said Divine. 'They were self-inflicted.'

If they've cooked this up between them, Resnick thought, I'll have them on a charge before they know what's hit them.

'It's true, sir,' Naylor said.

'True?'

'Yes, sir.'

'Your prisoner suddenly ups and punches himself in the face?'

'Threw himself against the wall, sir,' Divine said quickly.

'For the sheer hell of it?'

Here it comes, Naylor was thinking. Divine was beginning to smell his own sweat.

'Naylor?' said Resnick sharply.

'Something, er, was said, sir.'

'To Macliesh?'

'Yes, sir,' said Naylor.

'Yes, sir,' said Divine.

'Some remark was made which caused your prisoner to perform an act of grievous bodily harm on his own person?'

Both men nodded, neither spoke.

'You know my next question, don't you?' Resnick asked.

They did. Naylor looked at Divine and Divine looked with sudden interest at the notices pinned to the board behind Resnick's desk.

'Wait outside, Naylor,' said Resnick. 'Don't stray, I'll want to talk to you again.'

Divine knew now that it was going to be worse than anything the rugby association had dreamed up, worse even than the inquiry the time that black bastard had ended up in hospital.

'What was it that made Macliesh so angry?'

Divine wet his drying lips with the end of his tongue, but his tongue was dry too.

'What did you say that made him want to injure himself?'

'Nothing, sir.'

'Divine.'

'Sir...'

'Divine, there's youths out on the street now, down on the square. Pull up alongside them, stop them – wouldn't matter if they had half-a-dozen gold watches up an arm, a sack swung over their shoulder with swag stencilled on it – you know what answer they'll give you when you ask them what they've been up to?'

Divine tried not to look at Resnick's face, but he was finding it increasingly difficult to avoid.

'I'm waiting.'

'Sorry, sir, I didn't think...'

'That I wanted an answer. Of course I do, that's what questions are for.'

Divine wriggled as if his briefs were too tight for him, his shoes too small.

'The answer?'

'Nothing, sir.'

'They'd say?'

'Nothing. Sir.'

'And do you believe them?'

Let it rest!

'Well? Do you?'

'No, sir.'

'Then you know what I'm feeling now.'

'Sir, I just wanted to get some response.'

'It looks as if you succeeded.'

'After yesterday, him never opening his mouth.'

'You thought you'd change that?'

'It was only a remark, like. Something to get him going.'

Resnick didn't take his eyes from Divine's face now. 'You said.'

'Yes, sir.'

'You said what?'

'I . . . said what kind of a bloke was it who couldn't even get it up when his tart was dying for it. Sir.'

Resnick rested the side of his face in his hand for a moment and slowly sat down. He supposed callousness shouldn't any longer surprise him. Still, for several seconds, this took his breath away.

'Sir, if I may, sir. I don't think it was just what I said. The way he threw himself against that wall, smacking his head against it like he did.' Divine's voice petered out. He forced himself to try again. 'I was the one pulled him off, sir. Ask Naylor, he . . .'

'I was looking at your report the other day,' Resnick said. 'Just something made me take it from the file, I can't remember what now. There were statements from five witnesses, all attesting to the use of excessive force. A taxi driver who said he was as much a racist as the next man, but he didn't think you ought to be able to get away with that sort of thing while you were on duty.'

Divine started counting inside his head; stopped, worried in case Resnick should see his lips moving.

'You wriggled out of that with a reprimand in private and an apology in public and the stars must have been shining out of your behind that day because there was enough cocaine in that youth's possession to make half the city numb in its collective nose. But when you were reassigned to me I gave you fair warning. I dare say you remember?'

Divine closed his eyes without realizing what he was doing. He said, 'Yes, sir. I remember.'

Resnick stood. 'Outside and write it up.'

Divine continued to stand there, uncertain.

'Something else you want to say?'

Divine gave Resnick a look of incomprehension. 'This Macliesh, sir. Ask me, he's cracked. Got no need of a reason for doing anything. D'you know what he did when we were bringing him in? Pissed down Naylor's leg!'

Ten

I'm going to find out who's going round the place
whistling the Glenn Miller songbook, Resnick said to
himself, and make sure he gets some Ellington for
Christmas. Maybe it was a she. Did women whistle?
Times gone by, it used to be considered unladylike,
especially in public. Like smoking. Now when you
walked round the city centre every other female you
passed had a lighted cigarette in her hand. Those under
twenty-five, younger. What had they been telling him
on Radio Four that morning? A generation of smoking
teenage schoolgirls, using nicotine to cope with the
stress of having few job prospects, of contracting Aids.

Suzanne Olds was sitting on a steel-framed chair with
a sagging canvas seat and she wasn't whistling. She
wasn't twenty-five any more, either; the law was her
second career – Resnick wasn't certain what the first
one had been except he thought it had something to
do with marketing. Maybe she used to stand in the
middle of the pedestrian precinct and solicit passers-by
into giving information about what newspaper they
read, the size of their feet, which brand of baked beans
they bought.

'Ms Olds.'

She stood up with a sigh of impatience and ditched
the end of her cigarette into the lukewarm dregs of her
coffee. People starting late on a second career didn't
like to be kept waiting.

'Sorry about the delay. At least you've had a chance to speak with your client.'

She had a pale leather bag, the size of a fat wallet, hanging by a thin strap from her left shoulder; she picked a matching satchel from the floor and carried it in her right hand. Keeping step with Resnick, she was not far short of his height, five-ten or even five-eleven.

'Which should have been afforded yesterday. Your grounds for delay are spurious at best.'

'How come you got Macliesh?' Resnick asked. 'Did he ask for you personally or what?'

'Or what. I was the duty solicitor who picked up the phone. Not that, that . . .' She broke off as Resnick thought about opening a door for her, reconsidered, waited for her to push it open for herself and followed after.

'I can't believe your superintendent is going to apply for an extension, which means some poor fool from the Crown Prosecutor's has got to go into court and try to wangle another three days in remand.'

'Thanks for spelling it out.'

'I'll look forward to seeing Macliesh wheeled up before the Bench looking the way he does. Somehow I can't see any magistrate handing him back to you so that further inquiries can be carried out.'

'If the crime under investigation is serious enough . . .'

'Your rights to brutalize my client become enshrined in law?'

'Any brutalization your client has suffered has been at his own hands.'

'Just try making the court believe that.' She was standing her ground now, legs apart, blocking Resnick's path.

'The court isn't stupid. And it won't overlook the serious nature of . . .'

'Come on, Inspector. This isn't prevention of terrorism or anything like it. No one's accused of planting a bomb in a wall cavity or crating up bodies in the diplomatic bag. This isn't even some crazy, running amok with a sub-machine-gun. At best, this is ordinary, common-or-garden murder.'

Resnick looked for the irony in her eyes but it wasn't there, only contact lenses and the vague reflection of himself, filtered through sepia.

'Excuse me, Ms Olds.' He stepped around her and hurried on to the interview room.

It was a smaller version of his own room and the air was stale before they began. From outside the building the metallic crump of heavy machinery beat beneath the silences. Tony Macliesh smoked his solicitor's cigarettes, taking them down to the nub end before pressing them out in the metal ashtray that was one of the room's few adornments. His face had been cleaned-up and disinfected, plastered and bandaged; now the injuries appeared even more serious, Macliesh sitting there as if waiting to be auditioned for a touring production of *The Invisible Man*.

He was talking now, terse and jagged, but talking.

'Tell me again what you were doing on the Industrial Estate.'

'I already told you.'

'I want to get it right.'

'We was sizin' up this job.'

'The warehouse?'

'Right.'

'You and two other men? One with a Liverpool accent . . .?'

'I think that's what it was.'

'Whose name you don't know?'

'The other feller brung him along.'

'The other feller being your West Indian friend, Warren?'

'I'm not prejudiced.'

'He was the muscle?'

'He's got biceps out to here.'

'And you were the brains?'

'I had brains enough to know we were never going to get inside there in a month of Sundays.'

'Brains enough to claim to be out there recceing the place at the same time that Shirley Peters was murdered?'

'I didn't know nothing about that, did I?'

Resnick stared at him until he turned aside and reached his hand towards Suzanne Olds, who pushed a packet of Dunhill International in his direction.

'You know, without corroboration, that alibi doesn't mean a thing?'

'Find Warren. Ask him.'

'I'm here, talking to you.'

'Send him. Instead of all that scribbling.'

Patel barely glanced up from the smaller table, where he was writing as speedily as he could, sheets of A4 fanned out before him.

'What's he doing anyroad?'

'Making a record of what's said.'

'What I'm saying?'

'Yes.'

'Then I hope he's getting it down right.' Macliesh leaned sideways and jerked a finger towards Patel. 'You understand what we're saying, pal?' He moved his head closer to Resnick. 'Can he spell?'

'I thought you weren't prejudiced?'

'That's not prejudice. He's a bleeding Paki!'

'DC Patel has a degree from the University of Bradford.'

'They buy 'em, don't they?'

'Why skip, Macliesh?'

'I don't skip.'

'You got off a train in Aberdeen.'

'I was away to my job.'

'You don't have a job.'

'I was promised work on the rigs. I can always get work on the rigs. I've done it before.'

'Was this since you came out of prison or before?'

'Don't you come clever with me, you cocky bugger!' Macliesh's hands were knots of fist, for a moment in sight and then punched down hard into his thighs.

Suzanne Olds stared at him hard, willing him to unclench his fingers. She shook the cigarette pack at him, breaking his concentration.

'Sudden change of plan, wasn't it?' Resnick said.

'What change of plan?' He took a cigarette and laid it down, unlit.

'Night before, you were all set up for a burglary. You and your friends, colleagues, whiling away the early evening sizing up this warehouse, and the next thing you're off with your bag to the station, booking a second-class single to Aberdeen.'

'Fucking class makes a difference, I suppose?'

Resnick could see the violence now, jumping behind Macliesh's eyes.

'It almost sounds, Inspector,' said Suzanne Olds, 'as if you are disappointed my client thought better of committing a crime and went off in search of honest employment.'

'Almost,' said Resnick sharply, reacting against the smirk in her voice.

'But you are conceding that my client was in Lenton Industrial Estate at the time that Shirley Peters was murdered?'

'I'm not conceding anything.'

'Don't you!' growled Macliesh, twisting in his chair.

'Inspector . . .' said Suzanne Olds, wanting to draw him off her client, wanting to push her point home.

'There's the matter of witnesses,' Resnick said.

Macliesh twisted back again. 'I've given you witnesses.'

'Names.'

'Aye, names.'

'Names of people who can't be found.'

Macliesh swore and pushed his chair away from the table. At Resnick's back, Patel tensed with apprehension.

'Inspector,' Suzanne Olds said forcefully, claiming his attention, 'is it likely that my client would voluntarily confess conspiracy to burglary and name his accomplices in that conspiracy if it were untrue?'

'Which would you rather stand charged with, Ms Olds? Conspiracy to commit a crime that didn't take place or a murder that did?'

'No one in this room is charged with murder,' she said.

Macliesh had his arm towards Resnick, finger poking the space between them, his voice drowning his solicitor out. 'I didn't fucking murder anyone!'

'Did you love her?' Resnick asked.

Macliesh looked at the wall.

'Even after she threw you out?'

'She never threw . . .'

'I've talked to her mother, Macliesh. She got sick of you hounding her and hitting her and when you were

95

out of the way she put your stuff in the street and changed all the locks.'

Macliesh said something beneath his breath nobody in the room could catch.

'Not that that was sufficient for you to understand. Phone calls, intimidation, threats of violence . . .'

'There was no threats of bloody violence!'

'Then a lot of people are lying.'

'They're always lying!'

'You used your fists against her . . .'

'That's not . . .'

'Used your fists against her when you were together . . .'

'That's not true!'

'Signed statements. You beat her up whenever you felt like it, whenever you thought she'd stepped out of line, and in the end the only thing left for her to do was to get a court order made out against you coming anywhere near her.'

Macliesh crumbled a cigarette between his fingers. 'That vicious whore put her up to it!'

'Who's that, Macliesh?'

'That stupid tart, always putting ideas into her head.'

'You mean Grace Kelley?' Resnick asked.

'You sodding know I do!'

'Miss Kelley says that in addition to being violent, you were unreasonably possessive. That even after Shirley Peters had made it clear that in her eyes your relationship was over, you still continued to make it difficult for her to meet other men.'

Macliesh twisted round in his chair, wrenching his head from one side to the other.

'You were jealous, weren't you, Macliesh?'

'Stuff it!' Macliesh hissed.

'You couldn't live with the thought of her seeing other men.'

'Stuff it!'

'Didn't like the idea of her being alone with them.'

Macliesh sat with his head back, mouth open, working at the stale air.

'The chance of her fancying them. Loving them.'

Macliesh's chair went cartwheeling backwards and Suzanne Olds let out a shout and her pen went skittering across the floor.

'Letting them love her.'

Macliesh's shoulder hit the wall and then the side of his fist, flat of his hand, fist again.

'Difficult inside,' Resnick went on as if Macliesh was still sitting across the table from him, 'inside, when she never came to visit you. Lincoln.'

'Shut your fucking mouth!' Macliesh screamed.

'Thinking about it.'

Macliesh hit the wall first with both hands, fingers spread wide, then with his head.

'Difficult not to let those pictures keep forming.'

Again, and there was blood beginning to seep out on either side of the bandages.

'Inspector!' shouted Suzanne Olds. 'I insist that this is stopped.'

' "You as much as sniff another man," ' said Resnick, on his feet now, ' "and I'll bloody strangle you." '

Macliesh charged blindly, knocking the solicitor sideways and almost to the ground. His knee banged into a chair, his hip went hard against the table's edge. He was already stumbling when he made his lunge at Resnick, who sidestepped him with the contempt of a man outwitting an unfocused bull.

' "I'll bloody strangle you," you said, and that was what you did.'

Resnick's voice was strong and clear in the confines of the room. Patel had Macliesh's arm high up behind his back and was forcing the side of his face down against the table. Graham Millington came through the door fast, drawn by the noise, and stood there staring.

'Charge him,' Resnick said.

Suzanne Olds was standing with her body bent forward, arms crossed tight across her chest. She was shaking.

'The murder of Shirley Peters.'

Eleven

The house was paid for: not much more than two up
and two down, extension built on the back, kitchen and
bathroom, garden the size of a snooker table with grass
it took Luke about two days to reduce to mud. But no
mortgage. He'd settled that, the one thing he did settle,
prissying about with lawyers, bank managers and bits
of paper. 'I'll make sure things are right for you, Mary,
you and the children. You'll not want.'

Not want. Made him sound like one of those hymns
she used to sing at Sunday school. He will lay me
down in green pastures. Well, Highland Crescent wasn't
exactly green pastures, but aside from the rates,
insurance, the normal bills ... she knew families who
were paying out as much as two hundred a month to
the building society. Linda, who worked on electrical,
almost two hundred and fifty theirs came to, outgoings,
with the loan for the new furniture. Pounds. She didn't
know how they managed. She found coping difficult
enough herself, and that was without splashing any
around; if they went and stayed in that caravan at
Ingoldmels another summer she'd push the wretched
thing into the sea.

Last year he'd sent Luke and Sarah a postcard from
Corsica.

She'd torn it up before they came home from school.
What did they want to know about him and that po-
faced pound of string beans he'd married, sunning

themselves in Corsica? *The water is clear and warm but you have to keep in the shade in the afternoons.* If he had that much cash to throw away, he could pay for Luke's new shoes, a winter coat for Sarah, one of those recorder things they both kept pestering her about.

'Luke!'

It was starting to get dark already, you could see the street lights clearly. Shapes of the cars parked on either side beginning to blur. She hated it when the nights started drawing in so fast.

'Luke!'

She'd told him, she'd told him half-a-dozen times if she'd told him once: back indoors by half-past four. What if I don't know the time, he'd said? What do you think that watch is for? It's bust. What do you mean, it's bust? It won't work any more. Look. Then ask somebody. You've got a tongue in your head, haven't you?

Oh, Christ!

She rocked back against the edge of the open door. She shouldn't ... that wasn't ... what was she doing, telling him to go up to some stranger and ask the time? *Telling* him. All the air seemed to be sucked from her body. Her stomach cramped. Skin was cold to the touch. Goose pimples. *Telling* him. Please, can you tell me ... can you tell me ... can you tell me the time?

Pictures formed at the backs of her eyes and wouldn't go away.

'Mummy. Mummy! What's the matter?'

She forced herself to breathe, to smile at four-year-old Sarah pulling at the side of her skirt.

'What's the matter?'

'Nothing. It's nothing. Come and have your tea.'

'Luke's not here.'

Pushing the child through to the back room. 'That's

all right. We don't have to wait. You can have yours now. Luke eats twice as fast as you do anyway. He'll soon catch up.'

'Mummy . . .'

She sat the child down in front of a plate, bread and butter cut, spaghetti hoops on the stove, bubbling up the sides of the pan. Six fish fingers under the grill, two for Sarah and . . .

Mary's legs went at the knees, a moment, nothing more, enough to spill her across the narrow room; her hand, catching out, catching at anything, caught the handle of the kettle and sent it clattering across the floor.

Water pooled about her feet, luke-warm.

She was at the sink, squeezing out a cloth before she realized that Sarah was pressed against the door jamb, tears on her face, staring.

'It's all right, darling. Mummy just spilt the water. You go back and get on with your tea and I'll clean this up. It won't take a minute.'

She gave the girl a quick hug, felt her own tears pricking at her eyes. *Ask somebody. You've got a tongue in your head, haven't you?* Mary bent low with the cloth; the water seemed to have got everywhere. On the third trip back to the sink, she switched on the gas over the grill, tipped half of the spaghetti out on to a plate.

'Mummy?'

'Mmm?'

'Here's Luke.'

She spun round and saw him across the room. The street door had been open and he had come running in to stand there, still a little out of breath, head held to one side and a lick of brown hair falling across it.

'I'm not late, I . . .'

101

The flat of her hand struck sharp across his face. There were seconds when he seemed not to have realized what had happened, rocked back against the wall, feeling needling back to his cheeks, stinging him to screams and tears.

At the table Sarah sat with her head bowed, not looking, not wanting to look, crying too.

'Whatever's the matter with them?'

'With who?'

'The children?'

'Nothing.'

'Mary, you can't tell me ...'

'Mother, nothing's the matter with them.'

'They've scarce said a word since they got here.'

'That was only ten minutes back. Give them a chance.'

'You were here at close to six as ...'

'Oh, what does it matter what time we got here? What possible difference does it make?'

'Mary, it's not the time I'm concerned with.'

'Then ... then don't go on about it so.'

'I am not going on about the time.'

'All right, you're not ...'

'It's my grandchildren that ...' If Vera Barnett had been able to get from her chair quickly enough, she would have caught hold of her daughter's arm and kept her physically in the room. As it was, all she could do was stare at her, will her not to leave, to do as she wanted, just as she had done when Mary had been herself a child of small unvoiced regrets and sullen silences.

A moment later, the sound of water splashing back from the inside of the kettle, cups and saucers being shuffled along the draining-board. Luke knelt before the television, too close to images of black and white outlaws waiting for the overland stage, the sound turned too low to hear. Wedged into the corner of the two-seater settee, Sarah gazed at her grandmother's face, the sucked-in cheeks, the collapse of curls, grey against the grey of her neck.

When Mary came back into the living-room, it was with the tea things on a patterned metal tray, biscuits tipped out on to a cracked bone china plate. Avoiding her mother's eyes, she sat on the settee and held saucer in one hand, cup in the other. Over Luke's shoulder she watched the stage-coach passengers dropping money and valuables into a sack. Sarah, cuddling up alongside her, spilt milky tea on to the flowers of her dress.

'Well, this is very nice, I must say.'

Mary tried not to react to her mother's voice, the cold challenge of its irony.

'Nobody visits me for over a week and when they do it's like a morgue.'

For a moment, Mary closed her eyes and slipped an arm around her daughter, drawing her closer still. It was enough.

'That's right, you don't have to pay any attention to me. Why should you? Bring the children round for tea and sit watching some stupid thing on television. I don't know why you bother.'

Mary was up from the settee quickly, leaning past Luke so that he flinched, clicking the set off.

'That's not fair,' Luke's protest started but got no further.

Vera Barnett's head was angled towards her daughter in a look of petty triumph.

'There's no winning with you, is there?' Mary was unable to keep silent.

'What's that supposed to mean?'

'If we don't come to see you, that's wrong, and if we do, that's wrong too.'

'I don't sit here to be ignored.'

'Nobody's ignoring you.'

'That's not what it looks like.'

'You can't expect to be made a fuss of all the time.'

'Fuss! A civil word would be something. A kiss from my own grandchildren.'

'Mother, they kissed you when they got here. You know very well.

'A peck.'

'Oh, now you're being ridiculous!'

'Ridiculous, am I? Well, at least I know how to behave.'

Mary couldn't believe it. She was starting this all over again. 'Perhaps behaving's easy when you never get out of your chair from morning till night.'

'How dare you!'

Oh, God! thought Mary. 'I'm sorry,' she said. 'I didn't mean that.'

Whether she had meant it or not didn't matter.

'I suppose you think I like to sit here every day, day after day? I suppose you think I do it on purpose?'

Mary shook her head slowly. 'No, mother.'

Luke switched the television back on in time to see one of the posse tumble sideways from his horse and cartwheel through sagebrush and dust.

'These bones of mine – you think I'm a cripple through choice?'

'Mother, you are not a cripple!' Mary was on her feet, standing over her mother, staring down at her. Sarah pushed back against the cushions, watching and listening, making herself small. 'I know you have a lot of pain, I know it's difficult for you to move around, but you are not a cripple.'

'Well, I'm sorry.'

'What do you mean, you're sorry?'

'That I'm not ill enough for you to do what you've been wanting to do ever since . . . ever since . . .'

'Mother!' She had hold of her arms, lifting her forwards in the chair. She could see the envelopes of skin, like chicken flesh, spreading out from the corners of her eyes. After some moments she was conscious of the narrow hardness of her mother's bones beneath her finger ends.

Sarah was sucking in air noisily, not quite crying, while Luke pretended to be watching a man with a badge walk into a crowded, brightly-lit saloon.

Mary straightened and looked at her mother, daughter, mother again. She turned away and began to put the cups back on the tray. 'I suppose you'll be going out later,' said her mother, as Mary went towards the kitchen.

'Yes, mother, I shall be going out later.'

Mary smoothed down her grey skirt and reached around behind to lower the toilet seat. Sitting, she lifted her heeled shoes from the plastic bag she had been carrying and wiped a scuff mark from the upper of one of them with a sheet of toilet paper. Wriggling her feet down into them, she squashed the soft-soled flatties she'd been wearing into her handbag; the striped plastic bag she stuffed down behind the pipe that ran from the cistern to the bowl. She stood then, wincing as the back of her left shoe bit into her skin. Why hadn't she remembered to bring a plaster that she could have put on beneath her tights? Now she would have to hope that whatever they did, she wouldn't have to walk too far.

She flushed the toilet and unbolted the cubicle door.

Make-up bag resting on the narrow ledge – How did they expect you to balance anything on something that wasn't wide enough for a cat to walk along? – Mary applied some blusher, wondering again how it was she could still have freckles around her nose this far into autumn.

Lipstick.

At least, she hadn't had to go through this with her mother; the questioning she had had to endure all the time she was at secondary school and beyond. Where are you going? Who are you going to meet? Which pictures? And the hand that would reach out to smear Miners make-up across her face: don't imagine that's going to wash with me, young lady, you don't cover yourself in this just to go to the Odeon with a girl-friend.

True or false, true or false, it had never mattered.

You can't lie to me, I'm your mother.

Yes, mother. She pressed her lips together tightly and then pulled them apart, making a soft popping sound. Well, it's just as well you no longer ask.

An ageless woman in a bulked-out coat like tinted sacking came in, pushing a small boy before her. 'In there. Go in. In there, stupid!' The door slammed shut.

Mary slid the black brush into the mascara and lifted up her eyelid with a finger. That's what she'd have me looking like, done-for and sexless. Like her. God, she's not yet sixty herself. Doesn't she ever think about it? Ever? Mary clicked the mascara shut, pulled a comb a few more times through the ends of her hair. Not that that was why she went with them. Men. It wasn't for the sex, which was just as well because half the time there wasn't much sex at all. Oh, there was the talk, that and a bit of last-minute poking and grabbing when it was all too late and any interest she might have had had fallen away somewhere between the awkward silences and obvious lies.

'So,' she addressed her reflection aloud, 'it's a good thing I'm not desperate for it, isn't it?'

Behind her a toilet flushed, a door banged and for a moment the woman's eyes caught hers in the mirror.

'Look where you're going,' she said to the boy. 'You're always under my feet.'

Mary zipped up her make-up bag and put it away. Checking her watch, she saw that she still had twenty minutes, which was as well for she always liked to be there first and waiting. That way she had the advantage: she was always the one to pick them out, make the approach. That was the only way she would have it. That bit of control. Besides which, if she didn't like the look of them – the least little thing – she'd walk right off and leave them there. Wandering up and down, walk and turn, walk and stop, check the watch, the clock across the square, walk some more.

Once she'd come back more than two hours later and this whippet of a bloke had still been there, eyes glazed over, cigarette cupped in his hand, waiting in the slow fall of rain.

Tonight, though – Mary stepped out on to the street, pressing the button at the pedestrian crossing – she had a feeling it was going to be all right. The way he'd written, that had convinced her of that. Not full of himself, the way some were, making out like they were a cross between Sylvester Stallone and Shakespeare. He wasn't a wimp, either – some of them sounded as if they'd gone down on their hands and knees before they set pen to paper.

And that was another thing. She turned down past the post office, thankful she didn't have far to go, there was a blister coming up over her heel already. His writing. Sophisticated, that's what she'd have to call it. Ink, too, real ink, not biro. Almost fancy. Well, nothing wrong with a man who was a bit fancy. Maybe he'd fancy her.

Crossing the square between the lager drinkers and the pigeons, Mary smiled: her fancy man.

She asked for a port and brandy and took it to her usual place, moving a stool along to the curve of the bar so that she had a good view of the door without being right on top of it. That way she had plenty of time to be sure. Behind her the drummer was unfastening his cases, beginning to assemble his kit. Mary sipped her drink and tried to ignore the faint itch of sweat just below her hairline. Relax, she told herself. Relax: you'll know him when he comes.

Twelve

You didn't only find dust in disused rooms: once, pulling out the empty whitewood chest, he had found a baby bird. Cocooned in a spider's web and resting back on outspread wings, its beak and belly gave it the look of some prehistoric creature here in miniature. Days old, only hours. Carefully, he had prised the web from round about it, closed his mouth and blown away the dust; when he cupped his hand beneath the bird and lifted it up, the wings disintegrated at his touch. Between the pages of a book he found a letter from his former wife which contained the words *for ever*. Tonight, searching for Bud, who had not appeared at the sound of cat food being scraped into bowls, he had picked from between some old magazines a picture postcard from Ben Riley.

Come on in, the message had read, *the water's fine*!

On the front of the card, an expanse of land pushed back towards a range of mountains, snow at their peaks; the moon rising pale through a lot of sky. Not a sign of water anywhere the eye could see.

Resnick and Ben Riley had walked the beat together for the best part of two years. One Saturday in four they would walk down through the Meadows and over Trent Bridge, stand on the terraces and watch their colleagues sitting below, helmets off and on the ground beside them. On the way back, Ben would drop into the cycle shop and discuss the comparative merits of machines and gears, while Resnick flipped through the new releases in the jazz specialists along the street. Now Arkwright Street had been pulled down and most of the small rows of adjoining terraces along with it. Where they used to stand to watch the Reds, others now sat in executive boxes with the televisions tuned to the racing. Resnick had started watching the team on the other side of the river. And Ben Riley was out in Montana.

Resnick supposed that was where he was.

At first there had been letters, postcards from trips Ben had made – Custer's Battlefields; the Breaks of the Missouri; Glacier National Park; Chicago – and then, inevitably, Christmas greetings that arrived mid-January and for the past few years nothing at all.

On the way past the bathroom, Resnick heard a familiar, pathetic mewing. Pepper was curled asleep around the top of the laundry basket and, somehow, Bud had managed to get trapped inside it, pitifully tangled amongst Resnick's soiled shirts.

On the way to the kitchen, the cat purring, nuzzling the crook of his arm, Resnick lifted the stylus back on to Johnny Hodges. Ben Riley, he was thinking, had been the best man at his wedding. Resnick set the cat down by his bowl and smiled: just as well somebody was.

He broke a couple of eggs into a bowl, added milk, forked butter into the bottom of a pan. He grated in some parmesan and opened the cupboard for the Tabasco sauce. *Do you ever do anything in the way of exercise? You're starting to look a little plump.* Resnick tore the health club's free offer into four and dropped the pieces into the bin. When the butter was beginning to sizzle up, he tipped in the egg mixture, stirred it round a couple of times and then, taking a carton of cream from the fridge, added a more than generous helping.

It was still only mid-evening and there was no point in getting to the club before eleven. At a sudden thought, he gave the eggs a stir, turned the gas low and went to the phone.

Chris Phillips answered.

Resnick imagined that was who it was. He said: 'Is Rachel there?'

'No, she's at a meeting,' Phillips said.

Resnick said, 'Oh,' wondering whether he should leave a message and ask her to call him, meet him later.

'Can I take a message?' Phillips said.

'No, it's okay. Thanks.'

'Who shall I say called?'

'Em, Resnick. Charlie Resnick.'

'Didn't you ring the other night?'

Resnick set down the phone. When he took his plate through to the living room, Johnny Hodges was still playing. 'Satin Doll'. When he had started listening to jazz, Resnick had thought Hodges the best saxophonist in the world. Still, there were times when his sound was the only one that worked.

> when I listen to Johnny Hodges
>
> I am ashamed
> to carry loss
> like a sick-note
> like a dream of sailing

Come on in, the water's fine! It didn't matter that Ben Riley was somewhere on the prairie, that Rachel Chaplin wasn't home: right now, Resnick felt better than all right.

*

There were nightclubs in the city where men had to wear a tie before they could gain admittance and the toilets were swabbed out three times of an evening. There was one with a style bouncer who checked you over carefully and if you were found to be wearing anything from Marks and Spencer or Top Shop they wouldn't sell you a ticket. Resnick had heard rumours of another with a membership fee that was roughly equal to his monthly salary, where the furnishings were pure white and they played nothing but Frank Sinatra and Vic Damone.

The Stardust was squeezed between a pub and a stationery warehouse on one of the main roads through Resnick's patch of inner city. The music was solid reggae and calls to complain about the insistent throb of bass were almost as consistent. Cabs lined the pavement between two and four. The sign above the cash desk announced that members had to show evidence of membership when entering, but nobody seemed overly concerned about dress code. Non-members were supposed to be signed in by a member but Resnick showed his warrant card instead.

At the far end of the room, a singer with a full beard and a brightly striped woollen hat was holding the microphone too close to his face. There were a few tables, but most of the clientele were on their feet – lining the bar, leaning back against the opposite wall, mostly twos and threes with an occasional male on his own, staring off into the middle distance, swaying lightly. Others were dancing. A sinewy black was winding his way around a woman in a vast velvet dress who turned through a small circle, never taking her eyes from his face. Four girls swayed around a pile of handbags. The majority of the men were Afro-Caribbean in origin; almost without exception the women were white and when Resnick first came to the city they would have worked in one or other of the hosiery factories that lined the road leading out through Kimberley and Eastwood towards Heanor. He wasn't sure what they did now, these women. Even the old Players factory had been demolished now, the one on Prospect Street.

'Trouble?' The man running the bar was overweight and white.

'Guinness,' said Resnick, drawing in his stomach.

'Paying for it?'

Resnick placed a five-pound note on the counter and left the change where it lay. 'Know a man named Warren?'

'Warren Oates.'

Resnick looked at him, the studied insolence in his eyes.

'Rabbit warren.'

Resnick scooped the change away and dropped it down into his pocket. He made his way slowly across the room, skirting round the handbag girls and waiting for a slim-hipped man with dreadlocks and a bright red and green skinny-ribbed jumper to finish dancing.

'Jackie, this here's Detective Inspector Resnick.'

The woman blinked at him from a face that saw too little natural light. She turned with a shrug and moved away.

'New girlfriend?' Resnick asked, pleasantly enough.

'Slag,' said the man, leaning against the wall beside Resnick, head arched back, pelvis jutting out.

'I can see why you're such a success with the ladies,' Resnick said. 'It's your natural sympathy and charm. That and the obvious respect you have.'

'You come to me for lessons?'

'Information.'

'Lessons cost.'

'Information comes free.'

'Who says?'

'It was free last time.'

'You shut it about that!' He was close now, close enough to smell the sweetness of the marijuana.

'You were only doing your duty.'

'Shut it!'

'An honest citizen.'

'I grassed.'

Each and every way, Resnick thought, enjoying the joke.

'What you grinning all over your face at?'

'You gave up somebody because it was in your own interests to do so. Someone who'd been putting girls on the streets you thought were yours to work. The right time, the right place and now he's still waiting for parole.'

'You complaining?'

'Asking for more.'

'Get fucked!' Swivelling away.

'Warren,' Resnick said after him.

He hesitated, half-turned.

'I need to talk with somebody called Warren.'

The man turned away again.

'Maybe, before I leave, I should get up on the mike and announce that you're our newest recruit to the Neighbourhood Watch.'

He didn't stop walking, but he heard.

Resnick waited a while. There were other faces that he recognized; by that time more who recognized him, knew who and what he was. He began to count those in the club whom he'd arrested, seen sent down. At five, he stopped and went back to the bar. The woman,

Jackie, was standing there and when he put down his empty glass she spat in it.

'Guinness,' said Resnick to the barman. 'Fresh glass.'

The same short fur coat, the same shiny trousers. She was with a man Resnick had tried to turn over twice and failed; after that he'd got passed on to the Serious Crimes Squad but they hadn't had any more luck. With George Despard you needed more than luck: more than most money could buy. The man loitering by the entrance Resnick knew to be Despard's minder.

He waited until the couple had sat down at one of the tables and made his way over, careful to approach from the front. Despard wasn't the kind of man you risked going up to from behind.

Resnick nodded at George Despard. 'I hope you haven't left the Porsche parked outside,' he said to Grace Kelley.

'We came in the Ferrari,' Despard said.

Grace Kelley smiled. 'Hello, Inspector. Didn't expect to see you here.'

'What's a nice clean copper like me doing in a place like this?'

'Something like that.'

'Didn't expect to see you in here, either, George,' Resnick said. 'Not coming down in the world, are you? Hard times?'

'I've read it,' said Despard. 'Less of a ramble than most of his books. Course, you got to respond to the symbolism.'

'Christ!' said Grace. 'What is this? Evening classes?'

'A little self-improvement never hurt a soul,' said Despard solemnly.

'And you're sitting next to the living proof,' Resnick said to her. 'The very model of a self-made man.'

'My father,' Despard said, looking at Grace, 'he come over from Jamaica after the war. Played trumpet in a dance band. Not very good, but he was black and up West they still thought that was exotic. Used to wear a frilly shirt and shake the maracas whenever they did a rumba.'

Half the club was watching Resnick and George Despard talking, trying to figure out what they were talking about: the other half were watching the first half watching.

'His lip give out,' Despard continued. 'London was getting bad, more black faces and nobody figured them for cute any more. He took it into his head to move up to the Midlands, buy some little green-grocer's shop. Months before it happening, he would say to everyone, watch out for Notting Hill. Trouble brewing.' Despard was stroking the curve of Grace Kelley's shoulder, fingers lost in the fur. 'He didn't see it happening up here, too. First race riots in the country. Burned him out.' She wriggled her shoulder a little and he moved his arm away. Not far. 'So you see,' he said, 'I had to start from nothing, do it all myself. From that burnt-out shop to where I am today.'

'Regular phoenix from the ashes, aren't you?' Grace said.

'There you are,' said Resnick. 'You wanted symbolism.'

'I wanted a drink,' said Grace, looking round.

Despard signalled to his minder and moments later a bottle of brandy arrived with three glasses.

'Sit down,' said Despard.

'I'm on Guinness,' Resnick said.

'Sit down, Inspector,' said Despard. 'You don't want to disappoint a lady.'

Resnick pulled over a chair.

'You made quite an impression on her.'

'It's my dress sense,' said Resnick. 'Never fails.'

George Despard was wearing a lightweight blue suit, a yellow silk shirt and a muted red tie. The shoes on his feet were real alligator. Gold was tastefully placed at strategic parts of his body.

They sat for a while drinking brandy, saying nothing very much. The singer was taking a rest and a DJ had taken over. People were dancing again.

'What's Macliesh got against you?' Resnick asked Grace after Despard had lit another of her cigarettes.

'I did like you said. Went in and made a statement.'

Resnick nodded. 'I read it.'

'Well, then.'

'He seemed certain you were the one that had it in for him.'

'After the way he treated Shirley . . .'

'More than that.'

Despard was looking at her with bored interest. Over by the bar, his minder was standing close to the man Resnick had been questioning earlier. They didn't appear to be talking to one another.

'Seemed more personal than that,' Resnick said. 'Between you and him.'

'As much distance as I can find,' Grace said. 'Always.'

'Woman like this,' Despard explained, holding her hand in his, holding it over the table, on display. 'Woman like this, men always going to fuss with her.'

'Let 'em try!' Grace shook her head.

'Is that what it was?' asked Resnick. 'He made a pass at you?'

She leaned her head back and a trail of smoke lifted up from her nostrils. 'More like – what d'you call it? – the Denver Buckskins.'

'Broncos,' Despard corrected her.

'Whatever.'

Despard laughed and jiggled the brandy round in his glass. 'Tried to sack you, did he?'

'Not after I put my foot in his bollocks, he didn't.'

'Did Shirley know?' Resnick asked.

A quick, strong shake of the head. 'She had enough to worry about, poor love.'

'He said he'd do you an injury,' Resnick said.

'Not where you've got him.'

'For the present.'

'You're not letting the bastard out?'

'Not if we can help it.'

'Course you can help it. He did for her, didn't he?'

Resnick glanced away. 'He's got an alibi.'

'Of course he's got a bleedin' alibi! Even he's not that fucking stupid!'

'He's in court tomorrow. Let's hope he doesn't get bail.'

Grace looked at Resnick and then at Despard.

'Still,' Resnick went on. 'You'll likely be back in London pretty soon.'

'She won't come to any harm here in the city,' said Despard proprietorially.

'I'm not going to be here in the sodding city. Not if that maniac's wandering loose.'

'We'll still be able to get in touch with you?'

'I'm not skipping the country.'

'Your address . . .'

'That sergeant of yours, I give it him.'

There didn't seem a great deal more to say after that and Resnick didn't want to carry on sitting there, drinking George Despard's brandy. Guilty through association: it had happened to men more senior than himself. Besides, he might want to start telling Despard what he thought of him.

'Nice to see you again,' he said to Grace Kelley and although the smile she gave him was genuine enough, there was more than a trace of fear lingering behind it.

Despard offered his hand and Resnick shook it, firmly but quickly and walked away.

His man was waiting at the entrance out on to the street. Resnick was aware of him a fraction of time before he saw him, a slender shadow backed up against the wall.

'This Warren. He's at Victor's. The gym.'

Resnick scarcely broke his stride.

Thirteen

Through the night CID presence was token: two officers from three stations. This night Lynn Kellogg was one of them. She sat at her desk with a cup of not-so-hot chocolate, struggling with a letter to her parents. Somewhere they'd heard about the city bus drivers going on strike and refusing to take out the last buses on a Friday or a Saturday night. *I do worry about you so, Lynnie love. What you got to be doing that job for in a rough place like that? Least you could do is get a transfer to Norwich. That'd be a lot safer and you'd be closer to home, wouldn't you?* Welcome to Norwich, thought Lynn, a fine city. Well, this was a fine city, one with a bit of real life to it and the thing about real life was occasionally it bit back. As for being closer to home – every couple of months she'd get to be really missing them, the family. Weekend off, she'd make the slow single-lane drive over there, hugs and kisses and handshakes and inside of an hour she couldn't wait to drive away again.

'Boyfriend?' Jim Peel was a gangling man with sandy hair and a declining slope where his chin was supposed to be. One of a family of four brothers, all of them had joined the Police Force, following a father and great-uncle before them. Well, it was either that or campanology.

'Letter home. They're worried about the last buses not going out.'

'Afraid you'll have to walk?'

'Something like that.'

Peel took a pencil from his pocket and poked it carefully down into Lynn's cup, lifting away a heavy crust of skin.

'Thanks, Jim.'

He nodded and dropped the skin into a nearby bin, licking the pencil end clean. 'It's nothing new, you know. This business with the buses. I was talking to someone in the canteen, said they were doing it when he first came on the Force, that was '67.' Peel sat on a chair over at the far side of the room and leaned back until it was balanced on its rear legs, his shoulders against the wall. 'Shouldn't be surprised if it wasn't the same back when they had horse-drawn trams.'

Lynn nodded and looked through what she'd written. He was a nice enough bloke, Jim, but, God, didn't he rattle on! Sort of bloke her folks would wet themselves over if ever she invited him home to Norfolk for the weekend, perish the thought. She could just imagine him walking around with her step-father, nodding with interest as the relative merits of White Rock and White Cornish broilers were explained in great detail. Pretty soon they'd have graduated to the lesser types of fowl pest and her mother would be counting the months as well as her chickens.

'I'll get it!'

Jim Peel rocked his chair forward and pushed himself off the wall with the flat of his hands, but all Lynn had to do was stretch sideways.

'CID. DC Kellogg speaking.'

Vera Barnett was fifty-eight and looked twenty years older; thinning grey hair was sticking to her scalp with perspiration and her facial skin was loose and sallow.

The knuckles of her hands were purple and swollen. She sat in a tall armchair, high-backed, high-sided. One of her feet rested on a cushion.

'The children . . .' Lynn asked.

'I've told you, they're in my bed, sleeping. Poor lambs!'

'But how old . . .?'

'Luke's just seven and little Sarah, she's four.'

'They're all right?'

'Nothing's going to happen to them while I'm here.'

Lynn glanced round at the uniformed officer, standing patiently to one side.

'Your daughter has left them with you before?' Lynn said.

'Every week.'

'The same evening?'

Vera Barnett nodded and Lynn winced as she heard bones creak and grate.

'Do they often stay the night?'

'Never.'

'Not even for a special occasion? I mean . . .'

The mouth tightened. 'She's their mother and they're her children. She's no right. No right.'

'So you were expecting her to collect them?'

'Always.'

'What time would that be, Mrs Barnett? Usually, I mean.'

'Half-past eleven.'

'But the children would already be asleep . . .'

'They're no trouble. Wake up without a fuss. Go off when she gets them back home again, fast as anything.'

'So your daughter comes to collect them at half-past eleven . . .'

'Or earlier. Makes me a bedtime drink, helps me into the bedroom and off she goes till the next time.

122

Brings them over on the bus, two buses really, but she always gets a taxi home. Phones through for it the minute she arrives.' She dabbed at a damp patch of hair. 'I've known her have to ring back two, oh, three times; give some excuse like they couldn't find the number, rang the bell and nobody answered. I've got nothing against them, of course, but they're all, you know, these Asians. I don't know if I should like to be driving home with them, last thing at night.'

There was a lot worse, Lynn thought.

'I rang the hospital,' Vera Barnett said. 'In case, you know, she'd been in an accident. Well, you hear about such things.'

'Why are you so certain something's happened to your daughter?'

'What else could it be?'

'It is only . . .' Lynn checked her watch.

'Two fifty-two,' said the constable.

'It isn't three yet. If she's with friends. A party.' Lynn tried to smile reassuringly, but more and more she had a sense that the woman's fears were grounded. Cold was starting to seek out her stomach. 'There's plenty of time for her to turn up.'

'She's only once been late, really late, and then she rang.'

'Maybe, wherever she is, she was having such a good time, she forgot.'

'With the children here?'

Lynn rubbed the palms of her hands along the slightly rough wool of her skirt. If the woman was right, then all they were doing here was wasting time. Trying to reassure her wasn't working anyway: her mind was too firmly set on disaster.

'You've phoned round her friends?' the constable asked.

123

'It's the middle of the night.'

'Even so. If you're worried.'

'Besides, she doesn't have friends. Not like that. Not that she goes out with. People to talk to at work, but that's all.'

They had already had the story of a marriage gone wrong, blame liberally sprinkled, one thing they could be sure of, wherever Mary was she wouldn't have gone gallivanting off to see *him*.

'And you've no idea where she was going this evening, Mrs Barnett?'

Again the set mouth, eyes narrow with disapproval. 'None whatsoever.'

'Where she usually went on her evening out?'

'She didn't tell me her business and I never asked.' With effort she shifted round in her chair, arms resting along the wings, fingers gripped. 'Though I knew what she was up to, of course.'

Lynn looked at her expectantly.

'She was with a man.'

'Getting really worked up about it, wasn't she?'

'Her daughter gone missing? Hardly surprising.'

'Her daughter having it off.'

'Is that what you think this is about?'

'Don't you? If you've only got one chance a week.'

Lynn blinked and gave a quick shake of the head: another bloke whose ideas about sex were based upon the letters pages in *Penthouse* and mutual masturbation sessions in the showers after games.

'What would your mum say, then? You and sex.'

'Not a lot.'

'How's that then?'

'They don't believe in sex in that part of Norfolk.'

The house was in a short road, cars parked close at

either side. A light was on inside number 7, probably the stairs. All of the other houses in the street were dark.

'What d'you reckon?'

Lynn shrugged, tightened the wool scarf across her neck and rang the bell. It sounded, off-key, inside the house. Through the letter-box there was nothing special: a plastic ball on the carpet, most of the air gone out of it, a piece of Lego.

'Want me to try the back?'

Lynn took from her coat pocket the key Mrs Barnett had given them. 'Why bother?'

'Look, you're sure about this?'

The backs of her legs were sure; her arms, all the places where the chill touched her, tensing the nerves beneath the skin. The key fitted the lock almost too easily and the door swung open with the first pressure of her hand. Lynn stepped around it and looked – it had been held on the catch, but the lock had not been slipped down.

The light that had been left on was on the landing.

With her gloved hand she depressed the switch on the wall, close by a line of pegs bunched with coats.

'Hello!' The constable called. 'Anybody home?'

Lynn opened the door to the first room on the left, turned on the light. Somebody had gone round in a hurry, tidying up. Papers and magazines, Ladybird books, scooped up and set down again in uneven piles; toys squashed up into a corner. Clear across the top of the television, the curve of dust left after a single sweep with the duster.

'Shall I check upstairs?'

'Yes.'

She did not want to go upstairs. Not first.

'Careful what you touch.'

The back room led into the kitchen. Mugs on the table, plates stacked on the draining board, a pan soaking in cold water in the sink, rimed with orange. She heard him coming down the stairs too fast and turned to face him.

'This Mary – houseproud, would you call her?'

'Not exactly. Why?'

'That bed up there's a proper tip.'

'She's not . . .?'

The constable shook his head.

'The bathroom?'

'Not anywhere.'

For several seconds, neither spoke nor moved.

'What d'you reckon?' the constable asked, anxious to be doing something.

'Hang on a minute.'

She walked back into the front room, remembering something she'd only half-noticed. On the floor in the corner alcove, close by the drawn curtains, a handbag. Lynn used finger and thumb to ease it open. Make-up bag, purse, a pair of black flat-heeled shoes, bent double and squashed down. She gave the bag a slight shake. A packet of contraceptives, Durex Elite. Thought about taking it to the table and emptying it out then thought against it.

'Reckon we should phone in?'

She nodded, setting the bag back down where she had found it. Going through the hall, past the crowded pegs, something stopped her. Underneath matching yellow plastic children's coats, different sizes, hung two pairs of blue and yellow wellington boots, threaded together at the top with string. Muddy at the bottom.

'Wait here a minute.'

'What's up?'

'Just wait.'

Back in the kitchen, a step down from the rest of the house, Lynn remembered the cold and knew it had been more than the cold of anticipation. The door to the garden had not quite been pulled to. She touched it open and stepped outside. Stray ends of cloud moved grey across the moon. A bicycle without a rear wheel leaned against the wall. Her toe touched against something and she bent to pick it up. A high-heeled shoe, black, new.

A shape higher up the garden, stretching away.

'A torch! Get me . . .'

He had been standing closer than she'd realized and the sudden beam of light made her jump.

Oh, God! Oh, Christ! Oh, Christ! Oh, God!

Mary Sheppard was wearing nothing above her waist, a halfslip, coffee or beige, below. The other shoe stuck up from the ground, holding stubbornly to the toes of a foot that angled too sharply aside. One arm bent out sideways, the other reached in a curve above her head as though she had been trying to swim to safety. Dark lines like ribbons drawn through her hair.

'Get through to the station. Tell Jim Peel to come out here. I'll ring my DI.'

'Sure you're . . .?'

'Do it.'

Resnick was dreaming about a child playing with dolls: it was not a pleasant dream. The first sound of the telephone woke him with relief. Ten-past four. Dizzy jumped soundlessly down from somewhere above Resnick's head, instantly hungry.

'Hello?'

'Sir, it's DC Kellogg. Sorry to disturb you, but I think you'd better come out . . .'

As he listened, Resnick pushed his fingers into

127

Dizzy's short fur, the cat walking and turning so that the length of his body could be stroked without Resnick's arm having to move.

'Fifteen minutes,' Resnick said, standing, setting down the phone. Dizzy's high, crooked tail slipped around the door before him.

He arrived in twelve. One flap of his shirt hung down below a grey pullover and a sleeve of his jacket was bunched up beneath his herringbone overcoat. He wore a dark brown scarf but was bareheaded.

The ambulance had pulled in close to the line of parked cars and a police car sat in the centre of the street, blue light flashing, blocking traffic. A few lights had been switched on in the adjacent houses.

Resnick nodded to the constable at the front door and went inside. Lynn Kellogg was standing in the living-room, in the semi-darkness. That was not where he had to go. Jim Peel was talking with one of the ambulance men in the back room, a second man had the kettle on and was making tea. Out in the garden, Mary Sheppard's body had been covered over with plastic, a couple of coats.

Resnick reached out a hand and Peel, who had followed him, gave him a torch. First one coat and then the other, top then bottom. He guessed at the temperature. Thirty-odd degrees? The ground was hard beneath his feet in ridges. Earlier that evening it had rained and this would have been mud. A rough circle of it crowned the heel of the dead woman's shoe.

The upstretched arm, the fingers that were like marble.

Resnick guessed that by now they would be quite stiff, solid.

He did not need to touch them and so he did not.

He turned and looked at the tall DC, who blinked at him before angling his head away. Resnick switched off the torch and passed it back. The police surgeon was taking off his gloves in the kitchen, watching the ambulance man pour boiling water over several tea-bags.

'Why's it always the middle of the night, Charlie?'

Resnick shrugged and Parkinson eased the gloves into the side pockets of his Barbour.

'Can we get some light fixed up out there?'

'On its way, sir,' said Jim Peel. 'Being organized.'

The surgeon nodded and accepted a mug of tea. From an inside pocket he took a small leather-covered flask. 'No point in catching my death,' he said, unscrewing the top and tipping a shot of brandy into the tea.

'Sir?'

Resnick spooned two sugars into the offered cup and carried it through to the front of the house. Lynn Kellogg had moved across the room to be close to the window, as if she had considered opening the curtains but decided against it.

'Here,' Resnick said quietly.

At first he thought she wasn't going to turn around. When she did, he held out the cup and she took it automatically in both hands.

'How you feeling?'

She didn't answer, watching the surface of the tea, lightly rocking towards the rim of the cup.

'Lynn?'

The cup fell through her fingers and before she could fall also, Resnick had hold of her, the side of her face squashed up against his chest. The fingers of one hand were pressing hard into the corner of Resnick's mouth. In that light her hair looked no longer brown but black. Resnick thought about the woman lying under those coats in the cold of the garden; thought of Parkinson's stethoscope, the gilt edges of his bifocals, the rolled gold of the propelling-pencil with which he would make his notes.

The strange sound that vibrated through him was Lynn Kellogg's breathing. The tip of her little finger was hooked over the edge of his lower lip.

DC Peel appeared for a moment in the doorway and went away again.

Only when the breathing had begun to steady, did Resnick say, 'You okay?'

She leaned her head back and then to one side, eyes closed and then open. Suddenly embarrassed, she pulled her hand back from Resnick's face.

'I'm sorry, sir, I . . .'

'Best sit down.'

'No, I . . .'

He led her to the nearest chair. Called for somebody to bring two more teas. Lot of sugar in one. When he pulled back the curtains it was still dark, the soft grey darkness that seeks to swallow you up. Back along the street, the police car still leaked blue light.

'Charlie,' Parkinson spoke from the hallway. 'A word?'

The pathologist's report would have to confirm it, but cause of death appeared to be numerous blows with a heavy instrument to the skull. There were also signs of bruising on the neck, around the windpipe and immediately below the jaw. Bruising to the tummy area and above the hips.

'How many?' Resnick asked.

'Sorry?'

'How many is numerous?'

Parkinson pursed his lips. 'Ten or twelve, I'd say. It's

hard to be exact. I expect you'll get a better idea later on.'

Resnick thanked him and turned back into the room where Lynn Kellogg was sipping her tea, staring at the bundle of toys in the corner of the room.

'You didn't ask?' said Parkinson.

Resnick's head swung back.

'Somewhere between midnight and one.'

Resnick nodded and went on into the room. The scene-of-crime team was just arriving outside; one or two neighbours were standing on the pavement in dressing-gowns and slippers.

'There are two kids,' Lynn said.

Resnick had to bend low in order to hear her.

'Boy and a girl.'

'Where?'

'At her mother's. The dead ... at her mother's. It was her that called in.'

'I see.'

'Worried that something had happened ...' The voice choked and Resnick thought she was going to go again, but she caught herself and continued. 'She was worried her daughter hadn't come to fetch the children. I went out to see her. Promised I'd call round, check; she gave me a spare key.'

Resnick took the cup from her hand and set it down on the carpet. 'Will they be all right with her, d'you think? The kids.'

Lynn wiped a hand across her face. 'I don't know. She's ... there's something wrong with her, arthritis, I don't know. I don't think she could cope for long.'

Especially not, Resnick thought, after someone has told her about this.

'All right,' Resnick said, straightening. He rested a

hand lightly on her shoulder and gave it a squeeze. 'I'll sort something out.'

Slowly, she turned her face towards his.

'Before, sir, I'm sorry. I . . .'

'Is that boyfriend of yours at home?'

'I expect so. I . . .'

'Give him a ring. He could come out and fetch you.'

Resnick was surprised to see Lynn Kellogg's face break into a smile.

'What's up?'

'I'd have to ride on the crossbar.'

Resnick smiled too. 'I'll get someone to give you a lift.'

'I'm all right, sir. Honest.'

'You'll be better after a few hours' sleep.'

'My report . . .'

'You made it to me. Write it up when you come in tomorrow.' Resnick corrected himself. 'Today. The only thing I'll need before you go, the mother's address.'

Lynn Kellogg, careful to get up from the chair slowly, opened her notebook.

'Hello? Who is this?' Chris Phillips's voice was thick with sleep.

Resnick told him that he wanted to speak with Rachel Chaplin.

'It's half-past bloody five!'

'So it must be important.'

'Not so important it can't wait.'

Resnick sensed he was about to be cut off, but he heard the receiver changing hands and then it was Rachel's voice.

'Hello?'

'It's Resnick,' he said.

There was a pause before she replied. 'I presume this is more than a social call.'

He told her, evenly, about the murdered woman, the two young children, the invalid grandmother.

Rachel listened carefully, without interrupting, and then said, 'We do have an emergency duty team, you know.'

'I didn't think they'd do much more at this time than send out a message to the nearest office.'

'So?'

'I thought maybe someone should get out to the grandmother's house before the kids wake up.'

'You mean she hasn't been told yet?'

'That's right.'

'And you want me to do it?'

'I'd like somebody else to be there when I do. Someone professional, who'll know how to cope with her and can cope with the kids as well.'

'Why me?'

Resnick didn't answer.

'Give me the address,' Rachel said. And then she said, 'I'll meet you outside in twenty minutes.'

'Right,' Resnick said. He could hear Chris Phillips's voice raised in the background. 'And thanks,' he added, but by then Rachel had put down the phone.

Fourteen

Superintendent Skelton was wearing a light grey suit with the finest of red stripes; the jacket was on a hanger behind his office door. Resnick was surprised that it had not been covered in polythene. The superintendent had allowed the top button of his waistcoat to be undone. His shirt was a pale blue with a white collar, the tie darker blue with a red stripe a shade darker than the one in the weave of his suit. Resnick felt relieved he could not see his superior's socks.

'Take a seat, Charlie. You look knackered.'

Resnick had had the same clothes on since clambering out of his bed in the early hours of that morning. When Rachel Chaplin had pointed it out to him, he had tucked in the flap of his shirt. Graham Millington had lent him a spare tie. His underpants were beginning to itch and he remembered that he had climbed back into the pair he had taken off the night before. He hadn't even fed the cats.

'Coffee?'

'Thanks.'

He tried not to watch as Skelton, not slowly but with care, measured out an amount of beans, tipped them into the electric grinder, from there into the fresh filter paper he had slipped into the top of the machine. Skelton measured water up to the proper calibration on the side of the jug and poured it into the rear. He pressed a switch on the base and a light glowed red.

'Be ready in a couple of minutes.'

Resnick nodded; he was nursing an irrational desire to jerk the electric lead from the wall socket and chuck the whole business through the window, kit and caboodle.

'How's DC Kellogg?'

'Downstairs writing up her report.'

'Making it a bit of a habit, that team. Turning up dead bodies.'

Resnick looked at the superintendent, but made no reply. Coffee was dripping through at a steady rate.

Skelton shuffled paper across his desk. 'You've read Parkinson's report?'

'Sir.'

'Whoever did this, he wasn't just trying to kill her. Whoever did this . . .' Skelton paused, as if trying – somehow – to picture the murderer in his mind . . . 'was after something more. Those blows were sufficient to . . .' Skelton paused to glance again at the report . . . to 'puncture the cerebral cortex over the left hemisphere, splinter the left ventricle and the anterior horn. Damage to the medulla oblongata had impaired the passage of the spinal cord along the central canal. All that's without serious bruising to the rest of the body.'

'Someone with a lot of strength,' Resnick observed.

'Or anger.' Skelton rose and poured the coffee.

Resnick was just in time to wave no to milk.

'If this had been Shirley Peters, I wouldn't have been surprised. Jealous man, violent, strong – we know how much damage he can do when his temper is roused. His own face is evidence enough of that.' Skelton tasted his coffee and gave a little nod of satisfaction. 'Instead he uses a woman's scarf.'

Did it matter, Resnick wondered, woman's or man's?

'It takes a deal of effort, sir,' Resnick said, 'to throttle the life out of someone.'

'All the same, to cave in a person's skull . . .'

'But the scarf, sir. Maybe it was important – to Macliesh, I mean.'

'Go on.'

'If what was getting at him was her attractiveness to other men, well, mightn't he have chosen that on purpose?' Resnick shrugged, not too happy with the idea himself, now that he'd given it voice.

'Red, you mean? The colour. Part of making her attractive to other men. Signalling that she was available.'

'Something like that.'

'Been brushing up on your psychology of crime, Charlie?'

Sarcastic bugger! thought Resnick. 'No, sir,' he said. 'I think I saw it once . . . in a film.'

'Didn't think symbolism was much in your line.'

An echo sounded in Resnick's mind. He wondered how Divine and Naylor were getting on looking for Macliesh's alibi down at the Victor Gym. And whether simply sitting with George Despard and sharing his brandy had been enough to earn him the information or if there had been any more to it.

'Think there's any connection, Charlie? Couple of single women, thirties. Both . . .' – Skelton hesitated before finishing the sentence, his mouth suspended in a prim circle – ' . . . sexually active. Apparently.'

'Not a crime, sir.'

'I'm not suggesting it is.' Skelton's response was just a little too quick, forcing his voice up a register.

'No, sir.'

'What I am pointing to is a connection.'

'Yes, sir.'

'Shirley Peters was strangled, concurrent with or soon after engaging in sex...'

'Or immediately before.'

Skelton hurried on. 'The scene-of-crime report on Mary Sheppard shows that intercourse had taken place at roughly the same time as her murder.' He looked steadily at Resnick. 'On this occasion certainly prior to her death. Since it seems that one occurred upstairs in the bedroom, the murder in the garden.'

On the cabinet to the side of the double bed, a used condom had been found squashed up into a couple of tissues, presumably for throwing away later. Other tissues, used, were scattered across the carpet; another had been pushed under the edge of the pillow. There were traces of semen down the inside of Mary Sheppard's thighs, not a great deal. Splashes perhaps. Before or after? There was also staining on the sheet which might, when analysed, or might not match.

'Any luck getting Macliesh to agree to giving us a sample?'

Resnick shook his head. 'The blood he gave us inadvertently: there was enough splashed round the police cell. His semen and his pubic hair, he's being more prudent with. And I'm sure his solicitor's advising him to keep it that way.'

'She doesn't think it would disprove his involvement then?'

'No more than we do, I should imagine.'

'How's that alibi holding up?'

'I'm having it checked out now, sir. It looks as though we've found one of the men Macliesh put up.'

'And this Mary Sheppard's ex-husband? Not another man scorned, I suppose?'

Resnick shook his head. 'It doesn't sound like it.'

'Too much to hope for.'

'We contacted him in the Wirral.'

'Gone up in the world, eh?'

'Gone West, anyway. He's driving down now. Patel's waiting to take his statement.'

'He's identifying the body when he arrives, is he?'

'No, sir. The mother did that.'

'Thought she couldn't get about.'

'She can, but with difficulty. Social Services laid on special transport.'

'I would have thought she was best off leaving it to somebody else.'

'She insisted. Said it was her daughter and she wanted to do what was right. I think she would have crawled there on her hands and knees if need be, rather than let him do it for her. The husband. Ex.'

'No love lost then?'

'He left her all alone with his children when it suited him, he could leave well alone now. That was what she said, more or less. I think he'll be lucky to get an invite to the funeral.'

Skelton sighed, lifted the cup to his mouth but he had already finished his coffee. Resnick was thinking about Mary Sheppard on her hands and knees in that small back garden, trying in vain to make her escape. Had she stumbled, trying to run? Had the first blow driven her to the ground? Other, later blows, had they flattened her into the drying mud despite all her efforts to get clear?

'No neighbours queuing up to testify on this one, Charlie?'

'Not so far, sir.'

'And no weapon?'

Resnick shook his head. 'Not yet.'

'I've had three calls from the chief superintendent in

the last couple of hours,' Skelton said. 'You've briefed the DCI?'

'Yes, sir.'

'We've borrowed some uniforms for house-to-house, but it's likely not going to be enough. Not unless someone turns something up quickly. This isn't just a nasty little domestic, Charlie. The local paper's already got sex crime all over its news-stands. They'll be hoping for an extra few thousand on their circulation by the end of the day.'

Resnick stood up. 'Maybe we'll have a good lead by then, sir.'

Skelton stood also. 'Be nice to think so.'

Resnick opened and closed the door to the superintendent's office carefully, not wishing to disturb the coat. In the corridor his stomach groaned not once, but twice, three times; groaned and whined. Eating: something else he hadn't got around to in the last eight hours.

Two detective constables and a sergeant were coaxing reports from typewriters which could never remember the rule about *i* before *e* – except when it was an exception. Divine and Naylor had not yet returned from Victor's. Lynn Kellogg had been in, written her report, and been sent home again to lie down before she fell down. Millington had driven out to the Sheppard house, taking the scene-of-the-crime officer along with him: check and double-check. Patel ... where was Patel?

Climbing the stairs to the first floor, he was followed by a whey-faced man with heavy-framed glasses and a decided stoop. The dark suit the visitor was wearing had probably cost more than Jack Skelton's but wasn't being worn with anything like the same flourish.

'This is Mr Sheppard, sir.'

Resnick introduced himself, shook hands, offered commiserations. Sheppard's hand was damp and cloying and Resnick was reminded of squeezing the water from spinach, cooked and rinsed.

'I'd like to talk to you after DC Patel has taken your statement,' said Resnick, stomach rumbling.

'That solicitor wants a word, sir,' the sergeant called over, hand covering the mouthpiece. 'Olds.'

'She in the building?'

'Downstairs, sir.'

'Tell her to count to a hundred in tens and then come up.'

Resnick pulled his office door to and dialled the number of the local deli: everything from amaretti and asparagus spears to Patum Peperium Gentleman's Relish and Japanese rice crackers. He ordered one tuna mayonnaise and salad on dark rye and a chicken breast and Jarlsberg cheese with French mustard and tomato on rye with caraway: a quarter of German potato salad and two large gherkins.

By the time he put down the phone, Suzanne Olds was standing outside his door, the smooth lines of her face marginally distorted by the glass. On a day when suits were clearly the thing, she had favoured a red wool skirt, calf-length, over highly polished black boots. Underneath an autumnal check jacket, a brooch the size of a 50p piece had been fastened at the collar of a cream silk blouse. She was armed with the same two bags as before, one slung over her shoulder, the other gripped in her opposite hand.

Resnick got up to open the door but, before he could get there, she had interpreted his move and was inside.

'Shall I close it?'

'If you like.'

140

She closed the door by leaning back against it, holding the pose for just long enough for Resnick to do what he was supposed to be doing and register how good she looked.

'Take a seat.'

What he wasn't supposed to be doing was wondering why he had never found her attractive. He didn't think it was because they were adversaries, not that at all. He wasn't fazed by strong professional women. No, more a question of image – the one Suzanne Olds was forever presenting. Not because there was anything wrong with it, but because he could never, convincingly, find her inside it.

'I'm not interrupting,' she said, with a quick glance towards the telephone.

'Not for the moment.'

The eyes, that's where it was; where she wasn't. He had a sudden memory of Rachel Chaplin, the shine in that first held look across the foyer of the court, green, blue.

'My client . . .'

'Macliesh.'

'You'll be releasing him.'

Resnick looked over his shoulder at the calendar on the wall. 'Isn't that question a little premature?'

'In the circumstances?'

'The circumstances are that we are progressing with our enquiries. The court was happy for your client to be held on remand.'

Suzanne Olds crossed her legs with a faint swish of nylon. 'That was before, Inspector.'

'Before what, Ms Olds?'

'Before the second murder.'

Resnick was aware suddenly that it was raining outside; he could hear it blowing in flurries against the window-pane, a counterpoint against the muted ringing of telephones.

'What relevance are you claiming?'

'I should have thought that was so obvious as to be not worth stating.'

Resnick heard from his stomach and gave it a gentle pat or two. Hold on there, it's coming. He wondered if the interview would be over before his sandwiches arrived or whether he was destined to another hard-earned meal before an audience.

'That sounds like courtroom debate, Ms Olds.'

'And that sounds as if you've got either a serious digestive problem or an ulcer.'

'I'm gratified by your concern.'

'I'd be gratified if you would show some concern for my client.'

'Let your client show some concern for himself.'

'He's made a full statement, answered all your questions. Despite being the victim of the most unpleasant provocation.'

'Oh, come on!'

'Come on, nothing. You know as well as I do . . .'

'I know Macliesh jumped on the first opportunity he could get.'

'You're saying that your DC behaved in a thoughtful and responsible manner?'

'I'm not saying anything about the way my DC acted.'

'I'm not surprised.'

Resnick leaned back in his chair. Divine and Naylor had just come into the outer office. 'Are you prepared to advise your client to co-operate with us and allow intimate samples . . .?'

'No.'

'When that would allow us to confirm or disprove . . .'

'Don't waste your breath quoting the Police and Criminal Evidence Act at me, Inspector.'

'Then there doesn't seem to be any alternative other than being patient and letting us get on with our investigation as best we can. By other and, unfortunately, more time-consuming methods.'

Suzanne Olds shook her head, opened her shoulder bag and took out a packet of cigarettes. 'Do you mind?' she asked automatically.

Resnick surprised himself by saying, 'Yes.'

He didn't want the smell of cigarette smoke interfering with his lunch.

Suzanne Olds bit lightly down into the flesh inside her lower lip and dropped the pack from sight.

'Congratulations, Inspector.'

'What for?'

'Sidetracking me.'

'Is that what I've done?'

'I came here to talk about last night's murder.'

'I don't understand. Someone's retained you . . .?'

She shook her head, vigorously this time. 'Tony Macliesh is still my one and only client in this matter.'

'Then . . .'

'And he was arrested on the basis of emotional hearsay evidence, a quick and convenient culprit against whom you had and continue to have nothing that goes beyond the purely circumstantial. There is nothing which points to my client being at or near the scene of Shirley Peters's death or which links him directly and specifically to what was a violent and sexual attack. An attack which has been followed by another, more brutish than the first, in which my client could have played no part since he is being held in police custody.'

Resnick was on his feet. 'Ms Olds, there has never

143

been any suggestion of linking Macliesh with Mary Sheppard's murder.'

'Exactly. There is a sadistic killer out there, preying on defenceless women and instead of tracking him down you are clinging blindly to the wrong man.'

Resnick leaned forward until Suzanne Olds's perfume was inescapable. 'I'll try to put this as clearly as I can. What we have here are two quite separate murders, quite distinct. The means of death, the modes of killing are absolutely different, no connection. Neither is there any connection between the victims, other than the fact that, yes, they were female, and, yes, they were living alone – not living, that is, with a man.' He straightened up. 'Two murders, two cases, two inquiries, two murderers, ultimately, two convictions. As you will know, we currently have someone under arrest for the first murder; and, as you have said yourself, there is no way in which that suspect could have been involved in the second.'

Resnick sat down. 'I hope, for Macliesh's sake, you've got something better for him than this by way of his defence.'

Suzanne Olds got up and walked out. This time no pose; she didn't even think to close the door.

'Divine! Naylor!'

The uniformed constable who had nipped up with the brown paper bag from the deli got caught between them.

'Regular sandwich there, sir,' said Divine.

'Two, I hope,' said Resnick, putting the bag down on his desk. 'What luck?'

'We found him, sir, Warren,' Naylor said eagerly.

'And?'

The two DCs exchanged glances. 'He does a bit of

working out there, sir, keeps an eye on the gym, weights and that.'

'Evenings, he works as a bouncer round the clubs.'

Resnick was getting impatient; his sandwiches were getting stale. 'Can we get to the point, gentlemen?'

'Yes, well, the point is, sir . . .'

'The point is . . .'

'The point is he'll only speak to you, Sir.'

'Fine,' said Resnick. 'So where is he?'

Another quick look flicked between the two men.

'At the gym, sir, Victor's . . .'

'It's in one of those old warehouses . . .'

'I know where it is. Where's this Warren? If he wants to speak to me, I'm here. Why didn't you bring him in?'

'We suggested it, sir,' said Naylor, fidgeting a little on his feet.

'Uh-huh.'

'He didn't take to the idea, sir.'

Resnick rubbed at the far corners of his eyes and switched his attention to Mark Divine. 'You told him this was a murder inquiry?'

'Yes, sir.'

'And he still refused to co-operate?'

'No, sir. I mean, not exactly. He did say he would talk to you, sir. Didn't seem to have any problems with that at all. It was just the matter of his coming into the station.'

'Busy, was he?' said Resnick. Suzanne Olds's scent had cleared sufficiently for him to be able to make out the caraway embedded in the rye, the richness of the mustard. 'Too busy watching over all those weights?'

'He was on the Nautilus machine, sir. What he was pushing . . .'

'Not like you, Divine, to miss an opportunity to be

145

persuasive.' Divine fiddled with the knot of his tie; Naylor, meanwhile, had finished with the basic foxtrot and was progressing to something with more than a tinge of *paso doble*.

'He was a big feller, sir.'

'Arms out to here.'

'You've seen them body-builders.'

'Almost unnatural.'

'Besides,' said Resnick, interrupting them. He wouldn't be able to requisition another piece of carpet for another three years. 'You didn't want to antagonize him, make him into a hostile witness. Didn't want to risk starting up violence in a public place.'

'Yes, sir,' said Divine.

'No, sir,' said Naylor.

'At the gym all afternoon, is he?'

'Till four, sir,' Naylor said.

Resnick glanced across the desk. 'You two had lunch?'

They had not.

'When you get back from the canteen, get back in touch with Liverpool CID. Run down that description Macliesh gave us of his other so-called co-conspirator. See if they can't come up with some faces. And run this Warren through the computer. Sharpish.'

Resnick was just crunching through the first of the gherkins when his phone rang. Vinegar splashed on to his hand and started to trickle between thumb and forefinger towards his wrist.

'Millington, sir.' It was one of those connections that sound like they've been routed via both Poles.

'You still at the Sheppard house?'

'Sir.'

'And?'

'I think I've found something interesting, sir. I thought, if you weren't snowed under, you might pop out.'

'You're the one who sounds snowed under, Graham.'

'Sorry, sir?'

'Don't be. I'll be there as soon as I can.' He replaced the receiver with one hand, lifted the chicken and cheese to his mouth with the other. 'I'm off out to the Sheppard place,' he announced to the office. 'Tell Patel to hang on to the Ex as long as he can. I'll try and get to the gym on the way back.'

He took the stairs two at a time, brown paper bag swinging from his left hand.

'Bad manners to talk with your mouth full,' observed Naylor. He didn't say it very loud. The last time he'd done it at home – pork chops and apple sauce done in the oven, roast potatoes and parsnips – Debbie had given him a proper going-over. She wasn't going to come rushing home to cook him a meal just for him to spit it out all over the tablecloth.

Oh, God! Why did he have to think about Debbie?

When he'd raised his eyebrow inquiringly that morning, the way she'd shaken her head, the expression in her eyes, it was almost as if she was pleased nothing had happened. Although he knew them off by heart, Naylor looked across at Divine's girlie calendar and recounted the days.

Fifteen

Rachel Chaplin shared her office with one of the other seniors, a room no wider than the average double bed and not a lot longer. Papers spilled out from in-trays and spread randomly across both desks, photocopied articles with the relevant passages high-lighted, claim forms for necessary travel, memos. *While you were out* ... Whoever had decided that cerise was a good colour for memo pads?

While Carole, her colleague, had spent the bulk of the morning trying to arrange for an eighty-two-year-old man with two replacement hips to be transferred from a geriatric ward into a nursing home, Rachel had been sorting out emergency fostering for Luke and Sharon Sheppard. Trying to.

'No, the boy is seven and the girl's four. No, no, she's got a nursery place. Not the same building, but close. Um, five, ten minutes walk, no more.'

'You don't have any idea when a vacancy might occur? Yes, I do realize what it depends upon and without wishing that to happen. Yes, I see, in a coma for four days and the doctor has no idea ... Yes, that's right, if you would, please ring me. Right.'

'I don't think it would be a good idea if the grandmother didn't have access. She's not very mobile, that's the problem. Otherwise ... Look, I don't want to sound grudging, but can I get back to you? No, today, I promise. One way or another, certainly.'

'You do know what it's like in a geriatric ward? Then you know why I'm anxious he should be moved.'

'Hello, this is Rachel Chaplin, city office. Yes, fine thanks. You? Good. Oh, really? That's great. Listen, there was a woman you used to use for short-term fostering. I met her once at that case conference we both went to. Yes, that's the one. I was wondering . . . Where? Australia. Thanks, anyway. Bye.'

For the first time in maybe an hour both receivers were in their cradles. Rachel stood up and arched backwards, stretching the muscles of her back.

'Alexander technique, that's what you ought to try,' Carole remarked.

'Isn't that where you lie flat on your back and have someone walk all over you?'

'Not exactly.'

'Always resisted it. Reminds me of too many relationships.'

'You're all right, you and Chris.'

Rachel looked at her.

'I mean, he's not like that.'

'More subtle.'

'Why don't you get him to give you a massage?'

'Can't see him having the time.'

'Find it. Last thing you want is a bad back. Something like that starts to go and the next thing you know you're applying for a mobility allowance.'

Sitting back down, turning the pages of her address book, Rachel laughed. 'Thanks very much!'

'You're still a young woman, but that's when it all begins to go wrong.'

'You can say that again.'

'I'm working with it all the time. People who've never given their bodies a single thought and then suddenly they're sixty and looking around, wondering why bits and pieces are malfunctioning. I mean, if it were a car, you wouldn't . . .'

Carole broke off as Rachel's phone rang.

'Hello, this is . . . Chris? Anything wrong?'

She glanced across at Carole, who gave a quick smile before starting to dial a number.

'I was going to skip lunch,' Rachel said. 'I don't think I've got the time. Besides, I brought a sandwich.'

Continuing to leaf through her address book, Rachel's face set in a frown. She didn't want this.

'Look, Chris,' she said, interrupting him. 'I'll meet you by the church. Five-past. Now I've got to go.'

'Well, I suppose that depends on how you define incontinent,' Carole was saying.

Rachel closed the book decisively and rang the internal number of the officer in charge of domiciliary care.

The sheets, the duvet cover, even the mattress, all had been stripped and bagged, taken away to forensic for analysis and reports. Resnick sat on the iron frame of the bed. Graham Millington was squatting on his haunches, knuckles of one hand resting against the floor. The drawer of the bedside cabinet was open and empty. Between Resnick and Millington, spreading across the carpet, overlapped, the letters.

'It's raining.'

Funny, isn't it, Rachel was thinking, how suddenly, one day and for no good reason, all those banalities we exchange throughout out lives become so intensely irritating.

'I said . . .'

'I know.'

'Well, do we have to stand out in it, getting wet?'

'It was your idea.'

'Not to come here.'

'I didn't want to go far.'

'Surely we could go to a pub? Even if it's only for a quick half.'

Rachel went through the arched iron gateway and turned right along uneven flagstones towards the south porch. Surrounded by scaffolding, like so much of the church, it was in the process of restoration.

She took her hands from her pockets, unfastened the top of her coat. Pushing his fingers through his damp hair, Chris Phillips followed her out of the rain. A couple of solicitor clerks scuttled past them, cellophane-wrapped lunch inside white Marks & Spencer bags.

'So what was so urgent?'

He started to speak, checked himself, half-turned his head aside to where the rain glistened on the black of the railings and a couple of petals clung, pale, to the bed of rose bushes.

'You're not going to make this easy, are you?' he said.

If Rachel heard him, she gave no sign.

Dear Box 124,

As you can guess I'm replying to your ad in Lonely Hearts. I'd better come right out with it and say that I'm a bit of a way outside the ages you mention – forty-three next birthday – but thought I'd give it a go anyway. After all, what's the price of a stamp these days!

Seriously though, I *am* caring and lively. Given the chance, if you know what I mean! Used to be married and have one kiddie, who I see every other weekend. The wife, as was, lives in Lincoln now so, as I'm not running a car at the moment, the journey's a bit of a problem. But enough of my difficulties! (You don't say if you've been married at all, not a lot about yourself at all – slim, attractive, twenty-nine – that's good enough, I suppose!)

Anyway, to save me rambling on, why don't we meet up one evening and see how it goes? You can't phone me at the moment (no phone!) so just drop me a line and say when and where.

I really hope you do.

Sincerely,

John Benedict

'Rach.' (God! She *hated* it when he called her that.) 'I just want to know what's going on.'

'It's cold, it's windy, I'm eating a . . .'

'Enough, Rachel.'

'. . . sandwich and you're doing a very good impression of "deeply worried, Notts".'

'Rachel, enough.'

Count up to ten, Rachel, she thought, stop being such a shit.

'All right,' she said. 'I'm sorry. I've been trying all morning to sort out some kind of care for two kids who've still got to be told their mother's been murdered.'

He put an arm around her shoulders and she found herself trying not to flinch.

'I'm sorry, too,' Chris said. 'I understand that you're preoccupied,' (Preoccupied, is that what I am?) 'but the same could go for both of us.' He gave her shoulder a squeeze before stepping away. 'It's bloody typical, isn't it?'

'What's that?'

'You can't think about anything but work, which means you haven't got any time left over for us, and my stupid brain's so clogged up with what's happening

152

to us, I can't think about my job for more than five minutes at a time.'

Dear Caring and Lively,
   I don't want you to think I'm in the habit of replying to these things, though I will admit to glancing through them, mainly for a laugh. There was something about the sound of yours, though, that made me want to set pen to paper for the first time. I couldn't see you, of course, when I was writing, but somehow it felt as if I could. See you there, sitting and having your lonely breakfast, sliding the end of the knife into my envelope and opening it up.
   Why not give me a call?
   Maybe you'll be as attracted by the sound of my voice as I was by the words in your advert. We'll never know till we try.
   Yours,
                   Caring and Lively II (*Not* the Movie!)

'I just feel that I can't touch you, I can't talk with you, anything I do is wrong and everything I say is either stupid or insensitive or both.'
   'Chris . . .'
   'No, I mean it. I feel I'm offensive to you. That's what it is.'
   'That's not true.'
   'Isn't it?'
   'No.'
   'It's the way I feel.'
   Rachel stood with her face in her hands, leaning back against the parish notices, the poster for a concert of early music, details of the restoration appeal.
   'Rachel, it's the way you make me feel.'

Dear Miss Lonely Hearts,

I'm sure that you will already have received a mass of replies to your advertisement and so I suppose I shouldn't rate my chances of earning a response too highly. When you've been trying, one way or another, to find a true friend in this harsh world, someone who might turn out to be your soulmate, for as many years as I have, you learn not to set your expectations too highly.

In case there is something in my letter which strikes a chord, though, let me tell you a little about myself. I am thirty-nine, only ten years older than yourself you see, and have always lived the bachelor life, though not through choice. Whenever I do begin to become close friends with a nice woman, something always seems to go wrong. When this happens, of course, I always say to myself, stop making a fool of yourself and vow to stop even trying. But that never lasts, does it, and something inside you, a sort of a yearning I suppose you could call it, makes you want to reach out to somebody again.

I very much hope that you will write to me and if you do I hope that we will be able to meet. Something tells me that we might be able to talk freely and openly to one another.

In anticipation of your reply,

Sincerely,

Martin Myers

'It's this policeman, isn't it? This Resnick.'

'What is?'

'Come on, Rachel! Ever since you met him, you've not been the same. Not towards me.'

'Chris, you're talking about a man I've met on two occasions for a drink.'

'So you say.'

'What the hell's that mean?'

'If that's all there is to it, what's he doing ringing you up at all hours of the night?'

'He rang me this morning because . . .'

'Because he wanted an excuse.'

Rachel laughed in amazement. 'Oh, so he went out and engineered a convenient crime so he could meet me at half-past five?'

'You know that's not what I mean.'

'It's what you said.'

'What I *mean* is, he could have phoned through to the emergency duty team. That's what anybody else in his position would have done. Wouldn't they?'

Rachel walked past him to the edge of the porch. Rain was dripping steadily from the scaffolding, but otherwise it seemed to be stopping. There was a blue spray of sky behind the rooftops opposite.

'Wouldn't they?'

'Yes.'

'What?'

'Yes.' Turning to face him, not knowing who she despised most for the hurt in his eyes, Chris or herself.

Dear 124,

Let's get right down to it (as the actress said to the bishop). I'm twenty-six, five-foot-seven with my socks (and everything else) off and I weigh eleven stone. There are other vital statistics, but I'll hang on until I can swop them with yours!

I'm a plumber, got my own business, van and that. Work evenings a lot of the time, but since what I do's in my own hands (it is now, but if you play your cards right, nudge, nudge!) I could always meet you for a quick hour or so in the daytime. I don't know if you've got a job or not, but that might suit you better.

Give us a ring. I've got one of them answering machines for the job, so you'd better not get too carried away talking to that! Leave that for the real thing.

Go on, do it today and remember what they say about plumbers!

You won't regret it!

Love,

Dave

Through the railings they could see barristers going into the brasserie opposite. The sun was in the sky, the colour of egg white. The slightest burnish of pink had begun to show on the stone slabs of the wall.

'He fancies you, then, does he? Resnick?'

'Chris, I don't know.'

'Of course you know. Women always know.'

'Does it matter?'

'Then he does.'

'Chris . . .' She took, for a moment, no more than seconds, his hand in hers. 'I can't have this now, this . . . conversation. It isn't the time.'

'It never is.'

She was looking at her watch.

'You'll be home later?'

'Of course, I'll be . . . Whatever do you think's happening, Chris?'

'I know what's happening. I'm not a fool. What I want to know is why, and how can I stop it.'

Rachel turned the collar of her coat up against the ends of her hair. Hands were back in her pockets. 'We'll talk tonight, okay?'

'Okay,' Chris sighed. 'Yes, sure. You haven't got any idea when . . .?'

'No.' She paused. 'Chris . . .'

'I know. You've got to go.'

Along the path and down the worn steps, he didn't expect her to look back but waited, anyway, until she was out of sight. He used his hand to wipe the surplus

156

water from one of the benches by the front of the
church and sat down.

'How many, Graham?'
  'Forty-three.'
  'Same age as John Benedict.'
  'Sir?'
Resnick pointed at the letter at the top of its pile.
'Amazing, isn't it?' Millington said, adjusting his tie.
'What's that?'
'All these blokes out there. Needing to, well, go
through this sort of rigmarole.' He stood up, flexing his
legs where the muscles had been stiffening. 'I never
thought anyone took it seriously. Personal columns.
Computer dating. What sort of a state do you have to
be in to do that?'
  Resnick looked at him. 'Lonely?'
  'I still reckon . . .'
But Resnick cut him off. 'When you were getting
them out of the drawer, you were careful about touching them?'
  'Kid gloves.'
'I don't suppose we'll get any prints, but there's no
point in making it more difficult. Collect them up, will
you. Best get them back to the station.' He glanced
back down at the letters. 'One or two going to get
the kind of reply they didn't bargain for, I shouldn't
wonder.'

'Everything all right?' asked Carole when Rachel
walked back into the office.
  'Um, why?'
  'Thought you seemed a little preoccupied, that's all.'
  (So it had to be right; that's what she was.)
  'I've been thinking about these Sheppard kids and

157

now I wonder if fostering is the best answer after all. It might be better to leave them in the grandmother's home; there's room, so that's not a problem. Her lack of mobility had decided me against it, but maybe that could be coped with. Get someone to call in there on a regular basis. Morning and evening to start off with. It would be a way of getting the woman to accept help for herself anyway. Might turn out to be a better solution for her and the children. What do you think?'

Sixteen

Suddenly, it was a fine autumn day but Resnick had missed the rainbow. The sky was a wash of pale blue and the sun strong enough now to draw colour from the bricks. He walked along a narrow street between warehouses, four or five storeys high, substantial, the windows perfectly placed, proportioned. If you looked upwards to the curved arches of the roofs, it was easy to think you were in another city.

Resnick turned right, where the hardware merchant, greengrocer, the purveyor of yeast tablets, urine bottles and athletic supporters had all waited until their leases had expired and gone with them. He went down the hill past the video diner, a window crammed with art-deco furniture, men's clothing shops with names like Herbie Hogg, Culture Vulture.

The sign above the gym was purple neon, like hand-writing, Victor's Gym and Health Club. Bowed-glass windows showed sets of weights, dumbbells, leotards in violent colours. The reception area was a small bar: freshly-squeezed orange juice, vegetable shakes, espresso. The receptionist had stainless steel hair and the most perfect make-up job Resnick had seen since he'd got trapped in a department store lift with four assistants from the perfumery department.

She was looking at a tall coffee-coloured man who was lounging in an oatmeal sweat suit, limbs carelessly arranged for the best effect.

Neither of them paid Resnick much attention. From deeper inside the building came the muted sound of disco music, an irregular succession of grunts and thumps. Out here, nobody moved. Nobody sweated.

'Do I go straight through to get to the gym?' Resnick asked.

'Why d'you want to do that?' the girl said, not looking at him, concentrating on the man in the sweat suit. There was a plastic badge pinned to her loose pink top and on it, in lettering not unlike that of the sign, Jane was written in purple ink.

'Why do people usually?'

An eyebrow lifted, not far. 'You're not a member.'

'No.' He was beginning to feel like the Dynarod man.

'Oh, then you got one of those things we sent out. Leaflets. Three free sessions. Through the door, right?'

'Right.'

She looked past Resnick to the man. 'I told Victor it was a stupid idea.'

Something or somebody landed heavily on the floor immediately over their heads.

'You've got to hand it in,' she said to Resnick. 'The leaflet. Otherwise you can't get the sessions.'

Resnick shook his head. 'I tore it up.'

'All in one go,' the man said, 'or did you take it a little bit at a time?'

Jane thought that was very funny. The laughter broke from her and when she tried to stifle it tears came to her eyes and tight wheezing sounds caught in her throat. She was in danger of choking or, at the very least, of her make-up cracking apart.

'Easily amused,' Resnick observed.

'Jane, she's got a great sense of humour.'

'Don't you think you should do something?' Resnick

160

said, looking at the way her eyes were growing increasingly alarmed, trapped in the centre of her face.

He shrugged and moved lithely around the bar, a couple of well-placed pats in the small of the back, an energetic release of air and Jane was sitting up right as rain with a carrot and wheatgerm cocktail in her hand.

'I'm here to see Warren,' Resnick said. 'I was told he'd be in the gym.'

'Why d'you want to see Warren?' the man said.

'Why do you need to know?'

'We don't encourage folk walking in off the street and . . .'

It was getting tedious. Resnick took out his wallet and showed his identification.

'I'll fetch him,' the man said.

Resnick put the wallet away. 'I'll find him.'

There was just a moment when he thought the man might be about to try and stop him, but the muscles relaxed and a finger pointed along the short corridor. 'Up the stairs. Left. Straight ahead.'

'Yes,' said Resnick. 'Follow the noise.'

High-toned sweat and embrocation. Up here the effort was real and nobody bothered too much about keeping the backs of their shorts rolled over so that the designer labels showed. As weights were lifted and set down, the boards vibrated beneath Resnick's feet. A small-boned Chinese woman lay on her back, legs arched into the air, while a fifteen-stone instructor added another ten pounds to her load.

'That's not all she can do.'

Resnick angled his head to the right.

'Restaurant where she works. I was in there once. Nice place. Not your take-away. Linen napkins. Finger bowls. These guys came in from the pub; one of them, real foul-mouthed, objectionable. Sits there ordering the lagers, making remarks at the other customers. Everyone staring down into their chow mein, pretending it isn't happening. She goes over and tells him to be quiet or leave. He starts calling her a few choice things, so she says she's going to call the police. He grabs at her, misses, up from the table, trying again. She turns, cool as you like, one foot in his balls and the next one takes his eye out. Out. Well, dangling. They have to sew it back in casualty. Four-and-a-half hours. Can't see the scar, but he's got this dreadful squint.' He held out his hand. 'I'm Warren.'

'Detective Inspector Resnick.'

'I figured.'

The handshake was firm and smeared with sweat. Warren was a couple of inches shorter than Resnick, ageless, his skin glistened and, yes, his muscles had been nurtured to the point where they were awesome. He was wearing loose-fitting grey sweat pants and a black cotton vest that stuck to back and chest. Bare feet.

'Let's talk in here.'

Resnick followed him into a small room next to the men's changing-room, a couple of chairs and a desk, rosters pinned with bright yellow tacks to a hessian-covered board on the wall.

'Staff perks,' explained Warren, sitting down, gesturing for Resnick to do the same.

'You know Georgie Despard,' Warren said.

'A little.'

Warren laughed. His teeth were even, the one left of centre had a tiny gold star set into it. He said, 'Georgie says you've been on his case for years.'

Resnick shook his head lightly. 'Not any more.'

Warren laughed again. 'He's fly, Georgie.'

'How come you know him?'

'Him and my old man, they were up in the Smoke together. Years back. His folks had moved up here and, oh, that wasn't right for George. He wanted some action. My old man'd grown up there, like him. George went back. Fine times. I'd see 'em getting ready, suits, shiny suits. They'd start weekends up West on a Friday night, the Flamingo. Georgie Fame and the Blue Flames. John Mayall. That bloke who threw himself under a Tube train – what was his name? I forget it now.' He stretched back in the chair and sighed with the pleasure of remembering.

'I don't imagine all they got up to was dancing.'

Warren leaned easily forward. 'Sorry about not coming up to the station.' He shuddered. 'Something about those places.'

'As long as you're still willing to talk.'

'About Macliesh?'

'Unless there's anything else you . . .'

'Macliesh.'

'All right.'

'You've got him banged up for doing that woman.'

'He's in custody.'

'Not for long.'

'How's that?'

'I mean, for all I care about the bloke, he could stay there. It's where he's come from and he'll be back, one way or another. They always are. Don't know how to get on in the world, his sort. No idea of, you know, coming to terms with it.'

'The time I'm interested in . . .'

'The Monday night, right? When it happened. According to the papers, anyway. Has to be.'

'Has to?'

'That's when Macliesh has got me pulled in for his alibi.'

'You saw him on the Monday?'

'Met him here. In the bar. Him and Mottram.'

'Mottram?'

'Scouser.'

'Friend of yours or Macliesh's?'

'Macliesh'd never set eyes on him before. I know him from the States. Used to go over, every year, body-building contests, exhibitions, Mister Universe.'

'Mottram was a body-builder?'

Warren smiled and showed his inlaid tooth. 'If Mottram stood still on a grating, he'd go down it. No, he was working with a couple of fighters, corner work; he was a good cuts man. Then his fingers went.'

'Started to shake?' said Resnick. 'Stiffened?'

Warren was still smiling. 'Got into an argument with this bloke who had an axe.'

Resnick thought about it: not for too long.

'What was he doing here? In the city.'

'Drifting around. Bumming what he can. He'd been in that day, earlier. I told him to stick around and see what Macliesh came up with.'

'One thing I don't see,' said Resnick. 'How Macliesh was talking to you in the first place? I don't see the connection.'

Warren pulled a sweater up from the floor and slipped it on; the sweat was beginning to dry cold. 'If I'm going to carry on talking . . .' He glanced at the closed door. ' . . . it's just inside this room right? There's nothing else here to interest you, just Macliesh. Right?'

Resnick nodded.

Both men knew that the policeman would not forget whatever Warren told him, that he'd file it away, worry over it, use it how and when he could. They also knew that whatever was said, there would be no witnesses.

'Time to time,' Warren said quietly, 'if there's a job wants doing that might need a little muscle, people will put people in touch with me. It's nothing organized, just word goes round the clubs. Late, you know. They see me on the door in a made-to-measure suit, bow tie, looking hard. Like I say, people talk to people. I don't know who Macliesh talked to except that he ended up talking to me.'

'That Monday?'

'That's right.'

'Tell me about it.'

'We went down to this Italian restaurant along the street and he's going on about this warehouse out on the Industrial Estate, drawing maps all over napkins like a bad movie. There's security patrolling the place, that's why he wants me to hold his hand. Reckons he's got a stone-cold market for this stuff, computer parts, some bits and pieces of junk, I don't know.'

'This was Macliesh's idea? Top to bottom?'

'Of course,' Warren grinned. 'What d'you think?'

'What happened?' Resnick asked.

'There's security there all right, uniformed bloke in a van, probably done time himself, dog with him, some kind of attack dog, I don't know one from another except I hate all of them. Vicious bloody things. Then Macliesh starts seeing burglar alarms all over the place, reckons they must be on the direct to your boys. Real panic. We hang around for a bit, drive away, back, drive away again. By now he's not so sure about off-loading the stuff. Mottram's well down a bottle of malt whisky, well down, and I'm looking another wasted night square in the eye.' Warren rocked back in his chair. 'It's a blow-out.'

Resnick nodded. 'Hours? How long was Macliesh in your company?'

'Met him here, eight, half-past, by the time it was all over, half-one, two. Waste of bloody time.'

'You'll sign a statement?'

Warren looked at him for a couple of moments, finally sighed. 'Not if it means going to the station, but, yes, I suppose so.'

Resnick stood up. 'The officers who were in before, I'll get them to come down.'

'Now?'

'Now.'

Warren shrugged massive shoulders. 'Fair enough.'

At the head of the stairs, Warren said, 'Give your best to Georgie, then?'

'Don't bother.'

Seventeen

Vera Barnett had already told them. As soon as she stepped into the airless hallway, faint with furniture spray and lily-of-the-valley, Rachel knew. The dry turning of locks and fumbled chains had taken minutes; the obscured murmurings of apology and frustration from behind the door. She sat in a wheelchair, uncomfortable, blue slipper-socks pulled over wrinkled tights, a plaid rug laid across her lap. Most of the curl had gone from her hair and it clung like a wig, ill-fitting and grey. She was staring at the swollen knuckles of her hands as though they had betrayed her once again.

'Mrs Barnett, I . . .'

'I haven't got the strength.'

'That's all right.'

'Is it?'

Rachel moved towards her, a half-smile. 'I see the chair arrived.'

'It's no good.'

'It looks fine.'

'It's no good.'

Rachel moved around the older woman, taking the handles of the chair. 'You'll soon get used to it.'

'To being a cripple.'

'That's not what I mean.'

'What else am I doing in a wheelchair?'

Rachel started to back the chair round, wanting to

move out of the hall. The sounds of muffled tears came from another room, intermittent.

'We talked about that, Mrs Barnett. About how it might help you while the children are here, so you don't have to go chasing after them all the time and wear yourself out.'

'You talked about it.'

Rachel applied pressure to the handles and the chair rose up on its rear legs so that she could swing it round.

'Be careful!'

'I am. Don't worry.'

When the front wheels touched ground again, lightly, Vera Barnett groaned.

'Let's go into the living-room,' Rachel said.

'You won't get it through the door. Not without banging.'

'I'm sure we can manage.'

'It's too big.'

'It'll be okay.'

'Not made for it, places like this. They're not designed for cripples and invalids. Those wheels will take all the paint off, marks and scratches. It isn't going to be any good.'

Rachel brought the chair round adjacent to the electric fire, pressed her foot down on the brake and sat on the Parker Knoll chair opposite. 'If you really don't want it, Mrs Barnett, I could call through to the department in the morning and ask them to come and take it away again.' She looked at her evenly. 'Is that what you want me to do?'

Vera Barnett didn't say anything. She fidgeted her hands along the edge of the rug and looked at the bars of the fire. Apart from the scrape of the older woman's breathing, the only sound was the single repeated tick of the clock on the mantelpiece, between Luke's school photograph and a china dog.

'How are the children?'

Vera Barnett closed her eyes. 'How do you think they are?'

Rachel continued to look at her. The sound of crying rose up with a sharpness that broke on a silence of its own.

'Their mother taken away from them.'

'Did you tell them how . . .?'

'I told them she'd been in a accident. A motor accident. While she was out.' She looked at Rachel accusingly, expecting to be accused. 'What did you want me to say? That she'd been killed by some monster. Raped and killed. Murdered. Is that what I should have said?'

Rachel shook her head. 'No,' she said softly. 'No.'

'Quick and done with, that's what it was. Peaceful. That's what . . . that's what . . .' Her fingers were rubbing against the canvas at the side of the chair. 'She didn't feel any pain.'

Rachel guessed she had been holding in the tears for a long time, too long, and now they came in sobs that made the bones in her chest and head ache. Rachel stood beside her, one arm lightly against her shoulder, a hand between her hands.

'I'm sorry,' Vera Barnett repeated, over and over as her body shook. 'I'm sorry, I shouldn't be like this with you.'

'Yes, you should.'

'It's not your worries.'

'Yes, they are.'

Luke was standing outside the open door, not daring to come into the room. He was wearing pyjama bottoms and a T-shirt with a blue and yellow Snoopy that had run in the wash.

Rachel smiled at him reassuringly.

Vera Barnett's eyes were clenched shut as if trying to stop up the tears. Her fingers clasped at Rachel's, failing to grip, and then they began to pat at the back of her hand instead, light and awkward.

'I'm sorry, I'm sorry,' she was still saying. 'I'm sorry.'

Rachel looked away from her towards the doorway and Luke had disappeared. 'It's fine,' she said. 'Cry. It will do you good.' Despite herself, she glanced at the clock on the mantel, the slowness of time.

'It's for you, sir.'

Resnick hesitated near the top of the stairs as Patel looked down at him expectantly.

'It's that solicitor, sir.'

'Olds?'

'Yes, sir.'

Resnick pushed back his sleeve, looked at his watch. 'I'm late already.'

'She's being really persistent. This is the fourth time in the last hour. Her office has been trying to get hold of you all . . .'

'Tell her to speak to the super.'

'Superintendent Skelton's left, sir.'

Resnick continued downwards. 'So have I.'

Patel's reply was less distinct. As he slipped the catch and went through the station entrance, Resnick could not help but think there were times when his young DC failed altogether to approve of him.

Across the road, near the lights, the placard read CITY SLAYER AT LARGE. The vendor slid a last edition from beneath the plastic sheeting that was keeping his papers dry. Resnick crossed back towards the car park, reading as he walked.

> Police are still probing the tragic and gruesome death of a young mother, whose body was found severely battered in the garden of her own home in the early hours of the morning.

Resnick pulled the car keys from his pocket. The front of the paper was dark with rain. As he dipped his head, water dribbled down the inside of his collar and on to his neck.

> The man heading the police investigation, Det Supt Jack Skelton, said there was no apparent connection with a recent murder of another young woman, found strangled in her home. A man is still believed to be helping police with their investigations into this earlier crime.

'Careful, careful. Oh, please God, be careful!'

Rachel lifted her firmly, one arm bracing the spine, the other beneath the thighs, the hardness of bone through too little flesh. The bathroom was narrow, too narrow of course to admit the wheelchair, and the toilet at the far end, beyond the bath. On her own, Vera Barnett traced a careful progress, steadying herself with towel rail and wall, turning only once, one arm leant against the cistern, lowering herself painfully down. Once seated, she stayed there, waiting for her breath to steady, steeling herself for the same process in reverse. Often, it seemed to take all the strength from her and this evening she had no strength to give.

Rachel ignored the wincing and muttering and scooped skirt and petticoat back at the last moment, helped to ease knickers towards the knees.

How weak she was, that she should permit these intimacies to Rachel, a person that she scarcely knew and trusted less.

'All right, you can leave me now.'

'Let me know when you're through, I'll give you a hand.'

'I shall be able to manage. I shall have to when you're not here. However else d'you think I get on?'

'Call me,' said Rachel, closing the door. 'If you want.'

She went and looked in on the children. Sarah lay curled into a ball, facing the wrong way in the bed; the covers were a tangle leaving her mostly uncovered. Her thumb was in her mouth way past the middle joint. Luke had pressed himself up against the wall, mouth open, breathing through his nose. Maybe it wouldn't work, letting them stay here with their grandmother; maybe Vera Barnett's condition had deteriorated too far to allow it. If they could be certain of enough support, she would recommend giving it a few days, a week. Once Vera Barnett realized what there was to be gained from coping, her strength of will might be enough. Despite everything, Rachel thought, she was a resolute woman, Vera Barnett.

Rachel bent carefully down and rearranged the clothing over the little girl. Close, she allowed herself for a moment to touch the child's cheek, the back of her hand against the smooth warmth of her skin. Sarah stirred, the rhythm of her breathing changed but she did not wake.

When she went out of the room, Rachel left the door unclosed by some inches. In the bathroom, Vera Barnett was on her feet, forcing one foot in front of the other as she leaned sideways against the wall.

'You needn't bother,' she said, when Rachel went to take her arm, but she did nothing to resist her.

She was seated in the living-room with the television on and Rachel was mashing tea when the doorbell rang.

'Whoever can that be?' called Vera Barnett. 'Don't let anybody in. I don't want to talk to anyone. I won't.'

'I think it might be the police,' Rachel said.

'How's it going?' Resnick asked, shuffling off his damp coat.

Rachel raised an eyebrow. 'Could be worse.'

'Kids?'

'Sleeping now.'

'You told them?'

Rachel nodded towards the open living-room door. 'She beat me to it.'

'How's she standing up?'

Rachel smiled. 'Sitting down.'

They were keeping their voices low, whispering really, close in someone else's house, strange sort of intimacy.

'How are you?' Resnick asked. He was having to stop himself from reaching out a hand, touching her.

'We'd better go through,' Rachel said.

'Is she up to a few questions?' he asked to Rachel's back.

'I think so. If you must.'

Vera had propped herself more upright in the chair; her hands were loosely linked over the straightened rug on her lap.

'This is Detective Inspector Resnick,' Rachel said, biting back a sudden, irrational desire to call him Charlie.

Charlie, Rachel was thinking. His name is Charlie.

She left them and went to the kitchen.

They were drinking tea. A half-dozen plain biscuits

had been fanned out on a plate and ignored. They had listened to Vera Barnett on the subject of her son-in-law, her ironic surprise that he had found the time to visit the registrar, contact the undertakers; they had tiptoed around the subject of the funeral itself, the necessity of a 'proper' service.

'You told the woman officer that your daughter had been seeing a man,' Resnick said.

Cup rattled against saucer. 'I did no such thing.'

Resnick glanced down at his notebook. 'She was with a man,' he quoted.

'Of course she was. Who else did that to her?'

'But you knew . . .'

'No.'

'You said . . .'

'Where else would she be?'

Resnick took another mouthful of tea. He knew that Rachel was trying hard not to look at him while he questioned Vera Barnett; somehow he'd felt good about the fact that she'd be watching him at work, but that had been before it began.

'Obviously, Mrs Barnett, the sooner we can trace whoever Mary saw yesterday evening the better. So if you have any idea, any idea at all, who she might have been with . . .'

'My daughter and I didn't discuss such matters.'

'Never?'

'She didn't say and I didn't ask.' The line of her mouth tightened until the lips had altogether disappeared. 'She was free to do as she pleased. Whatever I might have said would have made precious little difference.'

'You haven't any idea who she might have been seeing earlier, in the last six months or so? No name she might have mentioned, even in passing?'

'No.'

'And you don't know if she had been seeing some-body regularly?'

A small, tight shake of the head.

'If there had been anyone, serious, I mean . . .'

'We were never close, not . . . not after the divorce. She seemed to think I blamed her for it in some way. Blamed her instead of him, running off after the first woman who gave him a second look, no better than an animal in heat. He ought to be ashamed of himself, leaving her and those two beautiful children, and now I hope he is. If he'd been there, this would never . . .'

She was crying again and Rachel went over and took the cup and saucer from her hands. Her eyes told Resnick what he already knew – go easy, don't push too hard.

He waited until she had dabbed at her face with a tissue and Rachel had rearranged the rug about her knees. 'We found some letters . . .'

'What letters?'

'From men. It looks as though Mary might have, um, put an ad in the local paper.'

'I don't understand.'

'To meet somebody.'

'To meet . . . ?'

'The personal columns, Lonely Hearts they call it, if there's no other way of meeting someone to go out with . . .' Resnick felt himself faltering under the woman's barely comprehending stare. 'Somebody else who's looking for a relationship.'

'In the newspaper? The daily . . . you're talking about the newspaper?'

Resnick nodded. 'Yes. It's quite normal. A lot of people . . .'

'Mary did this?'

'Yes. At least, we think so.'

'Mary . . .?'

The rain had diminished to a slow drizzle that fell like a blur across the street lights. Search in vain for a star in the sky.

'I could do with a drink after that,' Resnick said.

'I'm sorry. I must get back.'

'I can't even give you a lift?'

Rachel shook her head. 'I've got my car.'

Nevertheless, she continued to stand there; they both did. When Resnick unlocked his car she slid into the passenger seat alongside him.

'I suppose you had to tell her that.'

'I think so.'

'She won't understand. She won't begin to.'

'The names, once we've checked the letters out, we'll have to see if any of them mean anything to her.'

'But she's told you . . .'

'I know, but we'll have to check just the same.'

'It hardly seems fair.'

'Think what would happen if we failed to do it and it turned out to have mattered. What she can't remember today might be clearer tomorrow.'

Resnick switched on the engine and turned up the heater.

'I don't think I understand either,' Rachel said. 'Not really.'

'You're lucky,' Resnick said.

'I don't feel it.' The words were out without thinking and with emphasis.

'You mean more than this,' Resnick said, gesturing back at the house.

Rachel nodded. 'Uh-huh.'

'Chris?'

'It'll sort itself out.' She wasn't looking at him any more. He could see her reflected in the car window, three-quarter profile. For Christ's sake, thought Resnick, do something – say something.

'I've got to go,' Rachel said, opening the door.

She had one foot on the pavement when Resnick put his hand on her arm. As her head swung round, he made himself keep the hand where it was. 'Take care.'

She smiled ironically. 'Leave it to the professionals.'

Resnick's fingers were back round the steering-wheel. The door was firmly shut. As Resnick signalled and drew away from the kerb, he was wondering how soon after getting home Jack Skelton or the DCI would be on the phone, checking progress, feeling for the next move.

Patel had been pulled on to nights to relieve Lynn Kellogg and let her return to normal shift. In a way, it suited him well. Peel wasn't the pushy sort, kept himself to his copy of the *Daily Mail* and allowed Patel to get on with the studying necessary for his sergeant's board.

'Running before you can bloody walk, pal!' Divine had said, glancing down over Patel's shoulder in the canteen. 'Look at this,' he'd called to Naylor. 'Not content with taking over every tobacconists and news-agents in the sodding country, they've got eyes on the Force as well!'

Naylor, who was busily beating the books on his own account (well, Debbie's, if the truth were to be told), had shaken his head and said nothing.

'You know why our Asian friends didn't prosper in the Roman Empire, don't you?' Divine had asked in a loud voice.

Naylor and Patel knew they were going to be told anyway.

'All them straight roads, where'd they put the corner shops?'

The beauty of nights, Patel thought now, no Mark Divine.

After another two paragraphs, Patel realized that Peel was staring at him. Oh, no, not you too. Then he understood that there was somebody else in the office; someone else who was receiving a great deal of Peel's attention. Patel got up from where he had tucked himself out of the way, round at the foot of the L-shaped room. Grace Kelley was standing outside the inspector's room, looking in. She was wearing a bright red laminated cape and a matching hood; there were a couple of inches of bare skin between her black leather trousers and red high-heeled shoes. Her sweater had a deep roll at the neck and a turquoise brooch like a misshapen heart pinned to the appropriate place; the sweater was white wool and at least one size too small.

She smiled at Patel encouragingly.

'Inspector Resnick is off duty,' Patel said.

'All tucked up?'

Behind Patel, DC Peel sniggered and crossed his legs.

'He will be in first thing,' Patel assured her. 'If you could call back.'

'By then I shall be back to civilization,' Grace said. 'Cases are in the car and I've just filled the tank. I've run out of things a girl can do here.'

She winked at Patel and made a sinuous movement with her shoulders, causing her cape to slide further back from her shoulders. Patel was doing his best not to stare at the turquoise heart, but it drew his dark eyes like a magnet.

'Touch it if you want,' she grinned, moving closer. 'Real smooth. Like a baby's bum.'

She supposed; she didn't think she had ever got near enough to know and she'd be pleased to keep it that way. This one, though, this little rabbit with his great startled eyes, ready to bolt at her first false move – well, somehow she'd never got around to bonking any Asians.

'No?'

Through the clipped dark hair of his moustache, she could see the drops of sweat beginning to gather. Rather him, she thought, than the chinless wonder, leering away at the back.

'No, well. I'd best leave the message with you, then. If that's okay.'

'Of course.'

'Might not be nothing special, only, Shirley, you see, my friend that got . . .' She shrugged, not wanting to say the word. 'She told me once about this bloke she met, all right he was, good-looking and everything. That's not the point, though, is it? Point is, she met him through one of them ads. You know the kind – glamorous blonde, simple tastes, anxious to meet well-hung yacht owner.' Her brittle laughter broke loud across the almost empty room. 'Poor bloody Shirley! Little Miss bleedin' Lonely Hearts!'

Eighteen

Was it something about his generation, the fact of living alone? He chose two potatoes from the rack and washed off the surplus dirt before beginning to peel. Most people he knew, worked with, they operated in couples: that was the way it still was. For the rest, though, finding someone or making it work, which was the most difficult? He thought of Rachel, of the two of them in the enclosed space of his car, a tiredness he had not noticed before in her eyes. Dizzy was winding in and out between his feet and he picked the animal up and set her down again across the room. All the things he might have said; the warmth of her arm through her sleeve. *It'll sort itself out.* Usually, he supposed, things did.

When he reached up on to the shelf to take down the grater, he noticed that Pepper had fitted the curve of her body inside the largest aluminium pan, only the last inches of her tail curling over the rim.

No matter what, his mother had made latkes on Monday evenings, grating the potato as finely as if she had been turning a precision tool. The smaller pile of onion would stand ready in its dish, the egg beaten, oven warming. In a saucepan, thickened with flour, gravy from the weekend's meat bubbled slowly.

Happy or miserable – mostly, Resnick realized, thinking back, resigned – his mother, once married, would have known no other option. Like her potato pancakes, regularly she made her bed and once that was done there was nothing else but to lay down in it.

Resnick gave the mixture a final stir and began to grease the bottom of the heavy frying-pan. There were still a few slices of smoked Polish ham in the fridge, a spoonful of sour cream.

'Dizzy! If you end up getting trodden on, don't blame me.'

He was sliding the spatula under the nearest *latke* to turn it when the phone began to ring. The outside was crisp yet not too thick and didn't crumble when he lifted it up, set it back down.

'Dizzy!'

The cat retreated beneath the table and regarded him balefully.

'Don't say I didn't warn you.'

Surprised that Jack Skelton had not called already, Resnick was anticipating the superintendent's voice until his hand touched the receiver and he knew it would be Rachel. Distressed, needing to talk.

'Hello?'

It was Patel. Resnick recognized that careful voice instantly. He listened for several moments and then, 'How long ago?' he asked, and, 'Is she still there?', finally, 'She was certain?'

Resnick kept the phone in hand and depressed a finger to break the connection. It was he who would have to call Skelton.

'Different game now, Charlie. Different rules.'

It was still shy of seven-thirty and they were on the steps outside the station. Skelton was wearing his dark executive blue and with good reason. There was an extra shine to his shoes and a messianic glint in his

181

eyes that made Resnick wonder if he moonlighted as a lay preacher on his days off.

'This is where we see the technology swing into action.'

'Yes, sir,' Resnick said glumly.

'Buck up, Charlie. Think where you'll get with all this glorious back-up.'

Confused, Resnick thought.

'Come on,' said Skelton, gesturing around the corner to the car park, 'I'll give you a lift.'

In the normal run of things it would be down to the detective superintendent of CID to head the inquiry, but he had been farmed out to Cumbria to investigate an alleged conspiracy involving the sale of radioactive sheep. So Len Lawrence was going to bluff and bluster his way through running the station, while Skelton moved his family photos and running gear into the major incident room at Radford Road sub-station. No surprise that he was looking more than usually chipper.

'Who's on, sir?' Resnick asked, as two buses, one trailing the other, brought them down to second gear.

'Tom Parker is heading up the outside team, that's the good news as far as you're concerned. Howard Colwin's coming in to co-ordinate the inside.'

'Is that the bad?'

'Depends on your point of view. Colwin'll run a tight ship, we can be sure of that. I'll trust him to get an efficient routine established, see that it's adhered to.'

Resnick allowed himself a smile. He considered Skelton to be pretty well organized, but Colwin – everything that came across his desk was dated and filed, each phone call logged, he probably had the paper clips sorted according to colour and weight. Howard Colwin was the man for whom the term anal retention had been invented: he even walked into a room with his buttocks held clenched.

Tom Parker was different. Resnick spoke to the DCI by phone most mornings, keeping him up-to-date with what was happening. He just might be able to work some kind of deal with Parker.

'Hate all this, don't you, Charlie?'

They were driving along by the Forest, past three-storey Victorian houses, which one of the local housing associations was busy restoring and converting into flats. To the right, down through the trees, the Goose Fair site stood empty save for a succession of small men exercising smaller dogs.

'Sometimes,' said Resnick, picking over his words, 'I think it can get in the way.'

'Of *real* police work, you mean?' said Skelton, underlining the word ironically as he said it.

'Of the answer.'

Skelton checked his mirror, indicated, slowed, rechecked the mirror, turned into a parking space. Text-book stuff.

'I'm not satisfied we've got the right question yet,' Skelton said, getting out.

Resnick looked at him over the roof of the car.

'One murderer or two?'

Skelton locked the door and Resnick followed him past the young constable on duty by the entrance.

'If you do sort something out with Parker,' Skelton said, his voice lowered, 'I shan't go against it.' He favoured Resnick with a rare smile. 'Still room for initiative in the computer age. Not all modules and floppy discs, eh?'

He moved briskly off and left Resnick thinking.

The briefing room was set up with a blackboard, twin

flip charts on twin easels, two linked video monitors, a computer screen and printer, their controls mutually accessing via the adjacent office with the Home Office computer. Maps of the city gave the location of the murders. Photographs, black and white and colour, had been tacked to one wall. Resnick's eyes glided over them, remembering, refusing to settle.

Jack Skelton stood behind a desk, lists and rosters spread before him. To his right, one arm crooked back on his chair, was DCI Parker: fifties, thinning hair and gently spreading paunch. He was wearing a dark sports jacket and light trousers, one leg crossed over the other. Waiting for the superintendent to begin, he lit a cigarette and, seeing Resnick, winked.

Across from him, the other detective chief inspector, Howard Colwin, sat upright and looked directly to the front. He had less hair than Tom Parker and what there was had been greased and brushed until it looked no more than a thin line drawn tight across his scalp. His suit was dark brown with a light stripe, but his shoes were black. He breathed tightly, as if begrudging the air.

Skelton cleared his throat and looked at his watch. Resnick glanced round the room: two other DIs apart from himself, Andy Hunt and Bernard Grafton; Paddy Fitzgerald was the inspector in charge of uniforms.

'We'll make a start,' Skelton said, lacing his hands together and pressing down so that the knuckles cracked.

Colin Rich came through the door, head turned away, finishing a conversation with someone in the corridor outside. His brown leather jacket was fashionably loose, its wide belt undone and hanging free. He wore thick green cords, cut wide at the hips, dark brown desert boots. When he realized that Skelton was staring at him, he mouthed a quick 'Sir' and moved towards a seat.

'I thought perhaps the Serious Crimes Squad had decided against joining us,' Skelton said.

'We did think about it, guv,' said Rich, settling into an immediate slouch. 'Only we thought you'd miss us.'

'More like you nearly missing us.'

'Sir?'

'Perhaps you were misinformed as to the time.'

Rich shook his head. 'No, sorting out my team, that's what it was.'

Skelton nodded. 'Who's sorting you out, Inspector?'

Rich looked quickly at the others, pushed brown hair forward over his forehead and grinned. 'Don't know, sir.'

'Think again, then.'

'Sorry, sir, afraid I don't quite . . .'

'Who's sorting you out, Inspector?' Skelton asked a second time.

Colin Rich wasn't so preoccupied with himself that he failed to see which way it was going. Let them out of the station for half a minute and they reckon Montgomery's their bloody uncle. He sat up straight. 'You are, sir,' he said.

'How many men?' Skelton asked, looking down at one of the lists.

'Three, sir.'

Skelton checked, frowned, but let it go.

The CID teams led by Resnick and the other two inspectors would be five-handed: Resnick would have Millington for his sergeant, Naylor and Divine, Lynn Kellogg and Patel. There could be as many as ten or a dozen uniformed constables, depending on need – here and elsewhere. The task of routine checking, house-to-house verification, would fall in the main to them.

Everything would pass through here, here and the computer room. There were a couple of uniformed officers in there, also, but most of the job was done by trained civilians, experts. Every scrap of information gathered and thought to be even marginally useful was fed in, checked through the giant Holmes computer, and for all of that information fresh action was generated. If the days were allowed to turn into weeks, the possible leads would multiply endlessly so that, even if more officers were drafted in, checking everything became less and less possible.

But, since the Peter Sutcliffe case, that had to be the way of it. If the ongoing results of that investigation into the so-called Yorkshire Ripper had been pulled together in a more readily comprehensible form, lives would have been saved, a murderer would have been stopped sooner, that was the consensus. But Sutcliffe had been interviewed by the police and talked his way clear – whatever might have been lacking there could not have been provided by high technology. And when, finally, he was caught it was as the result of a piece of common-or-garden practice, a couple of working coppers suspicious about a stolen car.

'Coincidence or otherwise,' Jack Skelton was saying, 'both of these murders were turned up by members of Inspector Resnick's team and it's fair to say that he's got a march on the rest of us when it comes to a sense of what's going on. Once we're through looking at the videos shot by scene-of-crime, I intend to ask the inspector to fill us in on background. Doubtless there'll be questions you'll want to ask at that stage.'

'Yeah,' said Colin Rich under his breath. 'Like where's the bloody coffee? When can we expect to get out of here and get a drink? They open at eleven.'

Nineteen

'Well, Inspector?'

That well-groomed smirk was just what Resnick didn't need. Suzanne Olds got up lithely to her feet, the folds of her beige suit skirt falling back against her knees. She followed him into his office and sat without waiting to be asked.

She watched Resnick making space enough on his desk to rest an elbow.

'It's unfair to say, "I told you so..." ' She smiled brightly, arched her hand towards her hair, gleam of fine gold at the wrist. 'But impossible to resist.'

Liverpool CID had finally tracked Mottram down. Millington had driven up to see him: a fiery little man with a head like a polished walnut and hands like an angel. He had been plying his trade in a former cinema in Wallasey; instead of bingo, it alternated between smoking concerts and prize fights, same audiences, same reactions. Mottram was looking after a lean youngster with a wall-eye and a skin like smoke. When he threw in the towel midway through the fifth, the crowd went mad; he had to push the kid back to the dressing-room through a hail of coins and spittle and cans.

Millington had to look away as Mottram's needle joined the ruptured skin over the eyelid, a flap of it hanging free. Mottram talked while he worked, his

187

concentration never breaking, hands never less than steady.

'It was a foolish thing I know,' his voice was oddly gentle, like his touch, somewhere at the back of it a Gallic lilt, 'but there are times you can't help but think ... easy money, it's the old story I suppose. One night's work and you can walk away a rich man.' He used scissors to cut the thread. 'I was there right enough, your friend Macliesh and the big feller, Warren.' He patted the boxer lightly on the arm. 'You'll do.'

Turning towards Millington, he added, 'Now, Warren, if he should ever chance to go into the ring ... Ah, there's a prospect.'

'You'll make a statement?'

'You write it and I'll sign it.'

It was there on Resnick's desk: somewhere.

'How do you find anything?' Suzanne Olds asked, amused.

'I'm a detective.'

'This new murder – are you, um, getting anywhere?'

'We're pursuing our enquiries.'

'Let's hope they're more fruitful than this.'

Resnick glanced towards the door. 'Why don't you have a word with the custody sergeant downstairs?'

'Talking to you is so pleasant.'

'I think the custody sergeant ...'

'Sometimes,' said Suzanne Olds, standing, 'it's hard to be gracious in defeat.'

'Is that what this is?'

She looked at Resnick coolly. 'When you pushed my client over the edge in that interview room, you thought you had it gift-wrapped.'

'I was doing my job.'

188

'My God!' she laughed. 'I don't believe you said that!'

'How about doing yours?'

'Police liaison,' she said at the door. 'Part of the job specification.'

'They say it's never too late to apply for retraining.'

'Good day, Inspector.'

'Ms Olds.'

He had turned towards the roster on the bulletin board behind his desk when she swung back into the room.

'Is it true both these women met whoever attacked them through some kind of advertisement?'

Resnick hesitated before answering. 'It's possible.'

She shook her head, frowning. 'The same man?'

'We don't know.'

'My God!'

'What is it?'

'I've got a friend. She works in my office. Once every few months she starts to feel restless, decides it's time to try again. The last occasion we made up the advertisement over a bottle of wine at lunch.'

'Tell her,' Resnick said.

Suzanne Olds nodded, abstracted.

'And maybe you should tell me her name.'

It was the day of the funeral. Lynn Kellogg sat near the back of the high-vaulted church while, in the pulpit, the vicar remembered Shirley Peters from hastily written notes. It was cold – the stone floor, smooth wood of the pews – and the voices had all but disappeared before the hymn's third verse had come to an end.

Olive Peters was helped along the aisle of the church, up through the welter of graves towards the freshly opened ground. In that temperature it would have been hard digging. The blonde of her hair was growing out around the edges of a black felt hat, bought in haste by a relative who had misjudged the size. There were few enough of them there: a sister, cousin perhaps; a man with steel-grey hair who walked with the aid of a stick; a dumpy girl with red cheeks forever dabbing at her eyes; an undermanager from the office where Shirley had worked, pushing back the sleeve of his thick black coat to look at his watch. The sheath of flowers sent by Grace Kelley was rich with lilies and Christmas roses and whoever had written the note had misspelled her name.

Last in a ragged line, Lynn hesitated before going forward to the grave. She thought of her own mother, fussing in the kitchen, busy with the fire, head turning towards her at the sound of a door opening, ready to smile. She took a crumble of cold earth between her fingers and threw it down, surprised at the hollow sound it made.

'Ought to put that bugger in charge of MI5. Wouldn't be any *Spycatcher* if he had anything to do with it.' Graham Millington was sitting on the corner of a desk in the CID room. There were six others present and Resnick was the only one who was listening. 'Official bloody Secrets Act wasn't in it! Insisted on speaking to the super on the phone.'

'You got what we wanted.'

Millington sighed and started to pat his pockets for his cigarettes. 'Names and addresses of all their Lonely Hearts advertisers over the past two months.'

'Men as well as women?'

'Yes.'

'Replies?'

The sergeant opened the flip-top pack and shook down a cigarette. 'Difficult.'

'Difficult?'

'Impossible.'

Two telephones at different points of the room began to ring almost simultaneously.

'I thought you weren't smoking?' Resnick said.

'I'm not,' said Millington, pushing the cigarette down into his breast pocket.

'For you, sir,' called one of the officers.

'Who is it?'

'DCI Parker, sir.'

'Ask him, can I ring back in five minutes.' Resnick looked back at his sergeant. 'How impossible?'

'He'll hang on, sir,' said the man at the phone.

'Right.'

'Letters come through sealed,' Millington explained. 'Often just the one, sometimes up to half a dozen. All that's on the envelope is the box number, whichever ad's taken their fancy. The paper forwards them twice a week in batches. No way of knowing where they've come from.'

'There's one way,' Resnick said.

Millington grinned and shook his head. 'That won't help us with replies they've already received, sir. Whoever the bastard was wrote to Shirley Peters, Mary Sheppard.'

Resnick was starting to move towards the phone. 'He'll try again,' he said. Hoping that he would not; hoping that he would.

'Not without a warrant, sir. Confidentiality, you'd think it kept him in a state of grace. And him working for a bloody newspaper. They'd put a periscope up your waste pipe if they thought it'd give them something to splash across the front page.'

Resnick took the receiver from the DC. He listened for a few moments to Tom Parker before interrupting: 'Sir, it looks as if we're going to need a court order.'

'Mrs Peters . . .'

'She doesn't want to be bothered.'

'Mrs Peters . . .'

'Can't you see she doesn't want to be bothered?'

'Mrs Peters, if . . .'

Look! How many more times . . .?'

'It was good of you to come,' Olive Peters's voice was hardly above a whisper, but in any case Lynn Kellogg was no longer crouched down and listening. With as few as seven people the room was over-crowded; the vicar looked up anxiously from the red and grey settee as the man tried to force Lynn towards the door.

'I'll break this bloody stick over your head!' he was shouting.

'No, you won't.'

'Really,' said the vicar, putting a sandwich back on the plate, jam or bloater paste, it was difficult to tell which. 'Really, I think this is less than appropriate.'

'You've no business here.'

'That's not true, sir, I'm afraid.'

'You should be out after the bastard 'as done this, not coming round here worrying the life out of the woman. What in God's name d'you think you're play-ing at, round here worrying the life out of her now?'

'If I might suggest . . .' attempted the vicar.

'You can keep your bloody nose out of it an' all!'

'I merely . . .'

'I should think we've had enough of your claptrap for one day.'

'Take it easy now,' said Lynn, moving so as to place herself between them.

At the far side of the room, the dumpy girl with red cheeks pulled open a door seeking a way out and a broom toppled forward from the cupboard and struck her on the side of the face.

Olive Peters held the framed photograph of her daughter and herself tighter, cradling it to her chest.

'Rejoice that she's gone to a better place! Shovelled underneath that sodding ground, that's where she is.' He raised the walking-stick towards the ceiling. 'You must think we're all bloody soft!'

'Give me the stick,' said Lynn Kellogg.

'Will I, hell as like!'

'Yes,' said Lynn firmly. 'You will.'

Never taking her eyes off his, she held out her hand and kept it there until he put the stick, with slow care, between her fingers.

'I know what you're thinking, Graham,' said Resnick.

They were on their way down to the incident room, snarled up in the first flow of homegoing traffic. Millington had been wondering what his wife had bought for supper and what his chances were of finding out before it was dried-up or cold or both.

'Len Lawrence gets the chance to get his boots under the super's desk for as long as this takes. Why haven't you been treated the same? Senior sergeant in terms of years, experience, surely you ought to be in my office, getting the feel of things, establishing yourself? Something along those lines?'

'Something like that, sir.'

'There's another way of looking at it,' Resnick continued.

Isn't there bloody always! thought Millington. Driving over in Resnick's car, that was practically the only time he hadn't been thinking about it since the teams had been announced.

'If we get a good result here ...'

'Us and all the rest,' said Millington.

' ... that might end up looking more impressive on your record than a week shuffling bits of paper across the surface of my desk.'

And it might not, Millington thought. We might not.

Resnick applied the brakes too sharply as a youth on a skateboard swerved out in front of him. Both Resnick and Millington were thrown forwards against their seat belts as the engine cut out.

Immediately horns sounded behind them.

'Those things should've been broken up and burned the first time round,' said Millington savagely.

'In a hurry to get home,' said Resnick, turning the key in the ignition.

'Can't wait to spend his social security.'

In the end it was the girl with plump cheeks and now a strip of plaster over her right eye. Lynn had offered her a lift back into the city; too late to be worth going back to the office, she was meeting her boyfriend in the Pizzaland on the Market Square.

Lynn sat there with her, toying with a coffee while the girl drank Diet Pepsi and complained about not losing weight.

'Trouble is Darren likes to eat here of an evening, but I only ever have the vegetarian. Thin and crispy, not the deep pan. And the salad. Darren gets through a double portion of garlic bread as well as most of a regular pizza and he never puts on a pound.' She looked at the door as if she couldn't wait for him to arrive. 'I even went to aerobics for a couple of months but all that happened was I got short of breath.'

'Don't worry,' Lynn reassured her. 'It's more difficult for us than it is for men.'

'But don't you wish you weren't so big?' asked the girl, leaning back to get a better look at her. 'I bet you do.'

Lynn shook her head. 'In my job it's useful.'

'I don't know how you can,' the girl said, thoughtfully.

'Do what I do?'

'Not want to lose weight.'

'I suppose I never think about it.'

'What about your feller? You have got one, a bloke?'

'He doesn't seem to think about it either,' Lynn said. Probably, she carried on the thought, because he's too busy thinking about his lightweight bike to notice.

'You're lucky. Ever since I met Darren . . .'

'How did you meet him?'

'You'll never guess,' the girl said, her cheeks growing redder than ever, 'but I met him through the paper. Sort of, you know, a blind date. It was Shirley's idea. We put it in together, two girls want to meet two smart fellers who'll show them a good time. It was Shirley's idea. She used to do it all the time.'

Rachel made a final note in her work diary and closed her eyes. Only for a moment. It wasn't until her colleague touched her lightly on the shoulder that she realized she had fallen asleep.

'You all right?'

'Fine,' Rachel said, yawning and smiling self-consciously at the same time. 'Nothing a few good nights wouldn't cure.'

'Better get off home then. It's way past any sort of time.'

'Isn't it always?'

'Goes with the job.'

Rachel nodded, stood up and stretched, started collecting things together. 'Carole,' she said suddenly.

'Mm?'

'That spare room at your place?'

'Yes?'

'Is it still empty?'

Twenty

The principal item at the morning briefing was a confirmation from forensic: analysis of semen deposited at the scene of both crimes yielded a positive comparison. Male pubic hair found on the body of Shirley Peters and in Mary Sheppard's bed was also of the same type. Skin samples from beneath Shirley Peters's fingernails were not a conclusive match with those taken from Mary Sheppard. A small number of wool fibres removed from the carpet of the room in which Shirley Peters was found as well as from the settee neither matched each other nor anything connected with Mary Sheppard.

'The assumption we are working on, therefore,' said Skelton, 'is that both murders were the work of the same man.'

'Bloody brilliant!' said Colin Rich to no one in particular.

'What about the different MO?' asked Grafton.

'Forensic evidence and now the apparent link through personal columns, which seems to have been confirmed by a member of Inspector Resnick's team, seem more important. But not conclusive.'

'As long as we're aware of the dangers of tunnelling our vision too soon,' put in Tom Parker, 'that's the line we're taking. We're looking for one man.'

The names and addresses of female advertisers were being entered on the computer and each would be contacted and, as far as possible, a list of those from whom they had received replies would be taken and accessed. These names would be cross-checked and then matched with the criminal records file; any who were known, for whatever reason, would be seen first – in addition to men who had, for one reason or another, aroused suspicion in the women they had eventually met.

'How about the letters, sir?' Andy Hunt looked up at the superintendent, pen resting on the almost full page of his notebook.

'In what regard?'

'Well, we've all seen copies of those that Charlie found in the Sheppard house . . .'

'Good old bloody Charlie!' said Colin Rich with quiet scorn.

' . . . and we'd probably all agree that some of them seem a sight more chancey than others.'

'It's not always the ones as come out and say it,' said Tom Parker.

'That whining bugger,' said Grafton. 'What's his name? Minors?'

'Myers,' corrected Resnick.

'He's the one I'd put my money on.'

Colin Rich leaned across to the uniformed inspector. 'One weekend course up at the University and he thinks he's Sigmund Freud.'

'Give him his full title, then.'

'Professor?'

'Bloody. You forgot the bloody. Sigmund bloody Freud.'

'Funny!' said Rich, sitting back. 'Very bloody funny!'

'We have acquired the services of a Professor Ramusen from the Polytechnic's psychology department, who will look at letters with a view to picking out any which seem to suggest any kind of abnormality or deviancy. Any tendency towards violence.' Skelton paused, as if waiting for comments which were unforthcoming. 'I've been in touch with the Yard this morning about the services of a handwriting expert and I'm waiting on their response.'

After that it was wrapped up quickly. Uniforms were going back over the house-to-house checks in the area of the two incidents. The Serious Crimes squad would start picking up anyone thrown up by the computer as being previously known. Grafton and Hunt would divide the remainder between them, beginning with those who had made multiple replies. It was down to Resnick and his team to follow up the letters that Graham Millington had discovered in Mary Sheppard's bedroom, also the lead that Lynn Kellogg had picked up after Shirley Peters's funeral.

A warrant would enable them to add the identities of all those responding to personal advertisements from first post that morning, although, once Skelton's press conference, scheduled for eleven, had been reported, it was expected that the numbers of both replies and new advertisers would drop. Initially, however, it meant more legwork, more reports to be filed, more time.

'This time next week we'll be up to our collective arses in astrologists and bloody clairvoyants!'

Colin Rich leant against the wall beside the coffee urn, looking at the expression of distaste on Resnick's face at the sight of the coffee.

'Wait till you taste it, Charlie.'

Resnick lifted up the lid of the urn and poured it back.

'Champagne soon for you, I shouldn't wonder.'

'How's that?'

'Regular golden bollocks on this show, aren't we?'

Resnick shrugged and turned away. The sooner he got back to the station, the sooner the team could get to work.

'Too good for the rest of us already, Charlie?' Rich was standing close behind him, but his voice was loud enough to be heard by the rest.

Resnick continued walking.

'That's it, Charlie. You keep going. That way we can all see the way the sun shines out of your arse!'

'So what do they say about plumbers?'

It was a conversion job. Take an old house, large, garden on two levels with birch trees and wild strawberries thatching themselves across what had passed for lawns; gut it, aside from the central sweep of staircase and main load-bearing walls; fillet out the dry rot: spray for fungus and drill for damp; matching kitchen units, pine's out so this is a job lot in heavy wood and dark. Executive apartments in highly sought-after residential area, excellent amenities, easy reach of the city-centre. Penthouse flat with superb views available now for immediate viewing.

Dave Beatty had his head behind the waste disposal, most of his body to the waist out of sight beneath the sink. A small transistor was not quite tuned to the local commercial station and too loud. Divine reached over and turned it off.

'Hey!'

The shout was muffled. Divine kicked the toe of his polished black shoe against the sole of Dave Beatty's worn-down Adidas sports shoe. Not hard.

'What the hell d'you . . .'

'Come on out from there.'

'Who . . .?'

'Do yourself a favour, take a break.'

Beatty swung himself from under the sink and on to his feet. A wrench was gripped tightly in his left hand. Divine looked at him levelly, glanced at the wrench with a dismissive grin, and lifted up the kettle, testing the weight.

'Electrics working?'

'Yes. What's going on?'

Divine switched on the kettle and picked up a jar of instant coffee, setting it right back down again. 'No tea?'

Dave Beatty moved the wrench to his other hand and opened a cupboard; inside was a large packet of tea-bags and some sugar. He was conscious of Divine looking at him again, weighing him up.

'Five-seven,' Divine said.

'Look . . .'

'About eleven stone.'

'This is bloody silly.'

Mark Divine reached out slowly and took the wrench from Beatty's hand. 'But I still don't know what they say about plumbers.'

'If someone's sent you round here to check on me, you can tell them they're wasting their time. I said the end of the week and the end of the week's what I meant.'

Divine smiled and switched off the kettle. 'You want to be mum, or shall I?'

Dave Beatty didn't move.

'Fair enough.' Divine dropped a bag into a clean mug and went towards the sink to rinse another.

'Don't,' warned Beatty.

'You don't want one?'

'If you run the tap it'll go right through.'

Divine shrugged. 'Not very clever.' He put the

201

tea-bag into the dirty mug, poured water into both of them. 'You know what you're doing, I suppose?'

Beatty gave a short, humourless laugh, almost a snort. 'I'm fitting a sodding disposal unit, I don't know what you think you're pissing around at.'

Mark Divine stirred, added milk, pushed one mug – the used one – towards Beatty. 'Better put in your own sugar.'

Divine allowed himself another smile. This was fun: he was enjoying himself. Almost as much as he would have been if Beatty had decided to have a go at him with the wrench.

'Don't know what you're getting shirty about. Thought you said you could always squeeze in a quick hour in the daytime.'

'Said?'

'Well, be more accurate, wrote.'

Beatty's right eye blinked shut and a little nerve began to beat beside it; some of the colour drained from his face. He glanced at where the wrench lay close to the kettle, closer to Divine than to himself.

'Remember?'

'Listen, all that stuff . . .'

'Yes?'

'That stuff I wrote . . .'

'Yes?'

'It was just a laugh, you know, just for . . .'

'A laugh.'

'Yeh, you know. I mean, wasn't as if I meant anything by it.'

'Getting right down to it.'

'Eh?'

'Isn't that what you like to do? No monkeying around beforehand, strictly wham, bam, thank you,

202

ma'am, now where was that other little plumbing job you wanted fixing?'

'Jesus! All I did was write to her.'

'All?'

'Yes! Well, ask her. Ask her, for Christ's sake! It was just a bit of fun. You know . . .'

'A laugh.'

'Yeh, a laugh.'

'You said.'

Beatty was looking smaller, younger by the second – a kid from the estate just starting on his City and Guilds. His age was what he'd lied about, Divine thought, probably wanted to convince her of his maturity, man of the world, no make of faucet that can't be fixed.

Divine was staring him out the way he stared out the opposition across the other side of the scrum; the way he faced down a belligerent drunk after closing.

'Your tea.'

'What?'

'Don't let it get cold.'

'W-what?'

'Nothing worse than mashing good tea and watching someone let it get cold.'

Beatty brought the mug up towards his mouth and Divine feinted towards him. The edge of the thick mug banged against Beatty's teeth and the mug started to slide between his fingers.

'Easy!'

Divine steadied it before a drop could be spilt; he pressed the plumber's fingers tight around the circumference of the mug and held them fast.

'The truth?'

Dave Beatty drew in air too fast and began to choke

but still Divine didn't release his grip. He knew that all he had to do now was wait.

'All right, all right, only it was just the one time, after I'd been round there. To the house. You got to believe that. I mean, we kidded around, you know how it is. Joking, sort of thing. But she had, well, the kid was with her and so she couldn't, we couldn't . . . that was when I wrote them letters. Didn't even think, you know, she'd take them serious. Not till, till she called me. Got home one night from this job, emergency, bloke with five inches of water in his bathroom and half a hundredweight of sewage backed up right out to the street. She'd left this message on the answerphone. How she'd, she'd meet me. In the van. It was the only time. Honest. Honest.'

If the vein alongside Beatty's eye didn't calm down pretty soon, Divine was thinking, he'd haemorrhage all over the newly sanded wood floor.

'Is that where you did it?' Divine asked, beginning to picture it. 'The van?'

Beatty didn't speak, angled his head aside and nodded.

'Say again?'

'Yes.'

'You did her in the van?'

'I said so, didn't I?'

'Say it again.'

'Yes,' Beatty sighed. 'In the van.'

'Parked up some back alley somewhere, were you?'

'Jesus! What does it matter?'

'I want to know!'

'All right. We were down behind the Raleigh works, that cut-through that comes out by the pub. If you want any more details, ask her.'

'Ask her?'

'She's your bloody wife!'

'Is she?'

'And she's already opened her bloody mouth a sight too much or you wouldn't be here now.'

'My wife?'

'How else did you get on to me? I don't advertise that in Yellow Pages.'

'I haven't got a wife.'

'Chucked her out, have you? Serve her sodding right! I suppose you'll be after me for the divorce next.'

'I've never had a wife.'

'Come off it!'

Divine moved his hand close to Beatty's face, close enough to make him flinch, enough to get all of his attention.

'What the fuck's going on, then?' Beatty said.

'You're telling me exactly that.'

'But if you're not . . .'

Mark Divine took his warrant card from his inside pocket and held it out long enough for Beatty to read it. After taking another swallow of tea, he exchanged it for a notebook and ball-point.

'This woman you've been diddling, what's her name?'

'Melissa.'

'Not Mary?'

'Melissa.'

'You're sure about that?'

'Course.'

Divine grinned with anticipation. 'All right, then, let's see how much else you can remember – and I do mean exactly. Then we'll get round to your interest in another kind of advertising, also not in Yellow Pages.'

Martin Myers worked as a volunteer for a Church of England charity that provided soup, second-hand clothes and temporary accommodation for destitute men. Three afternoons a week, two lunchtimes and one overnight every other weekend. For a spell he had worked mornings in a healthfood shop, but there had been arguments with the full-time members of the collective and he had been asked to leave. While his mother had still been alive, there had been the attendance allowance, but now . . . well, his needs were small and since they had opened a café upstairs in the library he had something there most mornings and that seemed to last him through the day.

'I thought, since mother passed on, someone to talk to, someone nice and sympathetic. There are so many things that concern us, so much that has to be discussed; mother and I did, of course, she was wonderful, so alert, right up to, well, almost to the end. And now . . .'

Patel wrote it all down diligently, scarcely needing to prompt or interrupt, the whole meagre litany.

' . . . I did so want to be able to make contact, in some way to touch her, but, of course, she never wrote back.'

The man in the doorway stank. His clothing was more rags than tatters, bits of cloth wrapped round and round, only here and there a garment that could be recognized as such – trousers with a gaping rent in the upper leg, a cable-knit sweater as matted as the underside of a moorland sheep. He saw Graham Millington and smiled.

'Get on home,' the sergeant said.

'Spare us something for a cup of tea,' the man replied, the look on his face positively benign.

Millington stepped over him and went into the shop. Both knew the man hadn't had a drop of tea since VE Day: then it had been a mistake, as he liked to explain it, the hysteria of the moment. He didn't have a home to go to either.

Millington frowned at the insistence of the heavy bass, words walked over like ground glass. If he remembered he'd pick up that Julio Iglesias his wife wanted on CD. Not in this place, though, he wouldn't.

'Why d'you put up with that?' Millington asked the girl behind the counter. 'Enough to put off any customers that survive the sound barrier.'

'What?' the girl said, angling one side of her face towards him.

A tiny curve of stars ran round her ear, each smaller than the last.

'Him in the door, why don't you have him moved on?'

'Maurice? He's our unofficial doorman. Autumn till the first day of spring.'

'Goes south for the summer, does he?'

'Eastbourne.'

'He must be a public health hazard.' Millington was having to shout to be heard. 'Put in a call to the station, get him disinfected.'

The girl's face screwed up into a frown. All the while she was talking to Millington, she continued to take records from a cardboard box, check them off against a printed list. 'Rather have him in here than the police.'

Millington took out his wallet and showed her his warrant card. 'Darren Jilkes,' he said, hard-faced.

'Downstairs,' she said, pointing. 'Singles.'

Millington was surprised to observe that she was blushing, high red.

The basement had posters on the walls, singles in their sleeves in browsing racks and behind the counter. One of the assistants was wearing a Smiths sweat shirt and drumming along with his hands, using the ring on his little finger for rim shots. He had short brown hair, rather more than his fair share of acne and, even though the lighting was subdued, he was wearing dark glasses. His companion, bending to find something on a shelf near the floor, was almost as fat as he was thin. He was also quite bald save for a wisp of hair that hung down from the folds of his scalp and was graced at its end by a black bow.

'You Darren?'

No reply.

Millington reached over and lifted the arm from the record, more carefully than it deserved.

The second assistant stood up and when he did Millington saw that he wasn't only fat, he was tall.

'Not keen on The Fall, then?' he said.

'I saw you,' Millington said. 'Tag team match at Heanor Town Hall. Winter before last. The Oblivion Brothers. One arm out of joint and a broken nose. When the trainer pushed it back into place I got blood and snot all over my shirt.'

'Front row, was you?'

'Third.'

'Wondered. Usually women in the front. Lapping up all the sweat and grunt and squeezing their handbags further and further down between their legs.'

'You given it up or just resting?'

'Moved on to higher things. Got to be more to life than sex and violence, hasn't there?'

Graham Millington could feel a familiar nervous squirming in his stomach so clearly he was worried that they might have heard it across the counter.

'That's how come you're down here, is it? The search for higher things.'

'It's in the music. Always has been. Isn't that so, Darren?'

If it was, Darren wasn't saying.

'What's your real name then?' Millington asked. 'Always assuming it isn't Oblivion.'

'Sloman. Geoff.'

Millington nodded. 'And you're Jilkes, Darren?'

'What d'you want?' asked Jilkes.

'Always assuming,' said Sloman, 'that it isn't a record.'

'A colleague of mine was talking to young Darren's girlfriend last night. She mentioned something about meeting on a double-date.'

'So?' said Sloman, a touch belligerent.

Darren had gone back to not talking.

'The friend she went with on this date, her name was Shirley Peters. That afternoon, she'd just come from helping to bury her.'

Darren stumbled back a couple of paces, looking as if his legs were going to give way under him; they might have done if Sloman hadn't placed his open hand against the small of his back and held him up.

'I was wondering, Darren, who your friend was on this occasion; this cosy little double-date?'

Only a flick of the eyes, still it was a dead giveaway.

'Maybe,' Millington said to Sloman, 'you'd like to finish work early today and come down to the station with Darren here – always assuming you haven't got anything more important in hand.'

And in case the former wrestler decided against coming quietly, Millington lifted his walkie-talkie out from beneath the lapel of his raincoat and called in for some support.

Twenty-One

LONELY HEARTS KILLER ON LOOSE
Terror Rapist Stalks City

Skelton's press conference had gone down a storm. A brief paragraph detailing the setting up of the inquiry and the rest was a half-hysterical mix of warning and conjecture. There was a photograph of Jack Skelton taken that morning, the very model of modern police management. If the Force was being privatized, it would only take a few shots like that on the prospectus to send the populace scurrying for their piggy-banks and building society accounts.

There were also pictures of the victims: Mary Sheppard wearing a white dress and a little veiled hat, holding one of the children to her shoulder, a christening; Shirley Peters, a blurred head and shoulders, turning from the camera as if hearing someone call her name.

Resnick read down as far as his own name before pushing the paper aside and turning to the reports that had begun to arrive on his desk.

John Benedict had proved to be a sad-faced man with a vivid birthmark on his neck and shoes worn down by walking the streets pushing double-glazing leaflets through reluctant letter-boxes. It was the only work he'd been able to get since an allergy had prevented him from carrying on nights at the pork-pie factory.

He had responded to three advertisements in the space of as many weeks and Shirley Peters had been the only one to write back. It had been a nice letter, a note really, apologizing for the fact that she wouldn't be meeting him, but wishing him better luck with somebody else. You sound a nice man: that's what she had written. Considerate. Most people don't bother. So considerate and kind and when I read in the paper what had happened...

Benedict's eyes had filled with tears and Naylor had thought about the condition of the handkerchief in his pocket, wondering if it were clean enough to offer. But the tears hadn't actually fallen and Naylor had made up his mind to take some tissues along with him next time.

'These three you wrote off to,' Naylor had asked, 'are they the only ones ever?'

Benedict had shaken his head. There had been others, twenty-four in all over a period of eighteen months.

'I've still got them,' he had said as Naylor had been putting his pen away.

'Sorry?'

'The advertisements. The ones I replied to. I've got them. If, I mean, if you'd like to see them. I don't know if...'

Naylor had looked at the two-dozen cuttings, each less than an inch high, sellotaped near the top of separate pages in a cheap scrapbook.

'You'll be hanging on to this?' Naylor had said. 'In case we want to look at it again.'

'Oh, yes,' John Benedict had assured him, 'I like to keep a record.'

'Caring and Lively II' could not have been more different. Lynn Kellogg traced him to the food department of a supermarket, where he was in charge of the meat and delicatessen sections. Assistant manager: Peter Geraghty. He had been slicing pink salami when Lynn was taken across to him, thin folds of adulterated meat folding one over the other.

'Do people actually buy that stuff?'

'Can't get enough!'

He had taken a piece between forefinger and thumb and offered it towards Lynn's face. She had shuddered: Geraghty glanced around and then ate it. After only seconds, he drew the length of plastic-coated skin from between his lips and lobbed it into a nearby bin.

Lynn thought she might be ill; she thought it might be enough to turn her vegetarian. She asked Peter Geraghty about his interest in personal advertisements and he had assumed that she was the woman who received the letters.

'How did you know where to find me?' he had asked. 'I only put the phone number.'

'It's my job,' she had explained.

He lifted up the blade and removed the end of a roll of salami. 'I didn't know you could make a living at it,' he had said, and then: 'Hey! This isn't one of those visiting massage things, is it? 'Cause if I strip off and lie down on here, they'll be fighting one another to buy me by the pound.'

'This is serious,' Lynn had said.

'So am I.'

'I doubt it.'

She had questioned him inside the manager's office. Away from the women who worked behind the counter and provided him with a ready audience, he was calmer. More sober. Friday nights he went round the pubs with his mates, usually they'd finish up in a club or a disco, not always. Saturdays, the pictures. Sunday afternoons, ten-pin bowling. Tuesday evenings, he went to adult education classes.

'What in?' she had asked, expecting something like retail management, maybe car maintenance.

'Russian.'

Her surprise was inescapable.

'I'm not thick, you know.'

'I didn't say you were.'

'It's not so bad when you get into it. Besides, it's going to be needed.' She nodded: a friend of hers had been on one of the trips, three Russian cities in ten days, the food was terrible. 'You know they're going to take over the world.'

The jury in the child abuse case was out: work on the murder investigation had been so pressing that Resnick had all but forgotten it was still going on. By the end of the day, there would be a verdict. His impulse was to go down there, to the court; some part of him wanted to be there when the foreman of the jury stood forward, when the judge pronounced sentence, some part of him – knotted and hard, like a growth – that wanted to watch the expression on that man's, that father's face.

Was that what people got married for? Had children?

The phone went and Resnick picked up the receiver on the second ring.

'Charlie?'

'Sir.'

It was Skelton, back from lunch and checking round. If they could get somebody for this before the incident room had computer print-out like cheap wrapping paper, he would be a grateful and happy man.

'The lads from the record shop . . .?'

'In interrogation now, sir.'

'You're not having a go at them yourself?'

'I thought Sergeant Millington should take first crack. I'll spell him in a bit.'

'Don't let up on them, Charlie.'

'No, sir.'

'One of them's a wrestler, isn't he?'

'Used to be, I believe, sir.'

'Big lad, then?'

'Cow-pie type, sir.'

There was a pause at the end of the line, only slight. 'Those blows to Mary Sheppard's head. A lot of force was used there, Charlie. A lot of force.'

'Yes, sir.'

'Keep me posted.'

'Sir.'

The receiver was on its way back to the cradle when Lynn Kellogg knocked and Resnick motioned for her to come in.

'I thought you might be going to take a look at Darren and his friend, sir.'

They had not been taken to the incident headquarters: parading them in front of a couple of bored reporters at this stage wouldn't help anybody. Them especially, if they were eliminated from the inquiry.

'I wondered if I could tag along?'

Resnick nodded, reached for his coat. 'Think you put us on to something, then?'

'I hope so, sir. I'd like to . . .'

She half-turned away, recalling the moment when she'd stepped into the darkness of that small garden,

214

the cold biting at her exposed face and hands, blood drying darkly on to dark, dry earth.

'Let's get going, then.'

They were only just out of the room when the phone sounded again.

'Forget it,' Resnick said. 'You could spend the whole day answering the thing and never get anywhere. Besides,' pushing open the door, 'it's a little difficult to imagine that it's good news.'

Graham Millington had taken the wrestler for himself, Patel was along the corridor with his friend. A uniformed PC struggled along in the corner, sweating as he tried to keep up with question and answer, flicking his eyes anxiously at the sergeant – slow down, for heaven's sake, slow down!

Geoff Sloman seemed to be enjoying it. He leaned his considerable weight back in the chair, answering questions with all the enthusiasm of someone whose ambition in life has been to be stopped by one of those women with clipboards who haunt the streets outside Tesco's or Sainsbury's.

The first time they'd met the two women, they'd gone to a couple of pubs and then on for a pizza. Shirley had been quite a bit older, but he hadn't minded that and during a quick chat with Darren in the gents they'd decided that was the way they were going to divvy them up. They'd all shared a cab from the square. Shirley had been the first to get out; he'd thought about getting out with her, the old goodnight on the doorstep routine, all the while trying to get your toe in the front door, but the prospect of having to walk home later had put him off. Besides, by then he'd already arranged to see her again.

Five nights later, the four of them again, a few beers

and then into the Astoria. The music, it wasn't Shirley's scene at all, soon as she was inside and sitting up on the balcony she got this look on her face, like she'd got toothache in her ear. So, a quick word with Darren, do the decent thing, off out of there and round the corner for a curry.

Well, she was grateful.

Millington wanted a cigarette. The ends of his moustache were beginning to itch and he eased them back from his upper lip with thumb and forefinger.

'Tell me about it.'

Sloman shrugged his powerful shoulders. 'She asked me in for a coffee, gave us a Scotch, large one, laughing, "I never did know when to say when". Time for Frank Sinatra. No wonder The Exorcists had gone down like a barrel-load of sick.' He looked across at Millington. 'That's it, more or less.'

'Which?'

'Um?'

'More or less?'

'Wrong time of the month.'

'So it was less?'

'Definitely.'

'You're sure?'

'Bloody certain!'

Millington nodded and stood up. He paced around a little, letting the big feller watch him, much as he would have done in the ring. It had been Sloman who had broken his opponent's nose in the bout he'd watched: like splintering a match. Except for the scream.

'You must have been pretty pissed-off.'

'No,' said Sloman carelessly, one arm hooked over the back of the chair.

'All that hanging about. Evening's already buggered

216

up because she doesn't like the music. Curry's probably given you heartburn. Gets you on the couch and pours whisky down you and then she's making the excuses. I bet you were really pissed-off.'

Sloman unhooked his arm, touched the ends of his fingers together with surprising lightness. 'I wasn't on the couch.'

'Does that matter?'

'You seem to think it does.'

'The couch, the floor . . .'

'I was sitting on a chair, soft-backed, solid arms, wood. She sat on the couch, when she wasn't wandering around between the kitchen and the stereo. When she wasn't sitting on my lap.'

'Sticking her tongue in your ear.'

'My mouth.'

'And you weren't randy?'

'Maybe.'

'Frustrated?'

Sloman shrugged.

'Come off it, Sloman. You're expecting me to believe there's this woman, asks you in, all over you, gives you the old come-on, and then she looks you in the eye and says it's off the menu – all that malarky and you says thanks very much.'

'Something like that.'

Millington leaned forward across the desk and laughed in Sloman's face.

Sloman gave a slow smile. 'See,' he said. 'I'm used to it. All manner of provocation. You. Her. Blokes in the ring. How else d'you reckon I stayed in the game for even three years? You get some nasty bastards, agree to one move and do another just to make themselves look good, walk away, and then it's the back heel into the groin, smile and spit in your eye. If you

217

haven't got the self-control, where are you? You can't
afford to let it get to you, can't afford to get frustrated.
If you did and really lost your temper, well...' He
winked at Millington and flexed the muscles in his arms.
'... whoever it was, they'd be dead. Wouldn't they?'

Graham Millington looked as if he'd been in the ring
– through the wringer, anyway. He was down to his
shirtsleeves, which were rolled unevenly back over
his wrists. The striped cotton was sticking darkly to his
skin. He had a mug of tea in one hand, a cigarette in
the other and he wanted a stiff Scotch.

'Problems?' Resnick asked.

Lynn Kellogg stood close by the door, not certain
whether she should be there at that moment or not.

'Clever bastard!' Millington spat out.

Resnick sat on the edge of a scarred table and lifted
the unlit cigarette from between his sergeant's fingers.
'Tell me.'

'Sure he went out with her, once with this Darren
and a couple of times on their own. Nice woman, he
says, but he likes them younger. No hard feelings, no
regrets; they sodding shook hands at her front door.'

Resnick smiled: without looking over his shoulder, he
knew that Lynn Kellogg would be smiling too. Nothing
angered his sergeant more than suspected villains and
tearaways behaving like the presenters on *Blue Peter*.
Especially if they happened to be seventeen-stone and
bald as a Chinese hippie.

'Think he's telling the truth?'

'I can't bloody shake him.'

'Get anything out of his pal?'

'If you ask me, they're both as bent as last year's
clockwork orange.'

'It wasn't what I was asking.'

'No. His mate's given us nothing.'

'Then maybe there's nothing to give.'

Millington put down the mug with a thump, stood up as he pushed his hands deep into his trouser-pockets. He glowered at Lynn Kellogg, who averted her eyes but stood her ground. 'He's perfect for it!' Millington said, angry. 'He met her through one of those ads, he's built like a brick shithouse, knows his own strength and what to do with it. If he'd taken a few swings at the back of Mary Sheppard's head she'd've looked like she did – bloody tinned tomatoes!'

'Christ!' Lynn exclaimed below her breath.

'Take it easy, Graham,' said Resnick, standing. 'Maybe it's too perfect. And, what you were just saying, my guess is that tells us he's not our man.'

'What I said . . .?'

'According to you, we've got a big man who knows what he can use his body for and what he can't. All in all pretty controlled, wouldn't you say?'

Millington was looking at a spot on the floor midway between the inspector and himself.

'Graham?' Resnick persisted quietly.

'I suppose so, sir. Only . . .'

'Whoever did that to Mary Sheppard, sir,' said Lynn Kellogg, coming forward, 'whatever control he might have had, he'd lost it.'

Millington glared at her hard.

'She's right, Graham. Let it go. For now, at least. On your own admission, it doesn't sound as if we've got anything to hold him on.'

The sergeant shook his head, sighed back in his throat.

'I'll have a quick word with him, since I'm here,' Resnick said, moving towards the door. 'With the pair

219

of them. Ring through to the DCI to check, but my guess is, we'll kick them out with our thanks.'

'I'd like to think we were going to keep an eye on them, the wrestler anyway.'

'Oh, yes,' said Resnick. 'We'll keep an eye.'

Millington sat there until the inch of tea that remained at the bottom of the borrowed mug was clinging to the sides with an orangey skin. He knew that Resnick was probably right in his judgment and was finding it difficult not to hope he would be proved wrong. You might come out of this better placed than if you stayed back in the station with your boots under my desk, that was what the inspector had said. He hoped he would be proved right.

Graham Millington hoped for a lot of things.

He never quite understood why they didn't happen; at least, not until way after they should. And, sooner or later, he was going to have to go home to a wife who was understanding enough to realize that something was troubling him and who would bide her time before asking him, oh so gently and reasonably; what it was. And, reasonably and gently as he could, Millington would tell her. She would sit there, listening, nodding her head, reaching out from time to time to touch his hand, run her fingers down the side of his face. She would listen and nod and yes, it was a shame the way things were sometimes but it would all work out in the end. After which she would offer to make him a cup of tea, or, if things were especially bleak, to pour him a small malt whisky.

All the while, Millington keeping it screwed up tight inside, like a fist wanting something to strike out against, something to hurt, to damage.

The phone broke his thoughts.

'Inspector Resnick? No, he's not here. No idea where you can find him. Sorry.'

It was a petty thing to do, but right then it was all Graham Millington had.

Twenty-Two

Downstairs Billie Holliday was wearying her way through 'Ghost of a Chance'. Resnick had put on the record and at the first sound of the voice known that he couldn't listen. Up here at the back of the house it was little more than remembered sound. Softly, he moved towards the window. Bud's head nestled against his neck; his fingers stroked the side of the cat's belly as the purring grew louder close to his ear. Louder till it blocked out everything but his thoughts.

Sharon Taylor had smiled the first time that the social worker had shown her the dolls. Warily, not openly trusting, already she had learned that much. Still she had smiled, even as she took the dolls into her hands. Seven years old. Resnick turned back into the room. He had painted over the wallpaper, two coats, yet here and there the figures showed through: the arms and baggy suit of a clown; a horse with a dancer on its back, careening; the face of a bear.

Can you show me, Sharon . . . ?

Slowly, but without hesitation, the little girl had pointed at the other doll, the girl doll, and when the tip of her finger touched the place she had winced with the memory of the pain.

Resnick's face had struck the coldness of the glass through which he watched.

The lying little bitch! Almost the only time her father

had shown any emotion in the dock. . . . *just a bloody kid!*

Bud began to wriggle and Resnick bent forward and set him down, watching him trot from the room on silent paws. Resnick moved aside a bundle of old newspapers and sat on the bed. The whitewood chest-of-drawers he had painted, using stencils for decoration, had boxes piled on top of it. Carrier bags stuffed with who knew what rubbish leaned against its sides and each other. Dust had gathered in clots against the skirting. Resnick pushed himself to his feet. Hire a skip, clear it out, all of it.

You ought to get married again, Charlie.

He thought about Jack Skelton's well-satisfied life, fitting him like his three-piece suits, the family photograph framed on his desk. Where were his kids now? College? University? As well-adjusted as their father's ties.

Making coffee earlier that evening, Resnick had switched on the national news. In the north-east, a man had been arrested on charges of indecently assaulting a girl of ten, of gross indecency with another, younger. These had not been isolated incidents: police and Social Services were working on the assumption that other adults and as many as fifty other children were involved, the youngest of the children was believed to be the same age as Sharon Taylor. The same news bulletin gave details of a telephone hot-line that had been set up in London following the discovery of a child sex ring, offering refuge and advice to abuse victims. So far one hundred and forty had been interviewed: so far.

The children, from deprived backgrounds, were caught up in a maelstrom not of their own making. They have been abused and chosen because of their poverty.

223

Resnick looked again around the shrivelled room.
Yes, it hurt me.

The telephone was ringing and he hurried downstairs.

'Charlie, are you crying?'

'What kind of question is that?'

'Are you?'

'Of course not.'

'Then you're getting a cold.'

'It's possible.'

'What you need, increase your vitamin C. You do take it, don't you?'

Resnick moved the receiver away from his mouth a little so that she wouldn't hear his breathing.

'Are you still there?'

'I should have thought you had enough of looking after people.'

'I do.'

'Am I getting enough sleep, eating enough oranges?'

'Oranges aren't enough on their own, you need the tablets.'

'Rachel . . .'

'Okay.' He heard the smile in her voice. 'I'm sorry. Goes with the job. You get trained for it, paid for it. Sometimes it's hard to switch off. Chris says . . .' She broke off; it didn't matter what Chris said.

'Charlie, I've been trying to get hold of you half the day. Nobody seemed to know for certain where you were.'

'This inquiry, you get shuffled around.'

'I thought perhaps . . . I wondered if you wanted to talk.'

'Talk?'

'Yes.'

Resnick glanced away across the room. He hadn't

switched on the light and the red dot on the stereo glowed brightly. One of the cats settling and resettling in its basket was the only sound.

'I didn't know how you'd be feeling.'

'No.'

'Sorry, I'm not . . .'

'I don't know what I'm feeling either.'

There was a slight sigh at the other end of the line. 'I shouldn't have phoned.'

'No. No, I'm glad you did.'

For several seconds neither of them spoke.

'All right,' Rachel said eventually. 'Maybe later in the week.'

'Yes,' said Resnick. 'Sure.'

There was another, briefer silence.

'If you do want to get in touch,' Rachel said, 'you'd better call me at work.' And she hung up.

The newspaper was on the kitchen table, folded to favour the sports page: team selection, transfer speculation. Resnick took the whisky bottle from the shelf and put it back down; there was a bottle of Czechoslovakian Budweiser in the fridge, cold. He poured it into a long glass. The double murder was still on the front page, but now it was boxed, bottom left. The photograph of Taylor, head and shoulders, was half lifesize: the headline alongside it, two inches deep, GUILTY! At the end of a two-hour summing up by the judge, the jury had only taken twenty-seven minutes to arrive at their verdict. When Taylor heard the sentence of three years he had smiled.

Resnick read the paragraph again, remembering the way Taylor had stood in the dock with a careless, bored arrogance. And at the end of it all he had smiled.

'Castrate the bastard!' a woman had shouted from

the public benches and a police officer had escorted her, struggling, from the court.

In a side interview with Mrs Taylor, a reporter asked her what she had felt when she heard the verdict.

'Glad that Sharon hadn't gone through all that for nothing.'

And the sentence?

'Stunned. Just stunned.'

At the leniency of it? The severity? The smile?

'And when your husband is released, Mrs Taylor, are there any circumstances in which you might have him back?'

'I don't know. I really don't know. It's too early to say. I'm not saying I never would, but now ... My daughter and I have got to get on with our lives.'

Three years, Resnick thought, and he'll be out on parole in two. Some probation officer with the task of resettling him back into society, his debt paid. The possibility of returning him to the family home. Sharon almost ten, almost grown. All of them together, hour-long sessions in a windowless room, therapy. 'I'm not saying I never would ...' What did Resnick want? *Castrate the bastard*! There would be those in prison who would be less uncertain: they would take the smile off his face and no mistake.

Yes, it hurt me:

He pushed the paper aside again and stood up. An eye for an eye, is that what he wanted? If ever he had got close to Taylor after his arrest, alone with him, how hard would it have been not to take a swing at him? In court he had wanted to catch hold of him and shake him to make him understand what it was he had done. Resnick didn't think Taylor knew, really knew, but then, as he had said to Rachel, it was beyond his understanding also. All of it. That girl ...

Carole's son had taken a rucksack and his father's dog-eared copy of Kerouac and set off round the world. However far he got, a place was waiting for him to study medicine the following autumn. 'I think he'll be a better doctor because of it,' Carole had said. 'I truly do. And as for being worried, of course, I'm his mother, but, heavens, you can't fuss about them all their lives, can you? Or all of your own. Besides, he's got his head screwed on . . . and his credit card.'

Rachel doubted if Kerouac had stuck his thumb in the air with an American Express card in the back pocket of his jeans.

There was a poster of James Dean on the wall, another which proclaimed *I Ran the World*. In the corner of the room, opposite the window and close to the head of the single bed stood an anatomical model, one half of the body lifted away to expose the pale coils of plastic bowel, the workings of a plastic heart.

Rachel was trying not to stare at it. When she heard the footsteps on the carpeted stairs, she opened the file close by and picked up her pen.

'Rachel?' A soft knock at the door.

'Yes?'

'Can I come in a minute?' The door was opening.

'For goodness' sake, Carole,' Rachel smiled. 'It is your house.'

'Conditioned response,' Carole said. 'Mark had me knocking on his door and waiting to be admitted the day he got to secondary school.'

'Not all parents would have paid much attention.'

'I think they should. Don't you?'

'We all need our own space.'

Carole glanced back over her shoulder. 'Somebody's here to see you.'

Chris Phillips stood waiting in the living-room. The lines around his eyes were heavy and dark and his face was devoid of colour.

'Carole says we can talk in here.'

'Talk?'

'I'll make some coffee,' Carole said, passing behind Rachel's back.

Rachel stood at the entrance to the room, not yet going in.

'I've got the dog in the car,' Chris Phillips said.

The trumpet, tightly muted through four bars of introduction, pianist quietly chording behind; the same phrase repeated, inverted, the last note fading into the fall of wire brush against the snare and there, tight to the beat, Billie's voice.

I need your love so badly

The last word of the line is broken by the way she phrases, by the first of the saxophone's cold spirals, grace notes that glide and lift around her without ever once touching.

I love you oh so madly

When she was ten years old she was abused by her stepfather; within too short a time she had left home and was selling her sex on the streets. This is 1954 and she is turning forty but not very far. Dead in a hospital bed she will have a police guard close by and the money for her next fix of heroin tied to her wasted leg.

But I don't stand
A ghost of a chance with you

Twenty-Three

So much for the obvious. Photographs of Mary Sheppard and Shirley Peters were taken round to all of the clubs, pubs and restaurants within a mile radius of the city-centre; officers also checked with staff at all four of the cinemas and both theatres. One theatre usher, three bar staff, the relief DJ at Madison's and the assistant manageress at the Odeon were sure they remembered seeing Mary Sheppard on the night that she was murdered. Pretty sure. Well, of course it was dark, bright, there was an awful crowd, I was rushed off my feet. After more questioning, two of the bar workers and the woman from the cinema were sticking to their guns. According to them she was accompanied by a tallish man with long hair wearing a dark hip-length coat, alternatively by someone of medium height, balding, a greycheck sports jacket and blue jeans, or a man quite a bit older with a local accent and a beard.

No one recollected seeing Shirley Peters on the date that she was killed; no one once she had left from outside her house in a taxi, other than the driver himself, who claimed to have dropped her on the north side of the main square outside Pizzaland. According to the staff who'd been on shift at the pizza place that evening, she hadn't eaten there. They were certain enough to be believed. Several people did recognize

Shirley's picture, however, but none could tie it in with the date in question.

Who was she here with?

'In a crowd, crowd of girls, you know the way it is.'

'Never with a man?'

'Yeh, sure, with a man? Which man? Come on, just men. Yes, men. Nothing funny, you know, just it never seemed to be the same man. Yeh, shame, she was all right. Fun, you know. Fun.'

One of those who reacted positively to Shirley Peters's photograph was Warren. Resnick dropped in at the gym and found him working out on the heavy punch bag.

'Getting ready for a fight?' Resnick asked.

'Mug's game.' Warren straightened and swung his head towards Resnick, spraying sweat.

'I thought maybe your friend the cuts man had talked you into it. He seemed to think you'd be something special.'

'Something special for him to practise on, fine. But no, thanks.' He flexed his shoulders and started to arch his back, moving his legs a little on the spot, limbering down. 'You're not still running around after that Macliesh business?'

Resnick shook his head. 'Shirley Peters.'

'Shirley?'

'You identified her.'

'Right,' said Warren, realizing. He rubbed at his head with a towel. 'Couple of places I'm on the door, she used to go down a few times. I mean, enough so's I knew the face, but no more than that. Like I said to your bloke, I never knew her name, nothing about her.'

'Nor who she went around with?'

Warren let the towel fall across his shoulders, shook

his head. 'Not the one bloke. Least, I don't think so.'
He began wiping at the sweat glistening on his thighs.

'You know she was a friend of Grace Kelley's?'

Warren looked puzzled.

'From London. Came up to see Shirley but too late.
She stayed around long enough to enjoy the hospitality
of a mutual acquaintance of ours.'

'Georgie Despard?' grinned Warren.

'The same.'

'Small world,' said Warren, still grinning.

Resnick nodded. 'Thanks for your time.'

'That I've got plenty of.' Warren looked across the
room at the assorted pullers and pushers and pounders.
'Any day you want to come down and work out for an
hour . . .'

'Thanks. I'll think . . .' He stopped, a thought striking
him. 'Don't suppose you know a Geoff Sloman by any
chance?'

Warren gave it a moment before shaking his head.

'He used to wrestle. The Oblivion Brothers.'

'He was both of them?'

Resnick smiled. 'He's big enough.'

'No. You don't get the likes of them down here.
Acting class, make-up – that's more their style. But I'll
ask around if you like. Think he might have been throwing his weight about in the wrong places, do you?'

'Not really. But if you do pick up anything . . .'

'I'll give you a bell.'

Advertisers with the local newspaper's personal columns were still being interviewed and not without
embarrassment. Strapping toy boys turned out to be
holders of bus passes; the secretary of the Mothers'
Union kept the photographs sent in response to 'sexy
redhead seeks man hot enough to put out the flame'

231

between the pages of her Bible. Husbands blushed on being confronted before their wives and vice versa. One married couple realized they had both had advertisements for new partners printed on the same day. It was slow, but it was methodical.

Gradually men who had responded to adverts were being tracked down and questioned. Skelton and the rest of the inquiry team felt without knowing why that it was starting to slip away from them. They wanted something more positive, a lead towards somebody they could begin to lean on. Mary Sheppard's double-date had seemed to be it; the former wrestler, for all too short a time, had been an ideal suspect.

'I've been reading through the stuff on Sloman again, Charlie,' Skelton said. 'You don't think we gave up on that too easily?'

'We've got half an eye on him, sir.'

'Whereas we did have him in the station. Voluntarily. No question of a charge, no solicitor, simply a chat. We thanked him very much and showed him the door.'

'It was put-up or shut-up, sir.'

'You don't think somebody else might have got more out of him?'

'I think if Millington had come out of there and, say, I'd gone in, started asking more questions, putting him back over the same ground, I think then he would have got the wind up.'

'You didn't want another Macliesh?'

'That's part of it.'

'The rest?'

Resnick half-shrugged. 'Just didn't feel right.'

'You'll be fingering seaweed next, Charlie. Reading tea-leaves or the I Ching.'

'You want me to pull him in again, sir, then of course . . .'

'I don't think so. But your sergeant does.'

'Millington? He's been to see you about it, sir. I mean, direct?'

Skelton held out his hands in a gesture of pacification. 'He's not been behind your back, Charlie. Nothing like that. A word in the corridor, that's all it was. In passing. A question from me, a remark from him in return. Anything more and I'd want it through the proper channels.'

'Yes, sir.'

'Tendency towards the purblind, Millington, but not a bad copper for all that.'

Resnick nodded.

'I think like the rest of us – everyone except those civilians and their software – I'm hoping against hope we won't be forced into phase two.'

'Phase two, gentlemen, brings with it a widening out of the inquiry.'

'And enough perforated bloody paper to keep a ward full of gastric cases going,' voiced Colin Rich at the rear of the room.

'On the one hand this means we start to check all of the marriage bureaux and dating agencies. To begin with we'll restrict this to the city; if necessary we shall extend throughout the county. Nationwide agencies whose files are already computerized will allow us to access them for local names and addresses as soon as we provide them with the necessary warrants.'

Skelton paused to worry something stuck between his teeth with his tongue.

'Those little back hairs,' said Rich, 'they get everywhere.'

'With surgery,' Resnick told him, 'you could probably have your brain moved back above your waist.'

'The second and murkier avenue,' Skelton was saying, 'is contact magazines. There are a number of these readily available in the city. Sometimes an entire magazine devoted to people looking specifically for sexual partners, sometimes a section in one of the girlie mags you can buy at any newsagents.'

'As long as they're called Patel,' laughed Rich.

'If we broaden out the inquiry along these lines,' said Skelton, 'I don't need to spell out the size of the task. Nor the importance of stressing to your teams the need for careful work, methodical and precise.'

Outside there were streaks of cloud like skid marks across a pale blue sky. The frost that had fringed gardens and roofs that morning had barely disappeared. A couple more hours and the light would begin to go. Lynn Kellogg thought about her father, fussing around the long, jerry-built hen houses, the last half-inch of an extinguished cigarette tight between bloodless lips. Inside the house, her mother's voice rising and fading over snatches of misremembered *Family Favourites*: 'Oh, Bella Margareta', 'Shrimpboats are a-Coming', 'Buttermilk Sky'. There would be bread rising in the cupboard beneath the boiler; soup beginning to simmer on the stove. The smell of carbolic soap and chickens.

She took a tea and a cheese and onion sandwich and went to join Kevin Naylor, who was sitting with the remnants of double egg and chips, thoughtfully worrying over the entries he was making in a small black diary.

'Join you?'

'Yes, course. There.' He pushed the plate along towards one end of the table, folded the diary closed over his yellow Bic.

Lynn had seen two columns of figures, small writing, sloping backwards, alongside each. 'Trying to make ends meet?'

Naylor shook his head. 'I was listening to the radio driving in this morning. Some woman from the Royal College of Nursing going on about how badly they were paid compared to the police.'

'What are you saying?'

'I get fed up with hearing it.'

'Not as much as the nurses.'

'I dare say. That's no reason for us to be passed off as earning a fortune.'

'We earn a sight more than they do. Double nearly, starting anyway.'

'It's a different issue.' He glanced round the canteen, worried in case he'd made his point too loudly. 'Debbie says all that happens is the public end up thinking we're overpaid, when what's happening is that the nurses are underpaid.'

'Right,' agreed Lynn. Why did they have to grate the cheese before putting it into the sandwiches? All that happened was that it fell out all over the table.

'It's those blokes down in the City they want to go after, not . . .'

'Come on, Kevin, nobody's going after us.'

'Yuppies making sixty thousand a year . . .'

'We get a decent wage and others should get the same.'

'A year ago, I never knew what a yuppie was. Well, did you?'

Lynn raised a hand to greet someone across the room. Usually when you sat with Kevin it was a wonder to get more than a dozen words out of him.

'Anyway,' he said, 'I don't see as it is that much. Now we've taken on this new house . . .'

'Between the two of you, though, you must be bringing in a good bit.'

Naylor mumbled something inaudible.

'Skiing in Italy as well as a summer holiday. Or was it Austria?'

'That was Debbie's idea, not mine.'

'Still, you could afford to go.'

'Good job we did.'

'What's that mean?'

'When we could, that's what it means.'

'She hasn't lost her job? Kevin, they haven't made her redundant?'

He fiddled with the top of his pen, pushed his diary around the table. 'More like I have,' he said, not looking at her.

'What are you on about? You've not had a row, I mean you haven't split up? You . . .' She reached across the table and took hold of his arm. 'She's pregnant, isn't she?'

He looked around anxiously, waved his hand at her to keep her voice down. 'That's it, tell everybody.'

'Why ever not? Aren't you pleased? You must be really chuffed. How long have you known?'

'It's only just . . . I mean, we thought, she thought, you know . . . but for definite, just this last few days.'

'That's great! I'm really excited for you. Both of you. How's Debbie? I bet she's thrilled.'

'Sick.'

'Hmm?'

'She's sick. Every morning. Half-past four every morning, there she goes, out to the bathroom.'

'But that'll soon pass.'

'I hope so.'

'Kevin, it's not you that's in there throwing up.'

'I sometimes think I might as well be.'

'Oh, Kevin, stop it! You make it sound like a disaster. She hasn't found out she's suffering from some fatal disease, you know. It's a baby!'

'Keep your voice down!'

'I don't understand this,' Lynn laughed. 'You should be dead proud. Walking round telling everyone. Writing it on walls. I know I should be.'

'You haven't been sitting here trying to balance next year's budget.'

'No. And I haven't been worrying myself silly over radiation levels or the next ice age or whether I'm going to be hit by a bus the next time I step out into the street.'

'I suppose you're right. It's just that, well, we'd begun to get on our feet, put a bit of money away.'

'Kevin, Kevin!' said Lynn, shaking her head.

'What's wrong now?'

'Listen to yourself. You sound like my parents when I was a kid: scrimping and saving over every penny, a little in a shoe box under the bed for emergencies, coppers in an old marmalade jar for Christmas – start filling up New Year's Day and you might have enough for presents and a bottle of brandy.'

He looked at her seriously. 'I don't see what's so terrible about that.'

Lynn smiled ruefully and pushed back her chair. 'I've got someone to see out at the University.'

'Better get going myself.'

'Give Debbie congratulations from me.'

'All right. Only, Lynn . . .'

'Um?'

'Don't, you know, spread it about. Once Divine gets hold of it – you can imagine what he'll say.'

Quickly, she leaned back towards him. 'What Mark Divine has to say is worth less than a fart in a

237

thunderstorm. He's got two ideas in his head – and they're both the same. And if you're going to let the likes of him run your life for you, you're less the bloke that I thought you were.'

Patel was around the corner of the CID room, typing up reports on the interviews he'd made that day – a greengrocer seeking solace from seven kids and the irregularities of the rhythm method, a refugee from Colombia who wanted to combine visits to the cinema with language lessons, a chartered accountant who was contemplating suing a dating agency after three successive mismatches by their computer.

Two others sat in a huddle over their notebooks while around them phones sputtered to life at intervals.

Lynn Kellogg came in briskly, went straight to Mark Divine's desk by the window, lifted the calendar now displaying Miss November from where it was hanging and tore it into half, then half again. With a satisfied slap of the hands she dropped the pieces into the nearest metal wastepaper bin and left.

In her wake even the phones stopped ringing.

The narrow road that wound through the University campus was all hills, right-angle bends and ramps. After wasting five minutes looking for a parking space, she left the car on the grass above the lake and walked up the broad stone steps to the nearest entrance.

Behind a desk and grille, a porter in a dark blue uniform was speaking into a walkie-talkie.

'Professor Doria,' she said.

Words fell apart against a hail of static and atmospherics. 'Useless blasted thing!'

'I've an appointment with a Professor Doria.'

238

'Might as well give us some of them tom-tom drums, stand as much chance of making yourself understood.'

'I'm supposed to be seeing him at a quarter-past three.'

'Interview, is it?'

'Sort of.'

'We get a lot of mature students coming here these days. Can't say as I can see why. You'd have thought 'em old enough to know better.'

Lynn searched his face for some sign that he was making a joke.

'You want the next building,' the porter said. 'Out of here and sharp right, through the car park and through the arch, you want the door to your left. There's a porter there – ask him.'

She didn't bother. Along a corridor devoid of students or any other form of life, she found the name – Professor W.J. Doria – in white letters cut into a dark wooden strip and fastened beneath the frosted glass panel of the door.

She knocked, paused and listened, was about to knock again when the door was thrown open and she had a sudden impression of a mass of dark hair, a strong nose, two gesticulating arms ushering her inside.

'Professor Doria?'

Outside, above the building, the clock sounded the single note for the quarter-hour.

Twenty-Four

Rachel didn't phone again. Days passed. Resnick looked up the number of the Social Services office a couple of times and went no further. The DCI got all hot and bothered about a pork butcher from Gedling with a record of petty theft that had escalated on two occasions to aggravated burglary. When he was brought in for questioning his photograph was in the local newspaper and middle-aged women threw refuse at him when he was bundled across the street. Suzanne Olds had a field day and there were threats of a suit for harassment and unlawful arrest. Pepper's stomach blew up like a balloon and Resnick hurried him to the vet before he exploded all over the living-room carpet. Debbie stopped being sick. Behind Lynn's back, Mark Divine swore at her viciously, but whenever she walked into the office he lapsed into an angry, wordless grumbling. Graham Millington stopped by the record shop and talked to Geoff Sloman for an hour and the only thing he came away with was a new Sandie Shaw EP that he played once and promptly forgot. Jack Skelton was now getting up at half-four, so that he could run five miles before getting into work by six, but it didn't make any difference.

What made Lynn drive down to the incident room and get a copy of the computer print-out she could never be certain. It did worry her, days and weeks afterwards, that she had waited so long. All she could put her slackness down to were the images of babies, floating effortlessly and unbidden, around and around inside her head.

That was easier to understand.

The conversation with Kevin Naylor, his reluctance either to accept or celebrate. *You should be dead proud. Walking round telling everyone. Writing it on walls. I know I should be.* If Naylor was normally taciturn, he was Bamber Gascoigne and Russell Harty rolled into one when set against her Dennis. Dennis who went through life with all the expressiveness and verbal eloquence of the Man in the Iron Mask. She thought they had last made love five weeks ago, after *EastEnders* and before he nipped down the road for an unofficial meeting of the Osprey Wheelers in the side room of the pub.

Not only a cyclist, but a cyclist whose other hobby was ornithology.

Much as she hated the old joke about the woman officer who was the station bike, Lynn thought the only way she might raise some excitement from Dennis would be to kit herself out with a racing saddle and a pair of drop handlebars.

'Do you ever think about having kids? The two of us. Together.'

He was asleep, dreaming of sighting a ptarmigan while winning the final stage of the Tour de France.

'Sir?'

She knocked and put her head round the door. Resnick was rereading a report he'd already been through twice without taking anything in. There were scores of others, milling around on the desk. It was becoming close to impossible: no way did they have the personnel to keep up with the spread of action the computer was generating.

'Have you got a minute?'

Resnick laughed. 'Don't suppose the kettle's on, is it?'

'It could be, sir.'

'Here,' he said, sliding open the bottom drawer and taking out a jar. 'Thee and me and then it goes right back in here.'

Lynn smiled, redder-faced than ever.

Nescafé Cap Colombie – she frequently lifted it off the shelf at Tesco's, but it had never got as far as her trolley. At that sort of price it would have given Kevin and Debbie Naylor serious heartburn. It tasted okay, though; not bitter but more flavour than most instant coffee she'd tried. Trust Resnick to have his priorities sorted out. A man who looked after his stomach first and foremost, Lynn decided, even if his clothes did come a poor second.

'It's a call I made, sir. I'm not sure what or why but it's been nagging at me, off and on ever since.' She pushed the print-out towards him. 'Probably nothing. Probably a waste of time.'

Resnick unfolded the paper. 'It's detectives who don't listen to the little nagging voices that put the wind up me. Like wing-halves who'll only pass square instead of putting a foot on the ball, getting their head up and seeing what might be on.'

Lynn Kellogg looked faintly puzzled.

'Wing-halves,' Resnick said. 'Call them something else now.'

'Yes, sir,' said Lynn, uncertain.

It was quiet while the inspector read the dot-matrix print as well as he could. He went back over a few

242

lines and then said: 'So tell me about him, Professor Doria.'

'He's been at the University nine years, before that he was at Hull. Three years ago he was given . . .' She hesitated, worrying about her choice of verb, ' . . . the Chair in Linguistics and Critical Theory. He's . . .'

Resnick was shaking his head and continued to do so until Lynn Kellogg's voice faltered to a stop.

'Come on, Lynn.'

'Sir?'

'I want you to tell me about *him*. Not give me what I can get from the University prospectus and *Who's Who*. He isn't making you wake in the middle of the night with your scalp itching because he's got the Chair in anything.'

She cradled the mug in her hands. How did you put things like this into words?

'I think . . . part of it, he was this odd kind of mixture of over-friendly and distant, both at the same time. I mean, he sat me down, fussed about whether I was comfortable enough, warm enough, seemed in quite a state about my not being in a draught. He was like – I don't know, I've never met one, but from the television – those dons – is that what they're called? – living their lives in book-lined rooms in Oxford or Cambridge.'

'Open-toe sandals and sherry and a copy of Wittgenstein casually open on the easy chair,' suggested Resnick.

'Behind it all, though, all the time, he didn't mean it. Not any of it.'

'And the sherry?'

'On his desk.'

'Sweet or dry?'

Lynn smiled and shook her head. 'I didn't have any, sir.'

'But he did?'

'He said he always had – "took" was the word he used – always took a glass at four in the afternoon. Part of his daily ritual.'

'It was four o'clock?'

Lynn shook her head again. 'He said in honour of my visit he'd make an exception. A member of CID.' She flushed, remembering. 'That's what I mean, sir. That's pretty much what he was like all the time, what he sounded like.'

'Bit much to be suspicious of a man for that. In his circles it probably counts as being polite.'

'He was. And helpful. Couldn't have been more so. He agreed that from time to time he wrote off in reply to Lonely Hearts ads, confirmed the names we had and offered another that somehow we'd missed.'

'That's been checked out?'

'It's gone into the system. I don't know if it's led anywhere special.'

Resnick drained his mug of coffee. 'So there he is, this effusive academic, not a great deal for you to like about his manner, but that's not enough, Lynn, is it? That's not all.'

She looked towards the floor. The lace of Resnick's left shoe had come undone and for an instant she had to suppress her instinct to bend down and retie it for him.

'The fuss, the showing-off, I'm not going back on what I said, there was something false about it, but at the same time I think he was excited.'

'Excited?'

'It's not quite right, but it's the only way I can describe it.'

'And what by?'

'By my . . .' she turned her head away, towards the door, then slowly back. 'By my being there.'

'He must have young women in that room all of the time, tutorials.'

'It was more than that.'

'Even so that was part of it?' said Resnick, not wanting to let the idea go.

'Yes, yes. But more, well, why I was there.'

'The investigation?'

'I think so, yes, I suppose that's what it was.'

'He was interested in the investigation?'

Lynn bit gently down into the centre of her lower lip. 'Maybe, this sounds daft, it was something to do with me being in the Force.'

'A police officer?'

'Yes.'

'That was what was exciting him?'

Lynn sighed. 'It makes it sound as if he was kinky for handcuffs and uniforms.'

'Which you weren't wearing?'

'No.'

'And presumably you didn't brandish a pair of cuffs under his nose?'

She laughed. 'No.'

Resnick looked down at the print-out again, looked across at her. 'Go on.'

'All the while he was talking, telling me what I wanted to know, what I didn't, great long sentences and one word in every dozen I didn't understand, it was as if – yes, as though he was in another part of the room, listening to himself. Thinking how clever he was sounding.'

'Admiring himself?'

'Yes, sir. And . . .'

'And?'

'I'd be making notes, book on my knee, and a couple of times I looked up when he wasn't expecting it and . . . the way he was watching me. It was as if there were these eyes, set back, staring, staring out at me as though they were behind a mask.' She looked towards Resnick, plainly troubled. 'Looking at me from behind a mask,' she said.

'Clutching at straws a bit, aren't we?' said Tom Parker.

'Straw man, Charlie?' said Skelton.

'There's not a lot else, sir,' Resnick observed.

'Exactly,' said Parker.

'You're running a check on him, of course?' asked Skelton.

Resnick nodded.

'You don't think there's a danger of letting the girl over-react to the situation?' Parker said.

They were walking across the Forest, the three of them, glad for the chance to get some fresh air, which is what it certainly was. All three of them were wearing overcoats, Resnick had a blue scarf knotted at his throat, hands pushed deep into his pockets. Jack Skelton and Tom Parker were both wearing trilby hats, Resnick was bareheaded. On the slope to the left, two kids who should have been at school were playing chase, in and out of the trees. Further over towards the road, a middle-aged man was trying to fly a kite which the wind, contrary, refused to accept. A steady stream of cars and vans passed each way along the boulevard.

'She's a woman,' said Resnick. 'A sensible one. She'd not be knocked sideways by a bloke in a gown gawping at her knees.'

'Was he wearing a gown?' asked Parker, surprised.

'Probably not.'

'What does seem strange,' Skelton ventured, fifty

yards later, 'is that he bothers with answering those kind of things at all. I mean, other staff aside, the place must be crawling with young women and from what I hear, liaisons of that nature are no longer frowned upon.'

Resnick looked at the superintendent keenly, wondering what his reaction would be if his daughter came home and announced she was having an affair with one of her lecturers.

'Could be that's the thing,' suggested Parker. 'How's the saying go? Don't spill milk on your own doorstep.'

'Something like that.'

'Instead of charvering his students, he looks further afield.'

Skelton was looking far from happy. 'It still doesn't sound anything close to a case. Not even reasonable grounds for suspicion.'

'All I'm asking, sir, is permission to scratch around a little.'

'Charlie, we've got paperwork like dogs have fleas,' said Parker.

'I won't use the whole team,' said Resnick.

'Too bloody right!'

'You're a wonder for following hunches!' said Skelton, slapping his arms across his chest. 'Even when they're not your own.'

'She's got the makings of a good copper,' said Resnick. 'I think she deserves this one.'

'Just a couple of officers, Charlie.' Skelton was striding away again, leaving the others in his wake. 'We can't spare any more. We shouldn't.'

'No, sir.'

'And the minute it looks like a dead end,' said Parker, 'we're out.'

'Yes, sir.'

They were back at the station when across their shoulders the first few flakes of snow began to fall.

'Kellogg's report aside,' said Jack Skelton, letting Tom Parker go on into the building ahead of them, 'have you got anything else making your blood pump a little faster?'

'Not really, sir.'

Skelton stood there, snow fluttering against his face, and waited.

'One of the names on the list,' Resnick said. 'The women our professor admitted to meeting . . . I know her.'

Twenty-Five

The white and red horizontal stripes of the Polish flag hung across the porch window, facing outwards on to the uneven paving of the drive. The house, a Victorian delight of turrets and arches, stood back from the road behind sixty feet of dark shrubs and rose bushes pruned almost to the roots. To the left of the porch was a trio of narrow stained glass windows one above the other, predominantly blue and green. Above the cracking wood of the door, a larger panel of coloured glass, rectangular, depicted the Annunciation. Lace, rich and yellowing, shielded the interior from casual sight.

Resnick pressed the smooth white circle of the bell and heard it sound, off-pitch and distant.

He didn't think he had spoken to Marian Witczak for more than two years, probably hadn't seen her in eighteen months. In the days of his marriage, Resnick's wife had feigned at least a fondness for the dances which the Polish community organized regularly on a Saturday night. On his own, what was there to do other than join one of those tight male circles where one pair of arms, at least, was always within reach of the bar? Or stand eating smoked ham and *pieroqi*, pretending not to notice the church matrons pointing him out encouragingly to their stubbornly unmarriageable daughters. Besides, so much had changed: now a dance there was not so different from the Miners' Welfare, the British Legion.

A key was turned, bolts were slid back, top and bottom, finally a chain was loosed. Marian looked at him in surprise, confusion, pleasure.

'I thought you were from the auction rooms. I am expecting ... But, no, it is you.'

Resnick grinned a little self-consciously. They were the same age, Marian and himself, a matter of some months' difference, yet she always made him feel like a small boy who had come cap in hand to beat the carpets, sweep the leaves.

'I do not read the newspaper, of course, but I have seen your picture. You are always descending steps, Charlie, after giving evidence against some dreadful man. You always look so sad and angry.'

'I don't like having my photograph taken.'

'And this job that you do – do you like your job?'

'I remember you used to make good coffee, Marian.'

'Ah, this is why you are suddenly here?'

Resnick shook his head, smiled. 'No.'

'Of course,' the muscles of her face tightened, 'the knock on the door. I do not forget.'

'Marian, it's a November morning in England. I'm not the Gestapo.'

'Oh, yes,' stepping back to let him enter. 'The English way. What is it? *An Inspector Calls*?'

'That was a long time ago.'

She closed the door behind him. 'Yes,' she said, turning the key in the lock, 'now you have guns.'

Resnick turned and looked at her. 'Marian, I suspect we always had guns.'

The fireplace was carved black marble, inset with deep pink and white, and more than six feet across, almost as tall. The centre had been covered with tiles and a fifties gas fire burned low, frugal and utilitarian. Three arm chairs and a *chaise-longue* were covered in dark floral brocade and draped with antimacassars. An arrangement of dried flowers stood in a glass vase at the centre of a low table. Around the walls, stained oak bookcases held a mixture of leather-bound books and old orange Penguins. Above these the walls were hung with photographs: General Sikorski, Cardinal Wysznski, a villa overlooking the Mazurian Lakes, a family group picnicking on the lawns in front of the Wilanow Palace.

Resnick didn't need to walk over to the piano at the rear of the room to see that the music that was open there was Chopin, some polonaise or other, probably the A flat major, the only one he knew.

Marian came in with the coffee in a dented enamel pot, ardently polished; there were small white cups, bone china, sugar in a bowl with tongs. She was wearing a stiff green dress, belted tightly at the waist, flat shoes in soft green leather. She had quickly pulled her hair back and tied it with a length of white ribbon. Her eyes were dark, her cheekbones high and hard against her skin so that her cheeks seemed pinched and hollow. She was what would once have been called a handsome woman; maybe in her circle she still was.

'After the war,' she said, 'only one thing changed. When they came in the night and hauled you from your beds, they were no longer German.'

'Marian,' Resnick said, 'that was forty years ago.'

'When we were born, you and I.'

'Then how can you say you remember?'

For a moment she glanced at the walls. 'We know these things, Charles, because they happened to our families, our people.' She smiled at him, indulgently. 'Does it have to be with your own ears, your own eyes?'

Resnick looked away from her, down at the coffee, black in the cup. 'I think, yes, it does.'

'They should, I think, have christened you Thomas.'

There was nothing he could say. Thomas the apostolic detective: give me the evidence, where's the evidence? Dead without a body?

Marian spooned sugar into her cup, one, two, shiny silver spoonfuls.

'But your family had already left for this country and you, Charles, you have assimilated to perfection.' She balanced cup and saucer in the palm of one hand, stirring with care. 'No longer Mass at the Polish church, communion; no longer the socials and the dances. You speak with no trace of accent, we are waiting only for you to change your name.'

Resnick tasted the coffee, thick like bitter treacle. Somewhere in the house a grandfather clock chimed, several seconds later another, and another.

'You're not selling up, moving?'

'How could I ever?'

'You said you were expecting someone, something to do with an auction.'

'Oh, one or two pieces, nothing special; but the rooms upstairs, they are so rarely used. People used to come and stay, many people, and now . . . This is a large house to keep, there are many bills and I am alone.' She looked at him sharply. 'You know what this is like.'

Resnick nodded. 'The reason I came . . .'

'I know.'

He sat further back in the chair and waited.

'As I have said, the newspaper I will not read myself, but a friend, she told me, you are asking questions of those like me who are – the expression – lonely of heart.'

'I saw your name, on a list . . .'

'A list?' she said, a hint of alarm.

'We have been checking everyone who has placed advertisements, responded; checking and cross-checking . . . I didn't want to send a stranger to see you.'

'You are kind.'

'I was surprised . . .'

'That I would do this?'

'That you would look outside the community.'

Her face broke into a gentle smile and he realized, not for the first time, that she could be beautiful. 'Oh, Charles, you understand how well-known I am. For me to approach somebody else, a man, a man who is . . .' She regarded him for a moment, pointedly. ' . . . unattached, this is so difficult. I am too well-known here among people whose ways are not perhaps the ways of this world. Oh, there are men who have said things to me behind their hands when their wives are out of the room, propositions, Charles, but not proposals.'

She set down her cup and sat perfectly still. Resnick continued to watch, wait.

'It was a little over a year ago, I was feeling, perhaps you will recognize this, so alone I could no longer believe the sound of my own breath as it left my body. For three whole weeks I shut myself in the house; I went through piles of old letters, read diaries I had kept ever since I was a child in my country. I stared into the faces of old photographs until they almost became my own. For the last five days I did not eat, I drank nothing but water. If the telephone rang, I did not hear it.'

She reached out for his hand and he took her fingers between his own. How could she be so cold?

'One morning in the bedroom I saw a face in the glass and it frightened me. I had seen it before, faces like it after the flesh has fallen away and only the eyes seem alive, the way they are staring. You know where I have seen such faces.'

After a little time she withdrew her hand, straightened her back. 'You would like more coffee?'

'Please.'

When it was poured, she continued. 'The advertisement I sent, it was discreet without telling a lie. I told the truth about my age, about the kind of friend I am seeking – educated, a gentleman, "with fine tastes and intellectual pursuits", I said this.' She sighed. 'Even so, of the few replies I received, you would not believe . . . perhaps now you would. But there was one, the only one worthy of reply; a professor at the University, Doria.' Smiling, she angled her head towards the light from the window. 'A renaissance man. Truly, that is what he is.'

'So you met him?'

'Yes, but not immediately. You have to understand, I was now uncertain of what I was doing. Did I want to meet this man, no matter how charming his letters, how erudite? I felt vulnerable and I am not used to this. So for a time there was a correspondence, nothing more.'

'And he was satisfied with this?'

'Perfectly.'

'Yet you did meet him?'

'He was a clever man, he knew by now my interests. I have, he wrote, a pair of excellent tickets for the Polish National Symphony Orchestra, here in the city. Chopin, naturally. Elsner, Lutoslawski. Everyone I know is there. It is wonderful, all wonderful. Flowers are thrown on to the stage. The audience is on its feet, cheering. There are three encores. Doria – he is charming, he has brought for me a small corsage. He smiles at my friends and shakes their hands, stands a little behind me and to the side. When we walk back to our seats after the interval, he takes, for a moment, my arm. After the concert we go for supper, a few glasses of wine.' She laughed, remembering. 'Vodka!'

'A success, then?'

'Ah, that depends.'

'You had found your man with fine tastes.'

'Oh, yes.'

Marian stood up and moved across the room in the direction of the piano.

'You saw him again?' Resnick asked.

'The next day, the day after that,' Marian replied, 'the telephone it was ringing constantly. All the friends who had forgotten me when I had been so lonely. What a wonderful man, such a charmer, who is he, where did you meet him, you lucky woman, what a catch!' She folded her arms across her chest, switched them behind her back, fingers linked.

'The catch was this – amongst all those telephone calls, there was not one from him. Nor was there a letter. Only, the next morning there had been a card, thanking me for being such a good companion and suggesting that perhaps we might go together again, one suitable evening, to a concert.' She paused. 'Evidently, no such evening has proved suitable.'

After a while Resnick asked, 'You've had no further contact with him?'

Marian shook her head.

'And you've made no attempt to contact him?'

'Of course not,' she said sharply.

'Nor would you?'

'No.'

'But if he had called, you would have seen him again?'

'Yes, I think so. After all, wasn't he, as you say, what I had been looking for?'

'Really?' Resnick asked, shifted forward in the chair. 'What do you mean?'

'All the charm, the knowledge, you thought it was real?'

'As far as I knew.'

'Sincere?'

'Certainly.'

'And yet he never wrote or phoned? Doesn't that call all that sincerity into question?'

'Charles, he was honest with me, this man. I think so. He did not make a secret of the fact that this was the way he met women, a number of women. He liked, he said, the excitement of meeting someone for the first time, getting to know them in that way. He was not looking for something more permanent than that suggests.'

Resnick stood up. 'I'm grateful, Marian. For what you've told me as well as the coffee.'

'You are not suspicious of him ... these awful crimes?'

'I don't think so.'

He took his overcoat from her in the hall; wound his scarf about his neck. 'Did you find him attractive?'

Something seemed to pass across her face, across her mind.

'Oh, Charles, be sure of this, he is an attractive man. To women, I think so.'

'He's good-looking?'

'He listens; he makes you think that you are important. That you matter.'

Resnick hesitated: he wanted to ask Marian if anything had taken place between them, anything sexual.

She stood there, like a governess, watching him as he put on his gloves. He couldn't ask her.

'Charles,' she said when he was out on the step, 'at the end of the evening he took my hand, he kissed it, so quick I barely felt it. That was all.'

Resnick nodded, wondering if he were really blushing. 'Goodbye, Marian.'

'Next time,' she said after him, 'come only for the coffee.'

At the gate he raised a hand and walked quickly from sight, leaving her standing there, alongside the flag.

Twenty-Six

Rachel gulped at her tea, swore when the toast splintered apart as soon as she pressed the butter knife against it. On the shelf behind, Radio Four was moving from the weather forecast to the news headlines via a trailer for that afternoon's play. Through the voices she could just hear *Morning Concert* on Radio Three coming to an end in the bathroom. Files, diary, letters to be posted. She swept the pieces of toast from the table into her hand and deposited them in the plastic bin.

'Why don't you hang on? I'll give you a lift.'

'Thanks, Carole, but I can't. I promised I'd look in on the Sheppard kids first thing.'

'No problem, is there?'

'I don't think so. But if I show my face, grannie can have a moan at me instead of taking it out on the home-help.'

'You'll be in tonight?'

'Not sure. But I'll see you in the office later.'

'I've got a case conference all afternoon.'

'Carole, if I miss you I'll phone.'

'Just want to make sure I don't make too much lasagne.'

'Bye!'

There was a slam as Rachel closed the door. Her car was parked thirty yards along the road and she was about to climb into it as Chris Phillips got out of his.

Rachel thumped her bag down against the roof of the car and glared.

'Well,' Chris said, 'when else do I get a chance to see you?'

'I thought that was the point.'

'Jesus! How long were we living together? One week we're talking about moving out of the city and buying a new place together . . .'

'You were talking.'

'. . . and the next . . .'

'*You* were talking.'

'All right, I was talking about getting somewhere else, and the next we're not talking at all.'

'We talked the other night when you came round uninvited, have you forgotten that? We didn't only talk, we got to walk the dog round the block.'

'How can . . .? You used to love that dog.'

'I still do.'

'You used to say you loved me.'

'What do you want, Chris? I'm already late.'

'Oh, God!'

Rachel opened the car door and threw her bag across on to the passenger seat.

'I thought, well, I haven't seen you for a bit, I thought we could go out for a meal.'

'We don't go out for meals.'

'It looks as if we don't do anything.'

She nodded. 'That's right.'

'Rachel,' he said, standing close against the car. 'You said this was a temporary thing, while you thought things through, sorted yourself out.'

'And if I'd wanted to sort them out with you, Chris, I would have done it while we were still together.'

'Come and talk to me, for Christ's sake!'

'I can't talk to you.'

'That's nonsense.'

'Is it?'

'Absolute bloody nonsense!'

Rachel looked at him, her fingers round the door handle.

'You know you can talk to me. You can talk to anybody. It's not something you have problems with.'

'All right, then. I don't want to talk to you.'

'Wonderful!'

'I don't want to talk to you, Chris, and that's why. That's a great example of why. Because whenever I say anything that goes against what you want to hear, you don't like it.'

'Do you? Does anyone?'

'There's a difference between disagreeing and refusing to hear what somebody's saying.'

'I can hear you all right.'

'Yes, but you don't acknowledge it.'

'Oh, fine!'

'You don't accept it and move on. How on earth you manage at work I can't imagine. Not if that's the way you act.'

'My work's perfectly okay, thanks very much. The difference is that I know when I'm there and when I'm not, I can tell where one starts and the other finishes.'

'Meaning that I can't?'

'Meaning that if I react to you the way I do, it's because my emotions are involved.'

'And they're not at work, not with your clients?'

'No! Not in the same way, for Christ's sake!'

Rachel looked at her watch. She pulled the door open wider, got in and closed it firmly behind her. She turned the key in the ignition, gave it some more choke, tried again and put the engine into gear.

'You won't change your mind?' Chris said, bending towards the window.

Rachel indicated that she was pulling out from the kerb.

'Something quick to eat . . .'

He stood in the middle of the road, watching her car get smaller until it turned right into the main stream of traffic.

'How's Debbie?' Lynn Kellogg asked.

'Fine,' said Naylor, a little too hastily.

'She's been seeing the doctor?'

'Honestly, she's okay. She wasn't even sick this morning. That is, not really sick. Just . . .'

Resnick had half a pastrami and mustard on dark rye and a quarter of potato, onion and chive salad. What he didn't have was a fork. Lunching on his own he wouldn't have thought twice about using his fingers, but in front of his subordinates he had to set an example. He'd save the salad for later.

He bit into the sandwich and lifted up a brown A4 envelope with forefinger and thumb of his other hand, shaking it gently until three copies of a photograph slid down on to the desk.

'William James Doria, academic of this parish.'

Lynn Kellogg's already red cheeks deepened a tone. So he had taken her seriously. Well, good for him.

'I don't know if this is going to be any more than an irrelevant little side-show,' Resnick was saying. 'But I've had a word with the superintendent and he says we can take it a little way, see if anything shows. If we haven't got anything after, say, three days at the most, we'll chuck him back on the pile with the other also-rans and join the main party. Right?'

Both the detective constables nodded in agreement.

'Questions at this point?'

'How did we get on to him, sir?' asked Naylor.

'Lynn here interviewed him as a matter of routine. Just one more bloke writing off to box numbers. She thought there was something funny about him.'

'That's it?' Naylor said, surprised.

'He wasn't what he seemed to be,' said Lynn, emphatically.

'What was he then?'

'He was . . . creepy.'

'We're not so overburdened with suspects we can afford to ignore the gut reactions of detectives,' said Resnick, not wanting Naylor to show his lack of enthusiasm any further. 'Especially when they've been proved right in the past.'

Thank you, Lynn Kellogg thought. Thank you for that.

Maybe Naylor's spent too long teamed up with Divine, Resnick was thinking. Or perhaps that new mortgage and all that life insurance is weighing him down with care and safety.

'Is he at the Poly or the University, sir, this bloke?'

'University. Linguistics and Critical Theory.'

'What's that, sir?'

'Buggered if I know for certain,' said Resnick. 'But I know one thing, while you two are out snooping around, Patel is going to be finding out.'

Thinking a moment about Patel, Resnick wondered if the rye bread he was eating was the stuff they sent down by van from Bradford.

'How d'you want us to go about it, sir?' Lynn asked. Part of her wanted to take another shot at Doria, see if in some way she could confirm her initial feelings; against that, spending another twenty minutes alone

262

with him in that office was close to the last thing she wanted to do.

'Kevin,' Resnick said, 'Lynn got a list from Doria of all the women he claims to have met through these ads. It goes back two years and there are sixteen names.'

'I'm surprised he's got the time,' said Naylor.

'No? You should see his timetable. With a workload like that he could manage sixteen women a week.'

Resnick glanced across at Lynn, worried in case he'd just said something sexist, but her expression gave away nothing. He wondered if she had been the one who'd ripped up Divine's girlie calendar? One of these days he'd have to ask her.

'Anyway,' Resnick said, 'I want you, Kevin, to go and talk to them. Just gently. Do they remember him? Where did they go, how did he strike them? Oh, and was it just the one date or more?'

'Yes, sir,' Naylor said, writing quickly in his notebook.

'Two years is a long time,' Resnick continued. 'They might be in who knows what relationship by now; they might not want to be reminded. Nurse them along.'

Naylor blinked. 'Um, what, sir, am I looking for exactly?'

Did he try and strangle them with their own scarves or bash them to bits in their own back garden, Resnick said to himself.

'One,' he said aloud, 'did any of them come away from this Doria with feelings in some sense similar to Lynn's? Anything that suggests he might be a little bit odd.'

'Kinky, d'you mean, sir?'

'Not necessarily. But not necessarily not. And, yes, if there's some way of finding out what went on sexually, if it did, that might be useful, too.'

Resnick leaned across and pointed to one name.

263

'Marian Witczak. I know her. Seen her this morning. I'll write it up and chuck it in with the rest, but for what it's worth, she didn't think he was strange at all. Bright as a button and charming as Fred Astaire.'

'I always thought he was creepy, too,' said Lynn.

'Fred Astaire?' Resnick and Naylor almost chorused.

'Yes. He's so, oh, smarmy.'

'Tell that to Ginger Rogers,' said Resnick.

'Do you know,' Lynn said, sitting forward, 'all those dances they did together, they never as much as kissed, off screen, I mean. I don't think she even liked him.'

'Torvill and Dean,' said Naylor.

Resnick finished his sandwich and called the meeting back to order. 'Lynn, spend some time hanging round the campus, use the bar, the cafeteria. Talk to some students, see if you can find anyone who takes one of his courses; even better, someone doing research, a student he's likely to spend quite a bit of time with alone.'

Lynn looked up and nodded. 'You don't want me to go and talk to Doria again, sir?'

'No,' said Resnick. 'Not yet.'

Halfway home, estate agents and clerical assistants sitting alone in their cars and inhaling one another's lead and carbon monoxide, Resnick suddenly realized what he had failed to do. Failed to ask for. Annoyance at his own foolishness fired adrenalin through him and he swung out from the double line of traffic, warning lights flashing and headlights on full beam, one hand on the horn. Drivers heading in the opposite direction shouted and shook their fists, but moved over just the same. Resnick made a quarter of a mile before tagging across a series of residential side-streets and finally skirting a

264

roundabout that took him back into the same section of the city he had visited that morning.

'Charles,' Marian Witczak had the door held on the chain and was peering through the crack, surprise darkening her eyes. 'Something is wrong?' She closed the door so as to free the chain. 'Come in, come in, please.'

She looked at him anxiously, rubbing one hand against the apron she was wearing over her green dress. Instead of the soft leather shoes, there were thick multi-coloured socks on her feet.

'I forgot . . .' Resnick began.

'About Doria? But I have already told . . .'

'No, but the letters. The letters he sent to you.'

'Yes?'

'You don't happen to have kept them, I suppose?'

'Oh, Charles!' She laid her hand over his forearm, a gesture of affection. 'Of course, they would have given you – what? – clues. That is what you policemen are always seeking. The one strand of yellow hair, a button torn from a jacket, the fatal footprint – see, Charles, I have read many mystery stories. Many.'

'But after you read the letters . . .' Resnick made an empty gesture with his hands.

Marian smiled a little, remembering. 'Oh, I kept them, Charles.'

'You did?'

'My first love letters in twenty years. Almost twenty years. And I suppose I am not deluding myself to call them that. In the old-fashioned sense that is what he was doing, making love to me with his clever words, reassuring and clever – what he had been reading, seeing at the theatre, exhibitions, experiences that we might share if only I would relent.'

Marian set a hand towards her face and lowered her

cheek to meet it. The pendulum movement at Resnick's back seemed unnaturally loud.

'Your visit this morning made me think – about why after that almost perfect evening he did not wish to see me again.' She let her hand slide clear of her face, not looking at Resnick now but instead at some invisible spot on the wall close by the door. 'I think it was because he no longer felt it necessary. It was a game you see, a game of wits and he had won it. The moment my note to him arrived saying that, yes, I would be delighted to go to the concert with him, that was his victory. Of course, he had to carry the evening off in style, gain my approval further so that when we parted he would know that the instant he asked to see me again, I would so readily say yes.' She allowed herself a brief smile of regret. 'For Doria, that was enough.'

'Not for you?' said Resnick softly.

The smile broadened, changed, faded. 'Yes. No. Everything I have learned tells me that my answer should be yes, it was enough for me too.'

'But?'

'But if that had been his finger upon the bell, his face I saw when I opened the door . . .' She made a small shrugging movement with her shoulders. 'I am sorry about the letters. If you had asked me as little as three months ago I could have taken you to the drawer and shown you them all.'

'Never mind,' Resnick said. 'One of those things.'

'Those foolish things, eh, Charles? *The winds of March that make my heart a dancer.*' She half sang the lines, her accent more pronounced. *A telephone that rings, but who's to answer?*

She was standing close to him and her hands were in his; her eyes were glistening, but if there were tears waiting she was too proud to let them fall.

'Did you know an Englishman wrote that stupid song, Charles?'

'Jack Strachey,' said Resnick.

'What did he know of life?' Marian said.

Twenty-Seven

'Do you know there are idiots out there still dropping a postcard in the box, meet you by the lions eight o'clock, I'll be the one with a ferret down me trousers, and there's other bloody idiots trouping out there to meet 'em!'

Colin Rich had a mug of tea in one hand and a wedge of bread pudding in the other. He was leaning up against a plate-glass window, one storey up. Resnick put temptation behind him and tasted the coffee from the urn.

'It's as bad as these silly sods sticking bloody needles in themselves, or diddling some scrubber round the side of the pub without wacking a johnny on their plonker first. Daft bastards! Deserve what they bloody get!'

Resnick threw the coffee out of the window instead.

'How's the intellectual life, Charlie?'

'Quiet, sir.'

'Did you go to University, Charlie, I can't remember?' Skelton asked, scarcely looking up from the notes he was making with a meticulous hand.

'No, sir. Never got round to it somehow.'

'Lot of life on the campuses in those days, Charlie. Especially if you were in a bit of new red-brick. Spent more time sitting in and marching than studying, I'm afraid.'

Bet you got a First, though, didn't you, sir? Resnick didn't say.

'Matter of fact, anyone who dug deep enough into my record, they'd find me listed on a couple of Special Branch files – under Danger to the Security of the Realm, I shouldn't wonder. Look at me now.'

Resnick did as he was told.

Skelton set aside his pen, screwing the cap back first. 'Andy Hunt's getting hot under the collar about the chap who works on the railway. Two women said he turned nasty when they wouldn't let him have what he thought was his due at the end of the evening. Knocked one of them around a little, nothing too serious, though apparently she was sitting at the check-out at Sainsbury's with a black eye for a week. The second one, however, that was nastier. Pulled a knife on her and held it to her throat while she . . .' the superintendent's voice changed key . . . 'masturbated him.'

'Didn't report it at the time?'

Skelton shook his head. 'Neither of them.'

'This second lass, any chance she'll make a complaint now?'

'Unlikely. Doesn't seem to think her husband will understand.'

'If it goes to court, it'll come out whatever she wants.'

'Seems she's prepared to take that risk. Besides . . .'

'You don't reckon him?'

'Agreed to an intimate search right off. Paid no attention to his solicitor warning him not to. No comeback from forensic yet, but my bet is that the results will clear him, no matter how much Andy wants it to go the other way.'

'Somebody ought to have words with that man about his courting technique.'

'Don't worry,' said Skelton. 'Unofficially, somebody will. I thought I'd let Rich read him a sermon or two. Potential serious crime, after all.'

'At least they'll talk the same language.'

Skelton uncapped his fountain-pen, thought about writing something, stopped.

'My hopes lie with this laddie Bernard Grafton's come up with.'

'His psychiatric case.'

'Exactly. Spent nine months in residential care after finding himself up in court for exposing himself outside the nurses' home.'

'Wasting his time there, sir,' said Resnick. 'They must be sick of it.'

'There was some doubt about his intentions; he was worried himself he might have attacked one of them on her way back off shift. Nothing happened, other than in his mind, so there wasn't any charge. But the probation officer put in a pretty useful Social Enquiry Report and hence the treatment. Apparently . . .' Skelton turned over some pieces of paper on his desk until he found the correct one . . . 'while he was a patient he asked for a drug which would curb his sexual urges and was put on a course of Androcur. Things improved, chappie was released but the medication was terminated.'

'Things deteriorated,' put in Resnick.

'Quite. Nevertheless, by this time he'd given up being a Peeping Tom for more legal diversions.'

'I think I can guess,' said Resnick.

'He wrote off to two-dozen women in the space of three months and five of them agreed to meet him. One of these he passed up on, hasn't said why. One look at her outside the wherever it was and he scarpered. But the other four – well, they're still being interviewed, though none of them seem to have been in any doubt that they'd got themselves saddled with a right funny one. We should have full statements by this time tomorrow.'

'Sounds interesting, sir,' agreed Resnick, almost reluctantly.

Skelton stood up behind his desk, tapping the end of his pen lightly against it. 'Tell you something you'll likely find even more interesting, Charlie.'

'Yes, sir?'

'The fifth woman, the one he walked away from, according to him she was Shirley Peters.'

The melody of 'Moonlight Serenade' was unmistakable. Resnick zipped himself up and ran the tap as the toilet flushed and Graham Millington emerged, still whistling.

'It *is* you,' Resnick said, drying his hands.

'Sir?'

'Glenn Miller all over the place.'

'Yes, sir.' Millington squinted at his moustache in the mirror; why did it always seem fuller on the left than the right, no matter how carefully he trimmed it? 'I've got this tape I play in the car.'

'Don't you get fed up with it?'

'No, sir. That is, I don't know really.' He shrugged, waiting for Resnick to finish with the roller towel. 'Never thought about it, I suppose.'

'Perhaps you should.'

'Sir?'

'Think about it. For the sake of the rest of us.'

'Right, sir.' What is he on about, thought Millington, bemused. What's Glenn Miller got to do with anything?

'Anything fresh on your wrestler?' Resnick asked. They were heading back towards the CID room.

'Not yet, sir.'

271

'Tell you what to do,' said Resnick.

Millington stopped outside the door and waited.

'DI Grafton's pinning his hopes on a one-time psychiatric patient who ducked out on a date with Shirley Peters. See if you can get a word with him, find out why.'

Millington shrugged. 'Didn't fancy her.'

'Or he's lying about walking away from her without as much as a hello.'

'I'll get on to it, sir,' said Millington, pushing open the door.

'Sooner rather than later.'

Instead of following his sergeant into the office, Resnick turned down the stairs in the direction of the street.

Once you'd tossed out the junk mail, there wasn't a great deal left. Resnick ignored the persistent cries of his cats long enough to grind some coffee and dump it in the filter. A bit of Basie would serve to cleanse the good Major from his mind: there wasn't a moon in the sky anyway, just a drizzle of rain, falling like fine gauze through the dark.

'Dizzy! Eat that fast and you'll have indigestion the whole evening.'

There was a letter from a long-stay prisoner he'd nicked and seen sent down to Parkhurst, two sides of recycled paper explaining how he'd found peace through Buddha, though it hadn't done anything about the quality of the food. In a brown envelope, a second reminder about his subscription to the Polish Association. Resnick lifted his elbows and flexed his shoulders backwards, seeking to do something about the stiffness along his spine. He took his coffee black with a shot of Scotch, carrying it, along with the remaining letter, to his favourite armchair. The postmark was local, the writing small enough to have had the postman reaching for his spectacles. Resnick slit the top of the envelope open with the end of his spoon.

Dear Charles,
   I am not certain if forgetting the enclosed was a trick of the memory, or merely a straightforward attempt to ignore my own sentimentality. In either case, be so kind as to destroy it when it is of no further use to you.
   Sincerely,
                            Marian Witczak

Resnick slipped the card from beneath the paperclip which held it to the sheet of writing paper. It was cream in colour, an expensive, satiny surface, smooth to the touch. Pepper burbled at the side of the chair and jumped on to Resnick's lap where he turned twice and settled.

My Dear Marian,
   I can only hope your evening was as pleasant as mine. I cannot recall attending a concert with a companion who was both as charming and as apposite as yourself!
   Let us both look forward to the time when the future presents us with as suitable an occasion for mutual delight and stimulation.
   In friendship and admiration—
                            William Doria

A quarter of an inch from the bottom of the card, a horizontal line was broken at its centre by the embossed burgundy letters *W. J. Doria*. Above, the writing was in matt black ink, so studied that each word seemed drawn rather than written. The circles of the *o*s and *a*s were beautifully rounded, precise and not extravagant;

only in the capitals was there a flourish, a sense of abandonment – the way the lower stroke of the *L* swerved beneath the rest of *Let*, the sweep of the *W* in his own name, continuing until it almost met the *D* *of Doria*, dipping to dot the *is* along the way.

When Resnick had stared at the card long enough, he reached sideways towards his coffee cup, disturbing a disgruntled Pepper, who jumped clear of his legs in disgust.

He was bringing the cup to his lips when the phone rang, startling a splash of lukewarm coffee over the front of his shirt.

'I was about to ring off.'

'Sorry. I was busy pouring coffee over myself.'

'I hope you didn't miss your tie.'

'No chance,' said Resnick, rubbing at it with his free hand.

'Just want to be able to recognize you when I see you.'

'I thought you'd given up on me.'

'I had.'

Resnick shifted his weight from one foot to the other, switched the receiver from left to right. Was she serious?

'I've been trying to phone you,' Rachel said. 'Either you're somewhere else and nobody knows when you'll be back, or they don't know where you are anyway.' She paused. 'Charlie, you haven't given instructions that I'm to be given the runaround, have you?'

'Why would you think I'd do that?'

'I don't know. Maybe because I was sure you'd call me and you didn't.'

Resnick didn't say anything.

'You didn't try me at home, did you?'

'You told me not to.'

'I know.'

'What's wrong with . . .?'

'I think it's time we went out to dinner, Charlie.'

He was smiling. 'You think so.'

'Don't you?'

'It's a possibility.'

'It's twenty-past seven.'

Resnick looked across the room. 'Is that relevant?'

'It is if you're going to meet me at eight-thirty.'

'Tonight?'

'You haven't already eaten, have you?'

'No, but . . .'

'Fine. I get to choose the restaurant.'

'How come?'

'I'm paying.'

'Oh, no. If we're . . .'

'Charlie, just listen to me. It's a celebration. My treat. All right?'

He was picturing her that first day he had seen her at court. How could a disembodied voice conjure up so clearly the dark fall of hair against collar and face, the smallest splash of blue against brown leather?

'What are we celebrating?' he asked.

'Wait until I see you.'

'Okay. Do you want me to pick you up, meet you, what?'

'Meet me.'

'Where?'

'Between the lions, of course.'

What had Colin Rich said about the idiots out there? 'Aren't we a little old for that kind of thing?'

'Speak for yourself, Charlie!'

He had been.

'Half-eight, then,' he said.

'I'll try to be fashionably late,' Rachel said, a laugh in her voice.

'Not too fashionable, it's raining.'

'Charlie, I promise you, we won't notice.'

He wondered what she would say if she could see him standing there, grinning like – yes, Colin Rich had been right for once – like a happy idiot.

'Oh, and Charlie . . .'

'Um?'

'Whatever you're wearing . . .'

'What about it?'

'Change it.'

Twenty-Eight

To the north of the Old Market Square was the site of
the Black Boy Hotel, designed by Watson Fothergill
and where Resnick and his friend Ben Riley used to
drink early on a Saturday night before things started
to move too fast. Now it was an expanse of ugly brick
wall barely disguised as a Littlewood's store. On the
south side the front of the Running Horse hotel was
dated 1483, but the rubble behind it was more recent.
On their rare trips up from Hayward's Heath to visit,
his in-laws had stayed there and complained about the
service and the sound of the traffic.

The steps between the stone lions were peopled with
punks and kids in leathers, girls in coats from Top Shop
or Miss Selfridge trying not to keep looking at their
watches, a couple of lads in shirtsleeves being 'tough'.

Half of them, Resnick thought, have me figured for
a copper on duty, the rest are imagining something
worse. He knew Rachel was in the square before he
saw her, a tensing of the nerve-ends turning his head
and opening his eyes. She was crossing behind one of
the fountains, hands resting easily inside the pockets
of her camel coat, face glowing in the street lights and
the shine of wet paving. The heels of her boots clicked
a crisp rhythm against the steps as Resnick stepped out
to greet her. Her hair was up and her face lifted towards
him, smiling.

'See. I'm not late.'

'Not very.'

The corner of her mouth when it brushed against his cheek was almost warm, though her face was cold.

'Come on,' Rachel said, linking her arm through his and turning him to walk up King Street. 'We're going this way.'

He had no sense of it still raining.

The restaurant was on the first floor, alongside a Chinese supermarket. There were tables lining both sides of an L-shaped room, most of them occupied. The waiter who took their coats said, 'Good evening, Miss Chaplin,' in a voice that was already more East Midlands than either Hong Kong or Peking. He showed them to a table by the window and Resnick knew that this was where she usually sat, those times she had been there with Chris Phillips, possibly with others too; her place, her territory, her celebration.

A waitress in starched white brought Resnick a bottle of Chinese beer and Rachel a vodka and tonic.

'Cheers,' Resnick said, lifting his glass. 'To whatever.'

'Independence,' Rachel said.

The waiter opened large, leather-bound menus in front of them and stepped discreetly away.

'I'd never seen you as anything else,' said Resnick.

'All I can say is, I wish others saw me through your eyes.'

'You mean Chris?'

She drank a little more vodka. 'We had it all spelled out, the two of us. What it was about and what it wasn't. Lots of dos and don'ts. Top of the list: don't become possessive, don't become dependent. We spent evening after evening talking it through, testing one another, what we thought we wanted.' She laughed disparagingly. 'Making lists.'

Love, Resnick wanted to ask, what about love?

'Lists are all right for Tesco's,' he said.

'And as long as you remember to take them with you.'

'You're saying Chris got forgetful?'

She shook her head. 'We both did.'

Resnick was wondering for how much of his marriage his wife had lain aside her ten-point plan: how to find true happiness in easy stages and still be one of the six per cent in the country to own a dishwasher.

'Eighteen months . . .'

That long, thought Resnick.

' . . . and it was as if nothing had ever been said. We were like everyone else. What time will you be back for a meal? Saturday night we've been invited to a party, to dinner, a wedding anniversary.'

'Sounds pretty normal.'

Rachel looked at him over the rim of her glasses. 'Normal, Charlie? Is that the way you live?'

'The way I live may not be altogether through choice.'

'All right, but still that choice is yours.'

'Is it?'

'Yes.'

'How can you be so certain?'

She didn't answer. 'I'd stopped thinking of myself as myself,' she said. 'I wasn't me, I was part of a couple.' She finished her drink. 'I didn't like it.'

'Couple or not,' said Resnick, 'I can't see you – what? – feeling threatened, submerged, losing your identity.'

'Nor could I until it began to happen.'

The waiter was hovering, an encouraging smile around his eyes.

'Well, Rachel Chaplin,' Resnick said, taking her

hand, 'there's no doubt in my mind exactly who you are.'

'That's what I'm banking on,' Rachel said, moving her hand away to turn a page of the menu. 'Now, shall I tell you what's good . . .?'

The monkfish and black beans spat and sizzled from a patterned iron plate.

'Sit back, Charlie. No sense in spoiling a clean shirt.'

It had taken him minutes to find one, dry and rumpled and needing water splashed liberally over it before it could be ironed. He had used his thumbnail to remove a blob of horseradish sauce from his best tie, dark red with diagonal white stripe. The shoes that he had quickly rubbed over had soon had the shine splashed out of them while walking to meet Rachel.

Rachel was wearing a pale blue blouse, ruffed and tight at neck and wrists. Silver drop ear-rings that caught the light whenever she tilted her head.

'Stop staring at me, Charlie,' she scolded, not seeming unhappy about it at all.

'It's difficult,' he said.

'Don't waste your breath, Charlie. It doesn't suit you.'

'What?'

'Whatever you were about to say. Flattery.'

'All I was going to say was . . .'

'Charlie!' She pointed a chopstick towards him, admonishingly.

'All . . .'

'Just don't!'

He grinned and diverted his attentions to lifting rice to his mouth. Even if you picked the bowl up from the table and lowered your mouth it wasn't easy. Broccoli, pieces of chicken, slices of pepper, they were easy, but rice . . .

'How long do you think you'll stay there?' he asked.

'At Carole's? I don't know. Till I feel it's time to move or until I sense that I'm getting in the way.'

'Then you'll get a place of your own?'

'Yes,' she said. 'What else?'

Keep your eyes on the food, Resnick ordered himself, and don't say it. Don't as much as think it, because if you do, she'll know.

She knew anyway.

Men! Rachel thought, with a slight shake of the head. Why do they never learn?

'It upset you, didn't it?' Rachel asked between mouthfuls. 'The verdict.'

Resnick took his time before answering. 'Only because it made me think about it again.'

'Then you still don't want to talk about it?'

'No, far from it. I do – with you – only . . . I don't know what I want to say.'

'Or think? What do you think about it, Charlie, the sentence?'

'That it wasn't enough. That it could never be enough.'

'Charlie, what good . . . ?'

'I know, I know. All the arguments. Revenge and not reform. Lock a man up and the longer he's inside the worse he'll be when he comes out.'

'You say it as though you know it without believing it.'

Resnick picked up the wine bottle and Rachel set her hand over the top of her glass; he refilled his own.

'There's nothing that clear-cut. I understand about the loss of dignity, about recidivism . . .'

'But your job . . .'

'And what I do, more often than not, more often than probably I think is wise, results in criminals being shut away. It's what happens, Rachel. It's the law, part of it. At the moment you can't have one without the other, and if I believe in most of what I do, I seem to have to accept the rest.'

'Like Sharon Taylor's father getting three years?'

'That's easier to take than most.'

'Not for him.'

'Christ!' exclaimed Resnick. 'Don't expect me to feel sympathy for him.'

Heads were angled towards them, conversations lowered. 'Everything all right, sir?' The waiter bowed to one table. 'Everything satisfactory, madam?' to another.

'I don't.'

'He'll be out and on parole in two, less.'

'You know that they'll do to him inside, as soon as they know what he's in for.'

'Yes.'

'You make it sound as if that's what he deserves.'

'It's hard not to think it.'

Rachel slowly shook her head. 'I don't understand how . . . Charlie, I may not know you very well, but I don't think you're that kind of man.'

'What kind of man is he, for Christ's sake?'

'Charlie, don't . . .'

'All I know, if that had been my child . . .'

'Oh, Charlie.' She took his hand which had closed into a fist between hers and held it for a moment against her cheek. 'Don't punish yourself more than you have to.'

What am I doing? Rachel Chaplin thought when he

was away from the table. On my own for what, a week, and I'm calling up this nice, shambling man and dangling things before his eyes I know he can't have. And why? Because I've been in too many nights in a row? Because I needed something other than Carole's too-sensible chatter to wind down with after work? Because I always did like to do the things I know are courting danger?

She turned her head as she heard him coming back towards the table, a big man with broad shoulders who moved a little like a dancer. Was it then just because she found herself fancying him, this Charlie Resnick? No more nor less than that? The muscles of her stomach wall tightened, knowing that she could go to bed with him now, that evening as soon as the meal was over, and knowing that she wouldn't.

Reaching out with her chopsticks to take the last prawn, Rachel realized there were goose-pimples along her arm. Who are you not being fair to? she asked herself, dipping the prawn in the remainder of the plum sauce before putting it in her mouth.

Neither of them had driven. Walking down the hill back into the centre of the city, they hailed an empty cab almost opposite the pub where they had first gone for a drink. Resnick suggested that they drop Rachel off first and, although it was furthest away, she agreed.

They leaned back against the seat, one of Resnick's arms across her shoulders, the back of her left hand resting against his leg. After all the talk during the meal, neither spoke until the driver turned into the street where Carole lived.

'Charlie,' Rachel said, turning to face him, 'I'm really pleased you were in when I called, pleased you came. I've had a good time tonight.'

Resnick tensed, waiting for the *but*.

'I like you, Charlie Resnick, at least I think I do, I enjoy being with you, but nothing more.'

'What more is there?'

Rachel laughed and threw back her head. 'You're impossible!'

Resnick leaned forward and kissed the stretch of muscle of her neck. She twisted slowly against him, moving her head until he was kissing her mouth. As the cab slowed to a halt, Resnick's lips parted and her tongue slid over his.

'Time to go, Charlie.'

Resnick sighed, 'Sure.'

Rachel opened the door, reaching for her purse with the other hand.

'On me,' Resnick said. 'You paid for the meal.'

'Okay,' she said, getting out.

'Next time we'll swop around,' Resnick called.

Rachel raised a hand. 'Next time you phone me.'

'Right.' Resnick closed the door and the driver swung the cab into a U-turn. He looked through the side window, but she had already turned away and was walking slowly up the path towards the front door. A few seconds and she was almost lost to shadow.

Rachel shook her bag, patted her pocket, where had she put the key? There were no lights showing in the house which meant either that Carole was out or had already gone to bed, tired out. She didn't want to stand around in the cold and damp and neither did she want to ring the bell and risk waking Carole. The sound of the cab taking Resnick away had already faded.

'Never do it, can you?'

Harsh, the words broke the darkness for a moment that for her was timeless, Rachel's heart stopped. The bag slithered between her fingers towards the path. At first she could not place even the voice, much less where it came from.

'Always amazed me, someone as organized as you, half-an-hour to find a front-door key.'

Rachel's fear became anger as Chris Phillips stepped from the shadows towards her. She wanted to hurt him for frightening her, but he caught the swing of her arm easily and held it above the wrist.

She could see that the upper sections of his raincoat were close to sodden; he was bareheaded and his hair stuck close to his scalp.

'How long have you been spying on me?' Rachel asked, shaking herself free.

'For about as long as you've been lying to me.'

'I haven't lied.'

'No?' Chris angled his head slowly back towards the road, looking in the direction that Resnick's departing cab had taken.

'You said there wasn't anybody.'

'There isn't.'

'What was that then? Some fucking apparition?'

'That was a friend.'

'I'll bet!'

Rachel turned away and walked to the front door; a light had gone on in the hall, Carole alerted by their raised voices. Her finger was almost upon the bell when an open hand smacked past her, shaking the door on its hinges.

'Don't you turn your back on me!'

'It's too late for that, Chris,' Rachel said, facing him once again. 'I already did.'

'Oh, you're so clever, aren't you?'

'I'm not trying to be clever . . .'

'Comes natural, does it?'

'Chris . . .'

'Like lying!'

'How many times, I have not been lying. Why should I? What would be the point?'

'And whoring!'

Carole was standing behind the door, her silhouette fractured by the glass. 'Let me in,' Rachel called and before she had finished speaking the door was open on to the hall.

'Hello, Chris,' Carole said in a neutral tone.

He ignored her, staring at Rachel with the same mixture of hatred and desperation she recognized from so many of her clients. He made as if to follow her and smartly Carole pushed Rachel inside and leaned against the door. Phillips was trapped with one side of his body jammed up against the wall.

'Carole, you'd better let me in!'

'I don't think so, Chris.'

'Rachel and I have got things to talk about.'

'No, we haven't,' called Rachel.

'You heard her, Chris,' said Carole.

He leaned his weight against the door and forced her back some way but not far enough for him to squeeze inside.

'You shouldn't be doing this, Chris,' Carole said. 'Go home.'

'Not until that lying bitch comes back out here to talk to me.'

'I've nothing left to say to you,' said Rachel, back at Carole's shoulder, 'and if I ever did, this has made me see the pointlessness of it. Just go.'

'Go, Chris,' echoed Carole.

'And if I don't?'

'Don't be even stupider than you have already,' said Rachel.

'Send for the police, why don't you? Your friend the fascist can come roaring up on his charger and practise a bit of that well-known police brutality. That's what turns you on these days, is it? Handcuffs and truncheons in the back of a blue van.'

Rachel wrenched the door back from Carole's hands and slammed it forward again with all her weight and anger behind it. If Chris Phillips hadn't jumped back in time, he would have lost a couple of fingers at least. As it was, one of the panels of glass splintered across from corner to corner and the whole door reverberated in its frame for several seconds.

Deftly, Carole slipped the bolt into place, followed by the chain; lastly, she turned the key in the second, mortice, lock.

'Leave him,' she said.

They sat in the kitchen at the back of the house, Carole drinking tea, Rachel gin. Each time there was an unexplained sound they thought it was Chris, moving around outside the house, but neither of them referred to it. Rachel told her friend about the Chinese meal in specific detail, not missing a flavour or a dish. On several occasions during her narrative she considered going to the phone and calling Resnick, but she always stopped herself.

At half-past midnight, Carole went upstairs and, without switching on any of the lights, looked out. Chris Phillips was standing much where he had been the best part of an hour before, hunched in the middle of the path. She went quietly back down and poured Rachel another drink.

When next she went to look it was a few minutes short of one o'clock and both the path and the street were empty.

Twenty-Nine

If there was one thing worse to read than computer print-out, it was microfiche. Patel had been moving between the two for hours already, alternating between the main catalogues on the ground floor and the more specialized information that was kept up on the second floor. Annotations spiralled over his notebook: publications, articles, conferences, papers. All against the constant hum of the central heating and, below, the criss-cross of students between the issue counter and short loan, the photocopying machines and the coffee bar.

Patel realized that when he had gone to University, he had been so overjoyed at simply being there, buoyed up by the pride and enthusiasm of his family, that he had never been able to put the experience into any context. The first to arrive at lectures, one of the few to stay behind for the obligatory and bored, 'If there are any questions afterwards, of course I'd be very happy . . .', Patel had filled block after block of loose-leaf paper without his imagination ever truly becoming engaged. Revising, panicking, he had been unable to read most of his frantic scrawling, had difficulty in remembering the sense of what he could. Fortunately, for his family the degree was enough – he had needed to bribe no fewer than five fellow-graduates to obtain sufficient tickets for the ceremony – the grade immaterial.

The police recruitment officer had paid almost as little attention. 'One of them bright little buggers, eh?'

'Yes, sir. I mean, no, not really, sir.'

Patel still flushed at the memory.

He stood in a short, animated queue and tried not to listen to the argument, detailed and specific, the couple in front were having about the relationship between alcohol and orgasms. Sitting with his styrofoam cup of instant coffee and his Kit-Kat, he hoped for a chance remark about Professor Doria, but was unrewarded. A student with blonde hair sleek as a swimming-cap took her place in the queue, smack in Patel's eyeline. A university scarf was wrapped several times around the top of her short blue duffle coat; there appeared to be nothing below the thigh-length hem but long legs and yellow and white running-shoes. Chocolate melted over Patel's fingers as he hurried away, back to the stacks.

'I was wondering, sir, well, about a transfer . . .' Naylor stood back from Resnick's desk, feet together, fingers fidgeting with the notebook held against his stomach.

'Best give Graham Souness a ring,' Resnick said, not looking up. 'He's buying anything that moves for Rangers these days.'

Naylor blinked. The last thing he'd expected or wanted had been a joke – that had been a joke, hadn't it?

'It's Debbie, sir. You see, now that she's . . . now that the baby's . . . well, it's a matter of where's the best place for it to grow up and . . .'

Resnick contained a sigh and set aside his pen. Sleep was something he hadn't had a lot of, his working hours seemed to be yielding less and less time, the superintendent was ever more disinclined to let him go his own way.

'It's a backwater, Charlie,' Skelton had said. 'That's my worry.'

'Up the creek again without a bloody paddle!' Colin Rich had laughed.

Now this.

'I don't want you to think I'm not happy here,' Naylor was stumbling on. 'I am, and I've learnt a lot, from you, I mean, and if it was up to me . . .'

'Kevin, Kevin,' Resnick waved him into silence. 'A minute. All right?'

'Yes, sir.' Naylor was looking at the far wall, the words he hadn't been able to get out continuing to steeplechase around his head.

'First off, if it's a matter of loyalties, you owe more to this kid of yours than to me. Clear?'

Naylor nodded. 'Yes, sir.'

'Second, there's a specific transfer procedure and, while it's good manners to inform me, I'm not the person you should be talking to at this stage.'

'Sir.'

'And, thirdly, and for what it's worth, what you and Debbie might give some thought to is this – maybe the where of bringing kids up is less important than the how.'

'Yes, sir.' Naylor's toes were wriggling inside his shoes. What had he been doing, coming into the inspector's office and starting all of this?

'Now,' Resnick said, matter-of-factly, 'how've you been getting on with that list of Doria's assignations?'

Lynn Kellogg had found a pair of bottle-green dungarees near the bottom of her wardrobe; a bulky sweater that, when you held it to the face, still carried the smell

290

of poultry; a soft black beret; worn-down ankle boots and a pair of striped leg warmers. All right, it wasn't what this year's students were wearing, not exactly, but it had that magpie quality which told of jumble sales and hand-me-downs. After which, the first students she got into conversation with all had hooray voices, sports cars their daddies had bought them as eighteenth-birthday presents and were actually terribly disappointed not to be at Girton.

A couple of days of drifting along corridors and about the campus, sitting in the canteen over pie, chips and beans and apricot crumble, browsing the shelves in the bookshop, hadn't yielded much more than a sense of frustration. She heard Professor Doria's name directly once, loitering by the Linguistics section. The student, tall with bad breath, responded to the first of her smiled questions, then bolted midway through the second, leaving an unpaid-for pile of books in his wake.

Linguistics and the After-Text. New York and London. Oxford University Press, 1975.

'A New Look at Poetry and Repression'. *Critical Inquiry*, v (1979).

'Coming out of the Unconscious'. *Modern Language Notes*, xcv (1980).

Nietzsche and Woman: Provocation and Closure. Chicago, Ill, and London. University of Chicago Press, 1983.

'(You said all you wanted was) A Sign, My Love. Deconstruction and Popular Culture'. University of Birmingham Centre for Contemporary Cultural Studies, 1984.

Deconstruction and Defacement. New York and London. Methuen, 1986.

Patel took a break from Doria's list of publications and rested his head in his arms. The words were beginning to jump and blur. Until now he'd been the only one of his family not to need glasses. He wondered about taking a break; the rain had eased off and he could walk between the trees and down the hill to the Sports Centre, take a shower. He ought to do something before two-fifteen. Doria was lecturing to the combined second- and third-year groups of his course and Patel had every intention of being there. He had been into the student shop and bought a new A4 pad for the occasion.

'What I don't understand, sir,' Naylor was saying, 'is what he's doing with someone like this – what's her name? – Sally Oakes? I mean, I know there's nothing wrong with working in the Virgin Megastore, but that's all she does, and on top of that she's . . .'

'Young enough to be his daughter,' Resnick finished for him. 'It isn't unknown, Kevin. Older men and younger women, young women and older men.'

'I know, sir. But take a look at the others. A fifty-year-old Anglican deaconess and this one, a Local Studies librarian who spends all her spare time clambering over rocks in the Peak District, and the manageress of one of them posh clothes shops along Bridlesmith Gate.' He wrinkled his nose, perplexed. 'There's no pattern to it.'

'Likes variety, the professor.'

Naylor pushed two sheets of typing paper, sellotaped together, across Resnick's desk. 'Look here, sir. Eighteen months, four different women, each of them he takes out at least three times.'

'Sally Oakes, five,' observed Resnick. 'That's the most.'

'He's not waiting until he's through with one . . .'

'Or they're through with him . . .'

'Before he's on to the next. Look at the way they overlap.'

'With Oakes threaded through the middle, neat as you like, once every, what, six weeks?'

'Just about, sir.'

Resnick sighed and leaned backwards, taking the chair on to its rear legs. 'The last time she saw him was between two and three months back.'

'Yes, sir.'

'Why nothing more?'

'She told him she didn't want to see him again.'

'She told him?'

'Yes, sir,' said Naylor positively.

'Did she say why?'

'Got a regular bloke, sir. Didn't see any way she could go on meeting the professor.'

'Did she say how he took that?'

Naylor's eyes darted quickly away. 'No, sir.'

'You didn't ask?'

'No, sir.'

'Don't worry.' Resnick stood up and walked round the desk. How long was the gap between Sally Oakes finishing their intermittent relationship and the first murder? Without working it out exactly, Resnick figured it would be somewhere in the region of six weeks.

'Well done, young Kevin,' he said. 'You've done good work. Next thing, I think we should go and have another chat with Sally Oakes.' And he turned away to avoid the most excessive of Naylor's blushes.

The lecture room was steeply sloped, with curved rows of bench seats and writing surfaces focused upon a blackboard, a screen, twin easels peppered with a flourish of names in many colours, a podium. The room was three-quarters full: students whose pain of comprehension showed on their faces, those who wrote continuously, others for whom the briefest of notes sufficed; a balding young man with acne and an Aran sweater spent the whole hour designing an intricate spider's web with the finest of art pens; a girl, redheaded, front and centre, kept her eyes closed, an expression of bliss on her face.

Patel's attention seldom shifted from Doria.

The professor's technique was to speak in moderate tones from the podium, referring from time to time to a stack of five by three cards, each one moved to the bottom once used. This was interrupted again and again by a sudden swirl towards the matching easels, a name writ large across an A1 sheet, left for several moments before being torn away, screwed into a ball and hurled aside. Lists of books and articles that had been on the board when the lecture began were pointed at, prodded, underlined, extolled as essential. At inconsistent intervals, Doria deserted the podium to sit on or lean along the front bench, his delivery becoming more familiar as he dispensed anecdotes about the Late Quartets of Beethoven, the solos of Thelonius Monk, stories by Borges, Karl Schwitters, the pervasive influence of Brian Clough upon English football in general and the Forest midfield in particular.

Along with the others, Patel enjoyed these, laughed and at the same time struggled to understand their relevance.

Once, moving swiftly away from one of these brief alightings, Doria allowed his hand to brush against the red hair of the student seated in the middle. Patel could not see her face clearly, could only imagine that, if anything, it became more blissful.

'Remember, for Derrida, "writing" has a special meaning. For him, it denotes "free play", that part of any and all systems of communication which cannot finally be pinned down, which are ultimately undecidable. Writing, for Derrida, does not codify, it does not limit. Rather, triumphantly, wonderfully, it displaces meaning, it dismantles order, defies both the safe and the sane. It is,' Doria sang out, one arm aloft, 'excess!'

The last word echoed from the ceiling before fading to a slow silence. Seats went up, students shuffled out. At the podium Doria was reassembling his note cards into sets and placing each within a different coloured envelope.

Patel's head was buzzing. He looked at the top sheet of his pad, at phrases he had written down because they had struck him as important without clearly understanding why. It had been exhilarating, as he imagined skiing must be, diving beneath the Barrier Reef.

The girl with red hair had thanked the professor softly for his lecture but if he heard her then he gave no sign.

Patel was one of only three or four students dawdling behind. He was almost at the bottom step and heading towards the door when Doria's voice stopped him.

'I don't think I've seen you at these classes before.'

'No,' said Patel with deference. 'No, that's correct.'

'You are not taking one of my courses?'

'I'm afraid not.'

'Another in the department, perhaps?'

'Mechanical engineering,' said Patel hopefully.

Doria was looking at him keenly, smiling now with his eyes. 'I have long argued for a less rigid approach to inter-disciplinary studies,' said Doria with a tone of regret. 'Alas, breaking down such rigid barriers . . .' He smiled at Patel suddenly. 'What we want is a deconstructive approach to the formalism of the academic syllabus, wouldn't you say?'

'Yes,' said Patel. 'Yes, I would.'

He was conscious of the professor's eyes watching him to the door and he made himself turn, careful to take his time. 'Thank you for the lecture, Professor Doria. It was really interesting.'

Doria made a short bow of the head and shoulders and Patel left the room.

Thirty

'What's the coffee like?'

Kevin Naylor looked beyond the T-shirts and the cassettes towards the cafeteria. 'No idea, sir.'

Resnick walked closer: it looked like a Gaggia machine to him. 'Where does this Sally work?'

Naylor pointed towards the basement. 'Chart albums, all the rock stuff, it's down below.'

'Have a word with the manager, manageress, whatever, get the girl a break. We'll talk over there.'

He ordered a double espresso, which caused some confusion, and carried it to a table by the far wall. The cafeteria was raised up above the rest of the floor, spacious; there were green plants and video screens and if you could shut your ears to the inanities of the in-house DJ it was pleasant enough.

The coffee wasn't as strong as it could have been, not as strong as at the Italian stall in the market. They were probably using the wrong beans. He had almost finished it by the time Naylor appeared with Sally Oakes: even when you've got no clear expectations, thought Resnick, it's possible to be surprised.

For a start she was slight, her black T-shirt and jeans seemed to hang from her by default; he knew her age, nineteen, but he hadn't expected her to look it. Her light brown hair was cut in a fuzzy stubble that suggested it would fold back against the hand like fur. There was a silver stud, shaped like a star, in her left nostril, a chunky bracelet of ornamented black leather round her left wrist.

She looked at Resnick curiously before sitting down, as if wondering if she wanted to be there at all.

'Are you his boss?' she asked, nodding in the direction of Naylor.

'Sort of.'

Sally Oakes sniffed.

'Coffee?' Resnick asked.

'Coke.'

'Espresso for me,' Resnick said to Naylor. 'Large.'

When Naylor had gone to the counter, Resnick introduced himself.

'You got a cigarette?' she asked.

'Afraid not.'

Sally Oakes swung up from her chair and went to where a couple of young men were sitting at a table, eating baked potatoes. Resnick watched her lean over them, asking first for a cigarette, then for a light. He was certain that she didn't know them, nor they her.

'So what's he done, old William James?' she asked, letting the smoke drift up from her nostrils.

'Has he done something?'

'You playing me around or what?' She swallowed some of the Coke, her eyes shifting across to Naylor and back again. 'First him and then you.' She sniffed. 'Not me you're interested in, is it?'

Resnick stirred his coffee. 'What do you think he might have done? Always assuming that he has.'

'I don't know, do I?'

'Guess.'

She blinked her eyes rapidly in annoyance. 'Computer games for policemen, is it? Dungeons and dragons. Got to make a move or it all grinds to a standstill.'

'Something like that.'

She blinked again through the smoke. She knows, Resnick thought, she knows or at least she suspects, but she's not saying.

'How come you went out with him?' Resnick asked, switching tack. 'On the surface it doesn't seem made in heaven.'

'I thought it'd be a laugh.'

'And was it?'

Sally drew on the cigarette, angling her head to one side. 'No it wasn't.'

'Still you carried on going out with him. Over a year.'

'He was interesting. I never said he wasn't interesting.'

'But?'

'But nothing.' she shrugged.

'But you stopped seeing him.'

'I was going steady.'

'You could have carried on meeting him if you'd wanted to, said he was your uncle.'

'That what you get them to say, is it?'

Resnick grinned back at her. Naylor, who had been in the act of drinking his cappuccino, spluttered bubbles into it and finished up half-choking and with a cream and chocolate moustache.

'You'd have stopped seeing him anyway, wouldn't you?' Resnick asked. 'After that last time.'

'What d'you mean?'

'After what happened that last time.'

'What do you know?'

'Only what you'll tell me.'

Sally Oakes showed Resnick her profile and took two, three deep drags on the cigarette. The DJ severed his love affair with himself long enough to play Nina Simone's 'My Baby Just Cares For Me.'

'Can I have another Coke?'

Resnick signalled for Naylor not to hurry back.

'The first time, the first couple of times,' Sally Oakes said, 'I thought he wasn't really interested, in anything happening, you know, sex. Then I realized what he was interested in, what he wanted me to do ... well, he wanted to watch me, you know. So I thought, okay, fine, he wants to play with himself. I mean, if it was good enough for Elvis ...' She stubbed out the cigarette. 'Then, we'd been to this bar, a couple of bands were playing, just local, he'd been doing his usual thing of listening half the time like they were, you know, God's gift to music and the rest bending my ear about some high-faluting theory or other, honest, I used to switch off. So, we got to my room and I thought, okay, a quick run through the usual, but this time it's different and he's all over the place, trying to stick it here, there and everywhere and, Christ, I'm wondering what I've got myself into when all of a sudden he jumps up and he's off in the bathroom – I don't know what he's doing in there except I suppose he's jerking himself off, but when he comes back it's all those old jokes about cold showers and he just wants to sit there with a mug of Horlicks in one hand, the other inside my knickers and some German film boring the arse off Channel Four just for a change.'

Sitting with her back towards Naylor, who had turned a lovely shade of puce, she reached round for the glass and drank half of the Coke right down.

'Is that the way it went on?' Resnick asked. 'After that.'

'You're joking! If it had've been, that would have been it, then and there. No, he went back to fooling around for half-an-hour at the end of the evening and going through the tapes I'd brought back from this place. Hip-hop, that's what he seemed keen on.'

I'll bet, thought Resnick.

'Tell me about the last time, Sally,' he said. 'If you don't mind.'

'It was like before, the one I told you about before. One minute it's all four-syllable words and the next we're down to four-letter ones and he's got me rolling on the floor while he's...' She stopped and lowered her voice still further, her eyes fixed on Resnick's face. 'There are some things I don't mind, more than a lot of girls maybe, but I don't mind telling you ... he hurt me.'

'You mean, he hit you?'

'No. He hurt me.'

Resnick wondered what Millington and Mark Divine were laughing about and quickly decided he'd rather not know.

He'd taken Lynn Kellogg out from the University and sent her off to talk with Sally Oakes, see if there wasn't something else to be learned. The girl would most likely agree to make a statement now, but to what avail he still wasn't certain.

Graham Millington turned away from Divine, still laughing, intending to answer a telephone, and spotted Resnick.

'Got a minute, sir,' he said, hurrying forward.

Mark Divine picked up the phone instead.

'He's a hot one,' Millington enthused. 'No two ways about it.'

'You thought that about our friendly neighbourhood wrestler,' Resnick reminded him.

'Sloman,' scoffed Millington. 'Still wouldn't trust him further than Big Daddy could throw him.'

'But this is different?'

'Inspector Grafton's pretty set on him, any road.'

'Graham, we all get set on anything that looks more than halfway possible. We all want to see this thing over. Either that or some other woman's going to finish her evening like Shirley Peters and Mary Sheppard.'

'I know, sir, but . . .'

'I would have bet a couple of months' pay away it was Macliesh, domestic violence, open and shut. You went after Sloman because some of the facts seemed to fit, because he looked as if he could have done it. What's different here?'

What's the matter with the man, Millington thought? He's beginning to sound more like counsel for the defence.

'For one thing, sir, there's his mental history. I mean he's not only a psycho, he's a self-confessed sexual maniac into the bargain.'

'Confessed to the thought, not the deed.'

'He says.'

'Do we know any different?'

'There's a psychiatrist's report. According to that, if he comes off his drugs then he's likely to be as randy as a buck rabbit in season.'

'The psychiatrist said that?'

'More or less. I mean, that was the gist of it.'

'Thanks for the translation.' Irony was wasted on Millington.

'Then there's this business with Shirley Peters. He admits writing to her, owns up to going out to meet her. Now that's a Monday night just three weeks before she was killed.'

'But he still hasn't admitted more than that?'

'Of course he hasn't. He's not stupid, is he?'

'I thought he was. I thought that was the point.'

'What I'm saying, sir, it doesn't make sense; it doesn't fit. All the other women he contacted, he went ahead and met. The only one we know came to any harm, the one who was murdered, oh, no, he walked away, didn't he?'

'Then why mention it in the first place?'

'Sir?'

'Why tell us he as much as knew her?'

'The inspector reckons it was because he thought we had a list of who he'd written to, thought we'd got hold of the letters, I suppose. That way, he'd have to admit something, but no more than he hoped to get away with.'

'And all the time you were interviewing him, he never broke down on that part of his story, that he took one look at Shirley Peters, turned tail and never saw her again?'

'No, sir.'

'And your verdict on that, Graham?'

'No doubt in my mind, sir,' said Millington without hesitation. 'He's lying.'

Resnick wrote a memo for Lynn Kellogg, another for Patel, asking for a summary of what they'd learned as soon as possible. When he phoned Skelton, the superintendent was closeted with the chief constable, doubtless doing his best to pacify him and promise an early result. The DCI was there and Resnick asked him if they were anticipating making an arrest.

'Simms, you mean? Grafton's sex offender.'

'That's the one.'

'Unofficially, Charlie, I think the word is imminent. Unless you've turned up something stronger.'

Resnick assured him that he hadn't.

'Not holding out on us, Charlie?'

'Not for a minute,' said Resnick and rung off. What he would say at the next briefing session might be another matter, but for now he needed time to think.

A little over an hour later he was sitting in his favourite chair with Bud curved round the back of his neck, purring head tucked up against Resnick's chin while his tail coiled across it from the other side. He was listening to the animal's contented breathing, the occasional vehicle passing too fast along the road outside. There had to be a way of pulling it all together, but as yet he couldn't determine what that was. There had to be something he could do with a quarter of ageing mushrooms and half a red pepper that was more interesting than slicing them finely and folding them into yet another omelette.

When he allowed himself to be convinced that there wasn't, he lifted Bud gently down and went to call Rachel.

She came to the phone after Carole had all but given him the third degree.

'I've just been interviewed for a very exclusive position,' said Resnick, 'only I don't know what it is.'

'Sorry,' Rachel explained, 'she's interceding for me with Chris.'

'What's up?'

'Oh, he was waiting for me last night when I got back.'

'After I left you?'

'Yes.'

'Jesus!'

'It could have been worse, I suppose. He was upset. At first he was angry and then he was, well, violent, I suppose you'd have to say.'

'He didn't strike you?'

'No. Nothing like that. Carole got me inside, he hung about getting wet and then disappeared. He's tried ringing me a few times and I don't know if it's to be abusive or to apologize, because so far I've managed to avoid him.'

'There's nothing you want me to do?'

'There's nothing you can do.'

'Except what I called for.'

'Which is?'

'To save myself from another mushroom omelette.'

'Charlie!'

'You said it was my turn to ring you.'

'I didn't mean less than twenty-four hours later.'

'You weren't that specific.'

'I know. But, anyway, I've eaten.'

'Oh.'

There was a silence and then Resnick said: 'What were you going to do?'

'An early bath and then bed.'

Great! thought Resnick. Do it here!

'Did you hear what I said, Charlie?' Rachel asked when there was no reply.

'I was just thinking about it.'

'You're not turning into a dirty old man on me, are you?'

'Come over,' said Resnick.

'What for?'

'To meet the cats.'

She didn't say anything for several seconds and then what she did say was, 'How can I resist?'

The introductions went as well as could be expected. Dizzy treated her to his rear view within seconds, but that aside the cats were as polite as they usually were when Resnick had guests, which wasn't often.

'Can I get you a drink?'

'Vodka and tonic?'

'Difficult.'

'Gin?'

'Ah . . .'

'What have you got?'

They sat on the settee with two glasses of Black
Label and Art Pepper on the stereo playing 'You'd Be
So Nice to Come Home To'. Resnick didn't tell her the
title, he thought that might be going too far, but he did
point out the link with Pepper the cat and he was
starting to tell her something else when she leaned
across him and placed her finger to his lips.

'Charlie . . .'

'Um?'

'Shut up and let me listen.'

When he refilled their glasses, he found a worn copy
of Sinatra's *Songs for Young Lovers*. Rachel waited
until it got to 'Someone to Watch Over Me' before
asking, 'Charlie, are you trying to seduce me?'

'Am I?'

'Don't you know?'

'No.'

'Are you being honest?'

'Usually.'

'And now?'

'Absolutely.'

'Only if you are, trying to seduce me I mean, I
haven't got my cap in.'

'Oh.'

'And I don't want you to think I'm the kind of woman
who takes it with her wherever she goes.'

'Absolutely not.'

'But I do happen to have it in my bag.'

'Ah.'

He took her whisky glass and she kissed him; when he had set both glasses down, she kissed him again.

They kissed one another.

After some time had elapsed and two of the cats had tried to find some purchase on their shifting laps and given up, Rachel took Resnick's hand and pulled him to his feet. 'Don't you think it's time you showed me the bedroom?'

'Yes.'

'Then you'd better point me at the bathroom on the way.'

'What in God's name do you think you're doing?'

Rachel waited fully fifteen seconds and when the bathroom mirror didn't provide her with an answer she flushed the toilet and switched out the light.

'Are you all right?'

'Mmm.'

'No, really?'

'I suppose not.'

Resnick sighed and rolled over on to his side; his eyes were closed and his breathing was loud and too fast. He waited until it had steadied and then opened his eyes and stared up at the ceiling.

'Charlie . . .' Rachel snuggled beneath the crook of his arm, laying her arm across his body, the curve of her hand on his belly. ' . . . it doesn't matter.'

Resnick didn't reply.

'Honestly.'

'Um.'

She turned her head in towards him and kissed first his side and then, slowly, his chest, all the way to the hair that gathered thickly at the middle of his rib cage and tasted of salt and sweat.

'Don't think about it.'

What Resnick was thinking about was Sally Oakes, her scrubbed face and her skinny body and her voice. *No. He hurt me.* And behind that, like an echo that was off-key but always present, a little girl sitting in a room with dolls: *Yes. It hurt me.*

Rachel moved until she was laying with her body half covering his and he softly stroked her back from the nape of her neck to the base of her spine.

'Charlie,' she said in a murmur, 'don't stop. That's lovely.'

And after that she didn't say anything because she was asleep.

When she woke it was pitch dark, she was alone in the bed and the luminous hands of her watch told her it was close to half-past two. She slipped out from under the covers without disturbing the cat that slept near the foot of the bed, curled in on itself.

She found Charlie in the nursery, with his face up against the window, gazing out into the dark. Rachel pressed her cheek into the middle of his back and her arms wound around him. After a little while he turned to her and when she kissed him, she could feel the tears, not yet dry on his face.

'What are you crying for, Charlie?' she said.

'The children.'

'Which children?'

'All of them.'

Thirty-One

'Charlie.'

'Um?'

'Charlie.'

He turned against her, no more than half awake and startled by her voice, her closeness, the warmth and smoothness of her skin.

'There's something on my head.'

'Oh.' Reaching up, one of Resnick's hands inadvertently brushed against her breast. 'Dizzy, come down. Come on.'

He prised the cat carefully away, wary that Dizzy's claws would become entangled with the curls of Rachel's hair. Setting the cat down on the floor, Resnick waited for him to jump back and when he did, pushed him more energetically away. The fur of his tail fluffed out, Dizzy sulked out of the room.

'Jealous,' Resnick said.

'He's no need to be.'

'He'll get used to it.'

Rachel ran a finger down the inside of Resnick's arm. 'He won't have to.' Looking at her, close enough to see himself reflected in her eyes, Resnick's fingers closed around hers.

'What time is it, Charlie?'

He brought her arm up in the bed until he could read the hands of her watch. 'Ten-past six.'

'I have to leave by seven.'

It was already five-to and Rachel was drinking coffee and putting on her eye shadow; in the bedroom, Resnick was sorting through his shirts.

'You were married, Charlie. Why didn't you have any kids?'

'The only time we might have was right afterwards, the first year or so. But then it was me, I was the one who wasn't sure, wanted to wait. I was just getting into the job, I suppose, maybe I was frightened of the disruption, the responsibility, I don't know. Later, well, later it was different. There were other things on her agenda.'

She could see him through the mirror, loosening the top of his trousers to tuck in his shirt, watching her.

'How about you?' Resnick said.

Rachel was checking her diary, one arm in her coat: they were standing in the hall.

'Young professionals; it wasn't an issue.'

'And now?'

'Now, I don't think about it, not often, and, when I do, I still don't know if I want any. Sometimes...' She pushed the diary down into her bag and finished fastening her coat... 'But then I've never been sure enough or I suppose by now I would have done something about it.'

She felt him looking at her and knew what he was thinking. It didn't make her feel comfortable.

'Bye, Charlie.' She opened the door. Outside it was still quite dark.

'I'll call you.'

'No.'

Rachel watched as anxiety narrowed his eyes. 'It's my turn to call you.'

Jack Skelton had either found the time to buy a new

suit or discovered one in the back of his wardrobe that
Resnick didn't remember. He went through the briefing
session even more briskly than usual. The blow-ups
of the bodies were still tacked to the wall; the map
enlargements with their annotations in red and blue
marker; now two ten by twelve photographs of Leonard
Simms, one a right profile, the other frontal. In both
he looked startled, his eyes protruding slightly from
their sockets, cheeks drawn in as if catching breath.

'What I shall say to the press is this: a man has been
helping us with our inquiries into the deaths of Shirley
Peters and Mary Sheppard, neither he nor anybody
else has been charged, but we do confidently expect an
arrest will be made shortly.'

'Shortly,' said Colin Rich. 'Why not now?' As usual
it was difficult to tell whether he was asking a specific
question or thinking aloud.

The superintendent chose to answer. 'To present,
Simms has been here voluntarily. He asked to see his
doctor and that was arranged, but always said he didn't
want a solicitor. Now he seems to be changing his mind
on that score and I'm not convinced we have enough
evidence on which to charge him. He's still denying
any actual contact with the Peters woman and in no
way have we been able to link him with the second
murder.'

'That aside,' put in the DCI, 'laddie's very much our
best bet.'

'But in the meanwhile,' said Skelton, 'we continue to
explore other avenues.'

'Or blind alleys, eh, Charlie?' Colin Rich winked.

Resnick knew that, when he talked to Skelton, the
superintendent would tell him to put at least two more
of his team back on to the main inquiry. Contact maga-

zines, dating agencies, singles clubs: action was continuing to be initiated, paper work still piling up.

Patel had typed his report with the usual painstaking application of Tipp-Ex and an uncertainty, shared by the majority of the population, about the use of the apostrophe. Resnick held the sheets folded back against the counter and spooned the sprinkling of chocolate from the surface of his cappuccino. Names of publications, academic posts held, bits and pieces of biography culled from slender sources, what did it all add up to? Repression, defacement. He wondered if Patel's page of notes outlining Doria's lecture on Derrida and Deconstruction meant any more to him than a collection of words, shuffled together. Repression and defacement: provocation and closure.

'Moonlighting, Inspector?'

Suzanne Olds was standing behind him, reading over his shoulder. Resnick refolded the papers and slid them back into their envelope.

'A little heavy for before lunch, isn't it?' she said, taking the stool next to him.

'Research,' Resnick explained.

'A closet intellectual.' She took a pack of cigarettes from her shoulder bag and then a lighter. 'You're a surprising man.' She lit a cigarette. 'Open University, is it? Career move or just a hobby?'

'I didn't know you came here?' Resnick said.

'I must be honest, I prefer the espresso bar down stairs at Next but there wasn't a spare seat.'

'Coffee's better up here.'

'It's stronger.'

'Exactly.'

Suzanne Olds put a 50p coin on the counter and told

the girl to keep the change. 'How's the inquiry coming along?'

'We confidently expect an arrest to be made shortly.'

'Thanks,' she said, averting her head to release a film of grey smoke, 'I read the first edition.'

'Then you know.'

'From what I hear you've got some half-witted flasher doing his best to talk himself into the High Court.'

'You're not representing him?'

'I didn't think anybody was.'

'Besides,' said Resnick, 'if you read the rest of the piece, you'll know we let him walk away.'

'How far and for how long?'

Resnick gave his coffee a stir and drank it down in three swallows.

'You don't think he did it, do you?' She was leaning her head towards him and he still didn't like her perfume. There was, though, something about the way her skin stretched tight over high cheekbones . . .'

'Don't I?'

'Inspector, I've seen you when you're convinced a man's guilty. That interrogation of Macliesh . . .'

'I regret that.'

'Why?' Her hand was resting on his sleeve. 'I thought you were very impressive.'

'I've got to go,' Resnick said, putting the envelope into his inside pocket, getting down from the stool.

'You know,' Suzanne Olds said, 'you could be an attractive man if ever you decided to take the trouble.'

Resnick had no trouble in not looking back.

For Christmas they had pork: slices of it a quarter-inch thick that her father would slice away from the bone, golden-yellow crackling, roast parsnips and potatoes, apple sauce to which her mother had added a thimbleful of brandy at the last moment. Her mother had been on to her about it since her last letter, this Sunday's eleven-thirty phone call.

'You will be home? You will be here? Christmas Eve, your dad says. He could do with some help on the last delivery. Can't trust that lad to come in. Oh, and the bird for that inspector of yours...'

Lynn wondered how difficult it would be to arrange for a spell of duty that would carry her across into the New Year.

'Problem?'

She hadn't noticed Resnick coming into the office.

'No, sir,' shaking her head.

'You look guilty about something.'

'Christmas, sir.'

Resnick grinned. 'Didn't have anything to do with that, did you?'

Across the room two phones rang almost simultaneously and Mark Divine picked up one with each hand and said into the pair of them, 'CID.'

One caller he asked to hold a moment, cupped his hand over the mouthpiece of the second and gestured towards Resnick, who shook his head.

'He's busy at the moment. Can you call back later?'

Divine shrugged and set the receiver back on the cradle. 'Hung up, sir.'

Resnick turned back to Lynn Kellogg. 'You went to see the girl?'

'Sally Oakes. Yes, sir.'

'What did you make of her?'

'Weird. I mean, really strange. Brittle as a stick and that look of hers... I'm ten years older than her and she made me feel like I was back at school.'

It was interesting, thought Resnick, the way that

her Norfolk accent came back more strongly whenever she'd been thinking about home.

'And all that carrying-on with Doria, I don't understand how she could . . . I don't see how she could bring herself to tell me about it, never mind mess around like that with a man . . .' She sensed the way her line of thought was taking her and veered away with as much grace as she could. Noticing, Resnick gave her room, impressed.

'I'll say this for her, though, she sent him packing and she meant it. That's not easy at the best of times.' Look at me, she thought, sharing a flat and a bed with a man I no longer have any feelings for, simply because it's less of a problem than finding a way of telling him to pick up his bike and walk. 'She gave him his marching orders and according to her he's accepted it; she doesn't seem to have been intimidated by him at all.'

'Whereas you were, a little, on your own admission.'

'More than a little. He overwhelmed me, I think.'

'With words.'

'That and the whole set-up, the cosy little room, all those books I'd never read and never will, the sherry. It's a long way from Norfolk.'

'So are most places,' Resnick smiled.

'Sally Oakes, though,' Lynn continued after a moment, 'none of that seemed to bother her at all.'

'She switched off.'

'I suppose so.'

'Until he came out from behind all the talk, the language.'

Inwardly, Lynn Kellogg shivered and, as if sensing it, Resnick reminded her of what she had said about Doria after their meeting, what she'd said about his eyes.

'Yes, sir. Like he was looking at me from behind a mask.'

'If that's right, he doesn't let it slip often. From your report, there doesn't seem to be any gossip about him at the University at all.'

'Nothing sexual, sir. No rumours about affairs with students, though from what I heard he must be about the only lecturer who isn't having one.'

'It's all that reading,' said Resnick. 'Gives them a taste for it.'

'Really, sir? I don't see how.' A boyfriend had given her a well-thumbed copy of *The Story of O* once; she'd hit him with it.

'Just a theory. Talking of which, no sign of Patel, I suppose?'

'I think he's at the Never-Too-Late Club for the Widowed and Divorced, sir. They're having a tea-dance.'

'If he comes in, tell him I'd appreciate a quick tutorial, will you?'

By the end of Resnick's shift there was still no Patel; perhaps he'd fallen for a matron with a holiday home in France and a winning way with a foxtrot.

He slipped across the road to buy a paper and the headline informed him: DOUBLE MURDER – ARREST NEAR. Divine was going down the stairs three at a time and had to push out his hand against the wall to stop himself.

'Another call for you a minute ago, sir. Pretty anxious to know where you could be contacted. I thought you'd already left, so I advised him to try the station tomorrow.'

Resnick nodded. 'Any time?'

'I asked him, sir, but he said it didn't matter. But I think it was the same person as earlier.'

'Thanks,' said Resnick and carried on to his office.

316

He dialled Social Services and Carole answered. Rachel had gone out to see a client and was intending to go straight home from there. Resnick thanked her and said he'd ring her there later, if that was all right.

'You're welcome to try,' Carole said, 'but you might be lucky to catch her. I know she's driving up to Sheffield to see a friend as soon as she's changed.'

'Maybe I'll leave it till tomorrow then,' said Resnick. 'If you'll just say I called.'

'Of course,' said Carole. And then, 'You didn't phone earlier, did you?'

'No, why?'

'No special reason. Only the switchboard took a couple of calls but they didn't get a name.'

'Not me.'

'Ex-boyfriend, probably.'

'Probably.'

'Pest!'

Resnick turned over to the back page to discover that County were playing at home.

Even after Resnick had transferred his allegiance back over the Trent, he had stayed away for months on end. When he started going regularly again, the team began losing. His most regular period in front of the London Road stand coincided with a drop of two Divisions in as many seasons. Gloriously, he remembered a floodlit game when Villa stuck eight past them and their blond winger ran riot. This was under the lights, too, but that was where the comparison ended.

On this present occasion, the visitors had brought a couple of dozen supporters with them, lost in the spaces of their enclosure and looking as if they'd have difficulty summoning up enough enthusiasm between them to club together for a cup of Bovril and a warmed-over sausage roll.

Resnick stood on the edge of the usual knot of fort-nightly acquaintances, for whom a fondness for County's flaws and misdemeanours had made cynicism an art form. Straightforward abuse was reserved for referees under five-foot four, and former English internationals; the most abusive remarks of all were shouted in Polish.

It was hard keeping warm during a first half that produced seventeen off-sides, three corners and no shots on goal at either end. During the interval Resnick glanced at Patel's notes, folded now inside his programme. The second forty-five minutes were pure County: a through ball out of nowhere, a man on the overlap and a first-time cross that was met at the gallop and clattered into the net; after that, they left one player upfield, pulled back the rest and held out until the last five minutes when they conceded two goals, one to bad luck, the other to bad marking; with sixty seconds remaining, they were awarded a penalty and the final chance to equalize was ballooned over the bar.

'Any other side, you could have been sure of three points.'

Hands in pockets, Resnick nodded without turning his head, moving with the small crowd towards the exit.

'But, then, that's what makes them so exciting to watch.'

Something in the voice made Resnick look to his side then, slowing down.

'I didn't take you for a County man, Inspector. More of a Forest supporter.'

'A long time back.'

'We learn the error of our ways.'

They were standing opposite the entrance to the cattle market, people continuing to spill round them.

A single constable on horseback was guiding the straggle of visitors across the road to their coach.

'Professor Doria,' said Resnick, not knowing how he knew.

'William Doria, yes.' He extended his hand. 'Inspector Resnick.'

'That's correct.'

His grip was strong and he held it for slightly longer than was necessary. He was shorter than Resnick, but by no more than a couple of inches. He wore a black wool overcoat, longer than was fashionable; the bottoms of his trousers were tucked into thick socks, brown leather boots came up above his ankles. Thick hair, greying, showed beneath the brim of a trilby hat. A County scarf, black and white, was tucked under the collar of his coat.

'I recognized you from the newspaper,' Doria explained. 'Your photograph, a while ago now. A case involving the abuse of a young child, I believe. Sad, naturally, but in so many ways symptomatic of our time.'

Did that, then, make it any less sad, Resnick thought?

The last few supporters moved around the corner from sight.

'But now, of course,' said Doria, 'your energies are being expended elsewhere, the deaths of those two unfortunate women.' His eyes flickered. 'And now the revelation is imminent, the victim, I see, is soon to be brought to justice.'

'The victim?'

'It must always be, Inspector, the perpetrator in such cases, violence against the person, these women, that child, they are also the victim.' But not the abused,

Resnick thought, not the dead. 'Perhaps you don't agree?'

'I hadn't realized your field was sociology, Professor,' Resnick said.

'Neither is it and I find I have little sympathy with the view that would seek to discover the cause for aberrant behaviour in unemployment and over-crowding.'

'Then where would you look?' Resnick asked.

Without hesitation, Doria set his index finger over his heart.

'Inside us,' he said. 'Those needs whose expression of necessity subverts the rules of community, of family, all of those patterns by which we live.' Doria barely paused. 'But now, Inspector, I have scripts waiting to be assessed and you and I, I think, go in different directions. It was a pleasure to have met you.'

Resnick stood his ground as Doria turned confidently away and walked south along London Road towards Turner's Quay and the river.

Thirty-Two

'So what are you saying, Charlie, that he confessed?'

Skelton stood against the window, a silver rind of moon over his left shoulder. So far it was a clear morning, bright and cold, no sign of rain. Resnick had scarcely slept; had been at the station well before the first shift came on duty.

'Not in so many words.'

'Not in any words.'

'He said . . .'

'Charlie, you've already told me, three times. I know it off by heart. And it still doesn't mean what you want it to mean.'

He stood there, thought Resnick, telling me: *those needs whose expression of necessity subverts the rules of community, of family, all of those patterns by which we live.*

'He gave you a theory, Charlie. Like any other tuppenny-ha'penny academic. It only takes a dolphin to be washed up on a beach somewhere in the world for some expert to inform us that they're doing it to warn us we're damaging the ecology of the planet. Child abuse has become a growth industry for sociologists and child psychologists from Aberystwyth to Scunthorpe. Do you know how much a QC gets paid to chair a panel which will take two years to tell us what was right before our eyes in the first place?

'We're surrounded by people with theories for all

and sundry, Charlie, and the best we can hope to do is steer a course between them and use their knowledge when we've told them exactly what we want and nothing more.'

'With respect, sir, I don't think this is the same. It isn't abstract. He knew what he was saying, Doria, knew who he was saying it to.'

'Now what, Charlie? He was watching for you, waiting for you? Maybe he went to the match for the express purpose of seeking you out, striking up a conversation? Great shot! That bloke's a load of rubbish! Oh, by the way, I've got this confession I want to make if you can hang on till they've taken this corner.'

Facetious sod! thought Resnick. His All-Bran can't be working.

'I don't think it's impossible, sir,' he said.

Skelton moved towards his desk. 'I know it's not easy to find acceptable reasons for watching that miserable team, but this might be taking it a bit far.'

Resnick turned and started towards the door, smarting under his superior's sarcasm.

'Inspector . . .' Skelton began.

'What about the girl?' Resnick asked, stopping, his voice unusually loud. 'Oakes – what about her? We've her description of . . .'

'A bit of rough, isn't that what they call it, Charlie? You're always so much more in tune with these terms than I seem to be. If we started pulling in every bloke who treated his wife like that, we'd have more inside than out on the street. And don't waste that look of disapproval, I'm not condoning anything, you know that. I'm saying there's a certain kind of world out there and we're paid to work in it. Unfortunately, we have to live in it, too.'

'Yes, sir.' Resnick spoke flatly, looked back at Skelton tight-lipped.

The superintendent drummed his fingers across the papers on his desk before sitting down. 'Anything else?'

'No, sir.'

'And there's nobody still wasting their time round the campus, playing at being students?'

'No, sir.'

Skelton lowered his head. Dismissed, Resnick opened and closed the door with respect.

'Someone asking to see you, sir.'

Resnick snapped at Naylor so sharply that the DC collided with the door when he withdrew.

Certain that nothing now was going to make the day better, Resnick finished what he was doing before quitting his desk. There seemed to be more than usual activity around him, but he felt no part of it. Better to push away at the routine, keep his head down, sooner or later he'd stop feeling sorry for himself. Just about the last thing he wanted to do was talk to another human being. And he knew that it was neither of the people he would have been interested in seeing: had it been either Doria or Rachel he felt he would have known. It was Marian Witczak.

She was wearing a burgundy cape and her hair was tied back into a bun. She looked like Resnick's idea of a piano teacher with perfect pitch and a mother in a nursing home in the country.

She waited until she was sitting opposite Resnick, until she had made a slow and careful survey of his office, until she had politely declined coffee, before taking an envelope from her bag and placing it on the desk before him.

Like somebody depressing middle C.

Resnick looked at her questioningly for a moment. 'Open it.'

The card was the same as he had seen before, the same colour, size, texture.

My Dear Marian,

I am beginning to regret, quite strongly, that so many months have elapsed since we met. I find I am in urgent need of mature and stimulating company and conversation.

I wonder if you can bring yourself to overlook my inexcusable tardiness in communicating and agree to spend an evening with me?

Shall we say this coming Saturday?

Your sincere friend—

William Doria

Neatly printed, below the embossed name, were his address and telephone number.

'I discovered it when I went downstairs,' Marian said. 'It had been put through the letter-box early this morning.'

Or very late last night, thought Resnick.

'It was certainly delivered by hand. You see, it bears no stamp.'

Resnick read the note through again, as Marian would have said, searching for clues. He could find none.

'I thought – after the interest you showed before – I thought, Charles, that you would wish to know of this.'

'You're right,' said Resnick. 'I'm grateful.' And then, 'What do you intend to do about what he says?'

'My first intention, this will not surprise you I think, was to tear this up, this beautiful calling card. My second, and I do not think this will surprise you either, was to accept.' She looked at Resnick, as if waiting for a comment that didn't come. 'Do you think I am foolish?'

'Not necessarily.'

'That I have no pride?'

'Certainly not that. I know you have.'

She lifted up the card and glanced at it once again, although she must have been able to picture it by then with her eyes closed tight.

'This last evening, the one I told you about, it was such pleasure to me. He is so diverting a companion.'

'You've made up your mind,' Resnick said.

'Unless you tell me otherwise.'

'How can I do that, Marian? What you do is your own affair.'

'Unless you wish to warn me.'

'Of what?'

'Charles, that I do not know.'

Resnick tried to unscramble all of the voices that were vying for attention inside his head.

'You said that when you were with him before you felt no danger?'

'Of course not. Are you saying I should have done so?'

'The important thing is that you didn't.'

'I have said this.'

'Then ... where would you go?'

'I don't know, I thought he might choose. He seems to have so many interests. Except ...'

'Yes?'

'There is a dance, at the Polish Association.' For a moment her severe face softened into a smile. 'You remember those dances? Of course they are not the same, but I could suggest it.' She studied his face. 'What do you think?'

'Yes,' Resnick said with a certainty he had no right to feel. 'I think that would be the best idea.'

He didn't see Jack Skelton for the remainder of that day, suppressing his inclination to go to him with the copy he had made of Doria's card and say, 'There. What do you think all that's about?'

But what was it about? An educated man who liked the company of women, who liked to take them out and impress them with his erudition and, just occasionally, take them to bed. As the superintendent had said, if that tended to get a little excited, wasn't that the same for all of us at some point in our lives?

Doria like to play verbal games, that was what words were to him: like 'writing' he used them to disturb the ordinary, the run-of-the-mill and the commonplace. Where was the harm in taking hold of conformity and shaking it by the scruff of its rigid neck?

And the evidence – instead of evidence all that Resnick had were voices: Patel's describing his charisma; Lynn Kellogg, the way his eyes had held her from an otherwise immobile face; Doria himself, the knowingness that had accompanied the placing of his finger to his heart.

Voices: *hurt me*
hurt me

At three minutes past eleven the following morning (the officer at the desk would remember that time exactly), Leonard Simms walked into the station and said he wanted to confess to the murders of both Shirley Peters and Mary Sheppard.

Thirty-Three

'Don't do it, Charlie.'

The band was taking a breather and the disco had taken its place immediately below the stage, patterned lights and sixty-watt speakers. They had found a table in a side room, where most of the others were families, grandmothers left with the smaller children while their parents danced. To saxophone and accordion, Rachel and Resnick had waltzed, quickstepped, simply walked around the floor, slowly, in each other's arms. It had been the jiving that had finished them, a breakdown of arms and good intentions during a version of 'La Bamba' that had owed more to the polka than to a bar out in the *barrio*.

'Don't keep looking at me like that.'

Resnick had not steered Rachel far past the entrance before vodkas had been thrust at them, amidst cries of surprise and greeting: back-slapping and kisses and the pumping of hands. 'You're supposed to swallow it straight down,' Resnick had explained, leading by example. After the second, Rachel had, politely but firmly, refused. Now Resnick was drinking beer and Rachel white wine, but every now and again someone would pass by their table and set down another glass of vodka, close by Resnick's elbow.

Rachel reached across and took hold of his hand. 'Stop trying to make me fall in love with you.'

Marian Witczak allowed Doria to pin the corsage to the bodice of her black dress; his hands were supple and confident, but there was a flush of excitement in his eyes which she could not remember. He accepted the offer of sherry and they sat facing one another, he leaning back in the worn comfort of the armchair, Marian at the edge of the settee, running the rings round and round her fingers.

He talked about the courses he was teaching, the brilliance of one of his students – 'the most striking red hair, she would have Rossetti painting in his grave' – and the dullness of the others. He had visited London and Manchester to attend the theatre, exhibitions; a flight to Dubai, first-class, all expenses paid, to deliver a paper on Paul de Man. Most perfect of all had been a recital in Bath: 'Fauré, Debussy, of course, Ravel – I have never heard anyone achieve the sensuality of the final section of the *Sonatine* in such a way. A cliché it may be, my dear Marian, but I am willing to swear here and now that she did become as one with her piano during that interpretation. A perfect fusion!'

Doria smiled, finished his sherry and sprang smartly to his feet. 'Now! Shall we go to the ball!'

Resnick's suit, Rachel recalled, was the one he had been wearing that first occasion she had seen him, walking across the entrance of the courthouse. She smiled to herself, remembering the way he had stared at her, tried to hide what he was doing, disguise it, embarrassed; the way he had carried on looking at her, nevertheless, as if having no alternative.

'What are you thinking about?'

'Oh, nothing special.'

'You were smiling.'

'Was I?'

'I hope it means you're having a good time?'

'Charlie, of course I am. I don't understand why you don't come here more often.'

He grinned, boyishly. Another woman, Rachel thought, would be reaching across to push his hair back from his eyes, straighten his tie. 'I can only take this much alcohol once every six months.'

'Are you drunk, Charlie?'

'Probably.'

A boy, fair-haired, no more than three or four, lost his balance playing chase between the tables and fell against Resnick's chair. Turning, Resnick swept him up from the floor and held him at arm's length, looking at Rachel past the child's laughing face.

No, Charlie, Rachel thought, I'm not falling for that one, either.

'Charlie, how nice to see you.'

Resnick set down the boy and got to his feet. Marian was wearing long black gloves with her short-sleeved gown, which was tightly belted at the waist. Doria, alongside her, had on a cream suit with a loose, deeply-pocketed jacket, a white shirt and a midnight-blue bow tie.

Resnick kissed Marian lightly on the cheek.

'Charles,' Marian said, 'allow me to introduce Professor Doria.'

'William,' said Doria, shaking Resnick's hand. 'William Doria.' He gave no sign that they had already met.

Resnick stood back, gesturing towards where Rachel was sitting.

'Marian Witczak, William Doria, this is Rachel . . .'

'Chaplin,' said Doria, making a slight bow and offering her his hand. 'Rachel Chaplin, of course.'

When he straightened again, the academic's eyes were bright but gave away nothing. 'Perhaps we might join you?' he said.

Resnick glanced quickly towards Rachel before answering. Doria fetched two chairs and he and Marian sat opposite one another.

'A drink?' Doria said. And, with a smile at Rachel, 'Some more wine.'

'Thank you, no.'

'But . . .'

'Later, perhaps.'

The muscles of Doria's face were immobile, but his eyes were never still, never leaving Rachel for more than a second.

'Charlie,' Rachel said, standing, head inclined towards the music. 'Let's dance. It's a shame to waste Stevie Wonder.'

'Excuse me,' said Resnick, following her through to where the disco was still playing.

One dance led to another.

'You didn't take to him, then, the professor?'

Rachel had realized by now that if she covered twice as much ground as Resnick did, and let her arms swing wide, they didn't look a bad couple.

'You've met him before?'

'Never.'

'You're sure?'

'I don't think I'd forget.'

'He knew your name.'

Rachel swung away from him through a dipping circle and then back, one hand pressed to his chest. Her skin was glowing.

'Charlie?'

'Yes?'

'Shut up and dance!'

A shout went up from across the room as the last of the winning numbers was called from the raffle. Resnick crumpled up a crocodile of salmon pink tickets.

'I had a new student in one of my lectures the other day,' Doria was saying. 'A nice boy, Asian, not enrolled in the department, auditing, I suppose you would say. But it's flattering when people know who you are, your reputation. He seemed to want to stay behind at the end, some clarification he was seeking, I don't know. He was too shy, finally.' Doria hooked one leg over the other at the ankle. 'The reverse side of reputation, I suppose, it can place others in awe of one. But, then, you must find the same yourself, Inspector?'

'I don't think so.'

'Come now. I would have thought your function depended upon it, to a certain extent at least. Dealing as you must with the public, subordinates, even.'

'I don't think my subordinates are in awe of me, Doria.'

'William.'

'And I shouldn't like it if they were.'

'A Detective Constable Kellogg, is she one of your subordinates?'

'She is.'

'She came to, um, to interview me – is that the correct terminology?'

'It'll do.'

'A charming young woman, earnest. Not of the brightest calibre, possibly, but competent.'

'She's a good policewoman.'

'She was there under your jurisdiction, Inspector?'

'As part of a routine inquiry, yes.'

'Into the deaths of two women.'

'Yes.'

'You must be relieved that it's over.'

'Over?'

'National television, the six o'clock news, a man you previously suspected has confessed.'

'All manner of men confess, Doria.'

The academic uncrossed his legs. 'A brandy, Inspector? Or are you driving?'

'I'm not driving,' said Resnick, 'but I'll say no to the brandy, just the same.'

With a nod of the head, Doria rose and went towards the bar.

A woman in a purple trouser suit sat in one of the cubicles with the door open and carefully emptied the entire contents of her handbag out on to the floor. Quietly, she was singing to herself.

Rachel combed through the ends of her hair, twisting her head round so that she could see the back of it in the mirror.

'How long have you known Charles?' Marian asked, pretending to straighten the folds of her dress.

'Not very long. A matter of weeks.'

'He seems very happy.'

'I think he is.'

Marian touched Rachel's shoulder. 'You will forgive me, but I have known him for many years, and I know he would not be pleased at my saying this, but for a long time now Charles has needed somebody.'

Rachel pursed her lips at the glass and turned away.

The woman in the cubicle was picking up her belongings and replacing them inside her bag, still singing.

'Those flowers are lovely,' said Rachel, looking at Marian's corsage. 'Did your friend give them to you?'

'Yes,' said Marian.

'He has good taste,' said Rachel. 'Shall we go back?'

'The taxi will be here in a few minutes,' said Resnick.

'Oh, you are not going already?' Marian protested.

'Afraid so.'

'Then,' said Doria, standing with a flourish, 'Rachel must have one dance with me before you do.'

He stood with both arms extended, hands out palms uppermost, eyes shining, daring her to decline.

'Thank you,' Rachel said, 'I've danced enough.'

'I insist,' said Doria.

'Even so,' said Rachel. 'The answer's the same.'

'On some future occasion, then?' said Doria, resuming his seat.

Rachel just looked at him.

'You don't want to share our cab, Marian?' Resnick asked.

'No thank you, Charles. I think we'll stay a little longer.'

He took her hands lightly and kissed her forehead. 'Safe journey home.'

'Of course.'

'I'll ring you.'

'What does a nice, intelligent woman like that see in a creep like Doria?'

Resnick lifted his hand from the switch on the coffee grinder.

'She thinks he's charming.'

'As a snake.'

'You really didn't like him, did you?'

'Neither did you.'

Resnick poured water into the machine. 'Was it that obvious?'

She put her arms tight around him and rested her head in the small of his back. 'Charlie, you're always obvious.'

He turned to her and kissed her. 'Isn't that preferable to devious?'

'Certainly.'

'In that case,' he said with an expression that was half grin, half smile, 'when the coffee's ready can we take it to bed?'

'You see,' she said.

'See what?' Her face was inches away from his, less.

'Let it happen once and straightaway you're taking it for granted.'

'I'm not.'

'Oh, Charlie.'

'I'm not taking it for granted. Or you.'

'You just naturally assumed that because I jumped into your bed the last time I was here that I would again. Evening out, dance and a drink, bed. Right?'

Resnick laughed, squeezing her. 'Yes.'

She kissed him. 'One condition.'

'Of course.'

'I don't want to make love.'

How could he stop the disappointment showing in his eyes?

'I think I'd like just to lay there with you quietly and cuddle.'

'Fine.'

'Then let's have the coffee down here, before we go up.'

When Resnick rang, Marian picked up the phone almost immediately.

'Naturally I am home all right,' she said in answer to his question. 'What is the matter with you? Why all of this concern, sweet as it is?'

Resnick told her he simply wanted to be sure.

'Sure of what?'

'Doria, is he ...?'

'He left me after I had turned the key in my front door, Charles. A gentleman.'

'Good night, Marian,' Resnick said.

'Charles, you are a strange man.'

Rachel's shoulder rested in the crook of Resnick's arm. Pepper lay against her left hip, Bud had dared to find a space between the pillows and the bedhead. Miles made little snoring sounds from beyond her toes.

'I feel honoured, Charlie.'

'Mmm?'

'Your cats, the way they accept me.'

'They sense that you like them.'

'They're right.' She snuggled closer against him. 'Where's the fourth one?'

'Dizzy? Out prowling.'

'I saw Vera Barnett the other day, did I tell you?'

'No, I don't think so.'

'She's coping okay, except that she keeps scraping the bathroom paintwork with her chair and complaining when we won't come and redecorate it for her. The kids seem fine, not a lot of bounce yet, but fine.'

Resnick was stroking her breast. 'Doesn't it bother you more than you'll admit, not having any of your own?'

For several moments Rachel said nothing. Then she shrugged off his hand and pushed herself up in the bed until the cats had scattered and she was on her knees, facing him.

'You know what I am to you, Charlie, I mean, really? A vacant womb. A womb with a view to marriage.'

The garden was dark and in shadow. Slow and insinuating, Dizzy wound himself around the man's legs, pressing his fur against them, in and out. The man paid the animal no heed: he allowed nothing to deflect his attention from the upstairs window, behind which a shaded light still burned.

Thirty-Four

It was the first time Resnick had ever caught the superintendent at it, but there he was, running, head up,
even swing of the arms, straight as a die back to the
station. Resnick leaned against the post near the foot
of the steps and waited. The superintendent's running-
suit was light grey, loose-fitting, with fluorescent strips
along the arms and down the legs for use at night. A
small wallet was velcroed to the tongue of one shoe
for his key and some small change. Not one to be
caught short, the Super.

He eased his pace down with twenty yards to go,
raising a hand in greeting.

'Lovely morning, Charlie.'

'Brisk, sir.'

'Just been round the lake. Moorhens, deer standing
out in the water with the last mist still round them –
beautiful.'

Resnick knew that round the lake meant a run of
some mile and a half or more down to the park, along
a straight avenue of trees past the golf club, another
mile from there and then the same distance back, the
last section of that up a hill steep enough to make
casual cyclists get off and push. And Skelton was barely
short of breath.

'Sorry about the other day, Charlie. That business
over the University.' He was limbering down, jogging
gently on the spot, stretching his calf muscles and his

337

thighs. 'Tell the truth, I'd had a bit of an argument at home that morning. That daughter of mine.' He shook his head a trace self-consciously: it wasn't usual for him to admit to colleagues that he had a private life. 'Happens in the best-regulated of families.'

'Yes, sir. Of course it does. Everything okay now, I hope?'

'Oh, yes. Storm in a teacup.'

Resnick nodded understandingly. 'Good.'

'Better have a session later, Charlie. Now that things will be getting back to normal.'

'Yes, sir.' Resnick followed him into the station. 'Normal it is.'

Divine was still filtering information into the files, messages and movements; he glanced up and said good morning to Resnick with his usual hearty belligerence. Typical, Resnick thought, going on into his own office: the files aren't sorted, but the kettle's simmering ready for a top-up and the tea's been brewed these five minutes. Maybe he should try having a word with Divine about priorities, about his future. Though he doubted if the future for Divine stretched far beyond opening time or closing time, whichever was the nearer.

He sat behind his desk, wondering if Kevin Naylor and his Debbie had come any closer to making a decision about moving. He supposed he'd be sad enough to lose the lad, although to be truthful Naylor needed a bit of shaking-up before he'd ever get to make a good detective. Though getting out from under Divine's guidance wouldn't come amiss. Maybe he should send Lynn Kellogg out with Divine? Resnick allowed himself a smile: he wouldn't be surprised to discover that Divine was terrified of her.

'Sir?'

Millington came round the door with a freshly trimmed moustache and a couple of extra-strong mints underneath his tongue.

'Good weekend, Graham?'

'Not bad, sir. Wife got me doing a bit of grouting.'

'Sounds fun.'

'She's been on at me since summer. Wants it right for when her mother comes at Christmas.' He moved the mints into his cheek. 'Meant to ask you about that, sir. Any chance of getting on the roster over the holiday? Wouldn't mind doing quite a bit and there must be lots want it off.'

'See what I can do,' said Resnick. 'Anything before we get started?'

'One thing, sir. You remember those break-ins?'

'Videos and so on?'

'The Boulevard, yes. I had a call from that bloke I know.'

'The fence, you mean?'

'That's him. He reckons there's something iffy coming in later today. I know he's said that before and it fell flat, but this time, might be kosher.'

'He's calling you?'

'Yes, sir. I thought, if it's all right with you, I'd get young Divine to stick around. He's handy if anything turns nasty.'

'All right, Graham. Now let's get that tea in here before it sticks to the cup.'

He's in a cheerful mood this morning, thought Millington, going out into the main office. If I didn't know him better, I'd reckon he'd had his leg over the right side of breakfast.

'How did it go?'

Rachel glanced up from the sheaf of messages that

had come through from the emergency duty team. A fourteen-year-old lad with a history of solvent abuse found unconscious in an underground car park; an old lady of eighty-seven who was taken into casualty as an emergency and was found to have severe bruising which she claimed to have been caused by her sixty-three-year-old daughter; a ten-year-old boy who phoned through to the local radio talk-in programme and said that his uncle and his elder brother were both sexually abusing him.

'Fine.'

'I presumed last night was that at least.'

'What's that ...? Oh, Carole, I'm sorry. It was thoughtless of me. I should have phoned.'

Carole went to her desk. 'It's only that you said you were popping round for an hour for a chat.'

Rachel made a face. 'That's what I thought.'

'It's stupid of me, I know,' said Carole. 'I know you're free, white and over twenty-one and all that, but ...'

'Don't let the anti-racist development officer hear you using that expression,' smiled Rachel.

'Oh, God!'

'But I didn't mean to worry you. I know what it's like when you're sharing. If it happens again, I'll make sure and let you know. Then at least you can bolt the door.'

'To tell the truth, I was going to look up the number and ring there, but that made me feel too much like your mother.' She turned over a page of her diary. 'Anyway, if you're going to start spending weekends there, it'll be ...'

'Carole!'

'What?'

'Hang on a minute!'

'I was only going to say it will make things clearer.'

'Carole,' said Rachel, on her feet, 'I am not going to start spending weekends at his house. Not. What's the matter with everybody?'

'What do you mean?'

'You're as bad as he is, that's what I mean. You can't get me in there fast enough.'

'Is that what he wants then?'

'Does a cat have fleas?'

'Then where's the harm? You do like him, don't you?'

'Of course I like him. I'm not in the habit of going to bed with men I don't like. But that's not the same as . . . Carole, I've only just got out of one relationship.'

'You make it sound like a prison sentence.'

'Maybe that's because sometimes it felt like that.'

Carole looked away towards the window. She was biting down into her lower lip and thinking it was a sentence she wouldn't mind serving. Three years now since Mike had handed her the envelope because he hadn't been able to say the words out loud.

'Look,' Rachel said.

'What is it?'

'He slipped this into my bag this morning when I wasn't looking.'

Rachel put the two keys on the desk, one mortice, one yale.

'What are you going to do?' Carole asked.

'Take them back.'

Graham Millington was jubilant. Not only had he been proved right about Simms, the dirty little pervert, even though they were having some difficulties getting his stories to tally, now this. Proceeds from ten or more burglaries for certain; Naylor and Patel were round at a lock-up in Hucknall now making an inventory of the rest. VCRs, stereos, televisions, Walkmans up the wazoo! Brilliant! Even the dust-up had been fun in its own way.

'Where's Divine?' Resnick asked.

'Off at casualty, sir. Suspected broken collarbone.'

'And you?'

Millington shrugged. 'Bumps and bruises, sir. I'm okay.'

'You've seen the doctor?'

'No need.'

Millington had a swelling on his left cheek, flakes of dried blood at the corner of his mouth. His clothes looked as if they'd been round in the dryer without being washed first.

'See him.'

'Yes, sir.'

'I just had a word with the custody sergeant. He said it needed four of them to get Sloman into a cell.'

'He caught hold of the radiator and wouldn't let go. Nearly wrenched it out of the wall.'

'His colleague's got a nasty cut over his eye. I take it your report will account for how that happened?'

'No problem, sir. Sloman did it.'

'Sloman?'

'Yes, sir.'

'Try telling that to Civil Liberties.'

'No, it's right. What happened, Divine and I walked in on them, well, I had no idea it was going to be that pair, how could I? Course, they knew me straight off from the other business. Sloman panics, turns fast with a cassette deck in his arms and catches Jilkes smack in the face. He's down and moaning and Sloman goes for the door like he's bouncing off the ropes and looking for a knock-down. It was all Divine and I could do

342

to hang on to him. I mean, sir, he may not be in training any more but he's still a big lad.'

'Talking, though, I understand?'

'Reams of it, sir. Once he'd calmed down in the cells for a bit he couldn't stop. Sounds like this garage of his has got enough in it to restock Lasky's.' Millington touched his cheek gingerly. 'Tell you what did come out, sir.'

'Yes?'

'All those records that were nicked – you remember, that James Brown. He kept them at his place. Priceless, he says. Original American pressings some of them. Worth a bomb.'

'Don't forget to see the doctor, Graham.'

'No, sir. Oh, and, sir, there was a call for you.'

'Man?'

'No, sir, female. Name of Chaplin. Said she'd ring back later, either that or she'd catch you at home this evening.'

Resnick turned away quickly but not quickly enough to hide the look of pleasure that had come to his face. The randy old sod! thought Millington. He is having it off after all.

Thirty-Five

The first call came when Rachel was still in the office. Carole had left to accompany a new young worker on a difficult client visit and Rachel was trying to bring the accumulation of papers on her desk down to acceptable proportions.

'Hello, Rachel Chaplin.'

She had a bundle of photocopied articles for filing in her other hand, expectation in her voice because she thought it was probably Resnick getting back to her at last.

'Rachel?'

'Yes.'

'Is that Rachel?'

'Yes, this is Rachel Chaplin. I'm sorry, who is this?' Whoever it was, it wasn't Charlie. For a moment she remembered him calling her in the middle of a busy meeting, asking her to meet him for a drink.

'I wondered if you were still free tonight, but maybe I'm already too late.'

'Look, what's going on here? Is this some kind of joke, because . . .?'

'I understand, you're already fixed up, is that it?' The voice was low, insinuating, something about it that encouraged Rachel to picture the speaker's slow leer into the receiver. 'Or there's somebody else there in the office, am I right?'

'No, there's . . .' Mouth open, Rachel's breath caught and stopped.

'You're tied up, already catered for, I do understand, believe me. No surprise, the way you put yourself across . . .'

'The way I what?'

'I thought as soon as I read it, this is a woman who knows a lot about marketing . . .'

'As soon as you read . . . Read what, for God's sake? Tell me!'

'In fact if the girl on your switchboard hadn't said Social Services, that's the kind of job I would have thought you had.'

Rachel pushed her chair away from the desk, phone gripped so tightly in her hand that her fingers were beginning to ache. 'Listen, for the last time, I want you to tell me what you are talking about, because I honestly do not have any idea what is going on. Right?'

'Right. You're under a lot of pressure now. That's why you need to unwind, be relaxed. If you've got someone to help out tonight, I'll call again.'

'You . . .!'

'Hey, Rachel! There'll be other nights. Lots of them. And you don't have to worry about the office number any more – I'll get you at home.'

The connection clicked dead.

Gradually, Rachel became aware that below her hips her body was mostly numb; her chest was cramped. It took her more than a minute to be able to lower the receiver and when she did, her palm slithered with sweat. Slowly, she stood up and rested both hands on the surface of the desk by her fingertips. Rachel stayed there feeling the blood beginning again to flow around her veins.

You're under a lot of pressure now.

345

She looked over at Carole's empty chair, stood for a while at the window, cool of the glass against her forehead.

. . . as soon as I read it . . .

She wanted to ring Resnick, but he must be busy otherwise he would have called her himself. Besides, what could he do other than listen sympathetically, and was that what she wanted from him? Or herself? Leaning on him the first time anything went wrong? How could she say, Charlie, this is moving too far too fast, I think we have to back away a little, and, at the same time, Charlie, I need you?

Rachel went back to the telephone, stared at it for some seconds and finally picked it up.

'Jane, you put a call through to me a short time ago. A man.'

'Yes, Miss Chaplin.'

'He didn't give you, he didn't say his name, I suppose?'

'No, Miss Chaplin, I'm sorry.'

'All right, Jane, and thanks. Oh, look, I know it's not policy, but there's no chance you gave him an outside number for me?'

'No, Miss Chaplin. You know we never give out home numbers to clients.'

'I know, but did he ask?'

'No, Miss Chaplin.'

'Thanks, Jane. I'm leaving soon, so no more calls, okay?'

But when she replaced the phone, Rachel continued to sit there, hearing the voice, over and over, something in it laughing at her, teasing, and something else, some quality of speech that she could not define yet which kept prompting her memory.

If you've got someone to help out tonight, I'll call again.

'CID. Resnick.'

Why was it there was invariably a call just as you were about to go off shift?

'Yes, I know her. Yes.'

He had been leaning sideways in his chair, one knee resting against the edge of the desk, but now, instantly, he was straight and alert, free hand prising the top from a pen as he listened.

'Yes, understood,' Resnick said. And then: 'How serious?'

His mouth tightened and, for a moment, still listening, he squeezed the bridge of his nose and his eyes closed.

'Is she ... can she talk? I mean ... Got it. Yes, I'll be right there. Ten minutes, fifteen at most. Thanks.'

He dropped the receiver back on to its cradle, grabbed his coat from the back of the door. Lynn Kellogg was typing up the report of an interrogation she'd been involved in that afternoon, each laborious page initialled and signed.

'Lynn!'

'Sir?' she answered, getting to her feet.

'City Hospital. Intensive Care. Let's go.'

Carole's car was not outside, so she obviously hadn't got back from her visit as early as she'd hoped. Rachel had wanted to talk to her, but the prospect of taking a drink and soaking in a hot bath appealed to her almost as much.

The phone was already ringing when she slipped her key into the lock. Against logic, the back of her throat went dry. Shutting the door, she bolted it. Stupid! What

347

was she getting so paranoid about? Sliding back the bolt, she settled for the chain instead, then smiled at herself. Good old liberal half-measures!

At the far end of the hall, the telephone was mounted on a bracket, a small hessian-covered pinboard beside it, a pad on a circular table below, pencils and biros in a hollow donkey marked 'A present from Skegness'. A joke, Carole had explained.

Rachel stared: whoever it is, they can't ring for ever. Carole, Charlie, whoever it is.

When she had steeled herself to answer it regardless, the tone stopped and the suddenness of the silence shocked her. The house was so quiet. Rachel checked in the kitchen and the living-room and she was right, Carole didn't have any vodka. Well, okay then, a large gin and tonic with ice and a slice of slightly decaying lemon and maybe she could start to unwind, relax. Rachel made her drink and then hurried upstairs to run the bath. Five minutes later she had perched the glass between bottles of shampoo and conditioner, dropped her clothes on the chair by the door and lowered herself into foaming, hot water, steam already beginning to frizzle the ends of her dark hair.

. . . that's why you need to unwind, be relaxed . . . I'll call again.

Phones rang and were answered.

Resnick showed his warrant card at reception and he and Lynn Kellogg were pointed towards another door, a corridor, a lift.

'When was she admitted, sir?' Kellogg asked.

'Early hours of this morning.'

Their feet clicked loud on the tiled floor.

'Why did it take them so long to contact us?'

'Sounds as if notification went out, but nobody made the connection to us. It wasn't until she said herself . . .'

'Still took her a long time, sir. Likely more than twelve hours.'

'Who knows?' Resnick said, pushing the lift button. 'Who knows what state she's in?'

There were double doors at the entrance to the Intensive Care ward, the first of which was kept locked. They rang and waited for a nurse to take them through.

Wrapped inside two towels, Rachel came down with care: the heat and the alcohol had made her a little dizzy. A cup of coffee was what she needed and by then Carole should be home, it was surprising she wasn't there already.

As Rachel was crossing the hall, the phone began to ring and, by instinct, she picked it up.

'Hello, Carole?'

'Feeling better now, away from the rigours of the working day?'

Rachel slammed the receiver against the wall, struck it, twice, against the cradle before finally forcing it down into place.

'Bastard!' she yelled. 'You bastard!'

She ran back up the stairs, nearly losing her footing once; pulled on her clothes, rubbed at her wet hair; downstairs again, she picked up the local paper she had stepped over earlier, folded inside the front door. Squatting there she rifled the pages: *Cars for Sale, Household Goods, Funeral Services,* there, *Lonely Hearts.* Shaking, her finger traced down the column.

'Oh, God!'

Rachel swallowed.

Attractive Professional Woman wants to hear from

imaginative men with interesting ideas to help her unwind. Rachel.

She tore at the paper, pummelled it, beat at it with her hands.

Between the bandages and the widths of tape, between the carefully arranged pillows and the sheet, it was difficult to see much that was recognizable as Sally Oakes. Where her jaw had been broken, it was clamped in a wire frame.

Only the eyes were clear, but closed.

The doctor stood with Resnick at the foot of the bed; Lynn Kellogg sat as close as the drips would allow, glucose and blood.

'She was found in the road. Taxi driver on his way back to base. Said she stumbled out and collapsed right in front of him, all he could do not to run her over. He picked her up and brought her into casualty. Better if he'd left her there and phoned for an ambulance, of course, but it's always easy to see clearly after the event.

'Then again, he had no way of knowing the extent of her injuries. Blood about the face and clothing, there must have been a lot of that, but I suppose he thought, you know, falling, drunk. Naturally, there would have been no way, simply by looking, of knowing about the internal injuries, their extent.'

Listening, looking, Resnick said nothing.

The cats had come running the instant they heard the key turn in the lock. Dizzy – he would be the first – Pepper, Miles and – what was the scrawny one called? – Bud. Rachel pushed the door to and bent down, favouring Bud with an especial stroke. Dizzy showed her his backside and headed for the kitchen.

Rachel hung the keyring Resnick had given her from her index finger and followed, the other cats sliding in and out of her feet. It struck warm inside the house and she felt something about it that was immediately welcoming, quite different from Carole's home which was always oddly vacant when Carole herself wasn't there – like a place that had been sold a long time ago and was still waiting for the new owners to move in.

This, though, was different. She felt – understanding what she was feeling, the seductive danger of it – more at home here. Remembering where the cat food was kept, Rachel spooned some into their respective bowls. There was only an inch of milk in the fridge, Charlie would probably bring some in with him when he arrived. Dizzy had bolted most of his own food already and was stealing Bud's; when she tried to budge him away, he arched his back at her and hissed. Oh well, Rachel thought, not my business. She opened the nearest cupboard and put the keys inside.

The sergeant on duty at the station told her he was sorry but there was nobody in CID at the moment, he could transfer her to Central Police Station if she wanted. Inspector Resnick was who she wanted. The sergeant didn't know if the inspector would be back, but if he came in then the message would be relayed. Good evening, madam.

Rachel left the phone off the hook.

'Sir! Sir!'

The yellowing eyelids flickered, stilled, flickered again; finally, Sally Oakes's eyes stayed open and slowly tried to focus.

'You must be careful,' the doctor warned, touching

Resnick's arm as he went forward. 'She's in a critical condition.'

Resnick nodded. He sat opposite Lynn Kellogg, both of them watching anxiously as Sally Oakes's eyes fixed first on one, then the other. Recognizing them, she began to cry.

Rachel was leaning back on the settee, stroking Bud and reading through some typed pages she had found on the table, somebody's notes about Professor Doria, an explanation, of sorts, of a lecture he had given at the University.

> Excess is essential in literature, in art as well as society, because of its power to challenge from the inside and help to dismantle traditional and hidebound structures. It is for this reason that Repression, with its opposition to Excess, is always to be fought against and denied.

She felt the cat tense against her hand and a moment later the knock at the door.

Oh, come on, Charlie! Give me your spare keys and then forget your own.

'Excuse me, little one,' Rachel said, depositing Bud on the back of the settee, 'I'll be back in a minute.'

The slight hesitation of warning that Rachel felt as she was turning the handle was too little and too late.

'Miss Chaplin. Rachel. Such a surprise.'

'Professor.'

He already had one foot across the threshold. 'I called to speak with the inspector.' His eyes were reaching past her. 'He's here?'

'Is it important?'

'Oh, yes. Yes. I'm afraid it is. Otherwise . . .' He

placed his hand against the frame of the door. ' . . . one doesn't like to call unannounced.'

Rachel's mind was racing too fast for her to think with any clarity. 'If you wouldn't mind call back later. An hour perhaps.'

Doria's face slid into a lingering smile. 'An hour, Rachel. What difference would an hour make now?'

'We were just going to eat.'

'He's here then. Call him. No need for good food to go cold and spoil.'

Rachel brought the door back towards her and then pushed it forward fast, throwing all her weight against it. Doria's arm braced and slowly started to straighten: he was surprisingly strong.

Resnick knew that within minutes the doctor would insist on their leaving and there would be nothing he could do to resist. A nurse sat with her arms behind one of the pillows, holding Sally so that her back was clear of the bed. Lynn Kellogg held a notebook in front of her, Resnick steadied the pencil as she struggled to write.

Sounds came intermittently from behind the wired jaw but unintelligibly. All they could do was share the girl's pain as she forced letters through their crazed journey across the page.

The first Resnick understood immediately, watched with impatience as Sally's fingers forced down on the book.

DORIA

She began to write her own name then, partway through, the pencil slipping with a thick stroke diagonally across the page. Her eyes found Resnick's, willing him to understand. He nodded, waiting for her to continue. Again a line through her name, an emphatic dropping of her head that made her moan and had the doctor stretching past Resnick with concern.

'You'll have to leave.'

'One more minute.'

'Tomorrow, when she's rested.'

'Look, there. She wants to say something.'

Sally tapped pencil against paper, her eyes moved imploringly towards Lynn Kellogg, the doctor, back to the paper. Falteringly, her fingers shifted their grip and began another word.

R

Me, Resnick thought, she's going to write my name?

RA

What's going on?

RACH

'Rachel!' Resnick said, face close to hers. 'Is that it, Rachel?'

Sally Oakes's eyes moved up and down inside their sockets, saying, yes, yes.

'What about her, Sally? What about her?'

'Inspector! You must leave the girl alone.'

Resnick shrugged away the doctor's hand. Sally Oakes was willing him to look at the pages on which she had written. Her eyes were beginning to close though. The doctor signalled to the nurse, who carefully began to lower the pillow back down against the others.

'Doria and Sally,' Lynn Kellogg said. 'Then why somebody else, why . . .?'

Resnick was staring at the lines the girl had scored through her own name before writing Rachel's in its place.

'When this happened,' he said, leaning now right across the bed, 'he wasn't doing it to Sally, he didn't call you Sally, but Rachel. Is that it? Is that what you're saying?'

Yes, said Sally Oakes's eyes, just once before they closed. Yes.

Resnick was already running down the ward, Lynn Kellogg in his wake.

Rachel was backed up against the empty fireplace. The sound of her breathing was unnaturally loud, lips slightly parted. If she made a dash back towards the front door, to her right in the direction of the kitchen where she might find a weapon with which to defend herself, she knew that Doria would attack.

Whereas now he sat on the arm of a comfortable chair, that confident smile across his face and the teasing quality in his voice that was clear to her from the disguised call to her office.

With one hand he was loosely holding Patel's notes, while the fingers of the other pushed into Dizzy's fur, the cat purring with pleasure.

'It seems I misjudged him, this young man from the great subcontinent, there are errors here, naturally, but for one new to the subject, he shows a good understanding.' The smile froze, the fingers ceased to move and the cat went up on to its hind legs, pushing his head against Doria's hand. 'Deconstruction, possibly you have a little knowledge of it yourself? No? Ah, well. It seems there are others who do. More understanding than I might have wished. Yourself, for instance, the nature of your profession – understanding. Wouldn't you say?'

Rachel nodded.

'What you and your kind like to call the weaknesses of others. To be treated with compassion, therapy. Not like the answer our mutual friend, the inspector, lives by. Punishment. Incarceration. Repression.' Dizzy nuzzled against him again and smartly, with the back of

355

his hand, Doria knocked him away into the centre of the room.

The cat squealed, spat and ran.

Rachel gasped and made half a move forwards.

'He does know, doesn't he, your inspector? He does know.'

'Yes,' Rachel breathed.

'And you,' said Doria. 'You know.'

Rachel ran for the kitchen. She heard him behind her, glimpsed him from the corner of her eye. With a slam she threw two doors closed and each, in turn, was pushed open. She banged her hip painfully against the table, jerked open a drawer, another, too far, the contents spilling out around her feet and across the floor.

Inside the room, watching, Doria leaned back on the door and laughed.

Rachel, shuddering, saw the bread knife beside the board and seized it between the fingers of her right hand.

'Carole,' Resnick said, his voice unnaturally high, 'Rachel, is she there?'

'Who is that?'

'Christ! Resnick, Charlie Resnick. Is she with you?'

'I thought she was at your house. She told me she was going to take back the keys you . . .'

He ran for the car; Lynn Kellogg was behind the wheel with the engine running.

'My place,' he said. 'Fast. I'll call through to the station as we go.'

He imagined, he didn't know what he imagined, trying to blank out the worst excesses of his imagination and never quite being able, all through that drive that seemed endless but was less than ten minutes. All the

356

while wanting to be driving himself, yet knowing that they would arrive no more quickly and, besides, trusting Lynn's co-ordination more than his own.

'Which side of the street, sir?'

'There, left. There!'

Resnick jumped clear of the car too soon, buckled over and was close to losing his footing. Stumbling, he steadied himself against the open gate; stopped, finally, where Rachel was standing, quite still, looking back towards the house with Bud cradled within her arms.

At the first movement of his arm about her shoulders, she flinched.

'Are you okay?'

Her head moved up and then down, slowly.

'You're sure?'

'Yes.'

'He was here, Doria?'

'Oh, yes.' Rachel continued to stare back at the house.

Resnick moved his arm away and motioned for Lynn Kellogg to come and look after Rachel. Police sirens could be heard, distant but getting closer.

There was blood on the hall carpet and Resnick thanked God that it was not Rachel's blood. There was blood in thick clusters on the treads of the stairs, blood smeared over the walls and along the banister. Blood darkening the length of the landing until it stopped at the door to the small bedroom at the back of the house.

With the outside of his shoe, Resnick pushed at the door. Something stopped it and it would open no further. He set his weight against it, just enough to squeeze inside the room.

Doria lay, what seemed like pieces of him, close against the small bed. Where he had hacked at himself with that blunt, serrated weapon more blood had splashed up on to the walls, to join the paint Resnick had so zealously applied. Even so, here and there, fragments of the nursery showed through.

The final thing Doria had done was to slice open his throat.

Resnick, sick, pushed open the window and saw, below, Rachel Chaplin being led towards a waiting ambulance.

ALSO AVAILABLE IN ARROW, A COLLECTION OF COMING-OF-
AGE STORIES FROM SOME OF THE MASTERS OF CRIME
FICTION, SELECTED AND EDITED BY JOHN HARVEY

Men From Boys

'Terrific tales' *Independent on Sunday*

Featuring Mark Billingham, Lawrence Block, Michael Connelly,
Jeffery Deaver, John Harvey, Reginald Hill, Bill James, Dennis
Lehane, George P. Pelecanos, Peter Robinson, James Sallis, John
Straley, Brian Thompson, Don Winslow, Daniel Woodrell and a
novella by Andrew Coburn.

Little is perfect for the men in these seventeen crime stories and
nothing is straightforward. The worlds they inhabit are as different
as a deprived London housing estate and a rundown jazz joint in
Manhattan, but each of them is striving to determine what is right,
what will given them dignity, what will earn them self-respect. Some
succeed. Others fail.

In this acclaimed collection of stories, John Harvey has gathered
together some of the very best names in contemporary crime
writing. Together these writers answer what it is to be a father, a son,
a man.

'Bonus points to Harvey as editor for taste, virtuosity and some
weird kind of compatibility-spotting which detects kinship between
the most dissimilar authors. An original, outstanding collection –
readable and rewarding from start to finish' *Literary Review*

arrow books

Now's the Time

John Harvey

With his richly praised sequence of novels featuring Detective Inspector Charlie Resnick, John Harvey created not only an unforgettable character of great depth and complexity, but a realistic and richly peopled inner-city world of struggling heroes and feckless villains.

A woman is beaten; a charred body is found in a warehouse; another 4 a.m. call for Charlie Resnick. Gathered together in *Now's the Time* are twelve short stories featuring Resnick, including a new story written especially for this edition. 'Billie's Blues' reunites Resnick with the troubled and beautiful Eileen, former stripper and mistress of a gangland boss, and now on the run and in fear for her life.

From old foes to upstart pretenders, the city and the jazz-soaked, night-time world of Charlie Resnick come vividly to life.

'Without doubt the best cop on the Britcrime beat. Harvey has set a benchmark which the genre must now measure up to'
Literary Review

'Sad tales, beautifully told'
Time Out

'Both as a treat for existing fans and bite-sized introduction to Resnick's world for new readers, this is a must'
Val McDermid

'A perfect coda to the most accomplished crime series of the 1990s'
Booklist

arrow books

**Order further John Harvey titles
from your local bookshop, or have them delivered
direct to your door by Bookpost**

☐	**Men from Boys** (ed.)	0 09 946152 8	£6.99
☐	**Now's the Time**	0 09 943556 X	£6.99
☐	**In a True Light**	0 09 941674 3	£6.99
☐	**Cold Light**	0 09 942157 7	£6.99
☐	**Still Water**	0 09 942162 3	£6.99
☐	**Last Rites**	0 09 942163 1	£6.99

Free post and packing

Overseas customers allow £2 per paperback

Phone: 01624 677237

Post: Random House Books
c/o Bookpost, PO Box 29, Douglas, Isle of Man IM99 1BQ

Fax: 01624 670923

email: bookshop@enterprise.net

Cheques (payable to Bookpost) and credit cards accepted

Prices and availability subject to change without notice.
Allow 28 days for delivery.
When placing your order, please state if you do not wish to receive any
additional information.

www.randomhouse.co.uk/arrowbooks

arrow books

In a True Light

John Harvey

Sloane walks free from prison after taking the rap for a high-profile art scam. A failed painter, he is now a failed forger. Awaiting him are two policemen anxious to remind him of his sins, and a letter from a woman with whom he had a passionate affair in his youth. Dying now, she summons him to tell him that he has a daughter, Connie.

Sloane agrees to return to New York, a city of potent memories, and look for his daughter. But Connie is locked into a relationship with a man the police believe has killed once and will not hesitate to kill again. Sloane has to decide whether to walk away or stay and fight for her. And the deeper the police dig into Vincent Delaney's business affairs, uncovering underworld associations, the more Delaney feels cornered, and the more unpredictable he becomes . . .

'John Harvey writes the way we all wish we could write. Elegiac and eloquent, his stories are filled with the blood of true character. In *In a True Light* he is at his very best. It's a crime story, but it's also a larger story about redemption and consequences set to the beat of the human heart'
Michael Connelly

arrow books